The Scarlet Impostor

A

The Scarlet Impostor

Readers of those two splendid stories, "BLACK AUGUST" and "CONTRABAND", will remember Satanic-looking, unscrupulous Gregory Sallust. In this story he sets out to follow the slender broken threads of a vast conspiracy which would sabotage the Gestapo, bring down the Nazi Government and create a new Germany with which the Allies might conclude a speedy and honourable peace.

What a colossal task! To bring about a victorious peace without the sacrifice of a million lives. With incredible suspense we follow Gregory into war-time Germany, the Rhineland, Holland, London, Paris, Munich and Berlin.

Wherever he goes the Angel of Death follows him with dark, silent, unseen wings. Friends and enemies alike are scythed by the grim reaper through their contact with the Scarlet Impostor right up to the last terrible night of blood in the German capital.

Again and again the darkness of the war-time black-outs proves Gregory's only friend, and from their shadows emerges the beautiful Erika von Epp, only to light them for a moment before herself falling under the shadow of Death.

It is a stupendous story not only because of the breath-taking episodes which succeed each other with each skilful twist, but also because Wheatley has used facts on which to base his tale, and it is safe to say that it will become a classic among the spy stories of the present war.

Dennis Wheatley

DENNIS WHEATLEY'S WORK

has also been published in	The titles of his books are:
	FICTION
THE UNITED STATES	*The Second Seal* *The Haunting of Toby Jugg*
FRANCE	*The Shadow of Tyburn Tree* *The Launching of Roger Brook* *The Man Who Killed the King*
GERMANY	
	The Scarlet Impostor
ITALY	*Faked Passports* *The Black Baroness* *V for Vengeance*
SWEDEN	*Come Into My Parlour*
HOLLAND	*Three Inquisitive People* *The Forbidden Territory*
	The Devil Rides Out
SPAIN	*The Golden Spaniard* *Strange Conflict*
	Codeword—Golden Fleece
HUNGARY	
	The Quest of Julian Day
BELGIUM	*The Sword of Fate*
	Black August
POLAND	*Contraband*
	The Eunuch of Stamboul
CZECHOSLOVAKIA	*The Secret War* *The Fabulous Valley*
	Sixty Days to Live
DENMARK	*Such Power is Dangerous* *Uncharted Seas*
FINLAND	*The Man Who Missed the War* *They Found Atlantis*
PORTUGAL	
	SHORT STORIES
NORWAY	*Mediterranean Nights* *Gunmen, Gallants and Ghosts*
RUMANIA	
	NON-FICTION
BRAZIL	*Total War*
	HISTORICAL
————	*A Private Life of Charles II* (*Illustrated by Frank C. Pape*). *Red Eagle* (*Illustrated*)
RUSSIAN	(*The Story of the Russian Revolution*)
SERBIAN	**CRIME DOSSIERS WITH** **J. G. LINKS**
ARMENIAN	*Murder off Miami* *Who Killed Robert Prentice?* *The Malinsay Massacre*
ARABIC	*Herewith the Clues*

DENNIS WHEATLEY

THE SCARLET IMPOSTOR

A Novel

HUTCHINSON
Stratford Place
London

Hutchinson & Co. (Publishers) Ltd
London   New York   Toronto
Sydney   Cape Town   Melbourne

First Published 1940
Reprinted   1942
Reprinted   1946
Reprinted   1949
Reprinted   1953

Made and Printed by Litho Offset in Great Britain at
GREYCAINES
(Taylor Garnett Evans & Co. Ltd.) Watford, Herts.

FOR

MAX

AUTHOR'S NOTE.—Gregory Sallust, who appears
in this book, also appeared in "BLACK AUGUST",
but "BLACK AUGUST" was set in an undated
future, so, chronologically, this book should be
considered as preceding "BLACK AUGUST",
although the two have no relation whatsoever
except in that certain of the characters appear
in both.

Contents

CONTENTS

THE SCARLET IMPOSTOR

Chapter I

THE MAN WITHOUT A JOB

GREGORY SALLUST paced restlessly up and down his
private sitting-room at No. 272 Gloucester Road. Lean
and loose-limbed, his habit of walking with his head thrust
forward made him appear to have a permanent stoop. His thin-
lipped mouth was tightly closed, his lantern-jawed face betrayed
a sullen anger and the white scar which ran from his left eyebrow
towards his dark, smooth hair, giving him a slightly Satanic
appearance, showed with unusual plainness, as was always the
case when the muscles of his face were tensed by any strong
emotion. His grim, silent pacing resembled that of a very
dangerous, caged animal desperately plotting to break free.

Rudd was the only other occupant of the room. He acted
in the rather curious dual capacity of Gregory's man-servant and
landlord, and was now sitting on the edge of a settee, polishing
two large automatics with loving care.

When Gregory had gone straight from his O.T.C. to serve
in France during the last years of the World War, Rudd had
been his batman. After the Armistice Rudd had inherited a
long lease of 272 Gloucester Road, the ground floor of which
was a grocer's shop, and the upper part a strange caravanserai
mainly tenanted by transient students at the near-by London
University. The first-floor front was their shabby, incredibly
untidy common sitting-room, in which they played gramophones,
held bottle-parties and, when funds were low, cooked weird
meals on a small gas-stove.

As Rudd's sole income consisted of his precarious rents and
such money as he could pick up by doing odd jobs for the grocer,
he would long since have gone under had it not been for Gregory,
his one permanent tenant, who occupied the two best rooms of
the house, with a private bathroom, at the back of the first floor.*

*See *BLACK AUGUST* (Hutchinson)

Rudd's yellowish hair was close-cropped and bristling at the top of his head but allowed to grow in front into a lock which he carefully trained across his forehead in a well-greased curve. A small, fair moustache graced his upper lip, but as he always kept it neatly trimmed it failed to hide the fact that his teeth badly needed the attention of a dentist. His eyes were blue, quick, humorous and friendly. Putting aside one of the automatics he took up the other and glanced anxiously at his master.

"Don't take on so, Mr. Gregory, they'll be wantin' yer soon enough nah there's another war on. We'll be givin' the Jerries 'ell tergether 'fore the month's aht."

Gregory stopped his pacing and stared down at him angrily.

"Damn it, man! You don't understand. This isn't like the last war. Everything's cut and dried already. Haven't you heard the B.B.C. announcements? No commissions to be granted to anyone who hasn't had a previous commission in the Regular Army or is a technical expert, except by way of the ranks, and the training battalions are already jammed full of young men in their twenties."

"That's wot they say, sir. But wot abart the Intelligence or this 'ere new Ministry of Infermation? You speaks German as well as any Fritz, you know the old Continong like the back of yer 'and and you've done plenty of queer jobs fer the big boys in Fleet 'Street. Couldn't yer get a civilian billet somewhere?"

"Civilian billets be damned! I'm only thirty-nine and I want to fight, so why the hell shouldn't I?"

"Oh, orl right, sir, orl right! But the war's only a week old yet and we'll all get a bellyful of fighting before we put little old 'Itler where the monkey put the nuts."

"You've said it!" Gregory exploded. "The war's a week old and here am I, still kicking my heels. Every regiment I've tried is full up and there isn't the ghost of a prospect of getting in anywhere."

"'Ave a little patience, sir, do. The war ain't 'ardly started yet an' I don't need ter tell *you* that the old Boche'll take some beatin'. It'll be four years or the duration again this time an' the duration'll be longer than the four years, as it was larst— leastways, that's my opinion, nah they've made this tie-up wiv Russia an' can get orl the supplies they want through 'er."

Gregory nodded jerkily. "Yes, but they'll have to pay for the stuff, remember, and they're devilishly hard up. Besides, the Russians only wanted to encourage them to cut their own throats."

"Them Russians is a slippery lot," agreed Rudd, but Gregory turned on him irritably.

"For God's sake stop polishing those guns ! You've been at it for a week, and you'll wear the damned things out. I'm going across the landing to see if the rest have any news."

In the common sitting-room at the front of the house, it being Sunday morning, Gregory found four of the six other tenants. Hildebrand Pomfret, a cadaverous, disappointed novelist with whose own assessment of his literary gifts the public obstinately refused to agree, was discussing the war with a bald, paunchy man of about fifty named Beadle, while the two other occupants of the room, Griselda Girlie, pimply and bespectacled, and Ann Croome, a small, plump person with a heart-shaped face and magnificent violet eyes, constituted an attentive audience. As Gregory's glance fell upon Ann his lean face lit up with a sudden smile. He was not the least interested in her personally, but beauty in any form always pleased his artistic eye.

"Any fresh news in the last bulletin ?" he asked of no one in particular.

"Not much," Ann replied. "The Poles are still hanging on outside Warsaw, but the B.B.C. hardly tell us a thing about our own end of it. Griselda's just got her orders, though."

"What orders ?" Gregory frowned. "I didn't know you were in anything, Griselda."

"Oh, yes," the pimply-faced girl smiled palely. "As a medical student I'm naturally qualified for nursing. It'll set me back in taking my degree, of course, but that can't be helped. It was all fixed up days ago and they're sending me to Southampton. I'm off this afternoon."

"Well, the best of luck to you." Gregory looked across at Beadle, who held a minor Customs post. "As you're well over fighting age I suppose you'll stay on in the Customs ?"

Mr. Beadle shook his pink, bald head.

"No, not exactly. Examinations of neutral shipping for contraband have to be made by experts. As I was in the R.N.V.R. for many years they're giving me a commission and I shall be posted to one of the ships maintaining the blockade."

Gregory grunted. "How about you, Pomfret ? Once it gets going, I expect the war will be good for the sale of your books. It's a pity you don't write thrillers, though."

Pomfret shrugged his narrow shoulders. "I'm afraid I shan't have much time for writing, because I've been fortunate enough to secure a post in the Ministry of Information. Where my department will operate from I don't know, but I'm under orders to leave London at a moment's notice."

'God help us, if the Ministry's to be run by people like old Pomfret,' thought Gregory, and looked across at Ann Croome. "I take it that you, at any rate, will remain here to lighten our darkness, Ann ; or are you thinking of departing to some funk-hole in the country ?"

"Oh, no," she smiled. "I'm staying in London. My boss has got himself a job in one of the civilian departments of the War Office, and as I'm carrying on as his secretary, I've got a War Office job, too. What are you doing, Gregory ?"

For perhaps the first time in his life Gregory Sallust stammered and he felt sick with shame as he replied : "I—I hardly know. Something'll turn up, I hope, but for the moment nobody seems to want me."

Ann's violet eyes opened wide. "But that's impossible ! You served in the last war, didn't you ? And you're such a very knowledgeable person. You've travelled everywhere and done all sorts of adventurous things. Surely they'll give you a commission in something or other ?"

Gregory shook his head, and the cynical smile which she knew so well twitched the corners of his thin-lipped mouth.

"My dear Ann, this is one of the penalties we pay for being a Democracy. All commissions are to be given through the ranks this time, except to youngsters who served in the O.T.C.—and there's no wire-pulling. It's twenty years since I served in the Army. I don't know the first thing about the new weapons, drill or tactics, so I just don't qualify. About the only thing open to me is to become a Grey Angel."

"A Grey Angel ?"

"Yes. They were a corps of old crocks formed during the last war at the behest of the old women who made it their job to see that serving soldiers on leave had as little fun as possible. They used to meet the leave-trains and shepherd the returning Tommies across London so that they could be sent straight back to their homes in the country without even an hour in the great, big, wicked city, in case they felt like spending some of their cash on a night at the 'Empire' or going out on the razzle with lovelies like you."

His bitter laugh was cut short by the entrance of Rudd.

"You're wanted on the 'phone, sir. It's Sir Pellinore Gwaine-Cust."

"The devil it is!" Gregory was through the door like a flash, and a moment later was at the telephone in his own sitting-room.

"Lunch with you? Delighted. A chat beforehand—yes, I can be with you in twenty minutes."

Seizing his hat he leaped down the rickety stairs four at a time, erupted into the street, hailed a passing taxi and told the driver to take him to 94 Carlton House Terrace.

As the cab spun through the streets of war-time London, half-deserted in the September sunshine, Gregory's mind was racing. What did old Gwaine-Cust want with him? Was it a job? Was it? It *must* be! In the past he had successfully undertaken many dangerous commissions for Sir Pellinore. The grand old chap must have remembered, and have found him some niche in the war machine.

The taxi halted Gregory paid off the cabman and his finger had hardly touched the bell before the door of Sir Pellinore's town house was opened by a liveried footman. The man gave him a friendly smile, said that Sir Pellinore was expecting him and took him straight up to the luxuriously-furnished library on the first floor, with its tall windows overlooking the lovely vista of St. James's Park.

Sir Pellinore came forward to meet him and as they shook hands he drew himself up to his full, magnificent height. The elderly Baronet stood six feet four in his socks and could easily have thrown most men of half his age down the staircase. He had very strong, blue eyes under bushy eyebrows whose snowy whiteness matched that of his luxuriant cavalry moustache, and his bluff, genial manner effectually disguised the extremely able brain which lay behind his broad forehead.

"Sit down, my boy, sit down," he boomed, indicating a comfortable chair opposite his desk. He then sank back in his own and gently tapped together the tips of his long fingers.

"Thought I'd give you a ring just to see if you were fixed up," he said smoothly.

Gregory gave a rueful laugh. "I wish to God I were, but no one'll have me."

"I had an idea that might be the case," Sir Pellinore smiled. "Too old at forty, eh?"

"I'm not forty yet."

"Lucky young devil! Still plenty of years ahead of you in

which to show the gels a thing or two. Wish I were your age!
But that's beside the point. I need hardly ask whether you're
willing to serve?"

"Good Lord, no! I'd fight the Jerries again for the fun of
the thing but these Nazi swine make me see so red I hate their
very guts. I'll take any mortal thing you can offer me if it
means having a cut at them."

"*Any* mortal thing?"

"Yes, and be thundering glad to get it."

The older man nodded slightly. He was no longer smiling
and his eyes were very grave as he said: "From what I know
of you, Gregory, I believe you would. That's why I sent for
you. I want a man who is brave, intelligent, resourceful,
unscrupulous: a man who can be trusted without limit because
he will carry not only his own life but the lives of others in his
hands: a lone wolf with no dependants to mourn him if he should
die unhonoured while taking a great gamble—a gamble in which
the winning stake is a speedy peace that will save millions from
untold misery.

"In short, I want a man who is capable of handling the most
important secret mission ever entrusted to a single individual—
and I believe that you are such a man. Are you prepared to
risk having to face a firing-squad, or worse, by going secretly
into war-time Germany?"

Chapter II

THE THREE TRAILS

IT was a fantastic proposition which Sir Pellinore Gwaine-Cust had put up to him. Had it come from almost anyone else Gregory would have thought that they were joking, but he knew the elderly Baronet far too well to think that such a thing was even remotely possible.

Sir Pellinore was one of those remarkable products which seem peculiar to England. Born in 1870, the heir to a pleasant property on the Welsh border which had been in his family since the Wars of the Roses, he had come into his inheritance in the naughty nineties, while still a subaltern in a crack cavalry regiment. He had an eye for a horse and a pretty woman, and an infinite capacity for vintage port, but no one had ever accused him of having any brains. Distantly connected with Royalty and numbering three Dukes among his first cousins, he had always known everyone who mattered by their Christian names, yet not one in a thousand of the general public had ever heard of him. He had shot everything shootable, including men, and had become briefly famous during the South African War owing to a particularly well-deserved V.C., but as he had never courted publicity he had soon slipped from public notice once more.

Early in the reign of King Edward VII a crisis in his financial affairs had led him to resign his commission rather than sacrifice his ancient patrimony. Solely on account of his social standing some people in the City had offered him a directorship, only to find him a surprisingly regular attendant at their board meetings, where he displayed a jovially blunt persistence in acquainting himself with the minutest details of the company's affairs.

Soon, too, they discovered that any particularly tricky negotiations with Levantines or Orientals were best left to Sir Pellinore ; he had no brains, of course, but he possessed a strangely direct way of putting matters to such people. He was so transparently honest that they never quite knew what had come over them until they were back in their own homes. Other directorships had been accepted by Sir Pellinore, but he had always modestly declined the chairmanship of any company with which he was connected.

For his services in the last Great War he had been offered a peerage, but had declined it on the score that, as there had been a Gwaine-Cust at Gwaine Meads for so many centuries, the tenants would think he had sold the place if he became Lord Something-or-Other.

He had always dealt with his co-directors with that same disarming frankness which he displayed with the Levantines and Orientals, his formula being : "Well now, you fellers, just pay me what you think the job was worth—say, half what I've saved the company, eh ? That's fair. No cheating there. Mustn't rob the shareholders, must we ?" He was now exceedingly rich.

To his vast mansion in Carlton House Terrace Admirals, Generals, Diplomats and Cabinet Ministers came to unburden themselves when their affairs proved exceptionally difficult. Not for advice, of course, since everybody knew that Sir Pellinore had no brains ; but he was safe as the grave and a decent sort— one of the old school, in fact, with a curiously direct way of thinking ; an eye for a horse or a pretty woman, and an infinite capacity for vintage port.

His only son had died of wounds during the Great War and it was Gregory who, as a very young subaltern, had carried him back from the hell of battle at the imminent risk of his own life. Thus Gregory had come to meet Sir Pellinore who, times without number, had offered him lucrative, permanent posts in his own companies ; posts which Gregory had turned down owing to his loathing of routine and the possession of a private income just sufficient to render him independent.

He too, however, had a direct way of thinking. That was why they liked each other and why, whenever one of the great corporations which Sir Pellinore virtually controlled found its interests threatened, he would say to the board : "I think I can get you the man. Very able feller. Much more likely to get to the bottom of this business for us than one of those beastly agencies. If you care to leave the matter in my hands . . ."*
Now, it seemed, Sir Pellinore had said much the same thing to someone far more important than his co-directors and, as usual, the matter had been left to him.

Since the last Great War Gregory had taken on various dangerous enterprises demanding secrecy and brains besides his

*See *CONTRABAND* (Hutchinson), 17th impression, now 3/6.

commissions from Sir Pellinore, but never before had he been asked to undertake a secret mission in a country where he would be shot as a spy if his true identity were discovered. Nevertheless he replied without hesitation : "Certainly ; if you think I'd be up to the job, I'll go to Germany for you."

"Good man !" Sir Pellinore brushed up his magnificent white moustache with a sweep of his hand. "I felt certain you would, but I wouldn't have asked you if I hadn't known that you speak German like a native."

"Yes, my German's all right—but one thing puzzles me. You're obviously acting on behalf of the Government. Why don't they send one of their own Secret Service people ? There must be plenty of them whose German is as good as mine, and they've been specially trained for this sort of thing, whereas I haven't."

Sir Pellinore nodded. "Reasonable question, that. I'll tell you. Whoever goes to Germany for us will have to get in touch with a number of highly-placed Germans. In peace-time every secret service does all it can to identify the secret agents of its potential enemies, so that we can never be completely certain that any particular one of our men is not known to the enemy. If we were to send one of our permanent people and it so happened that he was known, he might be spotted despite the cleverest disguise, and that would be fatal not only to him but also to the Germans with whom we want him to get in touch. The only alternative if we wish to handle this business through regular channels is to send out a youngster unknown to the enemy purely through the brevity of his service. But, damn it, we dare not trust to some inexperienced junior a matter on which the fate of the world may hang. Only remaining possibility is to use someone like yourself ; someone whose courage and ability have been proved but who is entirely outside the service and would never be connected with it if arrested when in contact with the people we wish to approach out there."

"That's sound enough," murmured Gregory. "What d'you wish me to do ?"

Sir Pellinore sat back. "To make the situation clear, I propose to bore you for a few moments with some facts about the internal state of Germany which are probably already known to you. Anyway, they're more or less common property.

"Hitler came to power on the shoulders of the industrialists. They financed him owing to their fear of the Communists and in the belief that they would be able to use him as a puppet or

throw him aside after he had served their purpose. Well, they
backed the wrong horse, for Hitler has been their taskmaster
ever since. Nevertheless, he put an end to Communism as an
active force in Germany.

"As we well know, he also put an end to free speech and free
institutions, thus sounding the death-knell of some of the best
intellectual elements of the country as represented by the Social
Democrats. Such diehard Communists or Social Democrats as
escaped being shot or put into concentration-camps went underground. After a time, a few of them sank their differences and
got together, since when they have continued to fight Hitler
with subterranean propaganda, secret wireless stations and so
forth."

Gregory pulled down the corners of his mouth. "Don't tell
me you're sending me to Germany to start a revolution?"

"The German people are ripe for revolution."

"Sorry, but I don't believe that." Gregory shook his head.
"I'd take your word for it that a proved loss of £100,000 on any
balance sheet could be converted into a profit by a little jugglery
of figures, but I'm afraid that in this case your judgment is at
fault."

"Nonsense !" Sir Pellinore smiled, obviously pleased by this
compliment to his financial acumen. "Never was any good at
figures. You know that."

"No?" Gregory grinned. "Yet the father of all the Roths-
childs would have buttoned up his pockets and knocked off work
for the day if he'd heard that you were going to pay him a visit
in his office."

"What's that ?" The elderly Baronet looked up sharply.

"Well—you know what I mean." Gregory continued to grin
unashamedly. He knew his man and treated Sir Pellinore in
private as few of his co-directors would have dared to do.

"Insolent young devil !" Sir Pellinore returned the grin.
"Good thing there aren't many more of your kidney knocking
about. World wouldn't be fit to live in. But never mind my
financial dabblings. It's a fact that a very large section of the
German people are just itching to get their hands on Hitler and
his bullies."

"Don't you believe it ! All these tales of unrest are greatly
exaggerated. In any nation, the people shout for whoever gives
them bread. When Hitler came to power there were eight
million unemployed in Germany, and even if he put them into
uniform he gave them back their self-respect and assured them

of food, steady jobs and better housing. When I was in Germany six months ago I formed the opinion that at least ninety per cent. of the Germans were right behind Hitler—and there's nothing like war to unite a country. Apart from a handful of fanatics I doubt if anyone in Germany would be prepared to attempt the overthrow of the Nazi Government to-day."

"Very sound. That's what we all thought up to a week ago, but information received since has caused us to think differently. The German people are at the end of their tether. They've been underfed too long; their liberties have been too heavily restricted, and they've become so inured to hearing fiery speeches that it has proved impossible to imbue them with a new wave of patriotism. They had no objection to a little war with the Poles, but now it's come to a show-down with the British and the French their memories of what they suffered after their last defeat are too recent to allow them to enter this war with a fighting spirit.

"The issue of ration-cards to them before the war had even started was an incredible blunder, and there have already been food riots in a number of the larger towns. I know you'll think that the wish is father to the thought, Gregory, but you may take my word for it that the German masses are now ready to throw off the Nazi yoke."

Gregory shrugged. "All right. I'm glad to hear it. But what can the poor devils do ? They won't stand a chance against the tear-gas and machine-guns that the police will use on them."

"I agree." Sir Pellinore leaned forward impressively. "But they would if they were given a lead by the Army !"

"What's that ?" Gregory exclaimed with sudden interest.

"Surprised you, eh ?" Sir Pellinore gave a jovial laugh. "But just consider. D'you think that the German nobility likes having to kow-tow to the scum of the gutters who have used graft, treachery and murder to climb to high places in the Nazi party ? D'you believe that the cultured people can possibly sympathize with a régime which restricts personal liberty and persecutes those of their fellow-intellectuals who happen to be Jews ? D'you think that the High Command, all at one time officers of the Imperial German Army, like taking their orders from an ex-Corporal ? You know how proud those stiff-necked Prussian aristocrats are. Is it conceivable that they enjoy having their way of life dictated to them by a house-painter ?"

Gregory's eyes narrowed. "Theoretically, there's a lot in what you say, but surely they're all watched by the Gestapo ?"

"Yes. That's why we've got to be so devilish careful. One false step and Hitler would shoot the lot, however high their rank and however much it might damage his military machine."

"But do you really think there's any chance of the Army leaders getting together?"

"I have every reason to believe that certain of them already have an understanding. All they're waiting for is an opportunity to come into the open, destroy Hitler and his satellites, seize power themselves and call off the war."

"Then why didn't they do so on the night Hitler ordered the advance into Poland? Surely that was their big chance? Saving their country from being plunged into a fresh World War would have been a perfect excuse for a *putsch*, and the majority of the nation would probably have lined up behind them."

"There were two reasons for their not doing so. First, there is an Inner Gestapo consisting entirely of Army officers, and until these have been identified and eliminated any attempt to come out into the open would result in the disaffected group being denounced and executed before they could get the movement going. Second, these men are patriots and desire justice for Germany. They will not destroy Hitler before they have an assurance that when they take over the Government the Democracies will scrap the Versailles treaty once and for all and give their country a new deal."

"In that case, why on earth wasn't such an assurance given to them?"

"Simply because, although we know that this group exists, we have not been able to find out the names of the Generals composing it."

"Is that what you want me to get you?"

"Yes."

"H'm. And what have you got for me to work on?"

"Precious little, I'm afraid. I'll give you what I can in a moment, but in the meantime I cannot stress too highly the service that you will be rendering, not only to Britain and her allies but also to Germany herself and the whole world, if you can only discover for us the actual heads of this temporarily dormant conspiracy. Once we know who they are we can practically guarantee their safety, for by a fantastic stroke of luck one of our agents managed to secure from Berchtesgaden itself a full list of this Inner Gestapo of Army officers."

"I see. And if that could be passed on to them they could arrest or bump off all the Inner Gestapo before acting. This becomes really interesting. Now let's hear exactly what lines you can give me to follow up."

"Ever heard of a woman called Erika von Epp ? Very beautiful girl and no better than she should be."

"Yes. Isn't she the mistress of Hugo Falkenstein, the Jewish armaments millionaire ?"

"She was until recently, but her Jew boy-friend was popped into Dachau and is now believed to be dead. In any case, she got married last winter to a Count von Osterberg. She travels a lot and when last heard of was on her way to the United States, but she was over here a couple of weeks ago. Had a flutter with a young officer in the Guards. Good-looking young devil, and not half as stupid as he looks. One night when they were together she said something that set him thinking. She comes from German Army stock, of course, and she toasted the Imperial German Army with the words : 'It won't be long now before the house-painter is put where he belongs and the old families are back again to lead Germany on a new and saner course. The Generals only have to give the word and the Nazis will be destroyed overnight."

"An extraordinary indiscretion, of course, but Erika von Epp was crazy about this boy and they were both half-tight at the time. Fortunately he reported it to the right quarter, and Erika knows so much of what's going on behind the scenes that one can't help thinking there must have been something more than idle wishing in what she said."

"From any ordinary German girl it wouldn't have been worth a damn, but with her connections there may well be something in it. What's the next thing ?"

Sir Pellinore pondered for a moment, then : "You've heard of Tom Archer ?"

"The Communist leader ?"

"Well, he calls himself a Marxist, but Anarchist would probably be a more accurate description. Anyhow, he and his friends are so hot that the official Communist Party refuse to have anything to do with them. Clever feller, though, and dangerous. Just before the balloon went up he sent a letter to the Prime Minister. In it he urged further delay before declaring war, giving as his reason his conviction that there would be a revolution inside Germany if only hostilities could be postponed for a few more days and we were willing to meet a *new* German Government round a conference table with honest intent to give Germany a new deal. He actually offered to act as go-between.

The interesting point is, though, that Archer stressed the fact that he wasn't counting upon a rising of the German Labour people, but that it would come from some other quarter. Now, from what other quarter could it come save the Army?"

"You think, then, that the Socialists and the Army leaders have agreed to act together?"

"It would seem so, but our ultimatum was already drafted and could not possibly be held up any longer, on account of the Poles. Archer was grilled afterwards, of course, but in spite of promises, pleading and threats of D.O.R.A. he closed up like an oyster. Wouldn't say a damned thing for fear of endangering his friends on the other side."

"Anything else?"

"Just one thing more. I expect you've drunk plenty of Rheinhardt's hock in your time? Well, Herr Julius Rheinhardt, the senior partner in the firm, who lives in Traben-Trabach on the Moselle, was over here not long ago. He talked very freely to one of his co-directors in their London office and stated categorically that the Army leaders, the big industrialists and the Socialists are banded together in a pact to destroy Hitler at the earliest possible moment.

"Unfortunately the London director, a naturalized British subject, didn't come forward with the information until war had actually broken out, but he's absolutely definite about what Julius Rheinhardt said.

"Archer has proved a dead end; Erika von Epp, or rather the Countess von Osterberg, as she now is, may or may not be in America, but Rheinhardt is almost certainly back at his home in Traben-Trabach. He's your best bet. You must see him and induce him in some way or another to give you the name of one of his superiors in the conspiracy. Then you must go on in the same way until you reach the man right at the very top."

The expression of tense eagerness faded from Gregory Sallust's lean face and was replaced by a thoughtful frown as he asked: "But what happens if I do succeed in reaching him? I've no credentials to show, and even if I were to risk carrying any—well—he'd still have to entrust his safety to an unknown secret agent. He'd be out of his senses, surely, to do such a thing."

"Not at all. Once you can identify the man at the top the job's as good as done. The list of the Inner Gestapo of which I spoke is still in safe keeping in Berlin. There was no time to get it out before war broke.   Moreover, the last document to be sent to Berlin before our Embassy closed down was a letter, signed by responsible British and French statesmen.   It guaranteed that if the Generals would arrest the chiefs of the Nazi Party, call off the Polish war and support a new Government based on a free election, the Democracies would pledge themselves to a round-table conference and a new deal for Germany. That letter is with the list of the Inner Gestapo members.   If only you can secure these two documents and pass them on to the head of the conspiracy, the German Army will unquestionably depose Hitler and the peace of the world will be restored."

"You certainly didn't exaggerate the importance of this mission," Gregory murmured.   "When do I start?"

"It is a matter of extreme urgency," Sir Pellinore said quietly. "You will leave for Germany to-night."

Chapter III

THE REVERSED SWASTIKA

SIR PELLINORE GWAINE-CUST was a great gourmet and Gregory did ample justice to an admirable luncheon, during which they talked of many things, but they kept off the subject of the trip to Germany.

Refraining, for once, from lingering over the nuts and port, they returned to the great library overlooking St. James's Park and settled down to discuss the necessary arrangements.

"We shall send you over by plane, of course," said Sir Pellinore casually.

Gregory gave a rueful grin. "I suppose that means I'll have to make a parachute jump. I've done it once before, but I'm damned if I fancy the idea of coming down like that in enemy country at night ; especially as there's bound to be a black-out. I might land right in the arms of the village policeman."

"For that reason a parachute jump would be much too risky. The plane will land you on German soil."

Gregory raised his left eyebrow, and the old wound-scar above it whitened, accentuating the almost Satanic look which it gave to his lantern-jawed face. "A night-landing with no ground lights sounds a pretty tricky proposition."

"Providing the weather remains calm I don't think there's much likelihood of the plane's crashing. The pilot who will take you has done the trip a number of times before for practice."

"He hasn't had to do it in a complete black-out, though."

"True." Sir Pellinore smiled. "But we're not altogether without arrangements at the other end, so I think you may be reasonably confident of a safe landing."

"Good. Whereabouts is he going to drop me?"

"It's essential that you should make contact with Herr Julius Rheinhardt in Traben-Trabach at the earliest possible moment, but unfortunately the country to the south of Cologne is so thickly wooded and so mountainous that no secret landing-ground could be established there which we could use with even a reasonable degree of safety. The nearest, for your purpose, is in the flat country a few miles to the north-east of Cologne. You'll have to walk into the city, but once there you should find no difficulty in getting transport up the Rhine and along the valley of the Moselle to Traben."

"Have you any views as to the sort of kit I should go in?"

"As half the men in Germany are now under arms we thought that the most inconspicuous disguise for you would be the uniform of a German private."

"Don't like it." Gregory shook his head. "It might be all right later in the war, when thousands of them will be on leave from their units, but no leave will have been granted yet, and a stray private drifting about on his own would be liable to be questioned by any patrol and asked what he was doing snooping about the countryside instead of being with his regiment."

"You could say that you were on your way to join your unit. You will, of course, be provided with all the proper papers."

"I don't like it," Gregory repeated. "Some officious Railway Transport Officer will spot me as I'm travelling up the Rhine and probably bung me on the first train for Poland. They've got over seventy divisions operating there already so there's a big chance that the unit to which I'm supposed to be attached is among them."

"Well, you can go in civilian clothes if you prefer, of course, but . . ." Sir Pellinore broke off suddenly as the under-butler entered the room with a decanter and two big, bowl-shaped glasses. ". . . Ha! Here's the brandy."

"Have you still got any of that pre-war—I mean pre-1914— Kümmel?" Gregory asked.

"What, the original Mentzendorff?"

"Yes."

"Why?"

"Only that I've always found it an excellent aid to thought, and while I can get fine brandy in other people's houses you seem to have cornered all the pre-1914 Kümmel in London."

"Drat the boy!" muttered Sir Pellinore, brushing a hand over his fine, white moustache. "Another bottle gone, and even Justerini's can't find me any more, but I'd sooner you drank it than most people I know. At least you appear to appreciate the stuff, and I wouldn't mind a spot myself.

"Crawshay, bring me a bottle of Kümmel—out of the bin, mind; not that muck we have for parties."

"Very good, sir." The elderly under-butler bowed in the

doorway and disappeared as quietly as he had come. Sir
Pellinore looked across at his guest.

"I was about to say that very few men of your age in Germany
will be in civilian clothes these days."

"I know. If they're not in the Army they're all Brown-
shirts or Black Guards, or some other comic kit, and somehow
I don't fancy the idea of wearing petticoats."

Sir Pellinore leaned back in his chair and gave way to a great
gale of laughter. "No, no, Gregory. I've seen some damned
clever impersonations in my time but we could never make up
that lean, ugly face of yours to look like a woman's. I'd give a
packet to see you dressed as one, though, just for the fun of the
thing."

"Well, I'm afraid you'll never have the chance. Praise
Allah ! Here's the Kümmel."

The under-butler had returned with the cobwebbed bottle
still uncorked upon a salver. Sir Pellinore took it from him,
and when the door had closed behind the man he gently tapped
the wax off the top of the bottle as he said to Gregory :

"Never allow my people to uncork old liquor. Servants
don't understand that sort of thing these days. Cork's gone to
powder, like as not. If so, they push it in and ruin the stuff.
One thing I always do myself."

With a skilful sideways twist of the wide-spiralled corkscrew
he drew the cork, smelled it, wiped the lip of the bottle free from
dust with his finger and poured out two generous rations. For
a moment they both savoured the fragrance of the old liqueur,
then sipped it.

"By Jove ! How right I was to ask you for this !" Gregory
murmured. "Smooth as cream, isn't it ? But what a kick !"

Sir Pellinore nodded. "That's the stuff to give the gels, eh ?
But I bet you'd manage without it. Now, where were we ?
Ah, discussing your kit, of course. Well, in my view you'd
stand more chance of being questioned if you went in civilian
clothes than you would dressed as a German soldier."

"Soldier !" repeated Gregory, taking another swig at the
Kümmel. "You've said it. But I'm not going as a private,
who'd have to stand stiff as a ramrod before every bristle-haired
N.C.O. I'm going as a German General."

"Gad !" Sir Pellinore brought his huge first down on his
desk with a mighty thump. "Magnificent idea ! In war-time
a General is monarch of all he surveys. No one ever dares to
question a General."

"Not only that, but I'll be able to represent myself to Rheinhardt and his friends as one of the Generals who is in the conspiracy and they'll be much more likely to talk, then. I'll see if I can get myself a uniform from one of the theatrical costumiers this afternoon."

"Nonsense! Why shouldn't the department do the job? Plenty of German uniforms in the wardrobe. Bound to be. Only a matter of sewing on the right tabs, rank-badges and so on."

"You're right, of course. They'll be much more reliable about details than a costumier. We'd better leave it to them."

"We will. Never do anything yourself that you can get other people to do for you. Remember that, my boy. Better than any tip for the Derby. Lots of fools have paid me good money to get other people to do their work for them."

"I can well believe you," said Gregory succinctly. "West, of Savile Row, is my tailor. If they get on to him he'll give them my measurements as a guide for size and fit."

"Good." Sir Pellinore dialled a number and got through at once on a priority line to a house in one of London's remoter suburbs. After a short conversation the matter of the uniform was arranged, and replacing the receiver he turned back to Gregory. "What's the next thing?"

"Boodle," said Gregory.

"What?" said Sir Pellinore.

"Money—the sinews of war. I shall need German *Reichmarks*, and plenty of 'em."

"Of course. I've already seen to that. Knew you wouldn't let me down, you see!" Sir Pellinore opened a drawer in his desk and handed over a sealed packet which Gregory opened. It contained 5,000 *Reichmarks* in notes of various denominations, and a handful of silver.

"H'm," he reflected, "that's the equivalent of about £400 in our money if used inside Germany. Yes; that'll keep me in cigarettes for the time being. There's another thing, though. As a General I shall be immune from officious questioning, but I'll have to register at hotels and so forth, so I'll need an identity."

"Passport people will fix that for you this afternoon. They've plenty of enemy material to select from, and what they haven't got they can fake up for you so well that nobody'll know the difference. It's just a matter of your choosing any name you consider suitable."

"I'm afraid that's not good enough. True, the German Army's

so large that it has several hundred Generals ; but even so, most of the high officers must know each other, by name at least. If I happened to run into someone who was a keen student of their Army List and he'd never heard of any General of the name I was going under, I'd soon find myself in hot water. It would be much safer to take .the name of some existing General."

"The water would boil over right away, my boy, if you happened to walk into that particular General's command."

"Oh, I quite see that," Gregory agreed with a twisted smile, "and it wouldn't do to try to impersonate a General who's at all well known. I was thinking of trying to find one who is of the German Army, but not in it."

"What the devil are you talking about?"

"I mean a General who is at present outside Germany on a mission and can't get back—Military Attaché somewhere, or something like that. Or I tell you what ; better still, I'll impersonate a dead dug-out."

"A dead dug-out?"

"Certainly. Like every nation at war, Germany must be calling up innumerable officers who've been retired for some years but who're still active enough for training troops or garrison duty. We must find a man like that ; someone not very important but whose name would be vaguely known to a reasonable proportion of Army officers ; a man who might easily have been recalled from his retirement but who has actually died within the last year or so."

"If he had died, though, a certain number of people would be sure to know of it."

"A few, but not many. Unless he's a very big shot, nobody takes much notice of what happens to a General once he retires and leaves the way open for his juniors. If I ran into anyone who knew him personally I'd be in the soup, of course, but the chance of that is comparatively remote if we can find a man who has died after several years' retirement."

"How about age ? You don't look like a General who's been retired for several years."

"I don't think we need worry about that. When a man's passed his first youth he can easily add ten years to his age by the way in which he carries himself. Besides, though I hate like hell to do it, I shall shave my head like a typical Prussian, and when my dark hair's gone I think you'll be amazed to find how much older I shall look."

"Very well, then. I'll get on to the right people immediately you've gone and we'll try to trace a suitable defunct General for you. If we can, I'll have your papers made out in his name. If not, you'll have to put up with being a Colonel, but that would serve the purpose almost as well."

"Fine. Now, is there any other information at all that you can give me?"

Sir Pellinore put his hand in his waistcoat pocket and drew out a small, gold swastika which he pushed across the desk. "See anything queer about that?"

"Yes," Gregory replied at once. "It's a reversed swastika— the sort they call the male, as opposed to the female which the Nazis use as their symbol. The male swastika is a pre-Christian emblem which had much the same significance in ancient times as the Cross has had since. It was supposed to signify the power of Light among the Aryan peoples, whereas the female kind signified the power of Darkness. I've often wondered how the Nazis came to make such a howling blunder as to select the evil symbol for their own emblem."

Sir Pellinore guffawed. "Trust that type of wursteater to put his clumsy foot in it—just like sinking the *Athenia* at the very opening of the war. Well, Erika von Epp, or rather the Countess von Osterberg, to give her her new title, is the real owner of this little thing."

"How did it come to you?"

"That gay young blade in the Guards I was telling you about found it one morning caught in the top of his sock."

"Indeed?" Gregory raised his eyebrows, and the two men grinned at one another. "And how did it come to get there?"

"She had a violent infatuation for the young rascal—and that old scandalmonger, Brantôme, would have termed her *'une dame très belle et très galante.'* In our own more vulgar parlance, she's damned hot stuff. Our friend reports that she used to wear it tied to the shoulder-strap of her 'undies' with a little black bow It must have got loose one evening while they were having a romp together. Anyhow, he found it when he got home and passed it on to us at the same time as he turned in that bit of information about Erika's having toasted Germany's return to the good old days under the leadership of the Army chiefs. It may mean nothing, but on the other hand it may be an identification symbol that the conspirators are using. You'd better take it. It might come in handy."

Gregory picked up the little charm and put it carefully away in his notecase as he asked: "Anything else?"

"No. 'Fraid not. It's up to you now to trace the anti-Nazi leaders through Julius Rheinhardt, or, if he proves to be a dead end, through the Countess Erika. That Bolshie feller, Archer, is not worth wasting powder and shot on."

"All the same, I'd like to have his address."

"He lives at 65 Walshingham Terrace, Kennington ; just south of the river."

"Thanks. What time do I start ?"

"Be back here at 11 o'clock to-night. Your uniform and the necessary papers will be ready for you. There'll be a car here to take you to the airport and I'll come along to see you off."

"That's decent of you."

"No." Sir Pellinore's voice dropped to a lower note and he looked away a little quickly. "Either you won't come back, my boy, or having seen you leave England to-night I shall have been privileged to witness the opening of a new and happier chapter in European history."

Chapter IV

WINGS OVER THE FRONTIER

AS a taxi whisked Gregory back to Gloucester Road the streets appeared just the same as they had a few hours earlier. The sun was still shining; people were going about their Sunday occupations much as usual. Except that there was less than half the usual traffic, only the occasional heaps of sandbags protecting pavement lights, the strips of paper pasted across shop windows to prevent broken glass flying in an air raid and a sprinkling of figures in khaki really brought home the fact that there was a war on.

The London scene remained exactly the same as it had been when he had set out from Gloucester Road, but Gregory himself was a changed man.

The sullen, angry despondence of the morning had left him. A new elation made him infinitely more sensitive to the sights and sounds around him, yet he experienced none of the wild exhilaration which might have filled a younger man.

He was fully conscious both of the magnitude of the task before him and of its danger. To penetrate an enemy country in war-time with forged papers meant that he would most certainly be shot as a spy if he were once caught and put behind iron bars, while it was credibly reported that Hitler's secret police often beat their victim to a bleeding mass of pulp with thin steel rods before they finally dragged them out to finish them off with a bullet. What such swine might do to one of the hated English now the war was on was just nobody's business.

Nevertheless, being a cheerful cynic by nature, he was not unduly despondent. A true philosopher, he realized that all he could do was to take every possible precaution that his very able brain could devise; the rest must remain upon the knees of the gods. One thing that cheered him immensely was the knowledge that he was being sent out on a job that really was worth while, and it tickled his sense of humour to think that only that morning he would have jumped at the chance of a commission in an infantry regiment. Now, if only he could pull off this mighty coup, he would be able to serve his country as well as any Field-Marshal commanding a victorious army.

In his strong, sinewy hands, unshackled by orders or interference from above, there lay the possibility of being able to bring the war to a speedy and successful conclusion. All the armed forces of the Crown could not do more than that.

Immediately he reached 272 Gloucester Road he yelled for Rudd, and his ex-batman came tumbling up from the dark and mysterious cavern in the basement where he dwelt. One look at Gregory's face was enough to assure Rudd that he had got a job.

"So yer pulled it orf, sir ? Got the old gentleman ter wangle somethin' for yer ? I knew yer would. Wot's it ter be—Army, Nyvy, or the blinkin' Marines ! I don't give a cuss meself, s'long as I can lend a 'and ter shoot the Charlie Chaplin orf of 'Itler."

Gregory shook his head sadly. "I'm sorry, old friend, but I shan't be able to take you with me. Mine's to be a one-man show."

Rudd's face fell so suddenly that the change was almost comic. "Come orf of it, Mr. Gregory. Yer must 'ave someone ter look arter yer. Oo's goin' ter polish yer boots an' yer Sam Browne an' all, let alone mix yer mornin' pick-me-up when yer've been on the razzle ?"

"Sorry, Rudd, but I'm afraid it's impossible. I'm being sent abroad and I shall be living in hotels where I shan't need a soldier's servant—in fact, after the first few days I shan't be in uniform at all."

"Crikey ! They've bin an' 'ooked yer fer the Intelligence ! Some o' them Brass 'Ats must 'ave some brines in their 'eads arter all."

"It is a form of Intelligence, but that must remain absolutely between you and me."

"Mum's the word, sir," Rudd nodded, "an' yer know I ain't one ter talk. Why, if I even started ter let on what I knows abaht yer they'd 'ang yer as 'igh as the Crorss on St. Paul's. All the sime, it's a bleedin' shime they won't let yer tike me wiv yer."

"Yes. But I shall want you to help me here while I'm away," said Gregory quietly.

"Will yer ?" Rudd's blue eyes became round with surprise and delight. "Cor ! Just fancy yours truly bein' a blinkin' spy ! Blimey, that ain't arf a larf, that ain't !"

"You lying, drunken old reprobate! You know damned well you've done all sorts of dirty work of that kind for me before!"

"Not Secret Service, I ain't."

"No, but very much the same sort of thing ; watching people, finding out their habits, vices, weaknesses and the addresses of their friends. So what's the difference?"

" 'Struth, is that orl yer want?"

Rudd's disappointment was obvious and Gregory laughed aloud, knowing that his faithful henchman had pictured himself breaking into foreign Embassies to steal vitally important documents.

"Ever heard of a chap called Tom Archer?" he asked.

"Wot ; that ruddy Red?"

"Not so much of the 'ruddy'! He's going to be your bosom friend from now on."

"Don't go pullin' my leg, Mr. Gregory. You know 'ow I 'ates Communists—dirty lot of dogs, they are."

"Well, you're not going to hate them any longer. I'm serious, Rudd. This is a job of work just like any other. You can help me and serve your country by doing what I tell you just as well as you could with a rifle and bayonet, if not better."

"Orl right, sir. Seein' as it's that way, wot you sez goes, as per usual."

"Good. Then listen carefully. Archer lives at No. 65 Walshingham Terrace, Kennington. Got that? 65 Walshingham Terrace, Kennington. You've got to scrape acquaintance with him as soon as you possibly can. You're an Anarchist at heart—though not yet a member of any Party, in case he asks to see your ticket. You are also a pacifist."

"Wot, me? Me a pacifist? Come orf of it, sir! 'Ave an 'eart!"

"You're a pacifist, I tell you. You hate war, you hate the makers of war, and above all you hate that lying skunk, Adolf Hitler."

"Ah! Nah yer talkin' sensible. I could say a 'ole lot o' things abaht 'im wivaht drorin' breath ter take a pint."

"Well, you say them to Tom Archer and for God's sake keep off the British Empire else you'll spoil the whole box of tricks by pulling a Union Jack out of your pants or breaking into a drunken rendering of *Land of Hope and Glory.*"

"I get yer, sir." Rudd closed one eye in a knowing wink. "Yer want me ter lead 'im up the garden, like?"

"That's it. You're not half such a fool as you choose to make out. Your job is to get me every mortal thing you can about Tom Archer while I'm away. I want particulars about his family, his friends, his interests and his doings. If by any chance he should talk to you about the German Army you must do your damnedest to remember what he says, word for word, and immediately you get home you must write it down. Anything at all that he may say about Germany is of interest and any names that he may mention are to be carefully noted. I shall expect results when I get back."

"You shall 'ave 'em, sir, or I'll post meself as a Valentine to General Goering."

"Right. Now get me a complete set of clean underclothes ; socks, pants, vest, shirt—everything—and remove any tabs that are on them, the names of the shops from which they came, *and* the laundry-marks. They must be rendered completely unidentifiable. I'm going to have a sleep now, for God knows when I'll next get any. Turn on a bath, and call me at seven this evening."

At seven o'clock Gregory rang up to ask Sir Pellinore whether the department had managed to find him a suitable identity, and learned to his satisfaction that he would be stepping into the shoes of a deceased General of Engineers. He asked that everything possible about the dead man's career should be got for him, and rang off.

Having had his bath he drank two of his favourite cocktails ; concoctions of pineapple juice and Bacardi rum that Rudd had mixed for him, then sat down in his gaily-flowered dressing-gown to a light dinner.

After his meal he dressed in the clothes that Rudd had laid out for him, lit a cigar and settled down to refresh his memory of various places by the study of some maps of the Rhineland. He could take no luggage with him, except his shaving tackle and a piece of soap, so there was no packing to be done, and when Rudd announced at half-past ten that the taxi which he had ordered before black-out time, Gregory pocketed his big Mauser pistol and followed him downstairs.

"Good-bye, old chap." Gregory held out his hand.

Rudd wrung it until it hurt. "Take care o' yerself, sir. Best o' luck, an' send us a p.c."

Gregory smiled to himself as the cab moved off into the darkness. There would be no sending of postcards from the place to which he was going. At a cautious crawl the taxi ran through the black gulf of Knightsbridge, up Piccadilly and down St. James's Street to Carlton House Terrace.

In the hall Gregory was met by Sir Pellinore's valet, who took him straight upstairs to a bedroom where the uniform of a German General was laid out, with medal ribbons, boots, cap and all accessories, while in the adjoining bathroom razors and towels were in readiness.

Sir Pellinore's man shaved his head so closely that the dark hairs gave only a faintly bluish tinge to his bald scalp. After this Gregory produced his own razor and shaved his face very carefully, as he might be unable to get a shave on the following morning. The man then assisted him to dress, and when he went downstairs half an hour later with a stiff, strutting stride, he would have passed anywhere for the lean, dark-eyed type of German officer.

As he entered the library Sir Pellinore gave him one look and then roared with laughter. "Strap me! Gregory, what a guy you look, now you're as bald as a coot."

"You can keep your compliments for some other time," said Gregory. "It's the effect that matters."

"Yes, it certainly ages you. Damme! I don't believe I'd have known you!"

"Good! Now, who am I supposed to be?"

"General Franz von Lettow, of the 25th Engineer Regiment. Here are such particulars as I could get about you."

Gregory took the sheet of typescript that Sir Pellinore held out and glanced down it. "Franz von Lettow. Born January 12th, 1880, at Allenstein, East Prussia," he read. "Father, Civil Engineer ; mother came of small landed gentry. Educated at the Ruhm Schule, Königsberg, and the Engineering College of Königsberg University, military section. Entered the Army 1898. Posted to 10th Prussian Pioneer Regiment. Had little money and no influence. Married, in 1905, Fraulein Emmy Anholt, also without influence. Children of the marriage, three daughters, Hilda, Wilhelmina and Paula. Stationed in Cameroons 1911–1913. Served without distinction until the war of 1914–1918. As Colonel of Engineers, assisted his seniors in planning Hindenburg Line. Received Iron Cross of the second class. Eldest daughter, Hilda, died 1918. Second daughter, Wilhelmina, married, and emigrated to America in 1930. Her husband's name unknown. Third daughter, Paula, married *Herr Doktor* Paffer, of Leipzig, in 1933. After the Armistice, when the bulk of the German Army was disbanded, von Lettow was retired. Recommissioned in 1924 he again served without distinction until June 1934, in which month he was finally retired. Died January 1939 of angina, at his home in Allenstein."

"Just the sort of dead man's shoes you were looking for," commented Sir Pellinore.

"Yes. They'll serve admirably. The fact that he was recommissioned in 1924 shows that he was pretty competent at his job, but he was evidently of no special importance."

"Always has been difficult to get above a certain rank in the Germany Army without influence, and he was only a Brigadier when he retired. However, von Lettow is a good old Prussian name, and the department hasn't done too badly in getting those particulars at such short notice."

Gregory nodded. "I must memorize the names of these relatives of his and the dates; then I'll destroy this paper. As he was born in 1880, that makes me 59."

Sir Pellinore studied him carefully. "Having shaved your head certainly makes you look much older. I'd put you down as anything between 45 and 50, but the Army's a healthy life and if you'd lived carefully you might be a good bit more."

"Yes, I think I'll pass muster. Now, how about communications? You'd better give me the names of a few of your people who're still working in Germany so that I can keep in touch with you through them."

"I'm sorry. I can't do that."

"Then give me the names and addresses of some of the neutrals who're acting as post-offices for you."

"I can't do that either."

"Hell! Don't you trust me?" Gregory flared, and the scar above his left eyebrow grew suddenly livid.

"My dear boy . . ." Sir Pellinore raised a large hand in protest. ". . . such a suggestion is utterly absurd. Should I have chosen you for this mission if I'd had the least possible doubt as to your absolute discretion and integrity?"

"Sorry," Gregory muttered, "I'd forgotten for the moment that the reasons you thought of me was that you wanted someone unconnected in any way with the existing Service."

"Exactly. Any of our own people or post-offices out there may be known to the Gestapo and already watched. By making contact with any of them, you'd run the risk of being placed under supervision also, and that would be fatal to the whole enterprise."

"Then I shan't even be able to get a message back to you?"

"No. And it should not be necessary. Your task is to discover the Army leader at the head of the anti-Nazi conspiracy and to collect and deliver to him the two documents which are now lying in Berlin. In the meantime you must regard yourself as a lone wolf."

"I see. How about this list of the Inner Gestapo and the letter from the Allied Statesmen, though? You haven't yet told me where I collect them, and even when you have, I can hardly go to the chap who's got them and say: 'Please, I'm the Lone Wolf and I want you to hand over the Secret Documents.'"

"Of course not," Sir Pellinore smiled, "and for that reason we have allotted you a number. In view of the importance of your mission it's a very special number, too; one which has long been vacant and about which there can be no possible mistake. You are now listed by us as Secret Agent No. 1."

Gregory grinned. "I'm deeply flattered. And to whom do I introduce myself under this dramatic alias?"

"If and when you manage to identify the head of the anti-Nazi conspiracy you will proceed to Berlin. Go to the *Tiergarten* any morning between twelve and twelve-thirty, go in by the entrance nearest the zebra-house and approach the bench that you will see on your right. There'll be a man, or possibly a woman, sitting there eating their luncheon. Wait until they're alone, then sit down beside them and open a conversation by saying: '*One* war is very like another, isn't it?' They'll talk for a bit, then offer you a cigarette with the words: 'Will you have *one*?' You will reply: 'If you don't mind, I think I'll have *one* of my own.' After a while they will say: 'You're not a Berliner, are you? I wouldn't take you for *one*. From your accent I would judge you to be a Bavarian.' You will reply: 'I am *one*.'"

"No need for you to carry that precise conversation in your head," Sir Pellinore went on, "provided you remember that the word '*one*' must be introduced at least *twice* on both sides and that it then lies with you finally to establish your identity by speaking the last sentence."

"But '*ich bin ein*' is bad German," Gregory objected. "No-one would use such a phrase without a context."

"Of course not. That's the whole point. But you mustn't use it until you're satisfied that you're talking to the right person."

"I see. And then?"

"They'll say goodbye to you and walk away. You'll follow

at a discreet distance until they enter a house or someone else comes up and accosts you. In due course you will then be given the two papers."

"Right. That's all clear. Anything else?"

"No. Car's at the door but we've got a few minutes still. Always keep a bottle on the ice—or would you prefer something stronger?"

"No, thanks. Champagne's my favourite tipple and God knows when I'll taste it again."

When the under-butler had brought the bottle and emptied its contents into two silver tankards Gregory said: "What about your people having seen me in this kit? I suppose they're safe?"

"Safe as the grave, my boy. All picked men. Isn't one of them who hasn't been tested and proved completely trustworthy. I can't afford to have servants in this house who might talk."

"Of course. Silly of me to have asked such a question. Well, here we go!" Gregory picked up his tankard.

Raising his, Sir Pellinore drew himself up to his full six feet four as he proposed: "Success to your enterprise and confusion to our enemies!"

Having drunk the toast they lingered over their wine for a moment or two; then Gregory put on the heavy, field-grey great-coat that had been provided for him, slipped his own automatic into the pistol holster at his belt and followed Sir Pellinore out of the house.

In the lightless street a big Rolls was waiting, its blinds drawn. On the pavement and in the roadway Gregory glimpsed several shadowy figures in steel helmets and guessed that they were police posted there to turn back any casual pedestrian who might otherwise have noticed him entering the car. The Rolls purred, and they were off.

The car ran evenly, but at a moderate speed, since London's A.R.P. black-out was in full operation. As its blinds were drawn they were able to have the light on inside, and by it Gregory read and re-read the particulars of the late General von Lettow's career, until, by the end of the journey, he had thoroughly memorized them. When the car finally came to a halt he handed the slip on which they were typed back to Sir Pellinore.

"Thanks," said the baronet, glancing at his watch. "We've done it in just under the hour. Not so bad, as things are. This is Heston."

As they stepped out into the darkness Gregory sensed that

they were in a small, high-walled enclosure. They were met by more police and a young civilian who led them to a darkened doorway, through a light-screen and into an office where two men awaited them ; an airport control officer seated behind a desk and a young man of about twenty-five who was dressed in pilot's kit.

The airport official stood up, nodded to Sir Pellinore and said to Gregory : "I won't ask your name, but this is Flight-Lieutenant Charlton, who is going to fly you to Germany."

The young man smiled and held out a hand. There was something about his keen, grey eyes and his friendly, open face which inspired tremendous confidence, and Gregory felt at once that he would much rather make this dangerous flight with him than with some reckless young aviator of his acquaintance.

"I'm afraid you've been let in for a rotten job on my account," he smiled in reply as he took the pilot's hand.

Charlton shrugged. "Nothing like as dangerous as the sort of thing you're apparently going to do. I've been practising night-landings in Germany for months past and I think I can promise to get you safely to your destination, even in a black-out."

"I'm sure you will," Gregory agreed, "provided their 'Archies' don't find us."

"My plane's equipped for stratosphere flying ; we'll cross the frontier at 40,000 feet and there's not much likelihood of their being able to pick us up at that height."

"That's encouraging, anyway. Well, shall we go ?"

"Right. We may as well get off if you're ready."

The four of them trooped out on to the airfield. It was black as pitch outside but the airport man showed them the way by intermittent flashes of a torch especially constructed to throw light only on the ground. Charlton climbed into the plane, the interior of which was dimly lit by the glow of the dashboard lights illuminating an array of dials and instruments.

"Happy landings to you both," said the airport man.

"Good luck, my boy ! good luck, and a safe return !" Sir Pellinore muttered huskily, patting Gregory on the shoulder as he climbed into the four-seater beside Charlton.

"Thanks." Gregory smiled and lifted his hand. "I'll need it. But I always was an optimist, and with a little luck I'll live to knock back the last bottle of that Mentzendorff Kümmel of yours yet !"

Next moment the door of the cabin was closed and the

engine was revving. Charlton had already warmed her up before Gregory's arrival. Now he jerked his head towards the back of the cabin. "There are some rugs behind you. Better put one round you. I shall start to climb at once and it's going to be cold up there."

As Gregory reached for a rug the plane moved forward. Without a single bump it left the ground, and as the whole airfield was plunged in darkness there was nothing by which he could judge the exact moment of their take-off.

The silence was broken only by the steady purring of the engine as the small, fast plane climbed at high speed towards the stars. Gregory peered down through the cabin window. He had often flown at night, but was used to a landscape in which towns or villages and main roads were indicated from a great distance by clusters and long strings of lights.

Now, however, the whole country was shrouded in a pall of darkness, with only a tiny light showing here and there and giving little indication as to whether it shone from an isolated cottage or from a house in a thickly-populated area. There were a few moving lights, too ; the dimmed headlamps of cars ; but very soon these faded and the land beneath became indistinguishable from the sky above save for the darker tone of its background. It was impossible to tell, either from the stars above or from the few, scattered lights below, what part of the country lay beneath their ever-climbing wings.

As the plane gained height Gregory's ears began to pop, and knowing the drill he swallowed hard several times to ease the pressure. The altimeter showed 5,000 feet. A few minutes later they passed into cloud, but the needle moved steadily on, showing 7,000, 8,000, 10,000 as the plane climbed on into the empty heavens.

"We're over the coast now," said Charlton, and Gregory saw that they had reached 15,000.

The plane droned on. 18,000 ; 20,000. Charlton had already turned on the oxygen so that breathing was still quite easy, but it had become very cold and Gregory was glad of his heavy great-coat. The North Sea now lay far below them, with its lightless ships seeking to avoid the menace of German submarines, or waiting for daylight and a chance to hunt them out. 25,000 ; 30,000. A heavy frost had rimed the windows of the cabin.

Charlton glanced at his watch and checked his instruments. "We're over Belgium now," he murmured. But the plane was still climbing. 35,000 ; 40,000. In spite of the central heating, his coat and the rug, Gregory shivered. His hands were half-numbed by the cold and he envied Charlton his thick gloves.

Climbing no longer, but held steadily by Charlton at 40,000, the plane leaped ahead. Time seemed to hang interminably, although Gregory could see by the air-speed indicator that they were now doing 230 miles per hour. Suddenly Charlton cut off the engine. The silence that followed was uncanny, and Gregory looked up quickly.

"Anything wrong?"

"No." The pilot shook his head. "We passed the German frontier some minutes back, and now we're going to come down. From this height I can volplane for miles without having to use the engine."

"I get you. Their sound-detectors won't be able to pick us up, then. But how about your getting back? You'll have to use your engine to take off and climb again."

Charlton answered indirectly. "Were you in the last war?"

"Yes : the latter part of it."

"Then you'll know that different makes of engines have different notes. This plane is fitted with a German engine ; we have a few of them just for such purposes as this. If they pick me up when I'm climbing, they'll think it's one of their own planes."

"It's a wonder that our own coast batteries didn't have a slap at us, then, when we went over them at 15,000."

"They were warned. The listening-posts can distinguish a single plane from a flight, and the batteries in the area we had to cross were told to let us through."

"I see. But as this is a German engine, why don't you use it to come down? That would make for a safer landing, wouldn't it ?"

"It would. But it's important that we should land in silence, otherwise some busybody might come running across the fields to find out why one of their planes was landing where there was no aerodrome. Once I've taken off again it won't matter quite so much even if they do hear me."

The plane was gradually losing height as they talked, and Gregory's ears began to pop again. After some minutes they passed out of the clouds and scattered lights became dimly visible below them, being more numerous to their right front.

"Their black-out is not as good as ours," Greogry remarked. "That's a town over there."

"It's Cologne ; but their black-out is pretty good. They've got a more difficult problem than we have, because Cologne is much harder to hide than London. There's almost deserted country surrounding it ; just farm lands with villages dotted here and there ; whereas round London the suburbs spread out for twenty-five miles, merging gradually into the great, sprawling city. A night flier can easily locate it as a whole, but unless he can get low enough to pick up the Thames it's very difficult for him to discover what part of it he's over."

The plane was dropping rapidly now. The scattered lights grew brighter. When they had got down to 3,000 feet Charlton began to circle, going round and round for some minutes until at last he seemed satisfied and straightened out again. Away to the right the lights of Cologne seemed to be drawing together and receding, whereas the few, scattered twinklings in the darkness immediately below were spreading out yet rising rapidly to meet them. As he peered forward Gregory saw that one of these was blue, and that Charlton was heading for it. A moment later, most of the more distant lights had disappeared and the blue light could be seen to shine from a square window.

"The chap in that house is running a pretty big risk by showing you the way in," Gregory exclaimed.

"Such risks have to be taken, but as he's only a poor farmer he might get away with the excuse that he couldn't afford a thicker blind—the first time, anyhow. Besides, that room is only lit for a quarter of an hour at a time, and then only when he's had the tip that I'm coming over."

No other lights were now visible, and it seemed that they were about to crash head-on through the blue-curtained window when the plane suddenly curved away from it into the wind, bumped gently, and after running for a hundred yards came to a standstill.

As Gregory clambered out Charlton said : "Well, that's that. You see that star behind you, low on the horizon ? Head for it. The going won't be too good as part of it is over ploughed fields, but in about two miles you'll strike the Gladbach-Cologne road. Turn left along it, and a six-mile tramp will bring you to Cologne. All the very best of luck on your venture."

"Thanks." Gregory shook hands. "I couldn't have had a better man to help me over the first fence. Good luck yourself, and a safe return !"

As he slammed-to the door of the cabin and stepped back, Charlton switched on the engine. It roared for a moment ;

then Charlton turned the plane and taxied back across the rough grass until it was no longer visible in the faint starlight. Next moment Gregory saw the plane come rushing toward him again and the sudden gust of its passing hit him in the face as it took the air once more, climbing towards the stars on its way back to England.

As he glanced round he saw that the light in the blue-curtained window had been extinguished. The surrounding fields were dark, chill and unfriendly. Not a crack of light showed in any direction. His mission had begun in real earnest, now. He was a lone wolf without food or refuge and only his wits could save him from being torn to pieces by the ferocious enemy pack now that he was hunting in their territory.

Chapter V

A LONE WOLF ENTERS THE SHADOWS

TURNING towards the star that Charlton had pointed out, Gregory set off across the field. His boots were a little large, and though this was better than their being too tight, as he had an eight-mile walk ahead of him, he gave himself a mental rap over the knuckles for having omitted to mention the right size to Sir Pellinore. Evidently the department responsible for providing his General's uniform had made a pretty accurate guess by judging from his height, but carelessness upon just such small points might well cost him his life during the days or weeks that lay ahead of him, now that he was in enemy country.

When he had covered about 400 yards he encountered a fence, on the far side of which he found cultivated land. The crops had been gathered and a rough stubble rustled against his boots as he strode out across the uneven ground, thanking his stars that the weather had been good during the first week of the war and that the night was fine, for if his boots had been clogged with mud the going would have proved infinitely more tiring and difficult.

After a quarter of a mile the field ended and he struck grass again, but he had to cross several more stubble-fields before he reached a deep ditch and, scrambling across it, found himself on the open road. Turning left, he headed for Cologne.

The country was quite flat and utterly silent. The few houses that he passed showed blank, black windows and their inmates were clearly taking what sleep they could before facing the cheerless prospect of their second war-time Monday morning.

He saw no signs of military activity, but he had not expected to do so as he was nearly forty miles from the Belgian frontier and Germany was still at peace with Belgium. The nearest war zone was far away to the south of Luxemburg, well over a hundred miles distant. The only troops he was likely to encounter in this neighbourhood were anti-aircraft batteries stationed here for the defence of Cologne and the great industrial area further

north, where the plants at Düsseldorf, Crefeld and Essen would
be turning out munitions day and night. A faint reddening of
the sky to northward indicated the innumerable blast-furnaces
of Düsseldorf, which could not be entirely screened even in
a black-out.

Occasionally a lorry rumbled past or a car with dimmed
headlights crawled towards him in the darkness. At one point
he encountered a small party of revellers who were singing
drunkenly, at another an old woman who was pushing a hand-
cart. But there was little traffic, and each time anything
approached he stepped off the road to take cover in the shadows.

The six-mile tramp along the road was a dreary business,
but at last the scattered houses merged into disconnected rows
and Gregory knew that he was entering the suburbs of Cologne.

Glancing at the luminous dial of his wrist-watch, he saw
that it was just on 5.30. This meant that there was nearly
another hour to go until sunrise, but the sky was already paling
faintly in the east. He had not hurried on his way from the
landing-ground because it would have been dangerous for him
to be seen, in the conspicuous uniform of a General, drifting
aimlessly about the streets of the city before it was astir. Moreover, as an old soldier, Gregory had long since learned to conserve his strength and he never hurried over anything unless he
had excellent reasons for doing so.

Where a fence railed off an open field between two blocks of
houses he halted and sat down on the stile that gave entrance
to it. Plucking a tuft of grass he spent some moments dusting
his boots, as he knew that it would be a fatal give-away for a
German General to be seen about the streets in boots which
were not meticulously clean. Then he took out his case and
lit a cigarette.

That was another little slip, he thought, as he drew the
'fragrant smoke of the Sullivan down into his lungs. Sullivans
are not to be obtained in Germany, and if an occasion should
arise which necessitated his offering his case this fact might well
betray him. He would have to get some of those filthy German
stinkers as soon as possible.

Fortunately the case was of plain, engine-turned gold without monogram or initials, so he was able to retain it, but with
a reluctant sigh he took out the remaining Sullivans and, tearing
them into pieces, scattered the tobacco and paper in the long
grass behind him.

At a quarter to six a door banged in a nearby house and a

shrill voice called out something in German. That brought home to him as nothing had yet done that he really was in Germany. Shortly afterwards a light cart clattered by and Gregory stood up. It would not do for a General to be seen sitting dreaming at the roadside. German Generals were busy, practical people and not given to doing that sort of thing. The uniform would probably have big advantages later, but it had its drawbacks as well.

Stubbing out his cigarette he started off again towards the centre of the town and was soon walking on pavement. It was lighter now and there were quite a number of people in the streets. He came to tramlines, and passed a little group of workers waiting at the terminus for a tram to take them into the city. A solitary, grey-clad soldier was among them ; steel-helmeted, a gas-mask slung round his shoulders. He drew himself up stiffly and saluted. With a little start Gregory acknowledged the salute and walked on.

The fact that he was wearing a cap instead of a steel helmet did not matter. Actually, it was probably an advantage ; for except when actually on parade officers would certainly be permitted such licence behind the war zones, but he ought to have had a gas-mask. Evidently the department which had equipped him had not had one of the latest German pattern, and a British mask would have given him away. He made up his mind to rectify the omission as soon as possible.

The trams were running by now, but he noticed that their clanging, high-pitched bells were silent, doubtless on account of some regulation imposed by the German equivalent of A.R.P.

He had decided that he would make for the main railway-station, go in by one entrance and come out by another, and then hail a taxi as though he had just arrived by train, in order to reach an hotel where he could breakfast in a manner befitting his rank. But that little plan proved quite abortive.

The *Hauptbhanhof* yard was full of cars ; many were grey ones belonging to Army units and the rest all had some form or other of label pasted on their windscreens, reading 'Supply Service,' 'A.R.P.,' 'Road Control,' 'Police,' and so on. The station buzzed with activity ; people, most of whom were in uniform, came and went incessantly, but there was not a single taxi to be seen. Evidently the Germans must have taken them off the streets in order to conserve their petrol supply.

Somewhat cheered by seeing many other officers also walking, Gregory entered the stream of pedestrians moving towards the centre of the town and made his way to the Dom Hotel, which had been used by the British as their Headquarters during their occupation of Cologne twenty years before. A sentry outside it presented arms and Gregory acknowledged the salute, casually now, having become quite used to taking salutes during his walk from the station, but he was informed that the hotel had been taken over by the Administration and was directed to the Excelsior.

On arriving there he went straight through to the gentlemen's cloakroom, picked up the first gas-mask that he saw on a peg and, slinging it round his shoulders, walked out again. Crossing the street, he went round the corner, entered the Edenhof and going into the restaurant proceeded to order breakfast.

If he had had to content himself with the menu which was presented to him he would have fared badly, as rationing was already in force in Germany, but he knew that money would talk there as well as anywhere else in Europe, and in this little matter his rank would protect him from any charge of contravening the laws which some over-zealous witness might bring against him.

Looking the head waiter straight in the eye, he handed him back the menu, which listed only cereals, gave him a two-mark piece and gruffly demanded *Eier mit Schinken*.

"*Jawohl, Herr General*," replied the waiter swiftly, and turning to one of his minions passed on the order.

While he ate his ham and eggs and drank some passable imitation coffee he considered his next move. If he had entered the country dressed as a private, as Sir Pellinore had suggested, he would have carried a knapsack in which he could have brought a change of linen and other oddments that he might require ; but Generals do not carry knapsacks, neither do they carry suitcases, so he had had to content himself with slipping his razor, toothbrush and comb into one of his pockets.

It was clear, however, that he must have luggage if he were to stay in the country for any length of time. He could not just walk into hotels minus even an attaché-case and spend the night without arousing suspicion in the minds of chamber-maids and managers. It had been his intention to take a taxi round the town after he had breakfasted and to purchase his small requirements, but this was now out of the question.

Having paid his bill and had the ration-card with which the department had provided him punched, he went out to the reception-desk and announced to the weedy, C.3-looking clerk

who stood behind it : "I am General von Lettow. My servant
did not arrive at the station in Hanover last night in time to
meet me with my suitcase, so I had to leave without it. I am
now going out to buy a few things and shall have them sent
here. See to it that the porter has them all together in his office
when I return !"

The little clerk clicked his heels and bowed. "At your service, Excellency."

Turning away with a curt nod, Gregory went out to do his
shopping. After an hour he had bought at various places a
good-sized suitcase, pyjamas, a dressing-gown, two changes of
under-clothes, bedroom slippers, another pair of boots that
fitted him better, and toilet things. He almost gave himself
away at the chemist's by inquiring for hair-oil, but remembered
just in time that his head was now bald. He tried to get a torch,
but without success, as every torch in Cologne had either been
commandeered days before for military purposes or snapped up
by civilians as part of their A.R.P. outfits.

Having instructed the various shopkeepers that his purchases
should be sent at once by hand to the Edenhof, he decided to
go and have a drink at the big café on the *Dom Platz* in order
to give them reasonable time to make the deliveries, and seated
there at a small, marble-topped table with a big mug of the dark
Muniche Löwenbräu in front of him he studied the surrounding
scene with interest.

Workmen, high on a scaffolding, were busily removing the
stained glass of the rose-window from the great, twin-towered
cathedral opposite, and piles of neatly-stacked sandbags now
protected the fine stone carvings on the arches of its doors.

The café was one of those set aside for the use of officers,
but a few civilians were sitting about and taking their morning
beer. An elderly, grey-bearded man was seated at the next
table and Gregory thought that he would try out his German
on him, though he had few qualms about it. There are many
more dialects and local accents in Germany than there are in
England, so that even if his German were not absolutely perfect
any peculiarity of inflection would be noticed by his hearer only
in the same way that a Londoner might detect a slight touch
of the North Country or Cornwall in the speech of an educated
Englishman brought up in the provinces.

Having ordered a packet of cigarettes of a popular brand,
Gregory leaned across to the bearded man. *"Würden sie mir
Feuer geben bitte ?"*

The man quickly fumbled for some matches and Gregory took a light from the sulphurous flame. The thin, loosely-packed cigarette tasted as though it was made of hay, as it probably was, but Gregory knew that he would have to accustom himself to the taste. *"Danke,"* he smiled. "These are interesting times in which to live, are they not?"

"Yes, indeed, Herr General," his neighbour replied with nervous haste, and Gregory realized at once that he was too scared to talk to anyone in uniform. Another disadvantage of the kit that he had chosen ; but after all, it was not his business to go round seeking the opinions of individual Germans on the war. He must accept Sir Pellinore's statement that a considerable number of Germans were desperately opposed to it and to the Nazi régime, but they would certainly not admit as much to a General, even if there were not dozens of Nazis in brown or black uniforms strutting about within a stone's-throw of the café.

After remarking hurriedly that it was a good thing the weather was keeping so fine for the gallant troops, the elderly man rapidly disposed of his beer, paid his score and departed.

His table was taken shortly afterwards by two younger men, both officers, a Major and a Lieutenant. Having saluted Gregory, and with a formal : "You permit, Herr General?" they sat down and began to talk together in low voices.

Gregory's hay-filled cigarette had lasted for barely half a dozen puffs, so he took out another and again asked for a light.

The Lieutenant stood up with the rapidity of a Jack-in-the-box, clicked his heels and supplied it. Gregory stood up to take it and, bowing slightly, murmured : "Von Lettow." The Lieutenant jerked forward from the waist like an automaton and rapped out : "Kuhlemann, at your service, Herr General !" The Major sprang to his feet also, and bending abruptly at the waist, snapped : "Möller !"

Gregory returned their bows and asked if they would join him in a drink. Both accepted, and more beer was brought. Gregory opened the conversation by saying that he had arrived that night from Hanover and was on his way up the Rhine to Coblenz.

"Ha ! You are lucky, then, Herr General !" the Lieutenant exclaimed. "As Coblenz is our base for the Army on the Upper Moselle it does not need much intelligence to guess that to be your destination. You'll see some fighting, whereas we're stuck here in Cologne on garrison duty."

The Major grunted. "You'll get all the fighting you want Kuhlemann, before this war is over. It'll be a long show, just as it was last time. Don't you agree, sir?"

Gregory smiled. "It is good that young officers should be impatient to serve the Fatherland at the front, but we older soldiers who have seen war may be excused if we are content to wait until we are ordered forward into the battle. The struggle will be a long one, yes; but we shall emerge victorious."

"*Heil Hitler!*" ejaculated the Lieutenant.

"*Heil Hitler!*" echoed Gregory and Möller promptly, but the latter added thoughtfully: "It will be hard on the women and children."

"Yes, it will be hard," agreed Gregory, "but they must play their part without flinching."

"The poor devils are having to leave their homes already," Möller went on. "Look! There's another batch of them crossing the square."

Gregory turned in his chair and saw a dejected group of women and children staggering along under the weight of suit-cases and bundles. He had seen similar groups in the streets of Cologne earlier that morning, but had been too preoccupied with his own thoughts to wonder about them.

"They're evacuating all the towns in the Saar," remarked Kuhlemann, "but the minor discomforts they are asked to face are nothing compared to remaining there to be bombed to pieces by these English swine."

"They haven't dropped any bombs yet," replied the Major mildly, "except on the railway siding at Aachen. They're still busy distributing their leaflets."

"Have you seen one?" asked Gregory; "I tried to get a copy in Hanover but people were too frightened of the Gestapo to pass them on to anyone in my position."

The Major smiled and took out his pocket-book. "I've got one here, Herr General, if it would interest you to see it. We're supposed to destroy them, of course, but I kept it as an inter-esting souvenir.

"*Danke.*" Gregory extended his hand for the slip of paper. "It is not good that they should be passed freely among the civilian population, but among officers it is another matter. The loyalty of German officers can never be brought into question."

He read the leaflet through and handed it back. "What lies these English tell—but between ourselves we must admit that there's just enough truth in it to make it highly dangerous."

Möller laughed. "Well, it's not as dangerous as bombs would be, anyway, so we'll hope that they stick to dropping paper."

Gregory felt that sufficient time had now elapsed for his purchases to have been delivered at the Edenhof so he stood up, the other two following his example. Wishing them good luck, which sentiment they heartily reciprocated, he made his way back to the hotel.

His things had arrived, and he stood by while the porter packed them, in their wrappings, into the suitcase. He then inquired about the sailings of the Rhine steamers and learned to his satisfaction that one was due to leave Bonn for Coblenz at 1.30. The journey could have been made more quickly by rail but Gregory knew that had he actually been a serving officer he would have had a railway pass to his destination. To buy a ticket might create suspicion and to say that he had lost his voucher and ask the R.T.O. to supply him with another would have led to undesirable complications, so he had decided to make the journey by river steamer, on which it was less likely that he would be expected to produce a military chit.

The hall-porter summoned a street porter who took Gregory's bag and preceded him as he walked the comparatively short distance down to the river-side, whence the local electric trains start for Bonn. The line cuts across a bend in the Rhine where the country is flat and uninteresting, so that few people make the river trip from Cologne but prefer to board the boat at Bonn, and for a short, local journey of this kind it was quite natural that Gregory should take an ordinary ticket instead of producing a military travelling pass.

The old university town of Bonn was now empty of its students in their gay, many-coloured caps, and in their place were great numbers of refugees, for the colleges were being used to billet the women and children who had been evacuated from the towns immediately behind the Siegfried Line.

With a heavy-footed strut Gregory boarded the big, low-decked steamer and everybody made way for him as he forged ahead to a comfortable seat from which he could enjoy the view as they steamed up the Rhine. He had done the trip on numerous previous occasions, so when they came opposite to the Seven Sisters Mountains on the left bank and the Drakensberg, with its glass-verandahed restaurant situated high above the quiet little town of Königswinter, he went down to lunch.

This consisted of a very small portion of veal, boiled potatoes and carrots, followed by *Apfelkuchen*. There was plenty of bread to go with it, but no butter, cream or cheese. Another square of his forged ration-card was punched, he paid the bill and went on deck again to enjoy a lazy afternoon gazing out across the wide river as bend after bend of it opened out new vistas showing ruined castles perched upon nearly all of the heights that came into view.

At six o'clock they docked at Coblenz, and securing a porter to carry his bag Gregory went straight to the Hotel Bellevue, which stands right on the river-front. He registered at the desk as General von Lettow, and owing to his rank managed to secure a room on the first floor that had just been vacated. Having bought a couple of books from the stall in the hotel lounge he went straight up to his room and unpacked. Then he went out on to the balcony, and as he gazed down upon the scene spread out below memories came floating back to him.

To his left the river divided, and in this direction lay the most beautiful portion of the Rhine, with its famous vineyards of Johannesburg, Marcobrunn, Steinberg, Rudesheim and the rest. At Coblenz, too, the Rhine was joined by another great river, the Moselle, up which he meant to proceed on the following morning. The Moselle was beautiful also, he recalled, but with a more gentle beauty ; passing between less abrupt but more thickly-wooded slopes or lush water-meadows lying level with its banks.

He remembered his first visit to Coblenz, as a boy. It had been over Whitsun in 1913, when his father had taken him with him on a short business trip to Germany. That Whitsun Germany had held her first air pageant, a three-days' rally under the auspices of His Imperial Highness Prince Henry of Prussia, brother of the Kaiser. Over fifty crazy, flimsy planes made of linen and bamboo had gathered from all parts of Germany on the plateau above the town, and seven great Zeppelins had floated like huge, silver cigars above the airfield.

The Hotel Bellevue was then newly built, and had in fact been specially opened in honour of the occasion. Officers of the Kaiser's Army had thronged it, resplendent in their glossy cloaks of grey, green and blue. Their swords and spurs jangling ; the gold and silver eagles upon their *Pickelhaubes* glinting in the lights, Death's Head Hussars in fur toques and Jäger in forest green had made the place like a scene from a Viennese musical comedy.

Little Gregory had been thrilled beyond words by the martial splendour of it all, and on the last night he had been allowed to stay up to see the fireworks display at Ehrenbreitstein, the grim old fortress that crowned the hill on the farther side of the Rhine. Twenty-six years had not altered a line of this unforgettable picture save for the addition of hideous steel pylons carrying electric cables.

Yet—so much had happened since. His thoughts drifted to another occasion, a few years after the War, when he had stayed at the same hotel. His companion then had not been his father, but a very lovely lady. What marvellous times they had had together on that stolen holiday in the Rhineland ! He wondered what had become of Anita now. She must be getting on, and probably had children. Ah, well ! That was the way things went in this world. One could never hold happiness for very long ; one had to snatch it whenever it came one's way. With a little sigh he re-entered his room through the long windows and went down to the grill-room of the hotel for a meal.

It was packed with Army officers, but his rank soon secured him a table. As he there sat he sensed the tension about him. Few women were present, and there was no gaiety. The diners talked in low voices and many of them kept one eye on the door, through which an intermittent stream of orderlies hurried, bringing messages or calling officers to the telephone. Coblenz was an important junction and the supply base for the Western Front. And Germany was at war.

As soon as he had finished he went upstairs again and started to undress. It was over twenty-four hours since he had last slept and he was beginning to feel a little tired. He read for a quarter of an hour and then switched off his light.

Things had been easy so far—incredibly easy. He had secured his kit and accomplished over half his journey without the slightest hitch. Protected by his General's uniform, now that he was slipping into the part, he saw no reason why they should not continue so. After all, if one sees an English General in a London hotel or street it does not even occur to one that he might really be a German secret agent.

Turning over, he dropped into an untroubled sleep. But he might not have slept so soundly if he could have foreseen the desperate plight in which the following night was to find him.

Chapter VI

THE FIRST LINK

BY breakfast-time the following morning Gregory had planned the last stage of his journey to Traben-Trabach. The twin townships lay opposite to each other about thirty-five miles away up the Moselle as the crow flies, but considerably more by road or rail.

The road followed the twisting valley of the river, which included many huge loops in its erratic course, while although the main line of the railway ran directly across country to Bullay the latter half of the journey to Traben was by a branch line which, like the road, followed the bends of the river.

Rail would have been quicker, but once again he feared to arouse comment at the station owing to his lack of a military travelling voucher; if he travelled by car, however, he would evade the possibility of any such contretemps. Unfortunately it was impossible for him to hire a car, but he saw no reason why he should not commandeer one and he decided to do so.

With this idea in mind he walked from the restaurant to the entrance of the hotel, where he was able to keep a careful watch on arrivals and departures while screening his interest behind an open newspaper. The scene was one of considerable activity, for the hotel was crammed with officers and as they came and went they all seemed intent on urgent business.

To Gregory's annoyance every car that drove up was already being used either by Army officers or by uniformed Nazis. He did not want to risk coming into conflict with either, but at last a medium-sized touring car pulled up at the entrance, driven by a girl who wore an A.R.P. brassard on her arm. As soon as it halted a wiry, ferret-faced little civilian jumped out from beside her. Bustling importantly past Gregory, he thrust his way through the crush in the lounge and entered one of the lifts. No sooner was he inside it than Gregory folded his paper, strode across the pavement and saluted the driver.

For a moment the girl looked quite startled, but he gave her his most charming smile and said: "I regret to trouble you, Fräulein, but I have a most urgent duty to perform and my car has not arrived. I can wait no longer, so I fear that I must commandeer yours for military purposes."

The girl was a fair-haired, plump-faced female and his request made her look both scared and unhappy, but Gregory did not give her time to argue. Opening the door he got in beside her and said: ."You will drive me, please, to Traben."

"But—Herr Schnabel—" she began, but Gregory cut her short. "I regret, Fräulein, but we must not delay. I am already late and the matter is urgent."

To his immense relief she made no further effort to protest but slipped in the clutch and took the road that led towards the Moselle. Leaving behind the huge equestrian statue which stands at the confluence of the two rivers, they were soon speeding south-westwards down the wide *Autobahn*.

As the girl was obviously terrified of opening her mouth in the presence of anyone as important as a General, Gregory sought to put her at her ease by asking how long she had been in the Coblenz A.R.P.

He learned that her name was Greta Schultz and that she had been acting as driver to Herr Schnabel, the ferrety civilian who had bustled so importantly into the hotel, only for the past fortnight. Apparently no-one in Coblenz had thought that there was the least likelihood of Germany's being plunged into another Great War. Any danger of air-raids had therefore seemed immeasurably remote, and in consequence the A.R.P. organization of the district was hopelessly inadequate and they were now working night and day to make themselves reasonably secure. Herr Schnabel, a local Nazi of importance, had been made Chief Warden. He was a short-tempered man at the best of times and a fire at his home the previous night which had damaged both his uniforms had put him in a particularly evil mood that morning. Now that in addition he was harassed by his responsibility for the safety of the city's civilian population and had more appointments than he could possibly manage to keep, it was quite certain that he would be absolutely furious at having his car commandeered.

Gregory declared sententiously that military matters must come before civilian defence, and led the girl on to talk about the war. It soon transpired that she had no opinions of her own and that her views had been entirely formed for her by Dr.

Goebbels' Ministry of Propaganda. She retailed incredible stories of the tortures to which the Poles had subjected Germans living in Poland, praised Hitler as the liberator of the German people and spoke with unbelievable bitterness of Britain, the arch-enemy, who by her policy of encirclement was unquestionably responsible for the war.

About the Russo-German pact she was obviously completely puzzled and had no views to offer except that whatever the Führer did was right, but it was clear that the declaration of war by the Democracies had come as an appalling shock to herself and her friends, and that the bulletin issued the previous day, admitting that French troops were fighting on German soil, had filled them with dismay.

The road ran flat and smooth along the river-bank, winding its way south-westward in the direction of Trier and the southern corner of Luxemburg, less than seventy miles away, where fighting was in progress. The first part of the journey was not particularly interesting, but by the time that the tall tower of Cochem Castle had come in sight the river had become as beautiful as the upper reaches of the Thames. On one side, its steep slopes were covered with countless irregular terraces, built up from below or cut out from the hillside to catch every ray of sunshine which might help to sweeten the grapes of the carefully-cultivated rows of vines which were grown upon them. On the other, the deeper green of pine and larch woods rose unbroken from the river-bank to the crest of the hills that fringed the valley, while here and there sheltered meadows in which cattle were peacefully grazing lay along the banks of the river.

There was far more Army activity in this part of the country than there had been round Cologne and most of the traffic was of a military nature, but as soon as they had passed Boulay, where the main road and the main-line railway branch away from the river, the road became practically deserted. The villages of Zell and Enkirch lay sleeping in the September sunshine ; quiet, friendly places which, apart from a Nazi flag or two, had remained unchanged by the coming of Hitler or the war ; their inhabitants preoccupied with the tending of their vineyards and the vintaging of their wines as they had been through so many centuries.

Just before eleven they came in sight of the twin townlets of Traben-Trabach. The road lay along the south bank of the river, so they entered Trabach first. Passing below the ruined *Schloss* perched upon the wooded hillside above the town they pulled up at the bridge to inquire for Julius Rheinhardt's offices, and a policeman directed them over the river to Traben.

The river-bank there was lined with old houses, each with its vine-covered terrace overlooking the road below ; from the big, arched doorways under several of these terraces casks and cases of wine were being man-handled across the road to be loaded on to river barges. The policeman pointed out one of these as Herr Rheinhardt's, in which his offices were also situated. Crossing the river they drove round to the back of the house and entered a courtyard, where Gregory got out, ascended a few steps at the side of the yard, and entered a door marked *Bureau*.

The appearance of a General created quite a stir among the women and boys who were working there, and an elderly hunch-back quickly shuffled forward to ask the Herr General's pleasure.

It appeared that Herr Julius was making an inspection of some of his local vineyards that morning, as the vintaging was now very near and was, in fact, expected to start the following week. Introducing himself as Klein, the hunchback immediately offered his services as guide upon Gregory's saying that he wished to see Herr Rheinhardt as soon as possible, and they went out to the car together.

Beyond Traben the slope of the hill rose gently, being almost surrounded by a bend of the river, and the whole of it was covered with tall vines, differing from the low, French variety in that each was trained up a five-foot stake.

The car bucketted up a bumpy track until the hunchback called a halt and, getting out, clambered on to a low, stone wall whence he could get a view over the surrounding vineyards. Gregory followed, and climbed up beside him.

"Ha ! There is Herr Julius," exclaimed the little man, pointing. "You can just see the top of his hat." He was about to shout, but Gregory stopped him.

"One moment. It is no distance ; I will walk through the vineyards to him. You are to remain here. Go back and sit in the car."

Herr Klein obeyed without a murmur, and Gregory slipped down from the wall into the vineyard and went forward between two rows of tall vines.

It was intensely hot in the vineyard ; much hotter than up on the open road, owing to the slate which was scattered all over the ground to catch the sun's heat and reflect it up on to the bunches of grapes below the leaves so that they should ripen properly. After he had covered a hundred yards Gregory took off his cap to mop his bald, perspiring head and began to peer about among the vines for Herr Rheinhardt. As he moved the slate clinked beneath his heavy boots, so he began to tread cautiously, making as little noise as possible. Advancing a little further he caught the sound of Herr Rheinhardt's tread and a moment later saw a heavy, elderly man approaching down an adjacent lane between the vines, stopping here and there to examine a bunch of grapes with a professional eye.

Gregory drew back a little, putting another vine between himself and the winegrower. He had no introduction or credentials and it was absolutely essential that Herr Rheinhardt should be made to talk. He knew that in disclosing himself he ran a grave risk that Herr Rheinhardt might believe that he was being led into a trap, and would therefore promptly hand his unusual visitor over to the police in order to protect himself.

It was for this reason that Gregory had decided to tackle him while he was out here alone rather than wait until they had got back to the town, since should Rheinhardt react unfavourably the fact that he was out in the country would at least assure him of a flying start. Everything, he felt, hung upon Herr Rheinhardt's first reactions, so he had made up his mind to startle him out of his wits and take the consequences.

When the portly German had approached to within a couple of yards of him he said distinctly, in English : "You may vintage this crop, Herr Rheinhardt, but do you think you will live to drink the wine you make from it ?"

He waited, holding his breath, to see what the reply would be.

Chapter VII

WITHIN SOUND OF THE GUNS

"*HIMMEL* !" The stout man swung round as though he had been shot.

"*Wer ist das* ?" he added, peering anxiously between the vines, and Gregory caught the glint of sunlight on his thick-lensed spectacles. Swiftly he followed up his advantage, speaking still in English.

"Someone who could put you in a Nazi concentration camp to-night and have you shot to-morrow if he were not a friend, Herr Rheinhardt."

"*Wer ist das* ? *Wer ist da* ?" Brushing the vines swiftly aside with his thick, podgy hands the winegrower stumbled forward. His mouth was hanging open and his fat, pleasant face was contorted by acute fear.

"Don't be alarmed, my friend," said Gregory, reverting to excellent German. "No harm is coming to you. I have sought you out only to obtain information regarding your end of the movement in which we are both interested."

"What movement ? I know of none," Rheinhardt stammered, deferentially removing his hat as he caught sight of Gregory's badges of rank. "Anyone will tell you, Herr General, that I am a good German. I concern myself solely with my wine business and have no interest in politics."

"Oh, I'm quite sure of that," Gregory replied with a cynical half-smile. "All the same, you and I are going to have a chat together."

"At your service. But may I know whom I have the honour of addressing ?"

Gregory clicked his heels together and bowed sharply from the waist. "Franz von Lettow, General of Engineers," he rapped out formally.

"Why, then, did you address me just now in English ?" asked the winegrower.

"I used English with the idea of letting you know at once that my business does not concern ordinary military matters."

"It is not good to talk English any more."

"You regret that?"

"England is the best market for my wines, Herr General. Nearly half my business is done there and I have English friends of many years' standing. I am no less loyal a German because I tell you that I know the English much too well to believe that they deliberately plotted the encirclement of Germany with the object of destroying the German people."

Gregory decided that Herr Rheinhardt was not such a fool as he looked. He was at all events astute enough to express sentiments natural to one in his position instead of spouting a lot of nonsense about the British plot to strangle Germany. After a moment he said:

"I, too, know the English well. At heart they, like ourselves, are easy-going, home-loving people; slow to anger but bitter and tenacious enemies once they are aroused. I fought against them in the last war."

Herr Rheinhardt nodded, evidently unwilling to commit himself further. But seeing that Gregory remained silent, he asked: "If it was not upon some matter of supplies or billeting that you wished to see me, may I inquire the object of your visit, Herr General?"

"I was given your name," replied Gregory, "by a mutual friend who must remain anonymous. I have reason to believe that you and I have the same ideas about this war; unorthodox views, but of great importance to Germany. It is essential, therefore, that we go somewhere where we can have a quiet talk. Afterwards you can let it be known that I came to requisition certain stocks of wine. If that were my real object in visiting you we should naturally return to your office, so it is best that we do not stay chatting here for any length of time."

"The Herr General is mistaken," said Herr Rheinhardt mildly. "I have no opinions on the war, orthodox or otherwise. I shall do my duty as a loyal German. Now that the die is cast there is nothing else that any of us can do, however much we may have hoped in the past that peace would be maintained."

Gregory saw that having failed to fluster the winegrower into any incriminating admission, he was now up against a blank wall. The man would certainly not talk unless credentials of some kind could be presented to him, and there was only one rather doubtful card left to play.

From an inside pocket Gregory took out the small, golden, reversed swastika which had once graced the lingerie of Erika von Epp, and holding it cupped in the palm of his hand he silently displayed it to Herr Rheinhardt's view.

For a moment not a muscle of the German's heavy face moved as he stared down at the little golden charm. Then, to Gregory's infinite relief, he said: "The symbol of peace opens all doors among the right-thinking."

Gregory held his breath, and his momentary relief vanished as he wondered desperately whether the German's murmured phrase was some kind of password to which he was expected to supply the countersign. If so he was again at a dead end ; worse, the winegrower would know him for an impostor and, believing him to be a member of the Inner Gestapo, would warn all his friends against him, which would make his task next to impossible. But Herr Rheinhardt went on quietly :

"If you will lunch at my house we shall be undisturbed. In the meantime we had better talk about my stocks of wine to create the impression among my people that you are here for the purpose of commandeering some of them."

Gregory's face showed no trace of his intense elation. He merely nodded and fell into step with the German, who had already turned and was walking towards the road, separated from him by a row of tall vines.

Fräulein Schultz and the hunchback were waiting in the car. Herr Rheinhardt introduced the latter as his chief clerk, and as the car rattled down the hill the three of them talked of stocks, prices and vintages.

When they drew up in the courtyard of Herr Rheinhardt's house Gregory told Fräulein Schultz that she had better get herself some luncheon at the Hotel Clausfiest nearby and that she was to remain there until he sent for her. Having thanked him gratefully for the five-mark note which he handed to her she hurried away, while Gregory followed his host into the private portion of the house and Herr Klein was sent to fetch the stock-book to give cover to their deliberations.

While Rheinhardt ordered luncheon Gregory sat in a low-roofed parlour, mainly furnished with heavy, old-fashioned pieces dating from the eighteenth century. The room had no carpet or parquet, but its board floor was polished like a mirror and everything in it was spotlessly clean.

A copy of that morning's *Kölnischer Zeitung* lay on a side-table, and he filled in the time by reading the latest news of the war.

The Germans had now announced the fact that French

troops were fighting on German soil. They could hardly have done less, as the evacuees from the Saar Basin would now be spreading the news all through the Rhineland, but the official statement made light of it, pointing out that the French had penetrated only the no-man's-land between the Maginot Line and the Western Wall, which could be regarded as virtually neutral territory. It was stated with the utmost confidence that they would stand no chance whatever of advancing further once they had come up against the major defences embodied in the Siegfried Line.

Gregory felt that the Germans were right about that. In the last war it had proved impossible to break the German trench systems without immense loss of life, and, even then, the blood-baths of the Somme and Passchendaele had resulted merely in the formation of salients which had no strategic value what-soever as far as the speedier conclusion of the war was concerned. With the enormous superiority which modern weapons gave to defence over attack he estimated that it would need an advan-tage of five to one in man-power if the French were to force even a small sector of the Siegfried Line, and he hoped with all his heart that the Allied Generals were not going to repeat once again the crazy, tragic sacrifice of their men for gains of so little value.

The major portion of the war news was devoted to the Polish Front, and while the official communiqués blared out a pæan of triumph about Germany's successes in the East they issued a warning that the people must not expect the Army to continue its advance at the speed which it had been making during the past few days.

Gregory's mouth twisted in a cynical grin as he read. As an old soldier he knew how necessary that warning was. In some cases the Germans had advanced 200 miles in ten days ; a wonderful performance. But the fighting units must now be far in advance of their railheads. He had seen the great German drive for Paris in March 1918, when the British and French fronts were both broken, peter out from just the same cause. After ten days' desperate fighting the Germans had been forced to halt; although there were hardly any Allied troops left in that sector of the attack to stem them. They had covered only forty miles in that time, but even so reinforcements had been able gradually to consolidate the new Allied line and the last great German war effort had failed in its objective.

The Poles were great fighters. In 1920 they had been forced

back on Warsaw but had turned there and had held and broken the vast Bolshevik army which was then sweeping down into Europe. Now they had once more been forced back to their capital, but there seemed a good chance that in spite of the tremendous odds against them they would be able to hang on there until the rains came and Poland was turned into a sea of mud which would put the German mechanized divisions out of action for the winter.

Gregory's musings were interrupted by the arrival of Klein with the stock-book. A few minutes later Herr Rheinhardt joined them, after which Gregory and his host devoted three-quarters of an hour to listing wines suitable for the German Army canteens ; a solemn pantomime enacted solely for Klein's benefit. They were just concluding the business when a plump servant-girl, in a tight-waisted bodice and with numerous petticoats ballooning over her large hips, came in to say that *Mittagessen* was ready on the terrace. The hunchback bowed himself out backwards and Rheinhardt led Gregory through a pair of French windows on to a terrace overlooking the river and shaded from the midday sun by espaliered vines.

The first course consisted of delicious, freshly-caught Moselle trout, while on a side-table stood a big, glass bowl of peach *Bola* made of sparkling and still wine mixed and peaches which had been forked so that the wine should draw out their flavour.

For a while Gregory almost forgot the strange circumstances which had led to his receiving the winegrower's hospitality as he gave himself up to enjoying the simple perfection of such a meal in such a setting.

Now that the middle hour of the day had come, the loading of the barges below them had ceased, and there was not a soul to be seen either on the river or on the towpath opposite, along which ran the half-mile of gabled houses that composed the waterfront of Trabach. The river was about as broad as the Thames at Richmond, but there were no craft upon it other than the moored barges and it flowed unbroken, a swift but not dangerous torrent, under the bridge further downstream and on to the Rhine. Beyond it and the houses on the other bank a valley broke the contour of the wooded hills and led up into the forests of the Hunsrück, where wild boar and deer could still be hunted, but except at that point the great curve of the river was encircled by an unbroken range of hills, on the highest crest of which, above the town, the ruined castle stood out clearly against the skyline.

c

As is the case with so many of these small towns, cut off from the important centres of population by mountains and forests, both the town itself and the mode of life of its inhabitants could have altered very little in essentials, Gregory mused, since some robber Baron had lived in the castle and levied toll upon the passing merchants, who used the river as a highway for their goods long before the roads were made.

When he went to war the robber Baron would have exercised his feudal right to take the young men of the township with him, and despite their absence life would have gone on just the same ; but until a few centuries ago, when the Germans began to sell themselves as mercenaries to fight for any ambitious European King who would pay them, such wars were rarely more than local affairs.

His mind still wandering down the vistas of history, it occurred to him that the Germans had always liked fighting, and still did, for that matter. Long after the youth of other nations had come to regard war as a terrible business, to be entered into only under the dire necessity of protecting their countries and the things they loved, the young men of Germany were still brought up to believe that they should gladly give their lives on any battlefield to which they might be ordered.

Gregory had always thought that the reason for this extra-ordinarily marked difference between the youth of Germany and that of other States had a quite simple explanation. Wherever the Roman legions had penetrated, he reasoned, they had brought in their train road-makers, agricultural experts, law-givers, doctors, and poets who, once the tribes were subdued, had brought them the blessings of an ordered world, the culture of Rome, and the wisdom of the ancient civilizations of the East.

For four hundred years the *Pax Romana* had held in the interiors of most of the Roman provinces, from the Wall of Scotland to the Persian Gulf, and during this time nearly twenty generations of their inhabitants had gradually evolved from brutal savages into peace-loving husbandmen and craftsmen and prosperous merchants. The spiritual benefit brought by Rome to the whole of Southern Europe had been quite incalcul-able, and even after the fall of Rome the peoples of the old Roman provinces had never again relapsed altogether into the state of barbarity in which the legions had found them.

But apart from forays, the Roman legions had never pene-trated east of the Rhine or north of the Danube. The Teutonic peoples had never enjoyed the wonderfully civilizing influence of Rome, and throughout those long centuries, representing a period as great as that lying between early Tudor times and our own, the Germans had remained ignorant, cruel, and barbarous, in the depths of their wild forests. Even the civilizing influence of Christianity had not reached them until hundreds of years after it had permeated the whole of the Roman world.

It was that irreparable gap in the inheritance of the German mentality which had left them so far behind the other nations of the West as regards the true appreciation of spiritual values, so that the less complex among them still loved war for its own sake, and, when once it was in progress, rejoiced to wage it with cynical brutality.

It had been Germans of this type who had banded together after the Great War, and, carrying a bewildered and leaderless nation with them, had fought their way with savage directness out of the chaos and poverty of defeat. The tragedy of the present war, Gregory reflected, was due to the fact that such men, having achieved power, had drilled the rising generation into the deification of their own primitive type under the guise of Aryanism, and had inculcated the pagan worship of might as the only right.

At their head to-day another robber Baron had arisen, but one who was not content to call only the young men to his standard. As Gregory gazed down at the peaceful river scene he knew that not a single house in the little town could escape paying forfeit for the Führer's mad gamble with Germany's destiny. Every man up to the age of forty had already been called up ; soon other classes would be called until not a man remained, apart from the hopelessly unfit, under the age of fifty-five. Fathers and even grandfathers, as well as sons, would be dragged from their homes. Daughters would be pressed into women's units. The produce of the vines would be taken for the Armies, and a grim winter on the most meagre of rations would lie before those who were left.

Herr Rheinhardt must have sensed the trend of Gregory's thoughts, for he said : "I am afraid for the Fatherland. Men in your position and mine know that Germany has not the same powers of resistance as in 1914."

Gregory nodded. "Then, we at least started as a well-fed nation, and every man above the age of twenty had done his full period in the Army. Now, on the other hand, there is this appalling gap between old soldiers like myself and the young men who have been embodied in the army since Hitler decided on its expansion. Those who reached conscription age between 1919 and 1934 represent a very high percentage of Germany's manhood yet, with comparatively few exceptions, they have had only a few weeks' military service."

"*Wirklich* ! Also, we then had our colonies, each of which distracted the enemy from his main effort during the early years of the war. Together, they succeeded in occupying great numbers of the enemy's overseas troops, whereas now the whole weight of the French and British Empires can be thrown without hindrance against Germany herself."

"Unless Russia comes in with us," Gregory replied, "I can see no possible hope of victory."

Herr Rheinhardt shook his head despondently. "Russia would want her pound of flesh, and what good would her help do us if· we had to go Communist ? Our last state would be worse than our first."

Gregory gave a disillusioned laugh. "And to think that both the Army and industrialists like yourself gave Hitler their support because he promised to save us from the menace of Communism !"

Herr Rheinhardt shrugged. "What are his promises worth ? Those of us who have been in a position to travel in neutral countries and read a free, unbiased Press know that he has broken every promise that he has ever made. Yet, surrounded as he is by all the gangsters and criminals of the whole country, who spy upon everyone and everything, it will be no easy matter now to save Germany from him."

"The difficulties are immense, and the Gestapo is everywhere, yet it must be done, and it lies with people of influence like you and myself, who have the best interests of the Fatherland at heart, to do it."

"Speaking for my own associates, we are ready and willing to risk our necks whenever the time is ripe to move against these Nazi blackguards, but we would be powerless without a lead from the Army."

"You shall have it," Gregory assured him. "I cannot disclose the names of my superiors, but I am acting for some of the most important men among our Army leaders, and my purpose in making this tour of the Rhineland is to find out how well prepared the movement is down here, and in particular, how far we may rely upon the masses."

"I can speak for this section of the Moselle valley only.

Here, with the exception of a handful of young hotheads, everyone regards the war as a major calamity. Among the women this is particularly the case, and even those who previously had faith in Hitler are now of the opinion that he has betrayed them. They feel that nothing can justify his having overreached himself and plunged us into war with the great Democracies. Have you seen Wachmuller yet?"

Gregory shook his head, and was careful not to show his elation at having so soon discovered the name of a man who was obviously another link in the chain of conspirators.

"No," he said, "but I hope to do so within the course of the next few days."

"He can give you much more information than I can," Rheinhardt went on, "for being so noted a preacher he is in a position to tour the whole Rhineland without becoming suspect. He is in constant touch with our friends in all the important cities."

'So Wachmuller is a clergyman,' thought Gregory, as he asked, fishing carefully, "D'you happen to know if he's at home at the present time?"

"No," Rheinhardt shook his head; "but when you get back to Coblenz you can easily ring up his house at Ems and find out."

"I'll do so to-night, if I have time," said Gregory casually.

They talked for a little of the war in Poland and the threat to the Siegfried Line in the West, while they ate some roast veal and small, sweet grapes from the new crop, after which Gregory stood up to take his departure.

Before leaving the terrace they shook hands, and wished each other well in the dangerous game that they were playing for the salvation of their nation. Rheinhardt then telephoned to the Hotel Clausfiest, a few hundred yards further along the river bank, for Fräulein Schultz to bring the General's car. Having said in Klein's hearing that he would communicate in due course about the wines to be requisitioned, Gregory climbed into the car beside the girl and they set off to return along the quiet Moselle valley to Coblenz.

As they were driving out of Traben she asked him if he had heard the guns. He had not noticed them, so she pulled the car up for a moment, and as they listened he could hear a very faint, erratic rumble which showed that a bombardment was in progress some thirty or forty miles away, to the south of Trier.

They made the return journey without incident, and arrived back in Coblenz just as dusk was falling. Gregory was in good spirits, being highly satisfied with his day's work. The small town of Ems lay on the Lahn, another tributary of the Rhine, and was only about ten miles by road from Coblenz. He would telephone Pastor Wachmuller at once, and if he was at home he would go out to see him either that evening or the following morning.

As the car drew up he noticed that two Nazi Storm-Troopers were standing in front of the hotel entrance, and it was with a sudden apprehension that he saw them step forward. Next moment they were beside the car, and one of them said abruptly :

"It is the order of our chief that you should come with us, Herr General."

Chapter VIII

WHEN GREEK MEETS GREEK

THOUGH his brain was revving like a high-powered dynamo Gregory got out of the car with deliberate slowness. It would never do to show the least sign of fluster before these two brown-uniformed young men.

Where had he slipped up? What had he done to give himself away so soon? Or was his acute anxiety quite unnecessary? Perhaps he had only been sent for because he had neglected to fulfil some formality when registering at the hotel the night before?

"Who *is* your chief?" he asked quietly.

"He is Herr Schnabel," the taller Nazi replied, and immediately the situation was made plain to Gregory, for Herr Schnabel was the owner of the car which he had commandeered. When he had taken it he had been under the impression that it had belonged merely to an ordinary civilian engaged on A.R.P. work, but he now remembered that Fräulein Schultz had told him that Herr Schnabel was Chief Warden of Coblenz besides being an important member of the Nazi Party.

He cursed himself for not having given that piece of information the consideration it had deserved, but it was too late now, and his only course lay in trying to use his prestige as a General to bluff his way out of the awkward predicament in which his neglect had landed him.

"Oh!" he said. "That's the man whose car I was compelled to commandeer this morning, isn't it? I owe him an apology, but I'm sure Herr Schnabel would understand if I were free to inform him of the facts that made it necessary. Please convey that message to him."

"He wishes to see you, Herr General," reiterated the Nazi, "and we have been waiting here all day for your return."

"Where is he?" asked Gregory.

"At the Party Headquarters."

"I'm sorry, but I have no time to accompany you there now, as I have some urgent telephone calls to make. Please express my regrets to Herr Schnabel for any inconvenience I may have caused him." Gregory turned to glance at Fraulein Schultz, and added : "This lady is, of course, in no way to blame, as she merely acted under my orders. My compliments upon your good driving, Fräulein ; good night to you." With a quick salute he swung on his heel and strode into the hotel.

The two young Nazis came hurrying after him, and the taller said swiftly : "But, Herr General, it is an order ; a Party order ; and we cannot return to Herr Schnabel without you."

"What's that ?" Gregory swung round on him. "You don't seem to appreciate, young man, that Germany is at war. I have every respect for the officials of the Party, but in these days the military duties of an officer come before such matters as making amends to a Party official for having commandeered his car. I've already told you that I have important work to do."

The Nazi who did the talking was a well-built young fellow with rather nice blue eyes, but his expression did not denote any great degree of intelligence. He shuffled awkwardly for a moment before stuttering : "But—but, Herr General, it is an order, and Herr Schnabel says he *must* see you."

"All right, then," snapped Gregory ; "tell him that if he wishes to do so he must come to the hotel. It is intolerable that I should be bothered in this manner."

The one thing that Gregory was determined not to do if he could possibly avoid it was to put his foot inside the Party Headquarters, for if he did he might never get out again.

The senior Brownshirt shrugged resignedly, and looking at his companion, exclaimed : "Remain here with the Herr General, Otto ; I go to telephone."

He hurried off, leaving Gregory in a wretched quandary. By going straight up to his room and refusing the other fellow permission to enter it he could get free of him for the moment, but he could not prevent his standing outside the door. Even if he could trick or browbeat him into remaining downstairs, Herr Schnabel might now be appearing on the scene at any moment, so there was little chance of Gregory's being able to pack his things, pay his bill, and leave the hotel in a normal manner. If Schnabel caught him in the act of trying to make a speedy getaway he would have the best of grounds for suspecting that the car-commandeering General was not what he represented himself to be ; whereas, as far as Gregory knew at the moment, Schnabel had as yet no grounds at all for suspicions of that kind, but was just a self-important little official who was extremely irritated by having been put to considerable inconvenience. It seemed safest, therefore, to remain where he was, and attempt to bluff the matter out.

Simulating angry impatience, Gregory plonked himself down in a chair in the lounge, and bawled to a waiter to bring him a *Knickerbinechen*. A moment later he realized his error. This particular variety of German cocktail is made by putting Maraschino into a long, thin glass ; then the whole yolk of a raw egg, and topping it off with *Crème de Vanille*. German-made marks of the liqueurs were doubtless procurable, but eggs had been scarce in Germany for years, and now that rationing was in full swing it was unthinkable that people should wolf them publicly in cocktails.

When the elderly waiter began an apologetic protest, he cursed the man for a fool and told him that he had not said *Knickerbinechen* but *Kleinerbranntwein*, which is a small brandy ; but he caught the remaining Nazi, who was standing some feet away from him, glancing at him with sullen disapproval.

The fresh-faced fellow came hurrying back soon afterwards to say that Herr Schnabel was on his way round to the hotel. Gregory ignored the remark and sat in frowning silence until his brandy arrived. When it did, he tossed it off with the thought that if he wasn't darned careful it might be a long time before he had another.

As he set down the glass the little man whom he had seen hurrying from the car to the lift that morning came strutting into the lounge. Although he was still in civilian dress, the two Nazis jumped to attention.

On the old, if often fallacious principle that attack is the best form of defence, Gregory had determined to get in the first shot. Remembering that he was supposed to be a man of nearly sixty he lumbered up out of his chair as though it was an effort for him to get up quickly, drew his lean face into a thunderous scowl, and barked : "Von Lettow."

Herr Schnabel halted in his tracks, jerked forward from the waist and introduced himself, but he had hardly time to get his name out before Gregory growled : "Kindly explain this unwarrantable interference with my movements, *mein Herr*. That I had to take your car upon military business this morning was unfortunate, but I have already ordered your people to express my regrets to you, and there the matter should have ended. I have urgent work to do."

"By what authority did you take my car?" Herr Schnabel snapped. He had a ferret-face, narrow brow and light-blue eyes; Gregory had disliked him on sight.

"By the authority vested in me as an officer of the General Staff," he replied, "and now that Germany is at war I think you will find it difficult to produce any higher authority."

"In peace or war the authority of the Party is paramount, Herr General," retorted the Nazi chief, without hesitation.

Gregory knew well enough that he was on extremely doubtful ground. In peace-time the Party chiefs had been in a position to ride rough-shod over anyone, even high officers of the Army, but there did seem good reason to suppose that the situation had altered during the last week and that, except in matters concerning the heads of the government and the Gestapo, Army officers might have regained the almost limitless powers which they had enjoyed during the last World War in Germany and the territory of her allies.

"The safety of Germany is now in the hands of her soldiers," he said severely. "To hinder them in the execution of their duties is a punishable offence, and none who have the interests of the Fatherland at heart would ever do so."

"In the war zones that may be so," said Herr Schnabel, "but this is not a war zone, and as Chief Warden I am responsible for the safety of Coblenz. It is *you* who have hindered *me* in the execution of *my* duties. You had no right whatever to make off with my car."

"I had no alternative, since the car that was to have met me here failed to arrive; and my work is of the first importance."

"When we know what your work is, Herr General, we shall be better able to decide that."

"Since when has an officer of the General Staff been obliged to discuss his orders with a civilian?"

Herr Schnabel whipped a notecase out of his pocket, and displayed his Party card, secured in it under a mica screen. "Here is my authority, Herr General; a high officer of the Party is not a civilian, and as you are in my district you will please inform me what you are doing here."

"I have already told you that I have no intention of discussing my orders with anyone."

"Why not? I have told you what my duties are; what reason can you have for refusing to disclose yours to me? I demand to see your papers, Herr General, and if you refuse to show them I will call in the Gestapo."

Gregory knew that he was cornered. The Germans are not a very imaginative or clever people, but they are extraordinarily thorough, and produce some of the finest detectives in the world owing to the sheer, dogged persistence with which they follow up every smallest clue, despite endless trouble, until they can form some logical conclusion from the most insignificant of data. If once the Gestapo got their hooks into him he might just as well start right away to prepare his last will and testament—though it was extremely unlikely that any of his friends or legatees would ever see it.

It would have been unwise to have changed his manner too suddenly, but he allowed his features to relax into indifference and, producing his forged credentials, said: "This is a sheer waste of time, Herr Schnabel, and it would be absurd for us to delay our urgent affairs further by involving others in so trivial a difference of opinion."

The Nazi chief took the papers and glanced swiftly through them. "These seem to be all right," he muttered, "but they are only the usual passes. Have you no Army orders or other letters upon you?"

"If I had, I would not show them to you," retorted Gregory stiffly.

"Herr General," said Schnabel threateningly, "I regard this missing car of yours as most suspicious and I insist upon knowing your business in this area. If you have such letters, please to produce them."

Gregory shrugged. "Such letters as I have are upstairs in my baggage."

"All right, then; we will go up to your room, but your defiance of a Party Chief in my position is so unusual that in any case I consider that it should be reported to the Gestapo." Herr Schnabel glanced at his henchmen. "Weiss, Langleben, accompany the Herr General to his room while I telephone. If he refuses to produce his correspondence you have my authority to search his baggage."

With a curious, sinking feeling in the pit of his stomach Gregory watched the self-important little man strut away. He dared not risk a fracas in the lounge, where many people were sitting drinking, some of them already eyeing him and his companions with open curiosity. With a heavy step he walked towards the lifts, the two Nazis following.

When he reached his room the sullen-looking man who had been addressed as Langleben closed the door and took up his position just inside it, while the fresh-faced Weiss accompanied Gregory into the middle of the room and said, rather nervously : "Will you produce the papers, Herr General, or must I search your luggage ?"

Gregory shrugged again. "All this is quite unnecessary and when I have reported this matter to Army Headquarters your Chief will get a rap over the knuckles that he won't forget in a hurry ; but you are only doing your duty, young man, so remain where you are, please, while I get the letters from my suitcase."

He had no letters or documents of any kind, other than the passes he had already shown, with which to establish his identity, but he walked over to the suitcase, unlocked it, threw up the lid, and stooping down pretended to rummage in it. He was bending over it with his back to the two Nazis, and unperceived by them he undid his pistol holster. Next second he swung round with his automatic firmly clenched in his fist.

"Up with your hands ! Both of you ! Quick ! No arguing, or I'll shoot you where you stand ! You, Langleben, turn your face to that door. Weiss, right-about turn ; walk to the wall and glue your nose to that picture. Utter a sound and I'll shoot you both for the impudent dogs you are !"

He had caught them completely off their guard. Slowly they raised their hands above their heads and with ludicrously fallen faces obeyed his order to turn their backs to him.

In two strides he had crossed to Langleben, reached past him and turned the key in the lock of the door. A moment later he had disarmed them both, pressing his automatic against their spines as he did so, and taking not only their pistols but also their spare clips of ammunition, with the swift thought that it might come in useful later.

Having rammed their guns into the pockets of his greatcoat, he stepped back into the centre of the room and gave his next order. "Right-about turn ! Into the bathroom ! And if you shout when I've shut the door I'll come in and fill the two of you with lead ! Now, quick march !"

Still holding their hands shoulder-high they filed meekly past him. Once they were in the bathroom he removed the key and locked the door on his own side. Now that they were separated from him he had little hope that they would remain silent for more than a minute, but he had done the best he could to secure temporary immunity from a hue and cry.

To his chagrin he had to abandon his belongings, but even

had there been time to pack them he could not possibly have taken them with him. Without a second's delay he unlocked the bedroom door, pulled out the key and slamming the door behind him locked it from the other side.

He had not taken two steps down the corridor when Herr Schnabel came hastening round the corner and almost collided with him.

For an instant they stared at each other. Schnabel sensed that Gregory was escaping and Gregory knew that he was caught; the scar showed white on his forehead. Then the mask of pretence dropped from both their faces, and in their eyes undisguised hatred suddenly flamed. In that moment all the German's unformulated but instinctive suspicions that there was something not quite right about the self-styled General von Lettow were confirmed, and all Gregory's intense dislike of the mean-faced little rat who had cornered him came rushing to the surface.

Before the Nazi could open his mouth Gregory's left hand shot out, caught him by the throat and, swinging him round, forced him back against the wall. With complete ruthlessness Gregory raised his right fist and smashed it into the little man's face.

As his head was jammed against the wall he caught the full force of the blow. A gurgling moan issued from his gaping mouth, but Gregory knew that his own life depended upon putting the wretched man out, and with pitiless persistence he hammered the German's face with his right fist, banging his head against the wall with each blow until it began to roll about on his shoulders and Gregory knew that he had lost consciousness.

Letting Schnabel's body slip to the floor, Gregory grabbed his collar, unlocked the bedroom door again and pitched him inside, muttering to himself: "Well, after all, I'll bet that's no worse than the treatment the little swine has meted out to some of those unfortunate Jews."

As he re-locked the door loud shouts reached his ears. The other two had now plucked up sufficient courage to fling open the bathroom window and try to rouse the hotel. He had not a moment to lose.

To run would have been to court further trouble if he had met anybody, so controlling his pace he set off at a brisk stride down the corridor and round a corner which led to the back of the building. At the far end of the passage was a window which gave on to a fire-escape, as Gregory had found out when making a careful investigation of his surroundings soon after his arrival on the previous evening. At that time he had considered himself reasonably safe, but even so he was too old a hand to neglect the precaution of finding himself an emergency exit whereby he could leave the hotel in a hurry, and without passing through the lounge, if such a step should become necessary.

Thrusting up the window he looked out into a courtyard. Luck was with him, for at the moment none of the servants were working there. Swift, silent and agile as a panther he slipped down the fire-escape into the yard. For the benefit of anyone who might be standing at one of the back windows of the hotel he crossed it at an unhurried stroll, thanking his stars that dusk had already fallen, so that anyone looking down into the yard could have seen no more than the outline of a man in uniform. His rank and person would be quite unidentifiable.

All the same, he felt that he had landed himself in a most desperate plight. By this time the imprisoned Nazis would have secured assistance, for it would not have taken long to procure the pass-keys of his bedroom and bathroom. In another few moments someone would be running to a telephone, and the police and all their associated organizations, including the Gestapo, would be informed that an alleged General, calling himself von Lettow, had held up two Nazis and half-murdered a Nazi Party Chief after having behaved most suspiciously in commandeering a car for purposes which he had refused to reveal.

Within ten minutes the hunt would be up ; telephones buzzing, radios crackling ; and every policeman for miles around would have been warned to be on the look-out for a man, whose description would tally with his own, wearing the uniform of a German General.

Unless he could get rid of the uniform he would not stand an earthly chance of eluding the pursuit in daylight, but while darkness lasted there was still a hope that he might get out of Coblenz, at least.

For the first time since war had broken out he had real reason to be thankful that the threat of aerial warfare had brought A.R.P. black-outs in its train. It was now growing darker every moment, and before switching on their lights the people in the houses were pulling heavy curtains across their windows ; the street-lamps remained unlit and the only lights to be seen came from the small apertures in screens placed over the headlamps of cars.

Cautiously he made his way down side-streets, taking cover in a doorway every time anyone came along. Once he was challenged by a policeman for not having on the white armlet which was now apparently prescribed by law for all citizens of Coblenz who were out after dark, but a motorist nearly ran the policeman down a moment later and, taking to his heels during the ensuing argument, Gregory succeeded in getting away by diving into a near-by alley.

Finding himself back on the river-front near the bridge, he boldly crossed it, and having reached the east bank of the Rhine he turned south along it. There were fewer houses here, and soon all cover ended ; but he breathed more freely then, as there was less likelihood of his running slap into a police patrol, and as he trudged along he tried to formulate the least risky plan of campaign which he could adopt for the immediate future.

He was much too far from Traben-Trabach to try to secure a temporary refuge with Herr Rheinhardt, and in any case his late host would be under suspicion directly Fräulein Schultz had divulged the details of his trip of the previous day, so his best prospect seemed to be Pastor Wachmuller. Ems was less than ten miles distant, and as he had made up his mind earlier that evening to proceed there as soon as possible he had instinctively followed the trend of his thoughts and had left the town by the road that led in that direction.

If he could convince Wachmuller of his *bona fides* perhaps the Pastor would hide him for the next few days, while the hunt was at its hottest ; then provide him with a change of clothes which would enable him both to elude capture and to continue his mission.

But there was a nasty snag attached to that programme. If Wachmuller believed him to be a German General and the representative of the Army leaders, he might disclose a further link in the conspiracy ; but to induce him to provide hiding and fresh clothes Gregory would have to disclose the fact that he was not a General ; not even a German, in fact, but an English spy. It was hardly likely that the Pastor would be willing to give any particulars about his fellow-conspirators once this fact was revealed, even if he refrained from handing his dangerous visitor over to the police. Neither would he be well situated to gain information if he continued to pose as General von Lettow but admitted that the Gestapo were after him. The Pastor might give him clothes and hurry him into hiding, but the last thing he would be inclined for was a quiet talk.

After a five-mile tramp he came to a fork where the Ems road branched away north-eastward, inland from the river, and as he turned up it he was still undecided what course it would be best to pursue. For another mile he trudged doggedly on. If he had ever met the Pastor he would have been better able to judge whether he dared trust him fully, but he had not; and at the moment he felt disinclined to do so.

The stars gave him enough light to see by and in a field about half a mile from the river he noticed a haystack. It would be too late to tackle Wachmuller that night, even if he pushed on to Ems, as everybody turned in early now that social life had almost come to a standstill and light had to be economized. It would not be a good start to knock the Pastor up and pull him out of bed, so Gregory decided that he would sleep upon his problems. Entering the field, he began to dig a hole in the side of the haystack that was furthest from the road.

After twenty minutes' hard work he had made a little cave in the sweet-smelling hay, close to the ground. Crawling into it, he pulled the loose hay up over the opening and curled himself up as comfortably as he could. His thoughts were hardly conducive to peaceful slumber, but he tried to console himself with the fact that he had been thunderingly lucky to have got safely out of Coblenz and that the hole in the haystack was infinitely more comfortable than a stone cell in the local gaol.

Yet, before he managed to drop off into an uneasy sleep, he mustered all his courage to face the cold, hard truth. His General's uniform was no longer an asset but a liability; the Nazis had his description and he was a hunted man.

Chapter IX

DEATH INTERVENES

WHEN Gregory awoke on the Wednesday morning daylight was already filtering through the hay piled up at the entrance of his cave. Carefully pushing some of it aside he looked at his watch, to find that it was just half-past eight.

Peering out, he saw that the field was deserted. Only one house was visible, on a slope some half-mile away, and it was doubtful whether any of its occupants would be able to identify his uniform as that of an officer, even if they happened to be looking out of one of the windows as he crawled out of the haystack ; but if anyone there did chance to see him they might think that he was a deserter and inform the police or some local military authority.

However, there seemed little point in leaving his hiding place at the moment. It was quite certain that he would meet people if he started out on the road to Ems in broad daylight, and as the authorities in Coblenz would now be hunting everywhere for a man in General's uniform it would be a hundred to one on his being stopped and questioned. Feeling that the only thing to do was to remain where he was for the day he turned over and went to sleep again.

It was past noon when he awoke once more, and he was both hungry and thirsty. The Nazis having met him the night before on his return to Coblenz, had prevented him from getting any dinner, and it was now nearly twenty-four hours since he had eaten luncheon with Herr Rheinhardt in Traben.

Luckily, as an old campaigner, he had entered Germany prepared for such an emergency and he carried a large flask of brandy-and-water and a packet of slab chocolate. Breaking off a bar he ate it slowly and washed it down with the diluted brandy. It was not a very satisfying meal, but at all events it staved off any pangs of hunger.

The afternoon still remained to be filled in somehow so he endeavoured to sleep again, but a fitful doze was the best that he could manage and he was heartily glad when twilight came and made it possible for him to become active once more. In the meantime he had thoroughly sorted out his ideas and had decided quite definitely that the most important thing to be done was to get all the information he could from Wachmuller, and that therefore he must not disclose the fact that he was an English spy, but take his chance of being able to get away so as to utilize later anything that he had learned.

During the early afternoon the weather had changed ; dark clouds had rolled up in the sky and it had begun to rain. The rain would add to his discomfort on his walk into Ems, but on the other hand it would drive indoors everybody save those who were on duty or had some urgent job to do, and it brought dusk considerably earlier than if the sun had been shining. On balance he was by no means displeased by this break in the weather, and hoped that the same conditions were prevailing in Poland. If they were, the change would prove a perfect godsend to the Poles, as the cocksure Germans would soon find their tanks and motor vehicles bogged up to the axles in mud.

At six o'clock he ate another bar of chocolate and took a drink from his flask. Then he made his way out of the hole, pushing the loose hay slowly in front of him. Using it as cover he wriggled cautiously along the side of the haystack until he got to the corner, thus making it less likely that he would be seen, or at all events recognized as a soldier, should anyone be looking out of the windows of the house two fields away. Once he had the haystack between the house and himself he stood up, walked quickly to the road and set off towards Ems.

Bad-Ems is famous for its medicinal springs, and its delightful situation in the valley of the river Lahn makes it one of the beauty-spots of Southern Germany. A visit to the town is consequently one of the excursions most popular with holiday-makers in Coblenz, and Gregory had been out there on numerous former occasions in circumstances far happier than those in which he found himself at the moment.

The road wound up the valley so, his range of vision being limited, he was unable to spot cars either meeting or overtaking him until they were quite close and had to proceed with the utmost caution.

Wherever there was a hedge at the roadside he got into the field and walked behind it ; where there were woods he used them as cover, and each time he heard the noise of an approaching car when on the open road he turned his back to the direction from which it was coming so that its occupants should not see more of his face or rank-badges than was absolutely unavoidable.

Owing to these delays it took him an hour and a quarter to cover the three miles to Ems, and by the time he entered the outskirts of the town darkness had fallen.

As well as his own gun in his pistol holster he had the weapons of the two Nazis ; one in each of his overcoat pockets ; and though this triple armament tended to weigh him down it was comforting to think that if he were to get into any trouble out of which he could not bluff his way he had at least the means of putting up an extraordinarily good fight for it.

Having once entered Ems he abandoned all further attempts at concealment and walked briskly forward. There were few people in the streets but he passed occasional groups of A.R.P. men knocking up such houses as had not got their lights fully obscured.

Darkness now hid the pretty little *Kursaal* which overlooks the river in the centre of the town, and although Gregory felt certain that there must be a telephone kiosk somewhere outside, and had counted on it, he could not find one ; so, as he dared not loiter, he went boldly in by the restaurant entrance, which he knew from his previous visits. He had to inquire from somebody where Pastor Wachmuller lived and thought that he would get the information there more readily than by accosting the A.R.P. wardens, while for obvious reasons he had no intention of asking the police. A few officers, Nazis and civilians were sitting about drinking beer and *apéritifs* in the foyer of the restaurant but no one seemed to take much notice of him as he turned straight towards the bar, keeping his back to the room, and asked the girl if she could tell him Pastor Wachmuller's address.

She did not know it herself but obligingly turned it up in the telephone book, afterwards telling him the easiest way to find the Pastor's house, which was only a few streets away.

Gregory thanked her and got out of the place as quickly as he could without showing any obvious haste. Following her directions he found his way to a street of old, semi-basement houses ; they had no gardens, but their doors were reached by flights of stone steps leading up from the narrow pavement. By counting them he located the one in which the Pastor lived ; a biggish house near the middle of the irregular block. The door was opened by an elderly woman who told him that the Pastor was not at home, but that she was his housekeeper, and asked if she might take a message.

Gregory inquired when the Pastor was expected back and learned that he was not likely to be home much before midnight, as he was at the Church Hall with some of his women parishioners who gathered there every evening to roll bandages and knit woollies for the troops.

He said that his business with Pastor Wachmuller was urgent and suggested that the woman should go to fetch him, but this she refused to do, excusing herself on the plea that her sight was not very good and that she was terrified of going out into the streets during the black-outs as she might so easily be run over.

Having told her that his business was urgent Gregory could hardly suggest, as he would have liked to have done, that he might be allowed to wait for three or four hours in the Pastor's house until his return ; the only alternative was to go to the Church Hall and seek him out amongst his parishioners.

The housekeeper gave him directions and he set off once more, locating the Church Hall, not without difficulty, some twenty minutes later. From what he could see of it in the gloom it was a large, modern building, and directly he had passed the light-screens at its entrance he found himself in a long, barrack-like room where two hundred or more women were gathered round long trestle-tables busily engaged in war work.

He caught sight of the Pastor at once, at the far end of the hall, but before he could advance towards him a fat, middle-aged woman had fussed forward from one of the nearest tables to inquire his business. He said that he wanted a few words with Pastor Wachmuller and gave his name as General von Heintisch, since that of von Lettow was now much too dangerous for further use.

The woman bustled away to deliver his message and in the meantime he had to stand in the entrance of the hall with scores of eyes fixed upon him ; the appearance of a General at their meeting having aroused the natural curiosity of the women.

To his relief the Pastor came hurrying down the hall as soon as the fat woman had spoken to him. Gregory liked the look of him at once. He was a well-set-up man of about forty-five, with dark hair, greying at the temples and brushed smoothly back from a fine forehead, quick, intelligent eyes and determined features.

"What can I do for you, Herr General?" he asked, and lowering his voice Gregory replied :

"I'm sorry to have to drag you away from your meeting, Herr Pastor, but I have important matters to discuss with you : I've just come from Herr Julius Rheinhardt."

"I see." The Pastor gave Gregory a sharp glance and half-turned his head to make sure that they were not overheard. "In that case we'd better go to my house. Wait here a moment and I'll tell one of the members of the committee that I'll return later if I can but that I may not be able to get back this evening."

Gregory waited with what patience he could muster while Wachmuller went over to talk to some of the women, but he was considerably cheered by the fact that the Pastor had not inquired for particulars of his business and had apparently taken it for granted on learning that he had come from Rheinhardt.

Having collected his black soft hat and his cloak from a nearby peg the Pastor rejoined Gregory and they went out together. Immediately they were in the dark street Wachmuller said : "I have no idea what your business may be, Herr General, but Julius Rheinhardt is an old friend of mine and on his account I am delighted to receive you."

Although the Pastor spoke casually, Gregory sensed that the little speech had been dictated by caution and that Wachmuller had no intention of talking of those matters which interested him unless he produced some proper credentials, so he replied :

"Perhaps it will be better if we postpone our business until we get back to your house. In the meantime we shall have our work cut out to prevent ourselves tripping over kerbstones in this black-out."

After this they walked on in silence until they reached the Pastor's house. He let himself in with his own key and led Gregory upstairs to a comfortable, book-lined sitting-room on the first floor. As the housekeeper did not appear Gregory assumed that she had either gone to bed or was somewhere in the lower regions.

Directly they were in the room and the door had closed behind them, Gregory displayed the golden swastika in the palm of his hand.

"The symbol of peace opens all doors among the right-thinking," said Wachmuller, and added with a smile : "I thought you must be one of us as you came from Julius Rheinhardt, but one can't be too careful. Make yourself comfortable, please, and tell me what I can do for you."

"Thanks !" Gregory unbuttoned his great-coat and took it

off, glad of the opportunity to get rid of the rain-sodden garment. He then sat down and said quietly : "As you may have
noticed from my badges, I am a General of Engineers, but I've
been dug out from my retirement for this accursed war and
have as yet no actual command. In consequence, certain of
my superiors who know my views selected me as a suitable
man to send on a tour of the Rhineland ; ostensibly to inspect
bridges and so on, but actually to contact our civilian friends
and find out the state of public opinion in this part of the
country."

Wachmuller had produced a bottle of Schnapps and some
glasses from a cupboard. Having poured out two portions he
sat himself down in an arm-chair which had its back to a door,
in the wall between the bookshelves, which evidently led
into another room or a large cupboard.

"They made an admirable choice, I'm sure," he said, raising
his glass. *"Prosit !* Herr General."

"Prosit ! Herr Pastor," replied Gregory, lifting his, and after
they had drunk together Wachmuller went on :

"As our Army leaders are watched night and day by the
Inner Gestapo I quite understand that for any of them to make
direct contact with a number of well-known civilians would
immediately lay them open to suspicion."

Gregory nodded. "The difficulties of communication are
immense, but nevertheless if anything is to be done it's essential
that there must be the closest possible co-operation between
the Army, the industrialists and the Social Democrats."

"Something *must* be done," said Wachmuller firmly. "We
cannot allow this war to go on, bringing as it must unspeakable
horrors in its train to the whole German people."

"Do you honestly believe that a really considerable proportion of the people feel that way about it, as well as our own
group ?"

"I'm certain of it. As you may know, I have some reputation
as a preacher. In consequence I am asked to address many
congregations from the pulpit and constantly visit such towns
as Cologne, Frankfurt, Düsseldorf, Mainz and Wiesbaden, besides
many smaller places. That enables me to form a very shrewd
opinion of the state of things in this part of Germany. Hitler
may have given the people uniforms and bread, but he has
robbed them of even the shadow of freedom.

"Only the week before the war broke out a little girl in my
parochial school quite innocently let it out to her teacher that

her father had complained that morning of the margarine at breakfast and had grumbled that they hardly ever saw butter on their table any more. The teacher is a Nazi, of course, as all who are entrusted with the formation of the opinions of German youth must be if they wish to retain their jobs. She reported what the child had said ; she would herself have got into serious trouble if she had not done so and it had leaked out. The following day the father was arrested. None of his family know what has happened to him or where he is. He has just disappeared ; to a concentration-camp, of course, in which he will be confined indefinitely for correctional punishment without being tried by any court or even being given an opportunity to state his case. What, I ask you, can his friends and relatives feel about a régime under which such things can happen ; knowing all the time that they themselves may be the next to disappear for some equally trivial criticism of the Government ?

"That episode is typical of the sort of thing that is happening all over Germany. The people live in terror of being reported by one another, it is true ; but such terror is dangerous to the Government because the natural reaction has now begun. In spite of the announcement of most appalling penalties if found out they seize every opportunity to listen-in to the forbidden foreign broadcasts and to read the subversive literature which is being distributed in secret by revolutionary organizations."

"You feel convinced, then, that we would have the support of a large proportion of the masses ?"

"Undoubtedly. Even those who fell into the snare of Goebbels' propaganda and were in favour of a war of liberation to regain our old Polish provinces are taking a very different attitude now that they know we are faced with another war against the great Democracies."

"It is as well, then, that we took no premature action when the orders were issued for a march into Poland."

"At the time it was a disappointment that you did not, Herr General. We were hoping for a lead from the Army when the crisis was at its height, as the Generals would then have had a good case to present to the people—that they had carried out their *putsch* as the only method of saving the nation from being plunged into war. But in some respects their hand has been strengthened by waiting. Even those who were not at that time averse to the Polish adventure and did not believe that the Democracies would come in against us now realize that

Hitler has burnt his boats and has involved us in another struggle which may all but destroy the whole nation."

Gregory murmured his agreement, but his mind was swiftly planning his next move. Having got so far, he was now faced with an extraordinarily difficult task, for he had to try to trick the Pastor into naming one or more of those very Army leaders whose emissary he was representing himself to be. The only chance of doing so seemed to be to keep him talking on general lines in the hope that sooner or later he would let something out, so Gregory continued :

"All that you say tallies with what I have heard from other quarters, so if the *putsch* can be carried out efficiently I don't think there is any reason to doubt that the country will rise against the Nazis. Hitler has made so many enemies ; the Communists, the Social Democrats, the Czechs ; it was madness to overrun Czechoslovakia. The second we act the Czechs will murder every Nazi in their country. As it is we have to keep sixty thousand men there to prevent open revolution."

"Neither have the Austrians any love for their Nazi overlords."

"Quite so. Then there are the Jews. In spite of the deportations there are still five million Jews left in Germany and there must be thousands of them who would cheerfully give their own lives in an attempt to destroy Hitler, if they were not afraid of reprisals against their whole race. Once we have arrested the Führer and issued a proclamation disbanding the Nazi Party, the lower-class Jews in the great centres of population will fall upon local Nazi leaders like packs of wolves."

The Pastor nodded. "Lynching is a horrible thing to contemplate, and mob rule will have to be put down as soon as possible afterwards, but not a Nazi will be safe unless he is inside a prison or at his own local headquarters. That should have the effect of rounding them up for us so that once the Army takes over they can be tried for their crimes by proper tribunals. But as you say, many of them will be assassinated in the meantime, at their homes or in the streets, by the Communists and the unfortunate Jews whom they have so terribly persecuted."

"I have no particular liking for the Jews myself," said Gregory, expressing the views that he would be expected to hold as a Prussian Army officer, "but their persecution has injured Germany enormously. If the war goes on, thousands of lives will be lost among our wounded solely because we are so short of doctors owing to the Nazis' expulsion of the Jews from the medical profession. Moreover, we have lost innumerable financiers, writers and scientists, all of whom contributed to the life of the country."

"The Jews are not the only ones who have suffered amongst the intellectuals," Wachmuller took him up quickly. "Every writer of importance who has had the courage to use his pen to protest against our lack of liberty is either dead or behind barbed-wire in a concentration-camp. Those who are still free are silent only through fear of a similar fate; they have not forgotten the terrible things that have been done to their brethren. Apart from unscrupulous climbers who have joined forces with the Nazis there is not an intellectual in Germany who would hesitate to acclaim with joy the arrest of Hitler and his satellites."

Gregory listened attentively. He knew that they were only exchanging platitudes, but he hoped that in time those platitudes might lead somewhere, and in order to keep the Pastor talking he led the conversation to matters which had a close personal interest for his host.

"Then the Churches—" he began. "The Catholics who form so large a proportion of the South German people have suffered severely by the restrictions imposed upon them. Their Bishops will certainly support us against the Nazis and they will undoubtedly have the full approval of Rome."

"We Protestants have suffered hardly less," said Wachmuller earnestly. "That is a matter of which I can speak with authority, for I know the history of Hitler's relations with my Church chapter by chapter and verse by verse. Not one-tenth of it ever gets into the papers, but wherever an upright, God-fearing man has spoken to his flock and protested against some outrage by these Nazi beasts he has been treated like a criminal. Our Bishops to-day are shady characters; mere puppets of the Nazi Government; because no honest man will accept a diocese upon such terms. The rank and file amongst us know them for what they are and privately hold them in contempt, but scores of us each month are removed from our livings or forbidden to preach again under threat of imprisonment."

Full of righteous indignation the Pastor stood up and continued angrily: "It is not upon political grounds alone that my poor brethren are marked down. It is because the Nazi doctrine conflicts with that of Christianity. Hitler knows, and we know, that in spite of his legions of police spies he will never be the real master of Germany until he has destroyed all Christian belief within Germany's boundaries.

"I am a man of God, Herr General; yet I pray to God that an assassin's bullet may find Adolf Hitler before this year is out, unless you and your associates put him against a brick wall and shoot him for the murderer and anti-Christ he is."

From where Gregory was sitting he could just see the handle of the door in front of which the Pastor was standing. Owing to its heavy shade the light was not too good, but he suddenly had the impression that the door-knob was slowly turning.

Instantly his hand slid to his pistol holster. His fingers had barely touched it when the Pastor went on :

"When you see General Gra . . ."

At that second the door behind the Pastor was thrown open. Gregory had just time to glimpse a vague, black-uniformed figure in the shadows before there was a blinding flash and a report that sounded like a thunder-clap in the silence of the quiet room. Pastor Wachmuller threw up his chin ; his mouth fell open ; his eyes bulged hideously. His knees sagged and he collapsed, face-downwards on the carpet, without uttering a sound.

Gregory flung himself sideways at the very moment that the shot was fired. A second bullet thudded dully into the back of the arm-chair in which he had been sitting a fraction of a second earlier. As he had fallen to the floor he had lugged out his automatic, and lying there on his back he blazed off with it at the figure in the darkened doorway.

There was a cry and then a moan, followed by the thud of a pistol as it fell on the polished boards. Slowly the figure in the shadows crumpled and slid to the floor.

Wriggling to his knees, Gregory covered the assassin with his still smoking gun, but it was unnecessary for him to use another bullet. His first had taken the man in the shoulder and the second had got him through the heart.

He turned to stare down at the Pastor, but Wachmuller was beyond all human aid. He had been shot at close range through the back of the head, and the base of his skull was smashed in as though it had been hit with a sledge-hammer. Blood, brains and splintered bone seeped from the hideous cavity.

As Gregory got to his feet and stood for a moment in silence he was thinking, not of the unfortunate Pastor who, like himself, was only a pawn in the game, but with bitter fury of the fact that he should have been shot down at that particular instant.

If the assassin had held his hand for even one second longer Gregory would have learned the name of one of the Army leaders in the conspiracy, which would have been of immense importance to him.

Although he was now on the run himself he might still have been able to avoid capture and get in touch with the General whom Wachmuller had been just about to name ; or if that had proved to be impossible he could at least have endeavoured by a dozen different methods to evade the censorship and get the all-important name back through some neutral country to Sir Pellinore.

His eye switched to the dead Nazi, who was in the black uniform of an S.S. officer. He had a large, reddish, stupid face and an absurd little fair moustache. With angry frustration Gregory cursed the dead man for a brainless fool. Evidently he had been listening-in to their conversation, hidden behind the door. Had he waited only a second longer before killing Wachmuller he, too, would have learned the name of the anti-Nazi Army leader—information of incalculable value to his Party—but it was typical of that type of German to put his foot in it. After weeks or months of the most conscientious preparation they always loosed off their guns at the wrong moment, losing half the benefit of their carefully-laid plans by ill-timed action.

Gregory's racing thoughts moved at lightning speed. Only a second or two had elapsed since the S.S. man had fallen dead in the doorway when sounds of movement below caught his ear. Snatching up his overcoat he slipped it on and strode to the door, his gun still in his right hand. Opening the door quietly but quickly he slipped out on to the landing and stood listening. Excited voices came up from the hall below, followed by the sound of a footfall on the lower stairs.

One cautious glance over the landing-rail showed him the tops of uniform caps worn by men who were already running up towards him with drawn guns in their hands. The Nazi whom he had shot must have secreted himself in the room adjoining the library and left his men below to guard the exits of the house. Gregory was trapped ; his only chance of escape lay in getting away over the roof-tops before the Nazis had time to search the building.

With catlike swiftness he tiptoed to the foot of the upper stairs ; then, crouched and silent, he began to ascend. He had just reached a bend in the flight when the leading Nazis arrived with a rush on the landing below. By an evil chance one of them happened to glance up, and caught sight of him moving in the semi-darkness.

With a shout of *"Da ist jemand !"* he raised his automatic and fired.

The bullet crashed into the baluster-rail a few inches above the crouching Gregory's shoulder and sent splinters of wood-work flying into his face.

Then his own automatic spat as he pressed the trigger, firing between the balusters. The Nazi clutched at his throat; blood oozed between his fingers and spurted suddenly from his mouth. With a half-choked scream he fell back among his comrades.

The next second a fusillade of shots crashed out as the others blazed away into the gloom, but by that time Gregory was round the bend. As he sprang on to the upper landing he heard the killers come pounding up behind him.

Chapter X

THE FIGHT FOR LIFE

IN the dim light on the upper landing Gregory could just make out three doors, one of which was lower than the other two. There was no time to examine the rooms to which they led, as the slightest hesitation meant that he would be exposed to the bullets of his pursuers. He had to make an instantaneous choice. If the room he chose had a skylight there would still be the fraction of a chance that he might get away ; if not, he would be cornered and captured, or more probably dead, within the next few minutes.

The larger doors looked as though they led to bedrooms, whereas the lower one might well be that of the boxroom of the house—and boxrooms are more usually lit by skylights than are bedrooms.

Grabbing the handle of the lower door Gregory wrenched at it. Fortunately it was unlocked, and as it swung open he flung himself inside. For a second he could see nothing. The place was as black as pitch, but jerking his head upward with frantic anxiety he saw a long rectangle of dimmish light above him. It was a skylight ; he had been granted that hundredth chance of getting out alive.

How slender his chances were he knew only too well. If there was a key in the lock of the door it must still be on the far side, as he had had no time to remove it, and as people do not usually have bolts inside their boxroom doors it would be merely a waste of precious moments to fumble about in the hope of finding one.

Pouching his gun he reached down and groped about in the darkness. His hands came in contact first with a perambulator, then with a heavy wooden box. As he stooped to lift this and fling it against the door another fusillade of shots rang out. The house was old and the door a thick one, but even so several of the bullets penetrated the panels, and the fact that he had stooped just at that instant probably saved his life.

The heavy box now temporarily held the door, but the Nazis

were already battering on it and a faint streak of light showed
that their first assault had opened it a crack. Lying full length
on the floor Gregory set his shoulder against the box and drew
his gun again. Raising it and placing it against a panel on a
level with his head he pulled the trigger twice to give his pursuers
a taste of their own medicine. There was a yelp of pain followed by a blasphemous spate of curses, and the pressure on
the door eased a little. As it did so he wriggled back until his
feet touched something, and reaching behind him he found that
it was a ladder.

The Nazis charged the door again. It creaked under their
weight and the sudden broadening of the band of light showed
that they had now forced it open a good six inches. Judging
from its weight the box was probably full of books ; it had taken
a big effort for Gregory to heave it against the door. But there
was nothing but its weight to hold it in position, so a series of
determined assaults would soon force it back. If Gregory had
had more time he could have piled other things upon it, for he
could now see the faint outlines of a number of cases and trunks
in the boxroom ; but to stand up and move them would mean
exposing himself to any bullets that might come through the
door. He knew that he would have to risk such exposure for
a moment in any case, but he meant to do so only for the better
purpose of attempting to reach the skylight.

One of the Nazis emptied the remaining contents of his
pistol through the panels of the door and the bullets streamed
over Gregory's head. Immediately the smacking of bullets into
the far wall had ceased Gregory swung round, grabbed a rung
of the ladder and launched himself up it.

Another crash below told him that his pursuers had made a
further assault on the door, but by that time he was crouching
at the top of the ladder and fumbling frantically with the per-
forated iron strip by which the skylight could be adjusted at
various angles.

As he thrust up the skylight he glanced down and saw that
the door was now open a foot. A black patch, shoulder-high in
the band of light down its edge, could only be a man's arm
thrust round it. There came a rapid succession of flashes which
lit up the whole room as the owner of the arm sprayed it blind
with his pistol.

Gregory had always prided himself upon his marksmanship.
Raising his automatic he aimed carefully and let the fellow have
one in the shoulder. There was a cry and the pistol dropped

from a nerveless hand. Gregory heard it crash on the floor-boards as he wriggled out on to the roof.

Drawing the fresh night air gratefully into his lungs he let the skylight fall back with a bang and looked swiftly round him. The houses in the row were of the old German type with sloping roofs and many gables ; dangerous, tricky ground for any man to attempt to negotiate in the darkness ; but darkness was his friend, and if only he could manage to avoid slipping and falling headlong to the street they would afford excellent cover.

The rain had stopped, and a few stars were showing through a break in the clouds. They gave just a little light, and owing to his brief sojourn in the boxroom Gregory's eyes were by now accustomed to the darkness. He could see that he was standing upon a flat portion of the roof about two feet wide, and that it sloped sharply down on either side.

A tall chimney-stack some fifteen feet away, where the Pastor's house abutted on the next, showed as a patch of deeper blackness to Gregory's left, beyond the skylight. Drawing himself up, he stepped carefully towards it.

As he moved there came a sharp challenge from the roof of the neighbouring house : *"Wie gehts ?"*

"Fritz," he called out quickly ; that being the commonest German Christian name that he could think of on the spur of the moment ; but the challenge showed him that his position was even more desperate than it had been in the boxroom a few minutes before. The Nazis had posted men on the adjoining roofs, and if they had done that they would certainly have surrounded the whole block also. In a moment the men below would be scrambling up behind him, and he would be caught between two fires. Even if he could break through and reach the street he would find himself faced by the men of the cordon while the others followed in hot pursuit. It seemed that nothing now remained but for him to sell his life dearly.

"Fritz who ?" came the swift question.

Instead of answering, Gregory asked another question in reply. "Where is he ? Haven't you seen him ?"

"No !" shouted the other man.

"*Himmel !* Are you deaf and blind ?" Gregory cried urgently. "He came up out of the skylight less than a minute ago."

"He's somewhere on the roof, then. Must be behind you," said the German, moving forward and disclosing his position near the chimney-stack.

Already the sounds of feet below warned Gregory that the Nazis had forced the door of the boxroom and were streaming into it. Another moment and they would be dashing up the ladder. This was no time for scruples ; raising his gun he pointed it at the dark shadow by the chimney-stack and fired.

A gasp was followed by the sound of feet slithering on slates, the fall of a heavy body and then a shriek of fear as the Nazi on the adjoining roof lost his balance and went hurtling over and over down the steep slope until he pitched off over the gutter.

One of the men inside the boxroom sent a pot-shot crashing through the skylight. Lowering his weapon and firing blind, Gregory emptied all the bullets left in his automatic down through it, aiming at the spot where he knew the ladder to be. A whimpering moan followed by the thud of someone falling to the floor told him that one of his bullets had found flesh and bone. Before another Nazi could get up the ladder he turned and padded as quickly as he dared across the narrow, level stretch of roof to the point where the man on watch had been standing.

Halting there in the shadow of the chimney-stack he slipped a spare clip of cartridges into his own gun and pulled from his coat pocket one of those which he had taken from the Nazis at Coblenz. Crouching down and invisible in the darkness he waited, tense with the thrill of battle, for the enemy's next move.

Since his pursuers did not lack courage, it soon came. One of them scrambled out on to the roof, then another, then a third. Gregory held his fire, waiting to see whether any more would appear. There was just enough light for him to make them out as they crouched by the skylight, but they could not see him. Once he pressed the triggers of his guns he might never again have the chance of snaring them in so perfect an ambush.

The Nazis were muttering together. "Where is he? Which way did he go?" "Where's Förster?" "He must have killed him. That shot up here, just now." Cautiously they stood up to peer round, and Gregory let them have it.

Aiming both guns at the centre man he blazed off ; then slowly turned both barrels outwards while keeping his fingers pressed down on the triggers. The effect was like that of two machine-guns simultaneously spraying bullets outwards from a central point.

Cries, a gurgling moan, a curse cut short, penetrated faintly to him through the banging of his automatics. One Nazi crashed headlong through the skylight ; another rolled down the slope of the roof and pitched off ; the third slumped in a still, silent heap.

As he ceased fire to ascertain the result of his murderous attack Gregory could not tell whether the third man was dead or shamming. To make certain of him he took careful aim and put another bullet in his body, but he did not even moan. Gregory knew then, with a thrill of satisfaction, that he had scuppered the whole of the party which had broken into the Pastor's house.

But his elation was short-lived. As he drew himself upright a single shot cracked out from the roof beyond the skylight. Another Nazi had either been lurking there or had just come up, and had fired at the flash of Gregory's gun.

He felt a sharp pain, like the searing of a red-hot iron drawn across his left thigh ; staggered, lost his balance and slipped off the narrow, flat portion of the roof.

With a gasp he realized that he was about to die in the same way as the sentry whom he had shot on that very spot only two minutes earlier.

His pistols were knocked out of his hands as he fell ; one exploded and both clattered loudly as they slithered down the slates beside him. His hands clawed desperately at the empty air. As he rolled towards the gutter he glimpsed the double flash of his enemy's gun as the man put two more shots into the spot by the chimney-stack where he had been kneeling ; next instant he felt a terrific jolt which nearly drove the breath out of his body. His whirling descent had been brought up short against a gable which broke the outline of the gutter.

It was a quite small affair, and had he rolled down a single foot further either to the right or to the left he would have slithered round it to crash into the street forty feet below, but as it was it had caught him full in the centre of the spine, so that his head and arms were flung backwards on one side of the ridge and his heavy boots crashed on the slates at its other side.

For a minute he lay there, bent backwards like a bow ; then he cautiously eased himself up, scrabbling on the slates with his hands and feet until he was lying flat on the slope of the roof with his head uppermost and his feet wedged firmly against the gable.

The man who had shot him must have thought at first that he had fallen into the street, but a minute later would have heard the noise that he had been compelled to make as he hauled

D

himself up into a safer position. Gregory's fear that this had been so was soon confirmed. He heard the man stealthily approaching along the top of the roof, then saw him vaguely as a moving black blur against the skyline.

Very gently Gregory withdrew one of his hands from the flat surface of the slates and wriggled his third gun out of his overcoat pocket.

The man above had paused and was peering down, uncertain as to whether Gregory was still there or not, for he could not see him in the blackness.

Gregory knew that he was temporarily safe while he remained hidden ; to shoot would give away his position and would draw the enemy's fire in reply if his bullet went wide, but as he was a crack shot he decided to risk it. Resting his right hand on his left wrist as it lay on the slates in front of his face he aimed for the black blur above him. Placing his first finger along the side of his pistol, he very slowly squeezed the trigger with his second.

The flash of his gun stabbed the darkness : there was a loud cry, and the man above suddenly sprang into the air. But Gregory had not foreseen a possible result of his shooting. Next moment the man had pitched forward and came sliding down the roof towards him.

He had just time to jam his gun back into his pocket before he faced the peril of being swept from his precarious footing and whirled to the street with the wounded German.

Splaying his legs backwards like a frog round the sides of the gable, he lowered his head and clung to the slates with the flats of his hands. As he did so the German came tumbling, feet first, right on top of him. The Nazi would have gone right over the edge of the roof but for the fact that one of his hands came in contact with Gregory's right shoulder-strap. He grabbed it with all his strength, and though his legs were already well over the gutter on Gregory's right he succeeded in checking his fall.

The strain on Gregory was terrific. He was almost dragged over, but his leg-grip saved him, and the weight of the German was lessened almost at once as he managed to support himself by wedging one of his feet in the gutter.

Gregory turned sideways and lashed out with his fist in the direction in which he believed the man's head to be, but he missed it and barked his knuckles badly on the slates. The Nazi was still half on top of him, and with a swift wriggle he succeeded in throwing his whole weight on Gregory while he bashed at him with both fists, thus showing that he had been wounded only in the leg or body.

The fact that Gregory was lying face-downwards saved him from the worst effects of the blows; but, on the other hand, he was unable to get to grips with his enemy.

The Nazi was a big, heavy fellow who puffed and panted as he strove both to retain his balance and to knock Gregory out. Gregory was more wiry and since his fall had had time to get his breath, so he fought with silent ferocity.

Hugging each other in a bear-like grip, but not daring to move anything but their hands and arms for fear of falling off the roof, they struggled desperately until Gregory, now lying sideways and half twisted over, managed to get his hands upon the throat of the man above him. His was no amateur strangler's grip, for he did not press with the flats of his thumbs, but deliberately forced their points into the man's throat below his chin.

The wretched Nazi gurgled horribly; the pain must have been excruciating, but he could not scream. His hands loosed their hold on Gregory and began to flap wildly. For a full minute Gregory kept up the pressure, while he could feel the warm blood running over the backs of his hands from the places where his nails had gored the man's throat. Suddenly the Nazi slumped forward as though his neck had been broken, and Gregory knew that he was now unconscious. With a cautious heave he pitched the body from on top of him, and it disappeared into the blackness.

For a few seconds he lay there panting. When he could once more take stock of things, he could hear the Nazis in the street below talking round the body of their dead comrade while one of their officers issued fresh orders.

Easing his position carefully, he tried to haul himself up the steep slope of the roof, but there was not a thing to grip, and he had made hardly a couple of feet headway when he slithered back again to the gable that had proved his salvation. A second attempt met with no more success, and he realized with dismay that it was impossible for him to regain the roof-top. With that realization, a wave of black despair engulfed him. Sooner or later the Nazis would smell him out and pick him off at their leisure.

But his despair was only momentary, for it soon occurred to him that although he could not get up, there was a chance that he might be able to get down. Wherever there is a small gable breaking the gutter-line of a roof there is nearly always a dormer window below it. This new thought gave him fresh courage, and with the utmost caution he lowered himself round one side of the gable until his legs were dangling over the gutter. Very gingerly he began to feel about with his feet round the angle of the wall below.

It was difficult to judge what was below him in the darkness and at first he could find nothing with his groping feet. Lowering himself a little he tried again, and this time his foot struck something which gave out a low rumble, like the faint quivering of a drum.

With a sigh of thankfulness he realized that his luck still held. There *was* a window below the gable, and the upper half of it was open ; he had kicked the lower part with his foot, and it was the glass which had rumbled ; but it was going to be a devilishly tricky business to get inside it.

Just as he was about to make the attempt he caught the sound of fresh footsteps on the roof-top. Another party of Nazis must have come up through the skylight. Fortunately, the only man who had known his exact position was now lying dead in the street below, and providing that he could remain very quiet it might be some time before the new squad would be able to locate him.

Straining his ears until it felt as though their drums would burst he remained rigid, listening, until the Nazis above him spread out and began a systematic search for him along the roof-top. They were not to know that he had been wounded and was precariously perched upon a gutter some twenty feet below them ; they naturally supposed that he had stuck to the narrow, flat treads on the roof and was hiding behind one of the chimney-stacks, probably on one of the more distant houses.

From the sounds they made he could tell that they had split up into two parties and were moving in opposite directions with the intention of beating the roofs until they had cornered him at one of the extremities of the block.

Directly the group which had moved in his direction had gone past he lowered himself still further, until his whole body was dangling over the roof-edge and supported only by his elbows in the gutter. The houses were old, and the gutter bent under his weight until he feared that it might give way at any moment, and he dared not rest too long upon it. He had to make his attempt quickly or he might go crashing into the street without having made it at all.

Both his feet were now well inside the open window, but unless he could find some other support for the top half of his body immediately he let go of the gutter he would pitch backwards and descend head-first on to the paving-stones. Reaching down with his right hand, and supporting his weight with his left only, he felt along inside the top of the open window until to his immense relief, the tips of his fingers found a curtain-rail.

The rod was only a thin one, but he thought that it might bear his weight just long enough for him to gain sufficient impetus to fling himself in through the window. Drawing a deep breath he gripped the curtain-rail firmly, let go of the gutter and launched himself downwards, twisting his body as he did so. The thin rod snapped ; for a second he hovered in mid-air, his left hand flung out, his feet kicking wildly. Then he landed with a bump on the wooden window-frame, hanging half in and half out of the window. During his drop he had turned in the air so that he was now facing out across the street. With a desperate jerk he pitched himself backwards, banged his head on the upper part of the window-frame and fell in a heap on the floor inside.

Picking himself up he stepped forward into the darkness like a blind man, with his hands outstretched, until he came in contact with a bed. He did not dare to strike a light as the windows were uncurtained and to have done so would have given away his position, but to his relief the bed was unoccupied and he groped his way along until he found a door.

Pressing the handle firmly into its socket so that the catch should make no noise he turned it slowly and opened the door a fraction. A dim light filtering up the stairs showed him a landing. There were splashes of blood upon its floor, and next minute he realized that he was back in Pastor Wachmuller's house.

The door of the boxroom stood open. One dead Nazi was stretched out inside it ; another lay on his face beside him, groaning loudly. At first it seemed to Gregory that he had hardly improved his position. Almost certainly there would be Nazis occupying the hall below and on guard outside the door, as this was the house that they had raided and the centre of their operations. But on second thoughts he decided that even if he had been able to plan his movements he could hardly have done better than to return to the Pastor's house.

In all the others there would be civilians who, even if they had gone to bed early that night, would have been roused by all the shooting and excitement in their street. He could hardly have hoped to have got downstairs without one of them seeing him and raising the alarm, whereas here, in the upper part of Wachmuller's house, he was safe for the moment, at least. While the Nazis were probably already searching the other houses, this was the one place in which it would not occur to them to look for him.

For a moment he considered returning to the unoccupied bedroom and hiding in it, but he quickly abandoned that idea. When daylight came his pursuers would be able to get a full view of every roof in the block, and when they found that he was not concealed upon any of them they would resume their search of the houses. Every room, every cupboard and every cellar would be ransacked in case some anti-Nazi family had agreed to hide him. When that had failed the thorough Germans would conclude with their admirable logic that he must have got back into Pastor Wachmuller's house and search that ; so that to conceal himself in the bedroom would be simply to postpone his capture and death until the morning. The almost total darkness of the A.R.P. black-out was his one ally ; his sole chance of escape lay in acting while it lasted.

Having peered over the baluster-rail and seen that there was no one on the landing below, he tiptoed downstairs. The Nazi whom he had shot in the throat had been removed by his comrades, but splashes of blood on the wall showed where the wounded man had collapsed against it. The light was still on in the Pastor's sitting-room ; the door stood open. No sound disturbed the grim silence. Drawing his spare gun again Gregory edged his way round the corner of the door. The Pastor and the dead S.S. officer still lay there just as he had left them.

Returning to the landing he crept down the next flight of stairs. The hall was empty ; the heavy, wooden street-door shut. Still that uncanny silence. He wondered what had become of the old housekeeper. Either she was in the semi-basement or the Nazis had carried her off before laying their ambush. He paused for a moment in the stone-flagged hall, listening intently ; then, as he still heard no sound, he softly turned the handle of a door on his right and opened it a crack.

The room was in darkness, but opening the door a little further he saw by the light in the hall that it was the dining-room. Slipping inside, he held the door wide open for a second to get his bearings. It was a longish room with three tall windows ; the curtains of the farthest window billowed slightly from the draught. Having noted the disposition of the furniture he shut the door behind him and walked slowly forward into the darkness until he touched the table. Feeling his way along to its far end he turned half-left and took three good strides, which brought his outstretched hand in contact with the curtains of the farthest window.

Kneeling down on the floor he returned his one remaining gun to his pistol holster ; then very gingerly he parted the curtains a fraction. There was another, thinner, calico curtain behind them, evidently put up for black-out purposes, and he lifted it until his fingers touched the edge of the window-sill. Raising it a little more he peered out into the street.

At first he could see nothing except two spots of light some way to his left, on the roadway in front of the street door, but as his eyes grew accustomed to the darkness he gradually became able to make out the main details of the scene. The spots of light came from two black-out torches specially constructed to shine downwards, which were held by two uniformed men. Two others stood near them, and this group was evidently guarding the entrance to the house.

Farther along the street in both directions he could see other, smaller patches of light on the road, which clearly indicated that similar groups were posted at intervals to watch the exits of the other houses.

As all the houses in the street had semi-basements their first-floor windows were only about eight feet from the ground and Gregory saw that an easy drop from the window behind which he was crouching would bring him unharmed into the street below. But for how long could he hope to survive once he had gained it ? The street had apparently been closed both to traffic and pedestrians, and it was very quiet ; the stillness broken only by the occasional shouts of the Nazis as they called to one another.

Swiftly Gregory weighed up his chances. As a tall man, his toes would just about touch the pavement if he hung from the window-sill at the full stretch of his arms. He would have at the most only an inch or two to drop, but the rattle of his buttons and equipment against the woodwork as he wriggled himself through backward and the scraping of his toes on the wall as he lowered himself would cause a commotion in the utter stillness of the street quite sufficient to put the nearest groups of watchers instantly on the *qui vive*. Even in the shadows he would be shot before he had gone twenty yards.

He had already abandoned any idea of attempting an escape that way as absolutely suicidal when he suddenly heard someone speak in a low voice just below the window. Another voice answered with a monosyllable; then silence fell again, broken only by the faint, distant cries of men calling to each other while they still searched for him among the chimney-pots.

More from curiosity than for any other reason, Gregory raised his head slightly so that he could look down at the men who were standing below him in the street. As he did so another beam of light caught his eye. It came from the thin, horizontal aperture cut in the black-out shade of a motor-bicycle headlamp. He could make out the silhouette of the machine where it stood propped up in the gutter just in front of the men, who wore the flat caps of Nazis, and evidently it belonged to one of them.

Should he, or should he not? It would be a most desperate gamble, but any other exits from the house were sure to be equally well guarded, and if only he could seize the bike and get it going its speed would at least give him some chance of breaking through the cordon before he could be shot down.

"Nothing venture, nothing win!" muttered Gregory. "Here goes!" And coming up under the curtains he placed one foot on the low sill of the window.

For a second he paused there to make certain that the men below had not heard his movements. Apparently they had not, for they were still standing side by side just beneath him with their faces turned away towards the road.

Drawing up his other foot, he balanced himself in a crouching position, then jumped; not outwards towards the motor-cycle, but downwards, straight on top of the two Nazis.

He landed as he had planned, right between them, so that both of them were bowled over as he pitched forward on to his knees. Scrambling to his feet, he grabbed the handlebars of the motor-bike, opened the throttle, jammed the gear-lever into low, and, exerting every ounce of his strength, ran forward with it.

Time seemed to stand still as he forced the heavy, twin-cylinder B.M.W. along and waited for its engine to start firing. Both the men whom he had knocked over had begun to shout from the moment they had hit the pavement. The little blobs of light further down the street instantly began to move. Shouts, challenges and cries broke the stillness of the night as the waiting patrols sprang into action.

At last, after what seemed an eternity, there was a loud

explosion as the cycle backfired. Cursing *Ersatz* petrol, Gregory retarded the spark and dropped the decompression control. Another yard, and the powerful machine nearly jerked his arms from their sockets as it leaped forward, roaring suddenly into life.

When he landed in the saddle with a desperate spring he was already halfway towards the nearest group of Nazis. The road was narrow, and by seeking to avoid them he would only have presented a better target. Lying flat along the tank he jerked the throttle wide open and charged straight at them, the engine screaming deafeningly in bottom gear. They scattered and had evidently only just drawn their guns without having time to aim, as none of them fired until he had flashed by them and was roaring down the street towards the next group, which the light of his headlamp suddenly brought into view.

Still crouching low over the handlebars, he set his teeth and risked a racing change into second gear. By a miracle it came off, and the machine hurtled forward at even greater speed. The pistols of the Nazis ahead flashed almost in his face, but he had swerved a split second before, and their shots went wide. Scraping one man with his elbow he bowled him over, and raced on just as a shot from the first group, now well behind him, whistled past his ear.

An instant later a yell of pain sounded above the roar of his engine. A man in the second group had been hit by another bullet intended for Gregory and fired by one of the men in the first, who were now pounding vainly down the street after him.

Orders, counter-orders ; cries to stop him, to shoot him, to cease fire or they would kill one another, rang out in guttural German.

Behind him the darkness veiled a scene of consternation and confusion ; before him, at the end of the street, there waited yet another squad of Nazis, and although it was barely half a minute since he had thrown himself on the motor-cycle they had had that much more time in which to prepare for his reception.

They blazed off as he came charging down the street, but, gripping the handle-bars with savage determination he wrenched the machine right up on to the low pavement, skimmed inside an unlighted lamp-standard, roared past the group of men and bumped down off the pavement beyond them. Swerving again he careered first to one side of the street and then to the other until he shot round the bend, miraculously immune from the hail of bullets that were now striking sparks from the road-way and whining loudly as they ricochetted from the walls of the houses.

In his anxiety to get clear of Ems before a police cordon could be drawn across its exits he took a wrong turning, but he soon picked up his route again and striking the main Coblenz road slipped the B.M.W. into top gear. Regardless of all danger of a smash he streaked at over eighty m.p.h. past a police patrol which yelled at him to halt and two minutes later was clear of the town. At last he breathed a little more freely and eased up the speed of the machine. By the mercy of Providence and the use of his own quick wits he had escaped when escape had seemed next to impossible.

But how long would he be able to retain his liberty? He had no illusions about the odds that he was up against. The infuriated Nazis would already be bawling frantic orders down their telephones, raising the whole countryside against him. Had it not been that Ems was a small place and that his dash for liberty had been an extraordinarily swift one, they would have had a cordon drawn up to head him off before he had been able to get out of the town. They would certainly make certain of stopping him at some point further along the road, and the police in the whole Coblenz area were already on the look-out for him as General von Lettow. How far could he get before he was challenged and either halted or shot down?

He began to get out a mental balance-sheet and to start with counted his bag, but that consoled him little since he had now hopelessly bungled his mission.

What were eight Nazis when Hitler had a million of the brutes? If only Wachmuller had been able to give him the name of the General at the head of the conspiracy before he had been shot! Then there would have been at least a hope of getting that priceless information out of the country before he was captured. But Wachmuller was dead, and with him the trail had ended. More: Gregory felt certain in his own mind that he had been the unwitting cause of the unfortunate Pastor's murder.

He could not tell for certain how the Nazis had come to know of his presence in Ems, but he had evidently been recognized through the circulated description of 'General von Lettow' either by some police spy at the *Kursaal* café while he had been getting the Pastor's address from the barmaid or, more probably, by one of the women at the war workers' meeting in the Church

Hall. Whoever it had been, they must have telephoned Party Headquarters that he was seeking or actually with Pastor Wachmuller, thus enabling a squad of Storm-Troopers to get to the house before he and the Pastor had returned there. The housekeeper had doubtless been either gagged or removed ; the leader of the Nazis had hidden in the room adjoining Wachmuller's library, and the others, having sent for reinforcements, had then quietly surrounded the whole block while he had been talking to the Pastor.

All that would never have happened had he not been indiscreet enough to determine on seeing Wachmuller when he was himself wanted by the police on account of the previous night's affair in Coblenz.

It occurred to him that a second visit to Herr Rheinhardt might elicit further information and a fresh lead to another of the conspirators if he could escape, lie hidden until the present hue and cry had died down, and make his way to Traben-Trabach, but he suddenly recalled that he had made an irretrievable blunder at the very start by commandeering the car of a Nazi Party Chief for his first visit there. Fräulein Schultz would certainly have been questioned as to where she had driven the self-styled General von Lettow. She had no reason whatever to conceal such information, and even if she had, the unscrupulous blackguards whom he was up against would have wrung it from her by threats or torture. The unfortunate Herr Rheinhardt had probably been a prisoner for the greater part of the last twenty-four hours and perhaps was even now whimpering under the blows of the Nazis' rubber truncheons in some sound-proof cell ; if not already dead.

All that Gregory had accomplished, therefore, was the inadvertent betrayal of the two fine Germans who had been his only leads to further information.

And here he was, hatless, wounded, upon a stolen police motor-cycle, a fugitive himself knowing that in all probability death was waiting round one of the dark bends in the road to claim him. His only asset was the speed at which he could now travel. Any attempt to go into hiding in Germany was clearly useless now that all hope of pursuing his mission had been terminated through his having given away both Wachmuller and Rheinhardt to their enemies. The only remaining course was to try to get out of the country and sneak home with his tail between his legs.

If he could get as far as the Belgian or Dutch border he

knew that there were plenty of underground channels from the frontier villages by which he could cross into safety without going through the frontier posts. In peace-time a huge, illicit business in the smuggling of contraband through them was carried on which provided a prosperous livelihood for many thousands of peasants on both sides of the line.

Now that war had come the frontiers would be much more strictly guarded, but even so many such secret methods of evading the guards would still be in operation. All sorts of goods were very badly needed by the Germans, who would probably now be closing their eyes to illicit cargoes coming in from Belgium and Holland ; and where goods could come in men could go out.

Gregory still had a large sum of money on him, mainly concealed in his boots, and he had little doubt that if only he could reach the frontier in safety he would soon be able to find some avaricious peasant who, for a suitable remuneration, would smuggle him over into the security of a neutral country.

This thought cheered him a little but he knew that he was faced with many hours of desperate anxiety, if not worse, before he could attempt to put any such plan into practice. Besides being nearly a hundred miles by road from the Belgian frontier he was, in addition, on the wrong side of the broad waters of the Rhine. Unless he had himself ferried over he would have to cross a bridge before getting on to a road to the frontier, and both bridges and ferries were certain to be watched by the police.

Gregory's thoughts had been racing as swiftly as the speeding motor-cycle, and he was little more than three miles from Ems when he struck a fork of the road which branched away up into the dark hills upon his right. Having already decided that he dared not pass through Coblenz but must endeavour instead to find some side-road cutting inland behind the town he swerved uphill along the right fork.

It was not much better than a cart-track, and loose stones skidded from beneath his wheels as he leaned first to one side, then to the other, in negotiating steep bends. A few miles further on the road levelled out and ran across high, grassy, treeless country and Gregory realized suddenly that he was on a plateau behind Coblenz.

The knowledge that he had found a road which would take him past the city without entering it put fresh heart into him, and when the plateau ended he rode almost gaily, despite the pain of his wounded thigh, down the twisting road beyond its further edge. At the bottom of the slope the road levelled out again, and suddenly he emerged from it to find himself on the wide *Autobahn* which ran from Coblenz to Cologne along the banks of the Rhine.

Here there was much more likelihood of his meeting trouble but as there was no other road he had to take the risk ; the greater the distance he could put between the Ems-Coblenz area and himself the better. In any case, he was now running north-east, towards the Dutch frontier, and when he had left the scenes of his recent activities further behind he would have to devise some means of crossing the river.

Suddenly the engine of his motor-cycle started to stutter and backfire.

"Damn, blast and hell !" he exclaimed aloud, as the bike began to slow down. He knew enough of motors to recognize that particular noise when it came without warning after a machine had been running perfectly.

A moment later the engine petered out altogether, upon which Gregory gave vent to an Italian oath which is utterly unprintable, being probably the most blasphemous ever devised by man.

He had run out of petrol, and he was still no more than five miles from Coblenz.

Chapter XI

THE LADY OF THE LIMOUSINE

THE now silent motor-cycle ran on for a hundred yards. Gregory steered it to the side of the road, halted it, got off and jerked it up on its stand. Feeling for the petrol leads, he unscrewed and examined them. His surmise had been correct ; the tank was as dry as a bone.

Although petrol was rationed he might ordinarily have walked to the nearest filling-station and have succeeded in bribing a garage-hand with a hundred-mark note to sell him a couple of six-litre cans ; but he positively dared not do so now that he was a hunted man and still only just outside Coblenz, where the hunt for him was at its hottest. By this time, too, as he had stolen the motor-cycle from a Nazi, every garage for a hundred miles around would have been ordered by telephone not to supply him with petrol even if he produced a Party or Army permit, but to hold him until the police arrived.

It was accursed luck that such a thing should happen when, after so many close shaves during the night, it really seemed that there was a reasonably good prospect of his getting clear of the area in which he had got himself into such hot water ; but without petrol the bike was not only useless but actually dangerous. If he left it by the roadside it would be discovered either that night or early the following morning, and would give away to the police the road he had taken.

Turning towards the river he kicked back the motor-cycle's stand and pushed it up on to the edge of the grass which ran down to meet a sloping wall of stones set into the bank to prevent the river eating it away. The slope of the grass was the same as that of the stones, and together they formed a fairly smooth surface that rose steeply from the gurgling water.

Balancing the bike carefully, and holding its handlebars so that the front wheel pointed down the slope, he gave it a push and let it career down into the river ; then scrambled down after it to make sure that it was entirely submerged. The momentum of the weighty machine had carried it some ten feet

out from the river-wall, and peering down at the darkly flowing
water Gregory could see no trace of it. By daylight it might
be visible if the water was shallow, but he had to chance
that.

As he had had nothing to drink all day except a few mouthfuls
of brandy-and-water from his flask, which was now almost
empty, and the glass of Schnapps at Wachmuller's, he leaned
down, bathed his face in the cool river water, and cupping his
hands drank his fill. Gregory did not often drink water, but now
it tasted as good to him as a draught of Sir Pellinore's champagne
fresh off the ice, and had the necessity arisen he would cheerfully have paid a guinea a bottle for it. Having refilled his
flask he scrambled up the bank and turned his face towards
Cologne.

He was tired now, and despondent. Even his powers of
recuperation from hard knocks and the strain of danger were
beginning to fail him. It seemed quite certain that he must be
caught early the following morning. His only remaining chance
of evading capture for any length of time lay in reaching some
big town or city where he might elude the Nazis by mingling
with hundreds of other people in busy streets, but apart from
Coblenz, now definitely barred to him, Cologne was the only
city of any size in that part of Germany, and Cologne lay nearly
fifty miles away.

On the way to it there were only little places like Königswinter, where a stranger's presence would soon be noticed, and
the university town of Bonn, which was nearly as far away as
Cologne. Moreover, he was still in his General's uniform, which
was about the most easily identifiable thing that he could
possibly wear. To make matters worse he had lost his cap when
swinging himself in at the dormer window, a fact which the
Nazis would know and circulate ; as if it had not already been
found it certainly would be when the dawn revealed it, lying in
the street, to the men left in charge of the Pastor's house.

There seemed nevertheless to be absolutely no alternative
but to walk in the direction of Cologne with the intention of
putting as great a distance between Coblenz and himself as he
could manage while darkness lasted. Before dawn broke he
would have to endeavour to find another haystack or similar
hide-out in which to lie concealed during the coming day.

He had not gone a hundred yards before his leg began to
pain him. In the excitement of the fight on the roof-tops and
his subsequent escape he had hardly noticed his wound, and

had paid no attention to it, but now the pain in his thigh began to stab him angrily with every step he took, and he could feel the warm blood trickling down his leg inside his trousers.

Turning off the road he climbed down the river-bank again, removed his trousers, tore off the tail of his shirt, staunched the flow of blood as well as he could and carefully bathed the wound in the river water. He then made a rough bandage of the wet rag, adjusted it, pulled his trousers on again and washed the blood from his hands.

By careful prodding he had assured himself that the bullet was not in the wound, and he considered himself lucky to have got off so lightly. In his already difficult position the wound was yet another handicap, but he knew from experience that if only he could find some place in which to lie up for a few days he would soon be none the worse, as such flesh-wounds soon heal in a healthy body. A wet patch on his trousers just above the wound told him that they were stained with blood that had seeped through, but as he was still wearing his overcoat that would conceal the bloodstains from any casual observer.

Regaining the road he set off once more. The wound still hurt him, but not so badly as it had, and the bathing with cold water had lessened its tendency to become inflamed.

At a steady pace he limped along for a couple of miles, meeting no one on his way. As he saw from a glance at the luminous dial of his watch it was now past midnight, and he was cynically amused to think how many experiences he had passed through during the last four hours. In that time, too, eight Nazis and Pastor Wachmuller, all of whom had awakened in their beds that morning healthy and well and with no more than their normal shares of the world's cares, had passed from life to death. But what was that, after all, when literally thousands of people, women and children as well as soldiers, must also have died in that same space of time on the far-flung battle-fronts of Poland?

When he thought how he had been given a chance to stop that horrible carnage, a slaughter which was now going on hour after hour and might continue for years without intermission, yet had failed to do so, a new wave of despondency overtook him. He was very tired, and sat down to rest for a while on a low, stone wall by the roadside.

Taking one of the straw-filled German cigarettes from his case he lit and smoked it until, after a few puffs, it had burned down nearly to his fingers. Just as he was crushing out the stub he saw two tiny lights approaching along the road from the direction of Coblenz.

Instinctively he drew back to take cover behind the low wall, fearing that the lights might be those of a police car. Then a new recklessness suddenly surged up in him. What the hell did it matter whether it was a police car or not ? It had petrol, and was heading towards Cologne. He still had one pistol and plenty of ammunition ; the car was approaching slowly as its headlamps had been dimmed according to the A.R.P. regulations. He would hold it up at the point of his gun and demand a lift. If the car held civilians, which was unlikely, they would be too frightened of him to refuse ; if it held police, soldiers or Nazis, he would give battle. In the event of there being only one or two men in it he might succeed in shooting them before they could shoot him, in which case he would chuck the devils into the river and make off with their damned car.

Drawing his gun and slipping back the safety-catch he held it behind him in his right hand. He would have to walk into the faint beam of the headlights to bring the car to a halt, and he did not wish to invite any armed men who might be in it to draw upon him before he had at least a fighting chance to retaliate. A few steps brought him to the middle of the road. As the car approached he waved his left hand above his head, signalling it to halt, while he prayed with all his might for a lucky break.

The car stopped about ten yards from him and he walked up to it. If the people in the car were armed his position was about as bad as it could be, since after the blackness even the dimmed headlamps had momentarily dazzled him. As he regained his sight he saw, with a sudden sinking in the pit of his stomach, that the car was a big limousine Mercèdes and that its chauffeur was a soldier.

He was just about to whip up his automatic when the window behind the driver was pulled back and a girl's voice came clearly on the still, night air.

"What is it, Johannes ? Why have you stopped ?"

Stepping forward before the man could reply, Gregory grasped the handle of the car door and swung it open. Even in the darkened interior of the limousine he could see that the girl was its only occupant, and he addressed her in a polite but authoritative tone.

"*Guten Abend, Gnädiges Fräulein.* Forgive me, please, for

having pulled you up, but I have met with an accident, and I must ask you to be good enough to give me a lift to Cologne."

"An accident? Are you hurt?" the girl inquired quickly.

"*Es macht nichts*," Gregory shrugged, implying that he was making light of it. "Did you not see my car in the ditch half a mile back along the road? This confounded black-out! I've lost my cap and dirtied my clothes, but I can tidy myself up later. The important thing is that I should get to Cologne as soon as possible."

The girl had taken out a cigarette, and now she struck a match. Gregory guessed that the act was a mere excuse to get a proper look at him; as the match flared up he also got a good look at her. She was a blonde of about twenty-six, and although her features showed clearly that she was of German origin, hers was a type that one very rarely sees in Germany.

To start with she was extremely good-looking, which in itself is comparatively rare among German women, and for this reason Gregory thought that she might quite possibly be a fair Austrian. Her face had something of Marlene Dietrich about it, and although it was not over made-up her eyelashes were darkened and she wore lipstick, two things unusual among even smart women since Hitler had decreed that the females of the species who used such aids to beauty would no longer be well regarded. The hand that held the light to her cigarette had almond-shaped, painted nails, and a pair of long, slim, silk-stockinged legs with well-rounded knees protruded from under a black skirt which was decidedly short by comparison with the prevailing German fashion.

Her clothes immediately conveyed the information that she was something more than an unusually pretty German or Austrian girl. An absurd little pork-pie hat with long streamers, as once worn by the Widow of Windsor, was perched on the front of her head; a short, high-shouldered mink coat partly concealed her smart, black-frogged suit, and her high-heeled suède shoes were not designed for walking. Gregory, who knew about such matters, could see at a glance that her outfit had never been bought in Germany; it positively screamed of London, Paris or New York.

As she had a military chauffeur it was a safe bet that she was the wife, daughter or mistress of some high Army officer, but her identity did not at the moment concern him. His one anxiety was to get as far as possible from Coblenz.

Her quick, blue eyes had already taken in the rank-badges on Gregory's shoulders, and directly the match had flickered out she said : "I am going to Cologne, so I will give you a lift with pleasure, Herr General ; but how about your chauffeur ? Did he also escape with minor injuries only ?"

Gregory nodded. "The young fool is perfectly all right. I sent him to find the nearest garage at which he can secure help to get the car back on the road again. We hit a low wall as we ran off the road, but I don't think the car's seriously damaged ; I expect he'll be able to bring it on to Cologne early to-morrow morning."

Under cover of the darkness he brought his right hand from behind his back and replaced the automatic in his pistol holster ; then he climbed in behind with the girl and slammed the door. The chauffeur, who had heard the whole conversation, immediately restarted the engine, and the big Mercèdes rolled forward again at a cautious pace.

"You have been long in Coblenz, Herr General ?" asked the girl.

"No, *Gnädiges Fräulein*. I arrived only yesterday from Frankfurt. Permit me to introduce myself. I am Otto von Heintisch, General of Engineers. My present task is to inspect the bridges of the Rhine as quickly as possible, and to report upon them."

"How interesting !" she murmured, but she did not introduce herself in turn, and went on smoothly : "Have you seen any of the fighting ?"

"Not yet, although I hope to, of course." He would rather not have talked, but she seemed to expect it, so he added : "I was retired in 1934, and called up again only just before the outbreak of the war, so for the moment I'm really a supernumerary ; but I've no doubt that I shall be given an Engineer Unit in due course."

"Do you live in this part of the country ?" she inquired.

"No. My home is in Allenstein, in East Prussia. You know it, perhaps ?" Although Gregory had thought it wise to change his assumed name he was still using the particulars of General von Lettow's career. He had to have some sort of background and his memory had fully absorbed the particulars which he had been given about von Lettow, whereas if he started to invent details about the mythical Otto von Heintisch he might inadvertently contradict himself later on.

The girl shook her fair head. "No, I have never been in

East Prussia. Most of my life I have lived either in Berlin or
in South Germany."

"Except when you have been travelling," Gregory added
with a smile which was hidden from her by the shadows. "I
feel sure that the enchanting hat you're wearing didn't come
out of a German workshop."

"Correct !" she laughed. "I see, Herr General, that you
are something of a detective. I bought this hat in London
only three weeks ago. I like London ; it is so gay after our
German cities."

"I'm afraid you may get into trouble if you say that sort
of thing and it comes to the ears of the Gestapo," said Gregory
quietly.

"Oh ! The Gestapo !" He sensed rather than saw her dis-
dainful shrug. "I hardly think that my friend, Hermann Goering,
would allow them to interfere with me just because I said that
I liked London. Have you ever been there ?"

"No." Gregory noted that he had been right in his surmise
that she was someone of importance. "I would have liked to
do so before our bombers had destroyed all the principal streets,
but I'm just a German officer who has spent most of his life
in military duties, and when I retired I was not rich enough
to travel."

"*Ach ! Der Welt-Krieg* !" she exclaimed. "That and the
subsequent revolutions cost so many of us our private incomes
and estates. I am fortunate in that I have enough money in-
vested abroad to enable me to travel when I wish ; but for
most of our generation the tragic aftermath of the World War
has meant poverty and some wretched job, with a yearly fortnight at Norderney or on the Bodensee as the most that can
be hoped for."

"You flatter me, *Gnädiges Fräulein*, by placing me in the
same generation as yourself," said Gregory quickly. "I'm
old enough to be your father."

She laughed again. "From the glimpse I caught of you I
would not have thought it, and you have the voice of a youngish
man. I find it difficult to believe that you are really an old
dug-out."

"Oh, I'm not as old as all that ! I was only fifty-four when
I retired not so long ago, but I have a daughter of over thirty,
and I'm sure that you're nowhere near thirty yet."

"Thank you, Herr General. A woman's as old as she looks
and a man's as old as he feels, is that not so ?"

"A delightful saying and a very true one. It makes me feel much more like one of your contemporaries."

"Is your daughter married?"

"Yes; she now lives in America, but I have another, a few years younger, who is also married and living in Leipzig."

"*Ach so*! And have you any sons?"

"No. My children were all girls, and the eldest died when still a child, from ill-nourishment as a result of the war."

"How terrible for you! Were you at the Front when you lost her?"

"Yes. I was only a Colonel then, but I had some hand in the construction of the Hindenburg Line, and remained there until the collapse of the Home Front. My daughter died in 1918, a few weeks before the Armistice."

As they talked the car advanced at a steady pace. Gregory was leaning back comfortably on its well-upholstered cushions, relaxed at last after his stupendous exertions earlier that night. He was feeling rather more rested, and this easy conversation with a pretty girl was an oasis of delight after the endless desert of anxiety and strain through which he had passed. His only pressing trouble at the moment was that he was extremely hungry, having eaten nothing except a few bars of chocolate during the last thirty-six hours, but he hoped to devise some means of securing a hot meal on his arrival in Cologne. In the meantime he was content to close his eyes and breathe in the subtle, exotic perfume emanating from the girl at his side.

It was with astonishment and dismay that he suddenly heard her say: "You tell General von Lettow's story quite delightfully. What a pity that for my country's sake I shall have to hand you over to be shot as a spy directly we reach Cologne."

And he knew that the hard object that she had jammed into his side while she was speaking was the business end of an automatic.

Chapter XII

LOOK TO THY HEART

"I WOULDN'T move if I were you," she went on quietly. "The thing I'm holding to your ribs is a pocket Mauser; only a toy, but quite large enough to kill you, and as I come of an Army family I'm used to handling firearms."

The circumstances in which she had picked him up and her mention of von Lettow convinced Gregory that it would be useless, and therefore bad tactics, to attempt any kind of bluff. He was caught, and the best thing he could do was to admit it. His voice was under perfect control as he murmured: "Thank God for that! I'd hate to be accidentally shot by some flustered female. Now tell me, how did you find me out?"

"It was quite easy," she replied, with a hint of amusement in her tone. "I have many Army friends in Coblenz, and for the last two nights I've been staying at the Hotel Bellevue. It was quite natural that my friends should tell me of the peculiar behaviour of a certain General von Lettow, and that they had found, on turning up his record, that the real von Lettow had died early this year. Details of his career and a description of you were in all this morning's papers, and when you held up my car looking as though you had been dragged through a hedge backwards, though still wearing the uniform of a General of Engineers, it didn't take much detective ability to put two and two together."

"So that's the way it was. Well, congratulations on your capture. May I inquire what you intend to do with me?"

Her voice was cold as she replied: "I've already told you. I mean to hand you over to the authorities directly we reach Cologne."

"You were kind enough to add, though, that you thought it rather a pity that I should be shot."

"It is, especially if I'm correct in my belief that you're nowhere near as old as you pretended to be when impersonating the General."

"I'm not, but all the same I shall most certainly be shot if you do as you suggest."

"I see no alternative. You're an enemy agent, and your excellent German makes you a very dangerous one. You would pass even with the police as a German who had been brought up in the provinces, but you can't deceive me."

"What do you think I am, then?"

"I've travelled a lot," she replied, "and having heard so many foreigners speaking German really well I have a trained ear for such things. I believe that you're an Englishman, but in any case I'm convinced that you're a foreigner and a spy. Since my country's at war it is my duty to hand you over to the police, and I shall certainly do so."

"Now that seems a bit hard," Gregory protested, with pained politeness. "Of course you're right about my being English, but just now you were good enough to say how much you liked London. This war is bound to end sooner or later, and with luck it will end sooner. I was going to try to persuade you to lunch with me in London at the Ritz, when it *is* over and I've had a chance to grow my hair again. I'm sure we'd both find lots of interesting things to talk about; yet it seems that you're determined to rob us both of that pleasure."

He was trying to probe her mentality. Was she as hard-boiled as she appeared to be? If she was, he had got himself into a very nasty fix. As long as the car was moving he could not possibly escape without risking a bullet in his guts, a method of extinction which he had always heard to be particularly painful. Yet if he allowed her to take him as her captive to Cologne he would certainly find himself facing a firing-squad before he was much older.

"You're an audacious person, and I like audacious men," she said thoughtfully. "If our countries were at peace I might—just might—be tempted to accept your invitation: but as they are not, and you are my prisoner, I'm afraid that you will never lunch at the Ritz again, my friend, either with me or with anyone else."

"How very trying! Especially when the grouse must be so good there just now. And, talking of grouse, may I remind you that having caught your bird you've still got to cook it? If I decide to biff you over the head you may, or may not, be able to shoot me first. Personally, I find you so enchanting that I feel I could hardly bring myself to do so; but supposing I did attempt it, d'you honestly mean to say that your finger would close upon that trigger in a determined effort to send me to perdition?"

"I'm quite sure it would. So please don't try any tricks."
Her voice had abruptly hardened again. "I've already told
you that I'm well acquainted with the use of firearms. As long
as you remain perfectly still you're in no danger, but make
just—one—move—and I'll let you have the *entire* contents of
this automatic in the ribs. I don't intend to take half-measures
and risk getting hurt myself."

The further Gregory probed her mental processes the less
he liked the way things were going. It was no joke to be held
up at the end of a gun and when the holder of the gun was a girl
it was humiliating into the bargain. It was true that this particular girl was doing the job with a calm deliberation that
many men might have envied ; but that only lessened his chances
of putting a fast one over on her, and he had somehow got to
terminate the lift which he had so rashly demanded before the
car had proceeded very much further. Having failed completely
in his attempt to scare her he decided to try another tack,
and asked :

"Has it occurred to you that I'm a very desperate man ?"

"I knew that the moment I set eyes on you."

"You're very brave, then, to have wriggled that little gun
out of your bag with the idea of trying to corner me, when I
might have suspected what you were up to."

"There wasn't much chance of that, since we're in almost
total darkness."

"Darkness is always the friend of treachery."

"Treachery ?" she exclaimed angrily. "But I . . ."

"I was about to add," cut in Gregory, "and of lovers."

"What on earth are you talking about ?"

"I'm not going to tell you that I'm in love with you. But
by God, you *are* attractive. Perhaps you'll think I'm crazy,
but I'd give the hell of a lot for a proper chance to persuade
you to kiss me, and as things are I'll never get it unless . . ."

"Unless what ?"

"Unless you intend to be present at my execution, and the
sight of the preparations for the inevitable outcome of your
own handiwork fills you with a sudden wave of womanly pity."

"What nonsense !" She seemed to be half-annoyed, half-
amused. "You've only had one glimpse of my face ! Do you
tell every pretty girl you meet that you want to kiss her ?"

"Certainly not !" Gregory protested. "But you're different.
There's something about you, I don't know what it is, but
somehow it got me right away."

During his hectic career he had used the same formula, practically word for word, with at least a couple of score of good-looking young women. It was a safe bet, never failing to produce a suitable reaction. The only way in which the response of the present lady varied from those of most of her forerunners was that, instead of pretending to joke about it while half-believing that he really meant it, or accepting the statement with happy wonder, this young woman took it quite seriously and as her legitimate tribute.

"I'm sorry you feel like that about me," she said, "but I can quite understand it. I seem to have that effect on most of the men I meet ; and I *am* different from most girls of my age. It probably sounds extremely conceited, but I'm old enough to have proved to myself that I am blessed with brains and personality as well as looks."

"It does sound extremely conceited," Gregory agreed, "but the combination is extraordinarily rare and damnably attractive. I imagine that you also possess determination. Once you've really made up your mind about a thing you never alter it, do you ?"

"No. I may not look it, but I've got quite a lot of the male in my make-up. I'm not one of those poor, weak creatures who constantly have to claim the feminine privilege of changing their minds."

"Exactly," said Gregory, and as the car swung round a bend he gave a swift wriggle. At the same instant he grabbed her hand, so that her pistol no longer pointed at his ribs, but was forced down behind him towards the back of the car.

"That," he added, a second later, "is why, my lovely and determined friend, you compelled me to risk my life in order to change your mind for you. I'd loathe to hurt that nice little wrist of yours, but *by God* I'm going to unless you drop that gun."

His movement had been so sudden that it had caught her off her guard. For an instant he felt the tautening of the muscles in her wrist, and feared that she would pull the trigger before he could compel her to drop the pistol, but the muscles slackened almost at once, and for fear that it might go off as it fell, he quickly grasped the Mauser with his other hand, and drew it from between her fingers.

She relaxed with a faint sigh. "It was the darkness that proved your friend that time, wasn't it ? You'd never have caught me out like that if there'd been a light. I was a fool to amuse myself by letting you talk ; I'd certainly have shot you at your first movement if you hadn't distracted my attention, and if it hadn't been too dark to see you.'"

"Perhaps the darkness will prove a friend to both of us before we're through," suggested Gregory amiably, "but if it's any consolation to you, much older hands than you have been led up the garden path before now through over-indulgence in conversation with your humble servant."

As he was speaking he ran his hands over the miniature automatic and found that the safety-catch was off, so evidently she had not been bluffing, but had genuinely meant to send him to kingdom come. He made a wry grimace in the darkness as he thought of the risk he had just taken. He must have been nearer death at that moment than he had been when exchanging shots with the Nazis on the roof of Wachmuller's house, but his respect for the girl went up. Even to contemplate shooting a man took a lot of courage. She must be a real tough egg. But Gregory was a tough egg himself, and he always rejoiced to find similar qualities in others.

"And now that you're master of the situation may one inquire your intentions?" she asked quietly.

"Certainly. Should you be so indiscreet as to call out to your chauffeur or to pop your beautiful head out of the window in an effort to attract the attention of anyone we may pass it's my intention to fill you full of lead with your own gun. Please don't think I'm joking, either. I've already told you that I'm a desperate man. You know very well that if your friends catch me they'll shoot me, and I've no desire to quit this so-called vale of tears just yet if I can possibly avoid it. Have I made myself perfectly clear?"

"Perfectly, thank you."

"That's a good thing, because if you had any lingering doubts they might land you to-morrow in a nasty wooden box which would be lowered down a hole in a graveyard. Just keep that thought firmly in your mind, and I think we shall remain very good friends. It'd be a sin to rob the world of beauty such as yours, but I'm a professional sinner, and I'll shoot you as dead as cat's-meat if you don't do exactly as I tell you. To start with, you will remove your shoes and stockings."

"*Donner-Wetter !*" she exclaimed, suddenly stiffening. "Have you gone mad?"

"I'm no crazier than the proverbial Englishman. Kindly do as I say."

"But this, it is not—well, how shall I say—in the picture. No! I refuse. I will not half strip myself for your amusement."

"Dear, dear! What a fuss to make about removing a pair of stockings! If you only knew the number of lovely legs that I've seen with nothing on in my time! And in any case, I shan't be able to see yours in the darkness."

"No," she retorted, with abrupt frankness, "but you'd be able to feel them afterwards, wouldn't you? And I will not play."

"Just at this moment I'm not in a playing mood myself, so you need have no fears on that score. If you were as old as Methuselah and twice as ugly I'd still want you to take your stockings off, so for God's sake get on with it."

"In that case, it seems an extraordinary request. I really think you must be a little crazy."

"I'm not crazy, I tell you! Now, are you going to take those stockings off or must I taken them off for you?"

"No," she said hastily. "I'll do it, and if you dare to touch me I'll scream, whether you mean to shoot me or not."

Bending forward she kicked off her shoes, undid her suspenders, rolled down her stockings, and pulled them off.

"And now what?" she demanded angrily.

"Now pass your stockings over and listen to me. I'm going to tie your feet up. To do that I'll have to lean down, so I shan't be able to keep you covered with my gun. But I'm very much stronger than you are, and if you start any funny business while I'm tying up your feet you won't find dinner invitations come quite so frequently in future because I'll bash that nice nose of yours bang through the middle of your face. Get the idea?"

"So that's what you wanted my stockings for! Why on earth didn't you say so? Go on, tie me up, then. I value my nose very highly, and I'm certainly not going to risk it in an encounter with a brute like you."

"Easy, now, easy!" he protested. "All's fair in love and war, you know, and this seems to be a delightful combination of the two—at least, I'd like it to be that way. I haven't called you any hard names, so why should you start abusing me? You know quite well that I won't hurt a hair of your lovely head if you don't force me to by doing something stupid."

The safety-catch of her gun had been on for some minutes. Slipping it into his pocket he knelt down and lifted one of her feet. Gently pulling one of her toes he began : "This little pig went to market ; this little pig stayed at home. . . ."

"Don't !" she cried, jerking away her foot. "You tickle !" Then she laughed. "You are an absurd person, really."

"Not half as absurd as I would have been if I'd let you hand me over to a firing-squad. D'you mind giving me back your feet ?"

She stretched them out again, and he used one of the thin, silk stockings to tie her ankles firmly together. Then he put her shoes on again, so that her feet would not get cold in the draught, and raising them slightly he kissed the little pads of soft flesh on her insteps, first one and then the other.

She made no comment on this gallant gesture, so he sat back on the seat and said : Hands now, please. If I were a real ruffian I'd tie them behind your back, but that would be very uncomfortable for you, and, although I'm taking no chances, I don't think it's strictly necessary."

Holding out her hands until they touched his in the darkness she said : "You're really a sort of Claude Duval among secret agents, aren't you ? And to give you your due I find it very difficult to think of you as a ruffian at all."

"Now, that's charming of you," he murmured, as he tied her wrists tightly with the other stocking. "Quite the nicest thing you've said for some time. D'you know what they put on the gallant highwayman's tombstone ?

> "Here lies Du Vall : Reader, if male thou art
> Look to thy purse : if female, to thy heart.

"You encourage me to hope that we'll pull off that luncheon together at the Ritz yet, when the war's over."

"Don't you be too certain, my friend. You're still in Germany, and to judge from what was happening in Coblenz every policeman in the whole of the Rhineland is on the look-out for you. The odds are a hundred to one that the Gestapo will get you within the next couple of days, and when they do—well, I don't quite know now whether I shall be glad or sorry."

"Thanks for the warning, but I pity the poor devil who has the job of trying to arrest me, unless he catches me asleep. Now, to my deep regret, I must temporarily terminate this delightful conversation by tying my handkerchief over your mouth."

"*Ach, Himmel* !" she exclaimed. "Are you going to gag me

as well? Is that really necessary if I give you my word that I won't shout?"

"I'm afraid it is, but if you'll promise not to shout I'll leave the handkerchief quite loose so that you could if you wanted to. You see, I have to transact a little necessary business, and part of it demands that you should at least appear to be gagged."

"All right, then, go ahead. I do hope your handkerchief is clean."

"Fairly so, and there doesn't seem to be anything else handy that I could use. I'd like it to be my handkerchief, too, because then it might collect a little of that delightful scent you use. In any case I shall treasure it for ever afterwards on account of its once having been in contact with so lovely a mouth."

"You *are* a fool!" she muttered, as he adjusted the hand-kerchief and tied it firmly but not too tightly behind her golden curls.

Having dealt with her fairly and satisfactorily his next concern was with the chauffeur, who all this time had naturally been keeping his eyes fixed on the unlit road ahead which was extremely difficult to follow. Even had he chanced to glance into the windscreen mirror which normally showed him the interior of the car as well as the road behind him he could have seen nothing owing to the lack of lights.

Gregory's plan was already fully worked out in his mind and to begin with he sat down on the floor of the car with his back to the driver. Next he unlatched the near-side door with his left hand, holding it firmly so that the wind should not wrench it open as the car sped along, while with his right he drew his own heavy pistol and reversed it, clutching it firmly by the barrel. Then, bringing up his arm abruptly, he smashed the butt of the pistol with all his strength against the glass partition above his head, which was just behind the driver.

It was a risky procedure, as the shock and the flying glass might have caused the driver to lose control of the car, which would have resulted in a nasty smash; but they were running along a straight piece of road and keeping right down to a steady twenty-five miles an hour on account of the black-out. In any case, the risk had to be taken.

The car swerved violently as the heavy pistol crashed through the glass, but the driver soon had it under control again, steered it to the side of the road, jammed on his brakes and brought it to a halt.

Just as it swerved Gregory let the near-side door fly open

and grabbing the handle of the off-side door opened that too, but only a crack, and continued to hold on to it. The instant the car had stopped he pushed the off-side door open, slipped noiselessly out on to the road and gently closed it behind him. He intended the man to think, on finding the near-side door hanging open, that the passenger whom they had picked up was now some distance back along the road, having attacked the girl and afterwards leaped out of the car while it was still moving.

To have faked things so that they gave that appearance, yet to have succeeded in getting out of the car and keeping near it without having risked his neck, had been a tricky business depending upon perfect timing. In the ordinary way Gregory could never have accomplished it, but once more the darkness had proved his friend.

As he had calculated, immediately the car came to a stand-still the chauffeur turned, called out to ask what had happened, and receiving no reply jumped down from his seat. Thrusting his head through the open, near-side doorway of the car he asked what was wrong.

The moment the man had got out Gregory tiptoed swiftly round the back of the car, still clutching his pistol by the barrel. The chauffeur had just discovered that the dishevelled General to whom they had given a lift had disappeared, leaving the lady bound and gagged, and was reaching up to take the gag from her mouth when Gregory arrived behind him. Gregory waited for him to take it off and drew back a little ; then he lifted his pistol and with a savage, sideways swipe brought the butt thudding against the base of the chauffeur's skull just below his forage cap.

The man staggered, raised one hand to grab the side of the car, missed it, took a couple of unsteady steps backwards and collapsed in the roadway.

Gregory knew that it would be quite unnecessary to hit him a second time. As the man rolled over with a moan he put his head inside the car and said to the girl : "I'm terribly sorry that I've had to lay out your chauffeur, but I want his clothes, you see."

"I had an idea that that might be the case sooner or later," she remarked coolly. "I hope you haven't killed him, though. Johannes is a little stupid at times, but a very nice fellow."

"Don't worry ; he'll be all right after a few days in hospital. Our agreement about your not shouting still stands, doesn't it ?

Otherwise I'm afraid I'll have to replace that gag he untied for you, and tighten it up into the bargain."

"Yes. That stands, since you've still got the whip-hand of me, but don't be longer than you can help over changing. My legs are getting cold."

"Right ; I'll soon get through with it." He closed the door and, stooping, began to undress the unconscious soldier.

Johannes was considerably shorter than Gregory so his clothes were by no means a good fit, but that is not unusual in armies where a private must not only wear ready-mades, but take the best he can get if the Quartermaster has not got the right size.

Having stripped to his underclothes and buttoned himself into Johannes' uniform, Gregory pushed, pulled and shoved the limbs of the unconscious man until he had got him into the General's kit. Then, turning him over on his face in the road, he tied his hands behind his back with his braces and secured his ankles with a woollen muffler he had been wearing ; after which he again opened the door of the car and with a cry of "Mind your feet !" slung the unfortunate Johannes inside.

Leaning in, he arranged the unconscious man more comfortably and added : "I'm sorry to inflict his body on you, but you can use it as a footstool. I'm sorry, too, that we shan't be able to continue our little talk for a bit, as I now have to drive the car to our destination.

"Where are you taking me ?" she asked.

"Oh—Cologne," he answered casually. "I wouldn't dream of inconveniencing you more than was strictly necessary. I imagine that we've still got another twenty miles to go, so if I were you I'd have a short nap." The fact was that he did not feel that he dared risk attempting to cross the Cologne bridge with the car as there was a strong possibility that the police were examining all traffic there ; so he had already decided to abandon the car outside Cologne and from there seek other means of reaching the frontier.

With Gregory in the driver's seat the car started off again. He drove very carefully, keeping to the same unhurried pace that Johannes had maintained. It was only about a quarter past one so there remained several hours of darkness, and although he had much to do before daylight came he had no intention of risking an accident which would almost certainly land him in another mess.

The big Mercèdes ran smoothly on until, half an hour later,

the first houses of Bonn loomed up out of the black night ; upon which Gregory halted the car, got out and opened the door again.

"Sorry," he said, "but I'm afraid I've got to gag you properly now. We might be challenged by a patrol in the town. Johannes' papers should enable me to get through all right, but as my life literally depends upon it I can't trust even so charming a person as yourself not to forget your promise, quite inadvertently, and give me away."

She shrugged. "All right. I don't blame you ; although actually I have the queer, old-fashioned habit of keeping my word when I make promises like that."

"You make me feel an awful beast," he said softly as he climbed over Johannes' body and leaned across her. "I have that quaint, old-fashioned habit, too. Will you believe me when I say that I *would* trust you, if it was only my own life that hung in the balance ? But it's my job to get home if I can and make my report. Even the fact of knowing that I've had to quit Germany will enable my superiors to put someone much cleverer than myself on a job that may save the lives of countless other people."

"Yes ; I believe you." She tilted up her chin, offering her mouth, and Gregory, who could just see the outline of her face in the gloom, was devilishly tempted to kiss her. He knew, however, that she had held up her face merely so that he might apply the gag, and this time he tied it firmly behind her head.

His precaution proved to be unnecessary, as the car rolled slowly through Bonn without incident. Since they now had no great distance to go he did not stop on the far side of the town, but put on as much speed as he dared so that his beautiful passenger should not be inconvenienced by the gag for longer than he could help.

When they arrived on the outskirts of Cologne he slowed the car down almost to walking pace and peered ahead into the shadows on either side of the road. A few hundred yards past the first houses he found what he was looking for ; the starlight was just strong enough to show him a large, open field. Turning the car on to the grass he drove over the rough surface until he was a hundred yards from the road and quite certain that the car would not be visible from it while night lasted. Then he got out and opened the door of the limousine.

First he pulled out the unconscious Johannes and propped him in the driver's seat, his hands and feet still tied ; next he got into the car again, shut the door, sat down beside the girl and untied her gag.

After making a sucking noise with her lips and tongue to ease the muscles of her mouth, which had been held rigid for some time, she said: "Thank goodness that's over! What d'you mean to do now?"

"We're just outside Cologne and I've driven the car into a field, as you probably gathered from the bumping. I'm afraid you're going to have a rather uncomfortable night, but I've got to leave you here."

"Tied up like this?"

"Sorry; I've no alternative."

"You won't take my word for it that if you set me free I won't inform the police about you until to-morrow morning?"

"I daren't. Not only for my own sake, but for yours as well. It's impossible for me to drive the car further into the city, as it would soon be found wherever I left it and things would be set moving before I'd had time to get a good start. If I were to untie your hands and feet before I left you your first thought would be to get help for Johannes, and you'd find it more than difficult to account for that crack on the back of his head and the position of the car in this field without giving me away.

"Even if you decided to abandon him and walked along the road until you got a lift to your hotel, or wherever you intend to stay, the car would be discovered first thing in the morning. It's bound to be; because I've intentionally parked it in clear sight of the road so that you mayn't have to wait too long before somebody finds you.

"When the car's discovered the police will make inquiries. Johannes will have his own story to tell when he's well enough, and God only knows what the Gestapo would do to you if they were to find out that you'd gone calmly off to bed without having reported me. Whatever yarn you decided to spin them you'd find yourself in one hell of a mess before you were much older. For your own protection it's absolutely essential that someone must find you here, tied up in the car, so that there can be no possible suggestion that you connived at my getaway."

She sighed. "Yes; you're right, of course. How is poor Johannes?"

"Not too bad. I examined him just now; he's got a lump the size of an egg just above the base of his skull and it's bleeding slightly. When he comes to he'll probably be suffering from concussion, but the essential thing for anyone who has

E

concussion is that they should be moved as little as possible.   If I
allowed you to go and fetch help for him he'd be jolted about
for an hour or two by people heaving him into an ambulance,
taking him to hospital, undressing him, monkeying about with
his wound and putting him to bed, so he's really better off left
lying where he is. He'll be all right in a day or two and back
on duty in a week."

"I'm glad of that ; the poor fellow had done nothing to
deserve that awful crack over the head you gave him."

"I know ; but he just had to have it or I could never have
carried out my scheme for ensuring myself a decent start when
we arrived here. Anyhow, it may console him a bit, later on,
to find that he's the richer by a hundred marks. I stuffed a
note under his shirt after I'd undressed him where it's unlikely
that the hospital orderlies will find it if they get at him before
he recovers consciousness."

"What a queer person you are !"

"Queer ?   Why ?"

"Well, after all, Johannes is a soldier and you're at war with
his country. Most soldiers killed or wounded in a war never
know who fired the shot that hit them, so he's really no more
cause for complaint than any man at the Front ; yet you proceed to pay him compensation."

"One can look at it in that way, I suppose ; but even if he
is a soldier, striking a chap down from behind without warning,
miles behind the line, somehow seems quite different from
potting him in the trenches when he knows what he's in for and
is doing his best to pot you."

"How illogical !" she laughed.   "Think how expensive it
would be for airmen if they reasoned like that and threw bundles
of notes over every time they carried out night-bombing of
troop concentrations behind the lines ! All the same, though, I
do understand how you feel and I think it's very decent of you.
But are you quite sure you can afford to give away a hundred
marks ? You may need all the money that you've got to help
you out of Germany."

"Thanks ; but I've plenty left. And now I suppose I must
say good-bye."

"What do you intend to do ?"

"That's my secret !"

"You still don't trust me."

"I didn't say so ; but if you were grilled by the Gestapo
you might give something away quite unintentionally. As long

as you've no idea what I intend to do I'm protected against that."

"I wonder if you will succeed in getting through ?" she mused.

"I don't know, but I mean to have a damned good try. If I don't, I'll use the handkerchief with which I gagged you as a bandage for my eyes when I have to face the firing-squad." He laughed and patted the tunic-pocket in which the handkerchief now reposed.

"You're joking !" she exclaimed incredulously.

"I'm not, I assure you. All my life I've been a cheerful cynic. To adapt the words of an old English song : 'Good-time Charlie is my name, Drinking Champagne is my game.' I've never worshipped anything but beauty, and nothing that any artist ever created in paint or marble can equal the living beauty of a really lovely woman. If I'm caught you'll be the last beautiful woman that I'll have touched and talked to so it'll be very fitting that I use the handkerchief for that purpose, in spite of the fact that I'd always determined not to have my eyes bandaged if I ever had to die that way."

"I don't want you to die—now."

"Thanks. That's nice of you. It has something of the old chivalrous tradition of the days when wars were fought by gentlemen and enemies respected each other. I've always thought that one of the very worst things about modern warfare is this filthy inculcation of race hatred. You're a good German ; I'm a good Englishman ; but there's no earthly reason why we shouldn't retain our individualities and wish each other luck as long as we're not in personal combat."

"*Lieber Gott !* What a crazy business war is !" she exclaimed suddenly.

"I agree. We don't want to fight you ; you don't want to fight us. But untold misery is brought to both our countries just because a few men at the head of things can't get together, give way a little to each other and settle their differences amicably, as would be the case with the heads of two big business concerns."

"You said something just before you gagged me outside Bonn—something about enabling somebody much cleverer than yourself to save countless lives. What did you mean by that ?"

"Only that there's a scheme on foot to bring the war to a quick finish. I was sent out to start the ball rolling, but I've failed miserably. That's why I don't care so very much whether I'm shot or not, and took a chance on holding up your car when it might quite well have been full of armed S.S. men. Still, I suppose it's up to me to get back if I can to report the bungle I've made. Then someone else, who's a better man than I am, may be able to straighten out the mess and start something from another angle."

"From what I've seen of you I doubt whether they could find a better man. It must have been that you had extraordinarily bad luck."

"It's the other way round, I'm afraid. If I hadn't been monstrous lucky I'd be dead as a doornail at this moment ; I made two bad slips which I ought to have foreseen and avoided, and both of them were entirely my fault."

"I believe you're being hard on yourself. Even the cleverest of secret agents must fail to foresee certain eventualities at times. That you're really first-class is proved by the fact that you've managed to keep your freedom so far, although half the police in Germany have been after you for two nights and a day."

Gregory smiled, thinking of the row of Nazi corpses which must now be lying in the mortuary at Ems. "Well, apart from my job I haven't put up a bad show, I suppose, but it's the job that matters and I've fallen down on that."

"Will you promise me something ?" she asked quietly.

"Certainly : I'll promise you anything you like provided that it doesn't conflict with my duty or the interests of my country."

"Then if you do get back to England safely, promise me that you won't throw in your hand, but sort out the muddle you've made and have another shot at completing successfully the thing you set out to do."

"I don't know whether that's possible."

"You said that someone else might tackle the job from another angle. Why not do so yourself ?"

"Now that I've hopelessly botched the best lead there was it remains to be seen whether there *is* another angle from which it can be approached."

"Then promise me that if you can find one you'll use it yourself instead of handing it over to anybody else."

He laughed abruptly. "D'you realize that you're as good as inviting me to come back to Germany again as a spy ?"

"Certainly. I'm quite sure that a man of your courage would not allow that to daunt him."

"Maybe ; but I wasn't thinking of that. I meant to ask you whether you realized that you were expressing a wish for

the return to your country of an enemy agent ; one who might
be instrumental in sabotaging certain very important bits and
pieces of your war machine."

"That is a risk which I am prepared to take, since the
restoration of peace is your ultimate aim."

"In that case I give you my promise that if anyone is sent
to Germany again on this business and it lies in my power to
return, I'll do so."

She sat up suddenly. "Thank you for that. Now you must
go. You've still a few hours of darkness left, but every moment
counts if you're to get away safely."

"You're right. I've already lingered longer than I should,
but it's been well worth it. I must see your face again, though,
before I say good-bye." As he spoke Gregory took his matches
from his pocket and struck a light.

She was more beautiful than he had realized from his first
glimpse of her ; he gazed at her smile until the match burnt his
fingers and he was forced to drop it.

"Good-bye," he said, placing his hand gently over both of
hers and leaning slightly towards her.

"Not good-bye, but *Auf Wiedersehen*," she whispered, and he
felt the answering pressure of her shoulder in the darkness.

Bending his head he found her lips, which were held up to
meet his. After a long moment he crushed her hands between
his and murmured : "*Auf Wiedersehen, mein Liebchen.*"

With an effort he forced himself to relinquish her hands and
got out of the car.

"Good luck, dear spy ! Good luck !" she called after him,
"and do be careful on your way into the city."

"The odds are in my favour, at all events until morning,"
he called back reassuringly as he swung-to the door of the car.
"Darkness is my friend."

Chapter XIII

THERE'S MANY A SLIP

IMMENSELY cheered by his strange encounter with the lovely lady, Gregory set off at a quick limp across the field. The outcome of their meeting had been utterly different from anything he could possibly have anticipated when he had held up her car, or even after he had turned the tables on her and she had good-humouredly accepted his mastery of the situation.

A little over an hour before she had quite obviously intended handing him over, without the least compunction, to be shot, yet she had just kissed him with an ardour which only a woman experienced in the arts of love could have displayed, shown acute anxiety for his safety and begged him to seek some way of recommencing his mission although she knew him to be the secret agent of of an enemy country.

As he struck the road and headed for the centre of the city he thought, for the hundredth time, that women were truly weird creatures, though very wonderful. It was not until he had covered the best part of a mile that he suddenly realized that he had forgotten to ask her name.

This stupid omission annoyed him intensely. He knew that if he were still alive when the war ended he would not have a moment's peace until he had found her again, and as a result of his stupidity he might have the greatest difficulty in doing so. But it was now too late to go back ; the few remaining hours of darkness were precious and in addition he was compelled to economize his strength, for his leg was paining him again now that he had to use it and there was nothing to distract his mind from his wound.

As the houses became more numerous it occurred to him that he had better examine Johannes' papers and find out as much as possible about the man he was supposed to be, for now that he was wearing the uniform of a private he would have to answer questions if he ran into one of the patrols that were certain to be policing the city.

Turning into a pitch-black archway he struck a match and

quickly scrutinized the soldier's pay-book, from which he learned that Johannes' surname was Heckt, that he belonged to the 27th Bavarian Infantry Regiment and that he was married and thirty-one years of age.

That was oldish for a private, but like most men on back-area jobs he had probably been recalled to the colours only a few weeks before the outbreak of war. Gregory thanked his stars that Johannes had not been younger ; as he himself was slim and wiry he could pass for a man of thirty-one who had lived hard. That was the advantage of being one of the "lean and hungry" kind ; there was nothing to disclose one's real age except one's bearing, and that could be altered at will to a marked extent. He replaced the pay-book in his pocket, left the shelter of the arch and continued on his way.

The dark streets through which he passed were practically deserted and as far as he could he took cover in the deeper shadows whenever he heard anyone approaching, so that the only person he had met face-to-face by the time he reached the bridge was an A.R.P. man with whom he nearly collided on coming round a corner.

There were both civil and military police at the bridge-head and Gregory braced himself to face possible questioning ; but they were watching for a General on a motor-cycle, not an ordinary private and after a casual glance they let him pass without a challenge. Having crossed the bridge he entered the centre of Cologne with a considerably easier mind.

Avoiding the *Dom Platz* he walked straight to the station. As he passed its entrance, noise and the glow of shaded lights showed him that considerable activity was still going on there. Cologne might sleep, but Germany's trains must continue to run, carrying her troops and her industrialists from city to city.

Skirting the station-yard he turned down a street that ran parallel to the long steel-and-glass arches under which the trains drew in. After a quarter of a mile he found, as he expected, that the station-buildings gave way to a stout fence, made of railway-sleepers set on end, which enclosed the goods-yard.

He knew perfectly well that he had not the least hope of buying a ticket or obtaining a travelling-pass which would enable him to take a passenger-train to the frontier, much less over it ; but if the goods-yard were not too closely guarded he might be able to secrete himself in a wagon and travel out of Germany that way.

Crossing to the far side of the street he walked quietly down it, keeping a sharp watch on the fence opposite, and he soon discovered that soldiers were posted along it at intervals of approximately three hundred yards. From what little he could see they did not appear to be sentries, as none of them was marching up and down but merely pickets posted there at ease to make sure that nobody should climb over the fence into the yard.

He wondered for a moment whether, by choosing a spot exactly half-way between two pickets, he could get over the fence unseen, but decided that it would be too risky. The fence was about six feet high and its top could be made out with reasonable distinctness against the skyline. He could easily reach it without being spotted and crouch there unnoticed in the friendly shadows, but if one of the pickets saw him as he climbed over he might get a bullet in the back, or at all events become the object of a new hue and cry. That was a thing he dared not risk, as his wounded leg would prevent his outdistancing his pursuers, who would certainly come after him over the fence and into the yard.

It seemed that the only other possible scheme by which he could get into the yard depended upon starting a conversation with one of the pickets and either outwitting him or securing his assistance. Crossing the street Gregory approached the nearest man and opened up with the words : "Got a light, old chap ?"

"No," said the picket ; a big, bearded fellow who was evidently a reservist. "Don't smoke."

"Ah, well ; tastes differ. Leaves you more to spend on beer, doesn't it ?"

"I don't drink," replied the man gruffly.

Gregory itched to ask him whether he ate hay, and if he answered "no" to that let him have the old crack that he was no fit companion for man or beast ; but he suppressed the temptation and remarked instead : "Often wish I didn't smoke or drink, myself. Save quite a bit if I could bring myself to cut 'em out. With the price of everything going up all round money's that scarce these days you never know where to turn for the next five marks."

"Ah ; like so many people you live in Darkness, my friend," replied the man. "If only you could find the Light such trivial inconveniences would cease to trouble you."

Gregory had no desire whatever to find the Light at that moment. Darkness was his element and he would have been

supremely happy if he could have prevented the sun from
rising for another week ; but the man went on earnestly :

"People grumble at this and that only because they don't
realize that such trials as they have to face are sent them by
God for a mighty purpose : the regeneration of the human race.
It's only because people are greedy and selfish, like the English,
that our present troubles have befallen us. In the meantime
we must all do our duty to the Führer and the Fatherland
without flinching. Whatever sacrifices we may be called upon
to make let us rejoice in the knowledge that God knows our
every action and credits to our score every trial through which
we pass uncomplainingly."

"Quite," said Gregory. "Quite." Cheerful cynic that he
was he had always recognized that the history of England was
one long tale of grabbing other people's property, and he
rejoiced in the fact ; firmly believing that the British did far
more good than harm wherever they went and that it would
be no bad thing for everybody if the English-speaking races
ruled the whole world.

He always respected anyone's sincere beliefs, however, even
though he might not be able to subscribe to them himself, but
a fellow who believed in a combination of God and Hitler was
really too much of a good thing. Obviously the man would
prove quite unbribable and would refuse absolutely to give him
any sort of help ; so he added quickly : "Well, I'll be going now ;
must scrounge a light for my gasper. Good night."

The bearded picket's answering "good night" followed him
as he strolled along to the next man and tried the same tactics.

The second soldier was a weedy little man but he obligingly
produced a box of matches immediately Gregory asked for a
light.

"Have one ?" inquired Gregory, offering a battered packet
of cigarettes that he had found in Johannes' pocket.

"Thanks," said the man ; "don't mind if I do. The Sarge
has just done his round so he won't be snooping about in this
direction for another hour at least."

This piece of information was merry music to Gregory's ears
and he said casually : "Don't envy you your job ; standing
about half the night like this. Must get pretty cold towards
the morning."

"It does that." The man lit his cigarette and puffed at it,
cupping it in his hand. "What's your job ?"

"Oh, I've got a cushy billet, for the moment at all events.

I'm a clerk in the R.T.O.'s office. Hell of a lot of work to do with all these trains going through, and they keep us at it until all hours, but it's better than having to do guard or being sent to the Front."

"Wouldn't have minded having a bit of fun in Poland, myself," remarked the soldier, "but this war in the West's going to be different. The Frenchies has got field-guns what fire thirty rounds a minute, so a pal of mine was saying the other day ; and tanks that weigh near enough a hundred ton. If you ask me, it's going to be every bit as bad as what my Dad told me about the last war."

"That's right," agreed Gregory. "Blood baths for all and sundry. Four years or your life without the option."

"Four years !" sniffed the sentry. "I doubt if we can last two unless these Russkies come across with the goods. Why, look at the stuff they're giving us to eat already, before the darned war's a fortnight old. It isn't enough to support a well-grown kid."

"Makes you sick, doesn't it ? Especially when you know, as I do, that the Party leaders live on the fat of the land without giving a thought to chaps like us."

"Is that a fact ?" the man asked with all a scandalmonger's interest.

" 'Course it is," reponded Gregory, thoroughly enjoying the chance of conveying this piece of anti-Nazi propaganda, especially as it had a considerable basis of truth. "I should know, shouldn't I, being in railway transport ? What d'you think I do all day but check lists of things ? And half of them are luxuries from Holland and Belgium consigned to the Party H.Q.'s. You should just see the stuff they have ; caviare, champagne, all sorts of funny fruits that we've never even set eyes on, tubs of real butter, lovely, fat Dutch hams and Lord knows what besides."

"That's enough !" cut in the weedy soldier ; "you're making my mouth water. But it fair makes you sick, don't it ? I've got a wife at home and a couple of young kids, but we haven't seen butter in the house for the last six months."

"Same here," Gregory nodded, "only I've got four. It's cruel to see them, they're that thin. But listen here, chum ; you feel the same way as I do and fair's fair, isn't it ? And the blokes up top aren't giving us a square deal. Like to take your wife home a present ? One of those nice, fat Dutch hams I was talking about just now ?"

"You on the level?" queried the man warily; "I'll cut your guts out if you're one of them blasted Nazi spies."

" 'Course I'm not! I mean it about that ham, too, but I'll need your help."

"Nothing doing, mate. I'm not risking a month in cells."

"You don't have to. Just listen a minute. I was inspecting a train that come in from Holland to-day and I found the padlock broken on one of the wagons. When I got back to the office I turned up its number, and what d'you think was inside? Why! turkeys, geese and hams—all for the blinking Party Headquarters. Well, that train's still in the yard, on the siding. As the lock's broken it'd be as easy as pie for me to get into the wagon, see? I want one of those hams for my little lot at home. All you've got to do is to give me a leg-up over the fence and keep a sharp look-out so's I can get back over it with the goods without being spotted by your officer or one of your pals. If you're game to do that I'll bring you a fat ham for yourself, see?"

"Chum; I'm with you! How long's the job going to take?"

"Twenty minutes, about; half an hour at the outside. That all right?"

"Yes. You give three soft raps on the sleepers behind me when you get back, see? If I cough you'll know it's all right. If I don't, you'll know there's someone here and you'll have to lie low till I give you the wire that the coast's clear. How's that?"

"Fine," nodded Gregory. "I'll give three raps and wait till you cough. Well; the sooner we're through, the better."

"Sure thing! Up you go!"

As Gregory gripped the top of the fence the guard gave him a heave up from behind. He wriggled over and with a sigh of satisfaction dropped down on the other side.

In the huge yard there were scores of trains waiting in the sidings until engines could be found to take them to their destinations. His next problem was to find one which was being sent either to Belgium or Holland. As work was being carried on in shifts for twenty-four hours out of the twenty-four, faint lights were still moving here and there, where gangs loaded and unloaded cargoes, but now that he was past the pickets and actually in the yard Gregory had little fear of being challenged.

On the numerous occasions when he had visited Cologne during normal times he had stepped out of the Ostend train from Belgium on to a platform which had become quite familiar to him in consequence, and the knowledge of its position was the only thing which he now had to guide him in selecting one of the long lines of stationary wagons. Padding softly through the darkness and taking care to avoid the gangs of workmen, he made his way back to the passenger-station until he reached the ends of its long, low platforms.

There was enough light for him to see by quite easily here, as the glass panes of the station roof had been painted black, and shaded lights showed troops and civilians in the distance boarding one or two of the outgoing trains.

Having reached the end of the Ostend arrival platform, Gregory left the passenger-station once more, tracing the Ostend line that ran from it, and had not gone far before darkness once more closed in about him save for the low signal-lights of red and green which were burning opposite the sets of points so that the drivers might operate the trains.

As soon as he had retraced his steps to a spot opposite the goods-yard Gregory became particularly interested in these sets of points. He wanted to find one on the Ostend line from which there ran back into the goods yard a track having upon it a line of wagons which were already loaded for departure.

Having found the tracks he was seeking, he traced them back into the yard, thanking his stars when he found that on them there stood a long line of loaded wagons. As they stood near the entrance of the yard there was a fair chance that they would be dispatched early next morning or during the coming day, and although it was a considerable gamble there was a reasonable possibility that their cargo was booked for Belgium.

Fumbling in the darkness he soon discovered that the closed wagons were all padlocked, so that he would have to be satisfied with an open one. Climbing up he undid the cords holding down corners of the tarpaulins on several of them, until he found one that contained only wooden cases which could be moved about and which would not soil his clothes.

Scrambling up on to it, he turned back about a third of the tarpaulin and rearranged some of the cases as well as he could, making himself a little shelter which would suffice, at all events, to save him from being spotted by anyone who might make a merely casual examination of the truck's contents on its way to the frontier.

Bending nearly double, he pulled the tarpaulin over him and refixed it as well as he could, though he had to leave a rope dangling loose at one corner ; then he wriggled down in the pitch-blackness and stretched himself out at full length in the space which he had cleared between two cases and had concealed by piling two others above it.

He could not help thinking with regret of the unfortunate picket who was waiting in such eager expectation for his return with a fat ham, and had it been in his power he would gladly have compensated the poor fellow for his disappointment. As things were he would have given almost anything in the world, except another kiss from the Lady of the Limousine, for a plate of ham for himself.

On entering Cologne there had been no possible means by which he could get a square meal without running a suicidal risk of arousing suspicion, so it was now getting on for two days since he had had anything to eat except chocolate. He was desperately tired, however, and in spite of his hunger and the pain in his leg he composed himself to sleep with what fortitude he could muster.

A sudden jolting and clanking as an engine backed up to the string of trucks woke him, and the faint daylight which penetrated under the tarpaulin told him that he must have slept for a few hours at least. On peering at his watch he found that it was nearly midday. His first sensation was one of satisfaction at the thought that the train was moving instead of remaining, as it quite well might have, stuck for several days in the goods yard at Cologne ; his next was hunger. His stomach felt terribly empty, and only three bars of his packet of chocolate remained.

Breaking one off he nibbled it slowly ; then took a drink from his flask, which now contained a mixture composed of a very small proportion of brandy and an unduly large proportion of the river-water with which he had had the foresight to fill it up when he had bandaged his leg on the previous night.

The wagon bumped backwards and forwards, jolting him about as he ate his meagre breakfast, but at last the train got properly under way and chugged steadily along at a quite reasonable pace, and as Gregory had nothing more urgent to occupy him he proceeded to review his position.

If he could get into Belgium without being discovered at the frontier he must somehow or other get rid of his German uniform as quickly as possible and beg, borrow, buy or steal a suit. He had no passport, but once in civilian clothes he would be able to proceed to the British Embassy, whence he could telephone to Sir Pellinore and get things fixed up for his return to England.

Getting over the frontier was going to be the stickiest part of the business, since it was quite certain that every wagon would be searched on the German side for refugees and deserters and as the Germans are proverbially methodical the search would be a thorough one.

If he were to escape detection it was essential that he should improve his hiding-place. Crawling out of his hole he raised the loose corner of the tarpaulin and looked out. The train was running through flat country and there was a village in the distance. Gregory popped his head back. It was vital that he should not be seen by any railway ganger or officious house-holder living near the line who might telephone through to the next station and report that there was a deserter on the train, but by keeping the corner of the tarpaulin turned back he had plenty of light to see by and he set about the task of opening one of the cases.

It was no easy business as he had nothing but a jack-knife to use as a lever, but fortunately the Germans were by now using only thin wood for their packing-cases, for economic reasons, and after ten minutes' hard work he succeeded in prising open the lid of one of the cases under which he had been lying. It contained a consignment of German toys under a layer of wood-shavings. Putting the shavings aside Gregory threw the toys one by one, as far as he could without being seen, into the fields beside the line.

Next he piled the other big cases up on either side until he had cleared a space on the floor of the wagon large enough to take the case he had emptied and allow him just enough room to crawl into it. Turning the empty case on its side he pushed the shavings back into it so that they would make his hiding-place softer to lie in and provide a pillow ; he then heaved the other cases back on top of it, thus creating a snug hide-out, just large enough to hold him, right at the bottom of the wagon.

Having done all he could to conceal himself he tried to sleep again and managed to doze for a few hours, but to his annoyance the train halted in the early afternoon and when, after half an hour's wait, it still did not go on he feared that it had been side-tracked into another goods-yard. He had no idea where he was and as the hours dragged by he became acutely anxious. He had not even been sure, in the first place, that the train was going to Belgium. For all he knew it might have been switched over various points and be carrying him into the centre of Germany ;

or perhaps it was not on its way to the frontier at all, but had already reached its destination.

Hunger and thirst began to torture him so he ate another bar of his chocolate and had a sparing drink, praying the while that his slender stores would last him either until he was out of Germany or until he could find a good opportunity to leave the train under cover of darkness, if hunger forced him to do so.

At last night fell and he debated with himself whether or not to remain where he was for another twenty-four hours. He now had only one bar of chocolate and about a wineglassful of weak brandy-and-water left ; if he decided to stick it out he would suffer acutely during the following day, as he certainly dared not leave the train by daylight. For all he knew it might be left on the siding for a week before it proceeded further or was unloaded.

On the other hand he could leave the train during the night with comparative safety, but if he did so he would have to begin all over again the risky work of spotting a train bound for a neutral frontier, finding a suitably-loaded wagon and making himself some sort of a hide-out in the load ; while wherever he might try to get food in the meantime he would run the risk of being questioned, or even identified. It must now be a good twelve hours since the car had been discovered and its occupants examined by the police ; the radio and the evening papers would already have warned every German to be on the look-out for the fake General von Lettow, now dressed in the uniform of a private soldier.

At last he determined that he would remain where he was for some hours longer at all events, and leave the train only if it should remain stationary until just before dawn. To his joy the bumping started once more a little after one o'clock as the string of wagons resumed their journey, but during the next few hours they twice revived his fears by halting for periods of about a quarter of an hour.

His cramped position added to his wretchedness, for combined with his anxiety, thirst and hunger it rendered sleep impossible. To his relief, however, the train clanked away again after its third halt, although it once more bumped to a standstill half an hour later. Within a few minutes he heard two men talking in German on the tracks just outside his truck.

Instantly alert, Gregory wriggled down into his dark hiding-place and tensed himself to listen. Soon afterwards he heard the noise of the tarpaulin being flung back and a man climbing up on to the cases above him, and an instant later he just caught the flash of a torch penetrating between the cases. He lay very still, scarcely daring to breathe while the man rummaged about, but after what seemed an age the searcher muttered in German to his companion, the cover was replaced and they passed on. Relaxing, Gregory breathed more freely now, his hunger and thirst forgotten, for he felt certain that he had reached a frontier and had escaped detection by the examining officials.

If only he could escape the examination on the other side of the frontier, which was certain to be less rigorous, he was as good as safe. An hour or two of darkness still remained and he had plenty of money on him ; there would be any number of poor peasants in the frontier district who would be glad enough to sell him a suit of clothes for some of his German marks, and to keep their mouths shut, afterwards smuggling the marks back into Germany in payment for a consignment of illicit spirits. Gregory determined that he would leave the wagon as soon as possible after it had been passed by the neutral customs officers. To-morrow night, or the next at latest, he would be back in London.

Half an hour later the train moved off again, but soon jolted to a halt. After twenty minutes of unbroken silence he again heard voices, and straining his ears he listened intently. Two men near the wagon were talking in Dutch. He knew then that instead of being carried into Belgium he had reached Holland.

For the second time the tarpaulin was flung back, then a searcher climbed on to the wagon and began to poke about among the cases with something that rattled. He was thrusting a long pole down between them while his companion held a torch. Suddenly the pole banged on the floor of the wagon just by Gregory's head. He saw it as the torch shone down upon it, but the torch shone upon something else as well—some of the loose shavings that Gregory had been unable to scrape into the case when he had crawled into it in the darkness.

The Dutchman muttered something to his companion and they began to heave aside the heavy cases above Gregory until that in which he was crouching lay exposed. Next moment one of the men called out something sharply, and although he could not understand the actual words Gregory instinctively knew that the fellow was not speaking to his companion but was ordering him from his hiding-place. Then the long pole was thrust down again and jabbed him on the leg.

It was useless to lie there any longer. With a muttered

"Guten Abend" to-the men who had found him he slowly crawled out and stretched himself.

They returned his greeting quite civilly, motioned him to climb out of the wagon and escorted him along the railway track to the station buildings, where he was led into a small office.

One of the men said something in Dutch to an official who was seated there. The official in his turn looked across at Gregory and spoke in German.

"Hullo! Another deserter, eh? Well, you're out of your worst troubles, at all events, my friend ; but we shall have to intern you here for the duration of the war."

Chapter XIV

OUT OF THE GAME

GREGORY knew quite well that according to the laws of international warfare any soldier, sailor, airman or other member of the fighting forces of the combatant nations who penetrated into a neutral country in uniform and without an express invitation to do so was liable to internment. He had hoped that he might have remained undetected until he was far enough over the frontier to leave the wagon when it had been shunted to some siding and bribe someone to provide him with a change of clothes. Once out of uniform he would have been able to get back to England without difficulty as soon as he had managed to get into touch with London through diplomatic channels ; but making his way home presented an infinitely more difficult problem now that he had been caught.

For a moment he thought of telling the Dutch official that he was not a German at all, and asking to be sent under escort to the British Legation at The Hague, but he was not sufficiently *au fait* with the neutrality laws to take the risk. Since he was in German uniform to do so would have been as good as admitting that he was a British secret agent, and to ask the Dutch to facilitate his reaching the British Legation immediately after he had escaped out of Germany might be considered by them as a request to contravene their neutrality. Such an act would certainly be contrary to the interests of Germany and advantageous to Britain, so instead of helping him they might quite possibly lock him up in a fortress and refuse to allow him to communicate with the British Legation in any way. He therefore decided to say nothing for the moment, but to let them continue to imagine that he was an ordinary German deserter.

"I quite understand, *Mynheer*, that I must be interned," he said, "but I am very hungry and I am wounded in the leg. Would it be possible for me to have some food and the attention of a doctor ?"

"Certainly," replied the Dutchman. "We have already established a small concentration-camp outside Nijmegen for German prisoners. Directly you arrive there they will provide you with food and medical attention."

"Forgive me, *Mynheer*, but is Nijmegen very far away?" he asked in a tired voice.

The Dutchman smiled. "This is Nijmegen, or, rather, a suburb of it. The actual city is about four miles distant, but the concentration-camp is only about two miles from here."

As he spoke he signed to a couple of Dutch policemen, who had come in while he and Gregory had been talking, and gave them a brief order in Dutch. The policeman led Gregory out and through the station buildings to another exit, where a police car was waiting. Ten minutes later they were handing him over to an elderly Dutch Army Major in a large, barrack-like building which had apparently been a school, but which now contained the offices of the concentration-camp.

On the Major's questioning him in German Gregory produced the papers of Johannes Heckt and was duly registered in his name. The Major was gruff and surly, as he had been pulled out of bed to receive Gregory, and since there was still an hour to go to dawn the kitchen staff were not yet up; but on Gregory's asking whether it would be possible for him to have something to eat the Major gave instructions to an orderly, who left the room to return some minutes later with a mug of steaming cocoa and a large hunk of break and cheese. Having telephoned for a doctor, the Major went back to bed, leaving Gregory in charge of the Sergeant of the Guard.

The doctor, a fat, cheerful little man, turned up half an hour later. He bathed Gregory's wound, dressed it and assured him in fluent German that there was nothing for him to worry about, as the wound was quite clean and with rest and attention should be healing well inside a week. He congratulated Gregory on having succeeded in getting out of Germany, as he seemed to think that the German Army would have a hard time of it whichever way they might endeavour to break the ring which now encircled the Third Reich.

The Dutch soldiers who acted as warders also voted him a sensible fellow for bringing his personal participation in the war to so premature a conclusion by smuggling himself into Holland, and told him jokingly, in halting German, that he might find prison existence a dull one if the war went on for several years, but that at all events his life would be safe.

As he listened to these pleasantries Gregory appreciated anew the truth of the old adage: "There's many a true word spoken in jest." To be held prisoner for any length of time would be more than irksome and it was not going to be by any means an easy job to get himself out of this internment camp, but at least his life *was* safe. They little knew, he reflected, how near he had been to losing it on so many occasions during the last forty-eight hours.

With this comforting thought in his mind, he allowed himself to be led upstairs and down a long corridor on the third floor, where the sergeant opened a door and motioned him through the doorway into the room that was to be his cell.

He had already confirmed his original belief that the place had been a school until quite recently. It had been a large, expensive, high-class school for the sons of wealthy Dutchmen, but in view of the possibility of Germany's making a sudden onslaught through Holland in an attempt to turn the Maginot Line it had been considered to be too near the frontier for safety and the boys had been evacuated to the interior of Holland.

It was evident that each boy had enjoyed the luxury of a separate study-cum-bedroom on the upper floors, and these now made excellent cells, each being furnished with a bookcase, arm-chair, table, writing-desk, washstand and a folding bed which disappeared into the wall during the day, thus providing much greater comfort than any prisoner had a right to expect. The only alteration necessary to adapt them for their present purpose had been the affixing of iron bars to their windows and stout locks to their doors.

As soon as the sergeant had left him Gregory slowly undressed and crawled into bed. In spite of the uneasy dozes he had snatched while hidden in the wagon he was incredibly weary after the strain and exertions which he had undergone, and he fell at once into a heavy sleep.

With kindly consideration his Dutch gaolers did not wake him at the usual hour next morning but let him sleep on, and he was still asleep when the doctor came to visit him at four o'clock in the afternoon.

Having re-dressed his wound with the aid of an orderly the doctor told him that he could remain in bed for the time being but that they would see about fitting him with some crutches on the following day, as there was no reason why he should not get up provided he did not use his wounded leg.

The cocoa and bread and cheese in the early hours of the morning had done little but stay his hunger, so he again asked for food, and half an hour later was brought the first square meal he had enjoyed since he had lunched with Herr Rheinhardt in Traben-Trabach. That had been on Tuesday, September 12th, and it was now Friday, the 15th ; yet so much had happened since that the memory seemed months away.

At six o'clock a short, dark officer in the uniform of an Army Captain came to see him. The Captain had rather sleepy-looking eyes but a pleasant, genial smile. Introducing himself by the name of Bimigen he opened the conversation by inquiring in German after Gregory's wound and establishing friendly relations by offering him a cigarette.

Gregory accepted the cigarette, and reminding himself that although he was now wearing a pair of pyjamas with which he had been issued instead of Johannes' uniform he was still supposed to be a German soldier, he replied with the deference and in the tone which would be expected from a private talking to an officer.

The Dutchman sat down on the end of Gregory's bed and told him that it was part of his duty to discover the methods by which German deserters penetrated into Holland. He stated that he could not, of course, compel Gregory to give him this information, but explained that other things besides deserters might come through by the same means and that the Dutch Government was extremely anxious to protect the neutrality of Holland. He added that he would be frightfully interested to hear Gregory's story from the human point of view if Gregory were willing to tell it, because he personally thought that there was nothing so thrilling as a well-planned escape and he had read every book on the subject that he could get hold of.

Had the circumstances been different and Gregory a genuine deserter he would have told the sleepy-eyed Captain to go and teach his grandmother to suck eggs, as he knew perfectly well what the game was, and that the Captain was in the Dutch Intelligence Service. He already knew exactly how Gregory had escaped from Germany but he wanted to enter into a nice, friendly little chat in which the newly-arrived deserter might disclose facts about the state of things on the other side of the frontier. A private soldier might not know more than what he had seen with the eyes in his head, but even the dumbest recruit could not have helped noticing whether German troops were being concentrated on the Dutch border and, if so, to what regiments the men to whom he had recently talked in that area belonged.

As it was, Gregory was perfectly willing to give the

Dutchman any information that he could, and in consequence he allowed the friendly Captain to pump him to his heart's content, fell into every trap laid for him as though he were a complete dunderhead and answered truthfully every question except those relating to the circumstances in which he had been wounded in the leg and his own particular activities in the German Army.

Thinking that it might mislead the Captain to say that he had received his wound in Poland, as this could be interpreted to imply that German troops were being transferred from the Polish Front to the borders of Holland, he said that he had been wounded in one of the early skirmishes in between the Siegfried and Maginot Lines and had been evacuated to a hospital in Cologne. He went on to say that after this experience he had decided that he did not want to take any further risk of being killed or wounded, and in consequence had taken French leave from the hospital at the earliest possible opportunity and had persuaded one of the pickets at the station to let him through into the goods-yard on the pretext that he wanted to see a friend of his who was working there.

The Dutchman departed entirely satisfied, and after another good meal at half-past seven Gregory was left undisturbed for the rest of the evening. The lights clicked off automatically at nine o'clock and, turning over, he got in an excellent night's rest.

Next morning the doctor came again, fitted him with crutches and told him that he might get up that afternoon. He had hardly gone when a soldier warder appeared and told Gregory that there was a gentleman to see him from the German Legation ; whereupon a tall, thin, fair man came hurrying into the cell and the warder left them together.

The newcomer displayed none of the geniality of the sleepy-eyed Dutch Captain. It appeared that his job was to obtain particulars of all German soldiers interned in Holland, and he wasted no time in beginning his interrogation of Gregory, who at once handed over Johannes Heckt's papers.

The thin man noted their contents in a little black book, after which he snapped out : "And now, you scum, let me tell you something. You have been guilty of the greatest crime which any man can commit against his country. Our glorious Third Reich has been attacked, and needs every one of its sons to defend it under the leadership of our great Führer, Adolf Hitler. And you, a soldier of the invincible German Army, have chosen this, of all times, at which to become a deserter. You think that you are safe here for the duration of the war, *nicht wahr*? Well, that is so. But there will be an end to the war, and when Germany emerges victorious we shall bring you back and shoot you. Let that thought remain uppermost in your mind, day after day, as you skulk here in cowardly safety.

"In the meantime I will give you something else to think about. Now that I have your regimental number it will be quite easy for us to trace your relatives. You have a wife, so it appears from your papers, and there are doubtless others near to you. We know how to deal with traitors. Your wife and your relations shall pay something on your account. A family that breeds a deserter cannot be a good German family, and is only fit to congregate with Jews, so we shall put them all into a concentration-camp. Think of that, *Schweinehund*, while you are eating the good food that these fools of Dutchmen will give you!"

Gregory did not know whether to laugh or to hurl his crutches at the thin-faced, vicious brute. It was quite clear that, had he really been Johannes, that unfortunate's family would have been in for a very rough time. As it was, however, the real Johannes' regiment was certain to have been notified already that he was in hospital at Cologne, so that the mistake would soon be discovered and rectified. In the meantime it was up to Gregory to act his part, so he pretended great distress and sincere repentance of his folly, begging the man from the Legation to spare his family.

The rabid Nazi was adamant in his refusal to listen to any pleas for mercy, and evidently took a sadistic delight in the mental torture which he believed himself to be inflicting. For five minutes he openly boasted of the horrors of the German concentration-camp and the fact that now the Reich was at war even less food could be spared for the human offal inhabiting them, so that it was quite certain that the death-rate would increase enormously.

He then banged on the door for the orderly to let him out and, with a last sadistic thrust about the guards having free access to the women prisoners of the camps, so that if his wife survived he, 'Johannes', would probably find himself presented with a new family after the war when he was brought back to Germany to be shot, he gave a loud "*Heil Hitler*!" and took himself off.

"It's you who'll get shot after the war, laddie, not me,"

muttered Gregory as his venomous visitor left him. The war was being waged for the sole purpose of stamping out just such reptiles, and if the Allies should prove too soft-hearted to put him and his kind up against a brick wall there would still be plenty of decent people left in his own country to see to it that they got their just deserts. But for all that, Gregory realized on thinking things over that the Nazi's visit might be made to fit in admirably with a plan that he was already quietly maturing.

That afternoon he hobbled downstairs and met his fellow-prisoners in the recreation-room. As the war was still young there were only about twenty of them, and he found that they were divided into two bitterly hostile camps.

Seven of them were airmen who had lost their way while night flying, and had been forced down and interned in neutral Holland. These, led by a couple of rabid Nazis, were patriotic Germans. The remainder were all deserters who had crossed the frontier either through fear of being sent to the Front or because of a deep-rooted hostility to the Hitler régime. The airmen cursed their luck at having become prisoners so early in the war ; the others were only too glad to be sitting peacefully in Holland.

News spreads with mysterious swiftness amongst prisoners, and it was already known that Gregory was a deserter, so he was greeted with cheerful friendliness by the other deserters, and with angry looks of silent hostility by the airmen. Several of the former group were red-hot Communists and spoke openly of their hope that Germany would be defeated, since in their view the war was being waged not against the German people but against Adolf Hitler and his fellow-assassins.

Having sounded Gregory as to his political views one of the Communists began to mutter darkly about the prospect of a German Communist revolution while warning him that they must be careful what they said in case the Nazi airmen were to get hold of anything and find some means of communicating it to the German authorities ; but after some little conversation Gregory came to the conclusion that the fellow did not really know anything and was indulging merely in wish-fulfilment.

Back in his cell that evening he wrote a brief letter which he addressed to His Britannic Majesty's Minister at The Hague, and the following morning he applied for an interview with the Commandant of the camp.

His request was granted, and at twelve o'clock he was taken to the Major who had received him two nights before. Gregory handed him the letter and asked that it might be forwarded without delay to the British Legation.

The Major was an elderly man with a fine, flowing moustache and—now that he had not been roused from his bed in the middle of the night—a kindly manner. Gregory formed the impression that he was not a regular officer but a reservist who had been given this job of Prison Commandant on account of the excellent German that he spoke.

He twiddled Gregory's letter between his thumbs for a moment, then said : "Why should you, a German soldier, wish to communicate with the British Legation ?"

"Because, sir," Gregory replied, "I have relations in England and I'm very anxious to find out what has happened to them since the outbreak of the war."

"Humph !" grunted the Major. "I don't think I can send your letter. To do so would come under the official category of permitting you to communicate with an enemy country, and my connivance at such a thing would strictly speaking be an infringement of Dutch neutrality."

Gregory knew that this neutrality question was going to be the snag, whatever method he might adopt in an effort to get out of the concentration-camp by legitimate means, while if he tried to escape and failed the Dutch would put him in a fortress whence there would be still less chance of regaining his freedom before the end of the war. He proceeded therefore to use guile.

"Sir," he said, "at the moment I am in Holland, *ja* ?"

"You certainly are," agreed the Major, with a half-smile.

"And Holland is a free country, *nicht wahr* ?" Gregory went on. "All through history the Dutch have had a record second to none for their humanity and the high value they have set upon the liberty of the individual."

"Very true ; very true, indeed !" The Major sat back and stroked his fine moustache complacently, glowing with righteous pride in the virtues of his native land.

"And now that I am in Holland," proceeded Gregory with relentless logic, "I claim the protection of the just Dutch laws. I cannot think that such laws prevent even the convicts in your gaols writing to someone in Holland to inquire about their missing relatives, even if they are allowed to use the posts only once a week or once a month. As for me, I have committed no offence except to enter your country without a permit. Provided that I do nothing which is against Dutch law I cannot believe that the Dutch authorities would wish me to be treated worse than one of their own criminals."

"I see your point," admitted the Major. "I certainly see your point."

"Then, sir, I beg you, as a representative of your great and just nation, to help a poor prisoner to obtain news of his relatives by allowing him to send this letter."

"Well, well." The Major caressed the other side of his moustache. "Since you assure me that there's nothing in it which might make trouble for us, I think we could stretch a point and put it in the post. Naturally you must be anxious to know what the English have done with those of your relations who were caught there by the war. All right, my man, I'll see to it for you."

Fervently thanking the kindly Major Gregory saluted smartly, and was then led off by his guard. He would have bet a tenner that the sleepy-eyed Captain who had interviewed him two days before would be given the letter and would steam it open before it was finally posted, but this caused him no concern because its sole contents consisted of a formal request that the British Minister at The Hague would endeavour to find out for him what had happened to his half-brother, Otto Mentzendorff, who when last heard of was valet to Sir Pellinore Gwaine-Cust, 15th Bart., V.C., G.C.V.O., C.H.

There was a considerable possibility that the letter would be opened at the Legation by some underling to whom it would convey no more than its ostensible meaning and would then be put aside to be dealt with later, when the war had settled down and the initial rush of business was over. In that case he would probably have to possess his soul in patience for several weeks until the inquiry finally went through.

On the other hand, if the letter should happen to reach the Minister or one of the more knowledgeable secretaries of the Legation, Sir Pellinore's name would be certain to arouse their interest in the first place, while the painstaking enumeration of his full title and all the letters after his name would stimulate their curiosity to a pitch that would ensure prompt action. Anyone of intelligence in the Legation would realize that an ordinary German soldier inquiring for his half-brother in London could hardly be in possession of all these details. He might know that his relative's employer was a Baronet and a V.C.; it might even be credible that a punctilious valet, proud of his master's honours, had instructed his soldier half-brother to write to him care of Sir Pellinore Gwaine-Cust, Bart., V.C., G.C.V.O., C.H., but that "15th Bart." was a little touch which would be certain to arouse the curiosity of any English reader while hardly likely to receive particular attention from the sleepy-eyed Captain or any other Dutchman who might read the letter.

Gregory considered that the odds were in favour of his letter to the Legation being forwarded to Sir Pellinore without undue loss of time. When he received it Sir Pellinore might be momentarily surprised to learn that his personal valet was supposed to be a German named Otto, who possessed a half-brother, at present interned in Holland, who was anxious to have news of him. When, however, he noticed that the surname of the aforesaid Otto was Mentzendorff his thoughts would fly at once to his treasured Mentzendorff Kümmel and thence to the lean young man with the scarred face for whom he had broached one of the few remaining bottles on the eve of his departure into war-time Germany.

Sir Pellinore was not the man to ignore such a communication, especially when it came from Gregory, who knew that he would take instant and effective steps directly he received it. Once he had made a move, Gregory himself could take further measures which would ensure the days of his imprisonment being numbered.

That night Gregory penned another communication. It would ordinarily have run to about two thousand words, but by employing telegraphese he reduced the wordage to under five hundred and by using almost microscopic writing he got it on to one small piece of thin paper which he rolled up into a spill and tucked carefully away in his pocket.

Having done all that he could he then settled down to make the best of life in the concentration-camp. It was run on routine lines : reveille at half-past six, first parade seven o'clock, then roll-call, an hour's fatigues, tidying up cells, breakfast at eight and another parade at nine. During the morning the prisoners were employed on casual labour or building operations which were going on outside in the school grounds. The school itself had ample accommodation for the moderate number of prisoners now interned there, but the Dutch authorities evidently antici-pated that this number would be considerably increased as the war progressed, since they were erecting hutments in the grounds and putting up barbed-wire fencing all round the camp.

At twelve-thirty they lunched, and at two o'clock were set to work again, knocking off for the day at five, after which they

were free to amuse themselves in the recreation-room. Supper
was at seven-thirty, bed at eight and lights-out at nine.

Three more deserters soon arrived in the camp, and the
feud between the airmen and the deserters increased in bitterness
as each item of war news which came through was thoroughly
discussed. The Polish armies were still fighting hard but the
government had left Warsaw. At five-twenty on Sunday morning,
a few hours before Gregory had handed his letter to the Camp
Commandant, Russia had launched the Red Army against
Poland's eastern frontier, by then almost denuded of troops.

The German airmen "heiled" this news with cries of delight.
Now Germany would be able to show the world ! Russia had
come in against the Democracies, and the blockade of the
perfidious British was now definitely broken although the war
was barely a fortnight old. Russia would supply Germany with
wheat, petrol and military assistance. Was she not already
administering the *coup de grâce* to those dogs of Poles ?

The deserters also applauded Russia's entry into the war
but for very different reasons. Although they did not trust
Stalin they considered that Communist Russia would be more
dangerous to the hated Nazis as an ally than as an enemy. In
deference to his new friends Hitler would have to abandon his
attacks on Communism, and once the Gestapo had been ordered
to let up on the persecution of Communists their creed would
spread through Germany like wildfire and prove his undoing.
Russia and Germany would then form a Communist *bloc* strong
enough to ensure the agreement of the Capitalist Democracies
to a just peace, and that was all the deserters wanted.

Gregory had his own views on the situation, but did not air
them. For years past Russia had presented an unfathomable
mystery from which only one hard fact could be extracted : she
was no longer Communist. Stalin and his friends might talk
of themselves as Communists, but in actual practice they had
been running Russia for a long time now on lines approximating
very closely to those of the Nazis in Germany. Gregory did not
think that Stalin was particularly anxious to have another
workers' revolution in Germany, since its repercussions might
well undermine his own dictatorial powers.

On the other hand Stalin had certainly not entered the war
to help Hitler out, any more than he had been prepared to enter
it to assist the Democracies. For years after the Russian revolution Europe had treated the Bolsheviks as outlaws so they did
not feel that they owed Europe anything and with some

justification were interested only in their own affairs. If Germany, Britain, France, Poland and the rest chose to cut one another's throats, so much the better. The Union of Soviet Socialist Republics might perhaps rope them all in in the long run, but in the meantime Stalin's sole concern was the protection of Russian interests and he would not forget that Hitler had more than once turned his eyes towards the Ukraine.

Joe Stalin was not the kind of man to forget in a hurry ; his present move was obviously intended to make it quite clear to Hitler that although the Red Army had marched into Poland ostensibly to protect the White Russians and Ukrainians in Polish territory from the effects of war, with Russia in arms he could put out of his mind once and for all any thought of those lovely cornfields that covered countless miles of the Ukraine and ran right down to the Black Sea.

The more he considered the matter the more convinced Gregory became that Russia's entry into the war must have been a nasty jolt for Hitler. It had certainly terminated the resistance of the Polish Army considerably earlier than had been anticipated, for with rain, mud and luck they might have held out through the winter behind the rivers Narev and Bug ; but, on the other hand, instead of being able to leave conquered Poland to his police and reserve Divisions Hitler would now have to keep a big army there throughout the whole of the war in case Stalin should decide one night to play him the same sort of dirty trick as he had played on Czechoslovakia and Poland.

Contrary to all expectations large-scale aerial attacks by the Great Powers had not yet taken place, while the French were still only nibbling at the Siegfried Line and would, in Gregory's estimation, be able to do very little else ; so in his view the war in the West had not yet really started.

The wound in his leg made good progress, but on account of it he was excused duty with the other prisoners when they went out on fatigues for the hutment builders. He therefore had plenty of time to yarn with the Dutch camp guards, most of whom spoke a little German and who were mainly elderly, reservist N.C.O.s who had been given jobs as warders

Their discipline was firm, but they showed no animosity towards their prisoners ; on the contrary, they were even willing to do friendly services for them if approached in a reasonable manner. Gregory had soon established himself with them on an excellent footing, as for one thing he knew all about old soldiers' ways ; their likes, dislikes and customs, which do not vary very much in any army ; for another, he had come out of Germany with over four thousand *Reichmarks* still on him.

Without throwing his money about to an extent which would have caused comment he utilized some of it, that one of the N.C.O.s had changed for him into Dutch florins, to purchase decent cigarettes, soap and other small luxuries, giving a generous commission to the men who procured them for him. He found, too, that one of the guards could speak English, and by a little judicious bribery he persuaded him to listen-in each night to the British broadcasts and bring him a résumé of the latest news every day.

It was on the Thursday morning, just a week after he had left Cologne, that one of them came into the recreation-room where he was sitting to tell him that he was wanted by the Commandant. His poker-face gave nothing away as he followed the man down the corridor, but a sudden, suppressed excitement was gripping him.

One question only hammered in his brain. Had he been sent for on some routine matter, or had his letter to the British Legation at The Hague fallen into the hands of someone who had got into touch at once with Sir Pellinore ?

Chapter XV

A FANTASTIC FAMILY HISTORY

GREGORY'S excitement was caused by the fact that if he had succeeded in getting the Legation to communicate with Sir Pellinore and the astute Baronet had tumbled to it that it was he who had written from the Dutch concentration-camp, it was a fair bet that the British Legation had sent someone to interview him, and in that case it was going to be a very tricky interview indeed.

Nothing must pass between any visitor from the Legation and himself which might give away to the Dutch that he was not an ordinary German soldier, yet somehow or other he would have not only to confirm the fact that he was a British Secret Service agent working under Sir Pellinore, but also to pass on the particulars of a plan he had worked out to secure his release from the concentration-camp without contravening the neutrality of the Dutch.

If the British authorities were not able to arrange for his release it would still be comparatively easy to take matters into his own hands and escape provided he remained where he was, but if he were to slip up during the interview the Dutch would transfer him to a proper prison or a fortress from which his release would be much more difficult to negotiate, while escape would be next to impossible.

In the Commandant's office he found the elderly Major, the lazy-eyed Intelligence Captain and a pink-cheeked, innocent-looking young man in civilian clothes whose face reminded Gregory vaguely of a turbot. One glance at him was enough to tell Gregory that his clothes had been cut in London, and this opinion was confirmed as the Major said :

"This is Mr. Renshaw, of the British Passport Control Office at The Hague. He has come to see you in reply to your letter about your relatives in England."

"Thank you, sir, I'm sure I'm very grateful," replied Gregory with due humility, and the Major went on : "As a precautionary measure, to guard against your giving Mr. Renshaw any information about conditions inside Germany which might prove of value to the British, Captain Bimigen here will remain with you. I hope that you will give him no cause to interrupt your conversation and that you will confine it entirely to the subject of your relatives."

Gregory had foreseen just such a situation, and instead of replying he drew himself up on his crutches and saluted smartly as the Major left the room. Captain Bimigen then invited him to sit down, lit a cigarette and strolled off to pretend a deep interest in a large map hanging at the other end of the office.

Renshaw, who was already seated, started off by saying in stilted but correct German that Gregory's letter having been passed by the Legation to his department, they had made inquiries in London and it appeared that Otto Mentzendorff had left Sir Pellinore's service some time ago. He had, however, been traced to No. 272 Gloucester Road.

From this mention of his own address Gregory knew at once that Sir Pellinore must have spotted his true identity as soon as the Legation had forwarded his inquiry and that the fish-faced young man had been sent to confirm it and to sound him cautiously.

To clinch the matter Gregory replied at once : "*Ach, so* ! Otto wrote to me from that address once. It is a lodging-house over a grocer's shop, so he said."

Renshaw nodded, and went on to explain for the benefit of the listening Captain Bimigen that any reply to Gregory's inquiry would normally have been sent through the post, but that Otto Mentzendorff, who had registered with the police as an enemy alien on the outbreak of war, had mysteriously disappeared from the Gloucester Road address on the very day after he had received a letter from the Legation notifying him of his half-brother's inquiry for him.

The English authorities naturally wished to discover his present whereabouts, if only to make sure that no harm had befallen him, and Renshaw had therefore thought it worth while to take a train from The Hague and to pay Gregory a personal visit in the hope that he could give particulars of other relatives and friends of his half-brother's through whom the police might be able to trace him.

This piece of by-play very neatly excused Renshaw's visiting Gregory upon so trivial a personal matter, and Gregory proceeded to act up to the part which he was now called upon to play. If his half-brother was seeking to evade the police because he had committed some act contrary to British interests, he explained with embarrassed deference, he naturally could not be expected to give any information which might assist them to arrest him. If, on the other hand—as he was sure must be the case—Otto had merely got the wind up* like so many other enemy aliens caught by the declaration of war and was trying to get out of the country by some illicit means, it was obvious that the less trouble the police had in tracing him the better his case would be. On the whole, Gregory concluded, he thought it better to give all the information in his power.

Renshaw agreed that by doing so he could best help his half-brother, and eventually Gregory gave him one or two bogus names and addresses of imaginary people whom the equally mythical Otto had told him were friends of his whom he had met in England.

While they talked, Gregory glanced from time to time at Captain Bimigen's back in the hope that he would move a little ; he had seen at once that although the Captain appeared to be engrossed with the big map he was actually keeping a sharp eye on a mirror which hung beside it on the wall and in which he could keep both Gregory and his visitor under observation.

Renshaw had also spotted this. Knowing that Gregory would have to communicate with him by some means other than word of mouth if the visit were to serve any useful purpose, he picked up a sheet of paper from the desk and said : "Perhaps you wouldn't mind writing down those names and addresses for me ?"

Gregory saw that the fish-faced young man was by no means such a fool as he looked, and was giving him an opportunity of passing back any message that he might have with the sheet of paper. He had his little spill all ready in his left hand and was just about to pass it over under cover of the sheet upon which he had written when the wily Captain turned about, strolled slowly towards them, and, holding out his hand, said : "May I see those addresses, if you please ?"

"Of course, sir," Gregory replied, and handed over the sheet on which he had scribbled.

"Hugo Woltat, *Kellner*, The Queen's Brasserie, Leicester Square, London ; *Frau* Beamish, *Haushälterin*, 37 Euston Square, London, W.C.1.," read out the Captain, and passed the sheet with a polite smile to Renshaw.

Gregory was now distinctly worried as to how he was to

F

get his message across. The Captain was an opponent worthy of his steel and did not seem to miss many tricks. There was one he might not know, however, and Gregory decided to chance it. After a little more pointless conversation with Renshaw he said : "I am most grateful to you, sir, but I don't think I can tell you anything else," and stood up.

Renshaw rose at the same moment and held out his hand to say good-bye. It was another opportunity, but Gregory did not take it ; Captain Bimigen was far too wily a bird not to know that one.

Instead, as he began to hold out his right hand, which was quite clearly empty, he let his crutch slip on the polished floor, lost his balance and fell sprawling. Both Bimigen and Renshaw immediately came to his assistance, and having managed to fall so that his left shoulder was towards Renshaw he was able to slip the spill from his left hand into Renshaw's right as they both helped him to his feet.

Apologizing for his clumsiness, he took leave of Renshaw thanked the Captain and hobbled out, now extremely satisfied with his morning's work. It would be some days at least before he could expect his scheme to develop further, but if the plan which he had worked out for his release and described in the message which he had slipped to Renshaw were carefully followed, and if Sir Pellinore were to issue extremely careful instructions, he thought that he might with luck be back in England within a week or ten days.

The following day the doctor declared his wound to be sufficiently healed for him to abandon his crutches and he was put on light duty, which consisted mainly of sweeping various rooms and helping to wash up the crockery used by the prisoners at their meals.

The friendly guards continued to supply him with small comforts and all available news. He felt a touch of personal loss when he heard of the sinking of the poor old *Courageous*, since he had witnessed the Coronation Review at Spithead from her as the guest of one of her officers, but it was with cynical amusement that he learned of the Russian penetration into Poland and its unexpected depth.

By the end of the week both the Russians and the Germans were approaching Lvov, or Lemberg as the great, industrial capital of Southern Poland used to be called, and Gregory had little doubt in his mind as to who would get it. Climinty Voro-shilov, the Russian ex-workman who had risen to be Commissar of Defence, was commanding the Russian armies in person, and Gregory remembered the course of events in the Russo-Polish War of 1920. Tukachevsky—later shot during Stalin's purge of 1937—had then commanded the greatest army that the Bolsheviks had ever put into the field and but for his defeat outside Warsaw Voroshilov, who had commanded the cavalry on his southern flank, would have taken Lemberg then. The main Russian army having broken Voroshilov had had to call off his Cossacks when they had been within six miles of the town. That bitter disappointment of nineteen years ago would make him all the more determined to take it now.

The Russo-German *pourparlers* were apparently being held at Brest-Litovsk, where the Russo-German peace had been signed in 1917. It had been a brutal peace, dictated by the Germans to a Russia which lay prostrate and bleeding from the effects of war and revolution. Trotsky had represented Russia, and when he had heard that he would have to attend an official reception at which evening dress would be worn his Marxian conscience had pricked him and he had wired to Lenin for instructions. The reply had come promptly : "Go in a petticoat if you have to—but get us peace—peace at any price."

Things would be very different when the Russians met the Germans at Brest-Litovsk this time. Hitler might fly into one of his tantrums and bawl his head off at von Ribbentrop, but that would cut no ice. The Nazi Foreign Minister was reaping where he had already sown, and "Clim" Voroshilov would take the eagle's share for Russia from Germany's carrion crow.

As Gregory had anticipated, the French, despite their cheerful communiques, had been brought to a standstill. Flesh and blood could not stand up to the concentrated artillery and machine-gun fire that the Germans were able to bring to bear upon them now that they were actually facing the Siegfried Line, and the comparatively short length of the battle zone made it possible for the Germans to concentrate there a mass of artillery greater than any that had ever before been used on so narrow a front. The Somme, Verdun, even Passchendaele would have been nothing to what the French would have to face should they intend to make a serious attempt to break the Siegfried Line. But that applied equally to the Germans and the Maginot Line and, on balance, they were in a much more difficult position. The French could sit tight for years if need be whereas the Germans would have to attempt a break through in some direction or be gradually starved out. All things considered the war wasn't going too badly and some of the Nazi leaders must already be beginning to wrap wet towels round their heads.

It was on the following Monday, September 25th, that Gregory was again sent for to the Commandant's office. The Major greeted him kindly, saying in halting English :

"Why did you not tell me at once that you were an English-man ?"

Gregory, delighted to find that his plan had begun to develop, looked with pretended uneasiness at his feet. "Well, sir," he began, "you see, I *am* a German in a way, but that gentleman from the German Legation who came to see me the first day I was here put the wind up me. He said that if Germany won the war they'd take me back there and have me shot, so I thought I'd better get in touch with my half-brother, Otto Mentzendorff, in London, so that he could get me made British again."

"What is this ?" asked the puzzled Major. "You say you are a German in a way, but your half-brother can have you made British again ? Explain, please !"

"It's like this, sir. My mother is a German and I did my military service in Germany, and I've lived there all my life although I was born in England of a British father. I'm afraid it's a bit complicated to explain, really, but my mother is the widow of a German customs official and all she has to live on is her pension ; so if I'd disclosed the fact that I was British by birth and didn't want to fight when I was called up they'd have put me in a concentration-camp and stopped her pension, which would have meant that she'd have starved."

"Stop ! Stop !" the Major cried, breaking into German. "First you tell me that your father was British, then that he was a German customs official. That does not make sense."

"But, please, sir, my poor mother was not married to my *real* father. Soon after I was born she met Herr Heckt, of the German Customs Service, when he was holidaying in England, and married *him*. To hide the fact that she had an illegitimate child Herr Heckt got himself transferred from Herbensthal to Bremen before he sent for her to return and settle down with him in her native Germany. I was brought up as his son, Johannes Heckt. That's why I did my military service in Germany."

"But—but if your mother is German and you are illegitimate the fact that your father was English does not make you British."

"Excuse me, sir, but it does. If my mother had registered

my birth with a German Consul in England I'd have been German in spite of being born in England, but she didn't. On the contrary, she registered me as British with the British Consul in Bremen when she went to live there, so I am quite definitely British."

"Then surely the German authorities must have known of your British origin when you were called up to do your military training in the first place? Everyone living in Germany must have either a *carte d'identité* or a foreign passport. You couldn't have had both."

"I'm afraid I had, sir," said Gregory meekly. "As I've said, the whole thing is most horribly complicated. You see, my mother originally registered me as British in Bremen because she didn't want me to have to serve in the German Army, but after Herr Heckt's death she moved to Düsseldorf, and it was there that I was called up. We're only poor people and we didn't want to get into trouble with the authorities, so when they told me that I must do my time in the Army I thought it better not to argue about it, particularly as there was then no prospect of a war and I expected to live in Germany like a German for the rest of my days."

The Major tugged at his white moustache in half-irritated bewilderment. "I still do not see," he protested, "how you have managed to retain your British nationality or can claim it now?"

"I fixed it up three months ago, sir, through my half-brother, Otto Mentzendorff. He was in Germany then, visiting us, and I gave him my birth certificate and the papers from the British Consul in Bremen. He took them back to England with him and got them stamped at Somerset House just as a precaution. When the war came and I was called up I rejoined my regiment so that the German Government should continue to pay my mother's pension, but I didn't want to fight and thought that if I deserted I would only be posted as missing. I had already fixed up with my half-brother that if I should ever need to claim my British nationality I'd put through an inquiry for him; then he'd know just what to do. When I was first interned here I had no idea of putting the plan into action as I was quite content to stay quietly in Holland for the duration of the war, but as I told you, the visit of the gentleman from the German Legation made me change my mind. Otto knew what I wanted when the inquiry which you so very kindly posted for me got through to the British Legation at The Hague, and they passed it on to him through official channels. He was to show my papers to the British authorities and ask them to give me their protection and claim me as one of their nationals. He must have done so, if that is what has happened."

"I see. But this half-brother of yours, Otto Mentzendorff, is being sought by the English police as an enemy alien. Is that not so ?"

Gregory assumed a worried air as he replied : "So Mr. Renshaw informed me, and I can't understand it. He must have become afraid, as Mr. Renshaw suggested, and have posted off my papers to the authorities after he had disappeared and before he had had a chance to leave the country. I'm afraid it may make things difficult for me in England."

The kindly Major was by now entirely out of his depth. "But—but," he stuttered, "this relationship is beyond me. Your mother was German. Your father—your real father—was English. Herr Heckt was a German. Yet this half-brother of yours who is trying to leave England has a Russian name ! Please explain to me how this can be."

Gregory hung his head partly in assumed embarrassment and partly to conceal any signs of amusement which might be visible on his face despite his iron self-control. "It is painful, sir, but if you insist—it was like this. Before my poor mother met the Englishman who was my father there was a very hand-some violinist who played in the orchestra of an hotel where my mother worked for a time. His name was Mentzendorff, and he was not Russian but of German nationality. They loved. Otto, my half-brother, was born. When my mother met Herr Heckt, Otto was already four years old, and she did not dare to admit his existence. My own father was paying her a weekly sum under the English Courts, and this she made over to an English couple who brought Otto up. When Herr Heckt died Otto and I were both grown men, and because my mother so often spoke of her longing to see Otto again I traced him through his foster-parents and he came over to Germany often to see us. His birth was registered with the German Consul in London."

The Major had become as embarrassed during this recital as Gregory had pretended to be, and was obviously relieved now that it had ended.

"Well ! Well !" he exclaimed, with good-natured gruffness. "You certainly have a most extraordinary family history—but there it is." He shrugged expressively. "In any case, I under-stand that the British have allowed your claim, and that's their affair. Naturally we can't release you as you arrived in Holland without proper papers, but the authorities have acceded to the British Legation's request that you should be transferred to the British concentration-camp so that you may spend the duration of the war in company with those whom I suppose you prefer to regard as your own countrymen."

"That's very kind," said Gregory, "very kind indeed, sir."

"All right. You are to be transferred under guard this evening. The camp for British nationals is at Groningen, and you will leave on the six o'clock train to-night. You may go now."

Well pleased with the fantastic bit of muddled history with which he had bemused the Major Gregory withdrew to pack the few belongings that he had acquired during the ten days he had spent in the camp. At half-past five he was sent for again and handed over to a middle-aged Dutch Corporal named Jan Loon, a stroke of luck which he had not anticipated, for it was Jan Loon who spoke fairly good English and who, for a modest recompense, had daily brought him résumés of the British news bulletins.

The Corporal led him out to a waiting car with a military chauffeur and as they drove into the town Gregory informed the good Jan Loon of the reason for his transfer to Groningen and the curious circumstances which had resulted in his becoming a German soldier although British by birth.

Jan Loon said how sorry he was to lose so amiable a prisoner but took occasion to warn him that, good friends though they were, he must not try any tricks on the journey. Corporal Loon had his duty to do. He stated emphatically that he would not hesitate to report any attempt to escape, and said that any such report would certainly result in Gregory's being confined to cells when they got to the end of their journey instead of more comfortable quarters with the same good treatment as he had received at the camp at Nijmegen.

Gregory laughed heartily at the very suggestion that he might have harboured, even for a second, so absurd an idea as that of trying to escape from the Corporal's custody. He pointed out that since he was still wearing the uniform of a German soldier he would not be able to get a hundred yards on his own without being caught by the police. In any case he had nowhere to which he could escape : although he himself had succeeded in getting out of Germany all his family still lived there with the exception of Otto Mentzendorff, and he had disappeared. No, no; he was quite content to remain a prisoner in the hands of the kind Dutch people for the duration of the war.

Jan Loon was just congratulating him on his good sense as they pulled up in the station yard. Bidding the driver good night they left the car, and in the main booking-hall the Corporal produced a travelling-permit which he had stamped at the R.T.O.'s office while Gregory stood by, keeping a cautious but anxious eye upon the crowd that surged about him.

His anxiety was justified, for if any hitch were to occur during the next ten minutes of his secret programme the whole of his carefully-laid plan would be ruined. It was with immense delight, therefore, that he heard a hearty voice exclaim just behind him:

"Why, if it ain't Mister 'Eckt!"

Swinging round, he had barely time to flash a smile of welcome to his old friend Rudd before the Corporal glanced towards them.

"Why, hullo, Rudd!" Gregory extended his hand. "Fancy meeting you like this after all these years! It looks as though you've prospered."

Rudd's was indeed a transformed figure. He was wearing one of Gregory's smart, blue lounge suits with a Sulka tie, Beale and Inman shirt, Scott hat and Lobb shoes—all from Gregory's wardrobe. True, his borrowed plumage did not fit him at all perfectly, but its quality and texture denoted the rich Englishman at a glance.

Turning to Jan Loon, Gregory cried gaily: "Here's a coincidence! Corporal, shake hands with an old friend of mine. Mr. Rudd and I used to work together in the same business when I was in England ten years ago."

"That's right," Rudd grinned. "'Err 'Eckt, 'ere, was my boss, and a blinkin' good boss, too, even if 'e is a Jerry, if you'll pardon the expression."

"Pleased to meet. But it is not so," said Jan Loon solemnly. "Now, to-day, they prove him Englishman."

"Cor! Is that a fact?" Rudd's blue eyes opened wide. "Then wot's 'e doin' all togged up in a Jerry's uniform? Fer that matter, wot's 'e doin' 'ere in 'Olland at all?"

"I'm really half-and-half," Gregory explained. "Born British, but lived most of my life in Germany. My sympathies have always been with Britain, though, so I'm being transferred to the camp for British prisoners at Groningen."

"My! Now fancy that! Come ter think of it, I seem ter remember yer sayin' somethin' in the old days abaht yer 'avin' English relations."

"Are you still with the old firm?" Gregory asked.

"No fear! Got aht in 1931. Uncle o' mine left me a bit of dough, so I starts on me own. I ain't done so bad, neither. There's good profits fer a bloke wot knows the ropes, if you only 'as the cash ter run yer own ahtfit. 'Ere—wot trine you goin' by?"

"We haf the eighteen hours train to take for Arnhem, and to make changes there," supplied Jan Loon.

"That's my trine, too," said Rudd. "Look 'ere! We got ten minutes; wot abaht the three of us 'avin a quick one?"

"Understand not," said the Corporal.

"A drink, yer know; drop o' the pig's ear, or somefin'."

"I'd like to, for old times' sake," said Gregory, "that is, if Corporal Loon has no objection to joining us in a beer?"

"Beer!" repeated Jan Loon. "You like Dutch beer? Me, I like very much, but it makes me to grow fat. And the fatter as I get, the more beer I drinks." He laughed happily, and slapped his well-developed tummy.

The three of them went into the station buffet and sank three large lagers while Gregory and Rudd exchanged entirely fictitious reminiscences of an imaginary period during which they had been business associates. As they came out on to the platform a porter touched his cap to Rudd and indicated a first-class smoker into which he had put his baggage. Jan Loon made to move further down the train, but Rudd quickly intervened.

"Where are you a-goin' of? Can't we all travel together, friendly-like?"

The Corporal produced his voucher. "For me and my prisoner. We haf in the *derde klasse* to travel."

"Wot?" exclaimed Rudd indignantly: "On them narsty, 'ard little wooden seats? Not this time, you ain't. You're comin' in with me, an' I'll pay the difference."

"That's really very sporting of you," said Gregory.

"Not a bit of it, Mister 'Eckt; not a bit of it. You done me many a good turn when we was workin' for the old firm together, and it must come double 'ard on a gentleman like you, not only bein' a prisoner but missin' all 'is little comforts inter the bargain." With an imperious wave which had all Gregory's admiration Rudd beckoned up a railway inspector, and producing his wallet took out a sheaf of notes.

Corporal Loon, whose consent had been taken for granted and who actually had no objection whatever to travelling 'soft' if the Englishman was prepared to pay, translated Rudd's request to the inspector and the surcharge on the voucher was promptly paid over. The Corporal, his prisoner and Rudd then piled into the train, which steamed out of the station a couple of minutes later.

The journey from Nijmegen to Arnhem was quite a short one and took only a little over twenty minutes, but by the time they arrived there the three travellers were all talking and laughing together as though they had known each other for years. Rudd's high spirits were infectious, and although Gregory had sometimes to translate his Cockney witticisms into intelligible English for the benefit of Jan Loon, the rather stolid Dutchman was soon lulled by the cheerful innocence of their conversation into the belief that these two born thugs were simple, kindly people like himself, whose principal grouse against the war was that it might interfere with the continuous supply of good food and good beer.

It was quite natural that when they got out at Arnhem they should gravitate towards the station buffet. Gregory and Jan Loon had twenty-five minutes to wait for their train and although Rudd was not going to Groningen it had already transpired that he was on his way to Zwolle and would therefore be catching the same connection.

One beer, two beers, three beers, four beers. A dozen bottles of Holland's best passed down three thirsty throats and it was a merry party, provided with supper-hampers and an additional supply of good lager purchased by the generous Mr. Rudd, that tumbled into another first-class carriage on the north-bound train.

When the ticket-collector appeared Rudd again paid the excess fares of his companions ; then he drew down the blinds of the windows looking on to the corridor while the collector was still standing there, and tipped him lavishly getting Jan Loon to tell him that they didn't want their little party spoiled by some old woman or fusty old chap being pushed into their carriage, but that if he cared to send along three pretty girls they'd be obliged.

They ate their picnic supper in hilarious mood, drinking the health of the King of England and damnation to Herr Hitler ;

toasts in which all three participated with equal enthusiasm. The Queen of Holland's health also had to be drunk and that of the Dutch Army, represented by the person of Corporal Loon, after which Rudd suggested a bit of a sing-song.

He was the main contributor with Gregory in full support, while Jan Loon hummed the tunes as well as he could and solemnly kept time by waving a large, pink, right hand. The rousing chorus of "We're going to hang out our washing on the Siegfried Line", which Rudd had imported from England, was followed by old favourites such as "Pack up your troubles" and "Tipperary" until they eventually gravitated towards sleepy sentimentality, mooning out the sad strains of "Little Sir Echo" and "Roses in Picardy."

Having apparently exhausted his repertoire Rudd declared that he was going to have a bit of a sleep, and putting his beautiful Lobb shoes up on the opposite cushion of the carriage snuggled himself down in his corner.

For some little time Corporal Loon had also felt distinctly sleepy. Perhaps the considerable quantity of beer he had drunk was partially accountable for that, but only partially, for Gregory had reckoned on a good Dutch soldier's being able to sink practically any quantity of beer without either becoming drunk or necessarily going to sleep. Unknown to Corporal Loon, therefore, the entertaining Mr. Rudd had, in accordance with his instructions, slipped a little something into the second glass of beer the Corporal had drunk at Arnhem which would make quite certain of his falling into a harmless slumber before the train was half-way to Groningen.

He knew very well that he ought not to go to sleep with a prisoner in his charge, but the prisoner was obviously a decent fellow who would not wilfully get him into trouble and had himself pointed out how impossible it would be for him to get any distance in his German uniform without being caught ; an observation which was more than ever true now that they were right in the interior of Holland.

While the Corporal was pondering these matters he fell asleep, publicly announcing the fact a few minutes later by giving vent to sonorous and persistent snores.

The train rumbled on into the night. It had halted at Zutfen while they were supping and at Deventer towards the end of their sing-song. When it pulled up at Zwolle the Corporal was sound asleep. He was still sleeping when it stopped again at Meppel and Assen, but the noise of the porters shouting the

Dutch equivalent of "All change! All change here!" roused him a moment after it had pulled in to the platform at Groningen.

He sat up with a guilty start, but his first, sleepy glance round the carriage reassured him. The comical Englishman in the smart clothes had disappeared but his prisoner was still there and it was the presence of the figure opposite in the field-grey uniform that mattered to Corporal Loon. He recollected then that *de Heer* Rudd had said that he would be leaving the train at Zwolle.

The Corporal yawned and rubbed his eyes preparatory to standing up. When he glanced again at the figure opposite his blood suddenly seemed to chill in his veins. The uniform was the same, from the forage cap to the short, black top-boots, but the face was no longer that of the lean-jowled, saturnine Johannes Heckt who had been given into his charge.

Yet—somehow the little, fair, toothbrush moustache that failed to hide teeth badly needing the attention of a dentist was strangely familiar. As he stared at it the mouth below the moustache suddenly broadened into a grin and the unfortunate Jan Loon realised the trick that had been played upon him. His prisoner had swapped clothes with his friend, *de Heer* Rudd.

Rudd leaned forward and tapped the astonished, frightened Corporal on the knee. "Now don't go getting all excited, oid cock; you ain't goin' ter get inter any trouble as long as you act sensible, see?"

"Where? . . . Where? . . ." stammered Jan Loon, jumping excitedly to his feet.

"Where's the guv'nor? Oh, 'e's 'opped it, but it ain't fer me ter sy where 'e got aht. Look 'ere though, 'e tole me ter give yer this 'ere little *billy-doo.*"

With trembling fingers the Corporal smoothed out the brief letter which Rudd handed him. He was visualising courts-martial, cells, disgrace, the loss of his pension and all sorts of other calamities as the results of letting his prisoner escape. Striving to calm his nerves he hastily pocketed the fifty-Gulden note that Gregory had left folded in the sheet of paper and read the pencilled message, which ran:

Dear Jan Loon,

Never worry over trifles. You have to deliver a prisoner in German uniform who carries the papers of Soldat Heckt to the camp at Groningen and your prisoner is still with you. No one at Groningen has seen his face, so no one will know that he isn't the

A FANTASTIC FAMILY HISTORY

*same man who was in the camp at Nijmegen. If that is discovered
later you can always swear that the exchange must have been effected
just after you had delivered your prisoner.*

*If you report the matter you will only be court-martialled, so be
a sensible fellow, take your prisoner to the camp at Groningen, get
him signed for, go home and forget it.*

The Dutchman was no fool and he saw the sense of Gregory's
reasoning. With a little sigh he tore up the note; then he
smiled at Rudd and said : "You Englishmans haf trick me very
bad. But you treat me very good. Not many mens who make
escape think for poor guard so good."

Peering out of the carriage window his eye caught the flashing
lights above the buffet.

"Come on," he said. "It is only nine hours yet. You like
Dutch beer. I like very much. We haf one before I put you in
camp, eh, *Soldat* Heckt ?"

Chapter XVI

THE RETURN OF THE BROKEN REED

SIR PELLINORE GWAINE-CUST stretched out his long legs and regarded Gregory with a disapproving stare. "So Rheinhardt's sunk and the Pastor feller's dead. After four days in Germany you succeeded in raising the whole damned countryside against you ; then land yourself in an infernal Dutch concentration-camp and I have to get you out. A pretty performance, I must say !"

"Not at all !" snapped Gregory, the scar on his forehead paling. "I got myself out. It was my scheme, and a damned good one. Once I'd managed to get my plan back to you *via* the chap from the British Passport Control office, all *you* had to do was office-boy's work. It was child's play for you to apply for my transfer from the camp at Nijmegen on the grounds of my British nationality ; to send Rudd over to Holland with the instructions that I'd given you for him, so as to have him handy ; to find out on what day I was to be transferred when the Dutch had acceded to your request and to turn Rudd loose on Nijmegen station to carry out his orders. He and I did the rest between us."

Gregory did not need telling that he had made an infernal mess of his mission and would have been the first to admit it, but he was not the man to accept criticism from anyone else.

"Oh, you used your intelligence there," Sir Pellinore conceded a trifle more graciously, "except that you've landed that feller of yours—what's his name—Rudd, in jug for the duration. Pretty hard on him, what ?"

"For God's sake be sensible !" exclaimed Gregory angrily. "The Germans will have found out by this time that Johannes Heckt is still in Germany and that it was the man they were after—the spy posing as General von Lettow—who laid him out, pinched his papers and uniform, and was subsequently interned at Nijmegen under his name. If I had broken prison and laid out several Dutchmen in the process the Germans would soon have heard of it and have notified the Dutch of my doings in Germany. The Dutch authorities would have had something pretty hot to say to the British Government then, wouldn't they? We don't want trouble with Holland, so I had to think up a scheme for getting myself out of the country without assaulting any Dutchmen. By arranging that Rudd should take my place I succeeded in doing that very neatly. As for Rudd, you're going to get to work right away and secure his release through ordinary channels."

Sir Pellinore grunted. "I suppose you realize that all this is delaying my contribution to the successful prosecution of the war?"

"I don't care what it's doing. Anyhow, it won't take you ten minutes to set wheels in motion which will result in Rudd's release within a couple of weeks."

"Indeed? And how do you propose that I shall do that by employing above-board methods, when it was quite impossible for me to do so in your own case?"

"Simply by utilizing the differences that exist between Rudd's case and my own, and employing means to liberate him which would have been useless where I was concerned. I'm thirty-nine; Rudd is getting on for fifty. I'm of an age at which I'm still liable for military service; Rudd isn't, so he can be regarded as a non-combatant."

"You seem to forget that Rudd is not there as Rudd, but as Johannes Heckt, whose age I seem to remember your telling me is only thirty-one."

"Not so far as the Dutch authorities at Groningen are concerned. You see; before I passed it over to Rudd I took the trouble to alter the three to a five in Johannes' pay-book, so he is now officially fifty-one. Any medical board would substantiate the fact that he couldn't possibly be under forty, and what is more he suffers from night-blindness."

"And what the devil may that be?"

"A comparatively rare disease in peace-time, but one which became quite common during the last war and probably will during this one if it goes on much longer. On returning from the Front some of our less courageous soldiers found it impossible to see the lights in Piccadilly at night."

"Aren't any lights to see, this time."

"True, more's the pity; it makes for such a darned dull war. But quite seriously, night-blindness is a rare but genuine infirmity and it incapacitates men for active service. It proved a gift from Heaven to lead-swingers in the last schemozzle ; because if a man says that he can't see at night it's almost impossible for a medical board to trap him into admitting that he can."

"Very interesting. And you say your feller what's-his-name suffers from this convenient affliction ?"

"Of course he doesn't, but I've told him that he does and primed him about walking into a few brick walls at night during the next week or so in order to establish the fact with the people at the Groningen camp. Rudd will not hit anybody on the head so the Dutch won't have anything against him. In consequence, between the facts of his being over age for active service and a night-blindness case you should have no difficulty at all in applying for his release and getting him repatriated."

"Clever young devil, aren't you ?" muttered Sir Pellinore. "All right ; I'll have the matter put in hand."

"Thank you. And now, what have we got for dinner ?"

"Haven't the faintest idea, and why I should feed you at all now you're retiring into the obscurity of civilian life I can't think."

"Ah, well ; your chef has never failed us yet, so I suppose I can leave myself with confidence in his hands. I only raised the matter because I still hunger for exotic fare in spite of the picnic supper in the train last night and two good meals to-day. The food in the Dutch camp was edible but uninspired, and I haven't yet recovered mentally from having to go for four days on a slab of chocolate."

"If you'd played your cards properly you wouldn't have had to, but I'm sorry you had such a rough time. Frankly, Gregory, I'm terribly disappointed, too, that you've made such a botch of this affair. I was counting on you, you see, and I'd cracked you up to people in the War Cabinet as the one man who really might pull it off."

Gregory grinned suddenly. "That's better ! I wish you'd taken that line at first. I'm afraid eating humble-pie is not exactly one of my gifts, but you must know how dreadfully distressed I am at having let you down."

"That's all right, my dear boy ; you did your best, I'm sure. Let's say no more about it." Sir Pellinore stood up and stooped from his immense height to pat Gregory on the shoulder.

Gregory looked up quickly. "But I'm afraid we've *got* to

say some more about it ; and you're going to shelve that quaint idea of yours about my retiring into civilian life. The only reason that I got you to send Rudd out to Holland was so that I could return home myself with the least possible delay instead of sitting there for weeks in prison while you wangled some way of getting me out. I mean to have another crack at it, and we're starting in after dinner to discuss my next campaign."

Sir Pellinore stroked his fine, white moustache thoughtfully. He did not turn down Gregory's suggestion, as he knew the man with whom he was dealing and guessed at once that some plan must be hatching in that fertile brain, but after a moment's thought he replied : "I appreciate your attitude, but I don't see how you can attempt it again. Through ill luck your only leads in Germany have been short-circuited, so there's not much sense in your going back to poke around there like a blind-folded man."

"There's something in that, of course. Did you have any luck with the German Army List ?"

"Not much. Soon as you 'phoned me I had someone run through the 'G's.'" Sir Pellinore picked up a slip of paper from his desk. "You quite sure that sky-pilot feller didn't say : 'When we see General *von* Gra . . .' the moment before he was shot ?"

"Certain. He just said 'General Gra . . .' and the rest of the name was lost in the roar of the Nazi's pistol."

"Pity. Practically every officer of the German Army above the rank of Colonel received his first commission from the Kaiser, so it's still run by the old school tie crowd, nearly all of whom are '*vons*.' Best I can do for you is General Grabenhoff, General Grauwitz and General Gröner. First's an Army Service Corps man, second's an Austrian and the third's a Garrison Gunner now retired."

Gregory made a grimace. "No ; they don't sound a promising lot. An Army Service Corps man wouldn't run a thing like this, an Austrian would be too closely watched and a retired artillery-man doesn't sound a very big shot."

"Now if the syllable you heard had indicated someone like von Fritsch . . ."

"I thought he was killed the other day, out scouting on the Polish Front ?"

"He was. I meant someone of his eminence and integrity."

"Von Fritsch practically remade the German Army after

they threw the Treaty of Versailles down the drain, didn't he ?"

"Yes. I knew him well. Splendid feller. A good German if ever there was one. About the only one who dared to defy Hitler after he'd assumed power, too. Walked out on one of his ace speakers because he didn't approve of Nazi ideology, and made Hitler apologize for calling him over the coals about it afterwards. He was too big to kill so they retired him and made him Honorary Colonel of the 12th Artillery Regiment. But Hitler never forgets, and he cast poor von Fritsch for the part of Uriah the Hittite."

"You mean, he sent him to the front line on purpose, so that he'd get killed ?"

"Yes. He did that with a whole list of officers he wanted eliminated. Directly war was declared the Baron was ordered to join his regiment. He agreed, saying that he'd take command of it. Hitler said he was not to command it but merely to go with it and sent four S.S. men along as an escort. They never left him from the moment that he joined it, hoping that he'd be killed in action. But he wasn't."

"Good God ! Was he murdered, then ?"

"Yes. After waiting for three weeks they became impatient. Last Thursday, when he was observing the fire of No. 2 battery through his glasses, one of the S.S. men shot him in the back. In all history there has never been a more deliberate, cold-blooded assassination. And he was one of Germany's finest men."

"What in Heaven's name can one do with such people ?"

"Beat them to their knees, my boy ; then try them for their crimes before an International Court and hang them by the neck until they're dead."

"You're right, and even if it takes a year or two we'll do it."

"Yes ; but in the meantime thousands of decent folk are dying. We've got to try to stop that if we can. If only you'd got that name properly there might have been some point in your going back to Germany, but as it is . . ."

"We still have Tom Archer and Erika von Epp."

"As far as Archer is concerned I've already told you that we've tried everything we know on him but have drawn a complete blank. Erika von Epp is in America by this time, or more probably on her way south through Mexico. In any case, our people in the States have failed to trace her, so it's equally useless for you to go there."

At that moment the under-butler announced that dinner was served, so Gregory polished off his third glass of Amontillado and dropping their conversation for the time being they went in to dinner.

After washing down several portions of caviare rolled in smoked salmon with some yellow Zubrovka, the hay-scented Vodka favoured by connoisseurs, Gregory turned his attention to more solid fare, but meanwhile the butler brought round a magnum of champagne wrapped in a napkin and poured the best part of a pint from it into a large, silver tankard that stood near Gregory's right hand.

Having drunk his first draught of the wine he looked across at his host with quick appreciation in his dark eyes. "By Jove, this is good !"

"Should be," muttered Sir Pellinore. "It's Roederer 1920 and one can't find it on the market any more. One of the best *cuvées* that have come out of France in the last twenty years, in my opinion, but not up to the stuff we used to get before the last Great War. The 1900's and 1906's were positively magnificent."

Gregory nodded. "I remember the '06's, and the '11's were pretty good ; but whatever the vintage, how infinitely better champagne tastes out of a tankard."

"Always use 'em except on state occasions," volunteered Sir Pellinore. "Every drink has a vessel that brings out its best qualities. The finest Hock or Burgundy is hardly fit to drink out of a tea-cup, while for China tea nothing can beat the finest porcelain. Brandy must be drunk out of a glass which allows a big surface so that its esters can escape. Tastes rotten in one of those piddling little liqueur-glasses that people used to push round. On the other hand, though, it's no use putting liqueurs into brandy *ballons*. They lose their snap if you do ; they should be drunk out of little glasses filled to the brim. As for champagne, there's no question about it ; silver is the perfect medium for the King of Wines. No glass, whatever its shape, can touch a silver tankard.

"You don't appear to be feeling the food-shortage yet," Gregory remarked when they were half-way through the elaborate meal, "yet I hear that the Government is talking of bringing in rationing in October."

"Blithering idiots !" growled Sir Pellinore. "The work of the fighting Ministries has been beyond praise and the evacuation of the children from London was a splendid piece of work. You were here when that was carried out, of course. Some of the other Ministries, though, are behaving with incredible stupidity. There's no food shortage in this country and never will be. Damn it ! What's the Navy for ? And we've still got one, as the German submarines already know to their cost. Even in the first weeks of the war, when they had every possible advantage, they weren't able to sink anything like the tonnage that they sent to the bottom in 1917. They'll be launching new ones, of course, but only this afternoon Churchill announced in the House that we're trebling the number of our armed ships ; trebling the number, my boy ; think of that !"

"God help the U-boats, then," remarked Gregory.

"Exactly. And even as things are, the Seven Seas are ours. There are masses of food here and we're free to draw upon every friendly and neutral country in the world for more, yet the fools are planning to put the nation on rations. If that's not playing Hitler's game for him, Lord knows what is. We laughed at him for putting his own people on rations a couple of days before the war, yet here are we, with practically the whole world as an open market, talking of doing the same thing before the war's a month old.

"Last week they sent enough fish to Blair Atholl to have fed Birmingham. This week some crazy loon has suggested getting all the tea in the country and blending it together so that all individual flavours will be lost. Another lunatic instructed one of the biggest ham-curers in England that he was to stop making pork-pies because they were luxuries, whereas in actual fact ham-curers make their pork-pies from all the bits of pig which they can't possibly use for any other purpose. Luxuries, indeed ! And what if they were ? It's just such little tit-bits that keep the spirit of the people going. Besides, the British Army always has fought upon its stomach and the British Army to-day consists of every one of Britain's people."

"It certainly seems absurd to bring in rationing already, when we didn't have to until the third year of the last war, especially as we're now placed in so much stronger a situation," Gregory agreed.

"Another thing," Sir Pellinore boomed across the table. "Some fathead has issued an order that we're all to cut down our fuel and light by twenty-five per cent. Have you ever heard such nonsense ? The enormous economy effected by the A.R.P. black-out makes it completely unnecessary for any private household to cut down at all, and if they're afraid of a shortage why in God's name don't they give some of our thousands of unemployed miners a chance to do a job of work ? Nothing is more depressing than a cold house in winter, and one that's only half-lit. Not only are these restrictions bad for people, but they are also throwing thousands out of work and reducing the profits of countless commercial undertakings. Where's Simon going to get his taxes from, I'd like to know, if his colleagues send half the country broke ?"

"I gather from this evening's paper that the Ministry of Information is in a bit of a muddle, too," Gregory murmured.

"Muddle !" exclaimed the irate Baronet. "It's like Bedlam from what I hear. They've got nine hundred and ninety-nine people in it and only forty-three of them are professional journ-nalists. What d'you think of that ?"

"It sounds to me like packing an army of civilians off to the front with only four per cent. of professional soldiers among them," replied Gregory.

"That's exactly what it is, my boy, except that in this case the civilians are giving the orders. Goodness knows who have been given all these jobs, but it's quite obvious that most of them are utterly incompetent to handle such work. It needs ace-high, professional journalists, the best that Britain's got, to present the news in a manner which their experience tells them is most suitable for the papers to print. And people with imagination, too ; big advertising men who know how to sell a story or an idea, and best-selling authors the magnitude of whose sales proves their capability to interest the public. Such people are born, not made, and they're being wasted—stalled out by a lot of little nobodies who couldn't learn to write a saleable story if they took correspondence courses for twenty years."

"Yes, and what a story there is to tell in the might of the British Empire if it was handled by the right people—authors who have world-wide sales and whose names on the tops of articles would mean something in neutral countries. But what's the cause of all this muddle ?"

"The whole thing's the result of our having left the preparation of these wartime Ministries to the senior Civil Servants. How can you expect a man who's spent thirty years of his life dealing with roads to know anything about butter ; or a chap who's been adding columns of figures in the Treasury all his days to write a thrilling account of a brilliant air action ? Having got their jobs these people are sticking to them, and without a proper knowledge of necessary qualifications they've taken on all sorts of Toms, Dicks and Harrys who're eager to serve. They daren't sack these people now, because that would mean loss of face. In consequence, the thousands of offers of service which are arriving from the big industrialists and leaders of public opinion who could really do the jobs competently and restore public confidence in the Ministries, are being thrown in the wastepaper baskets without even the courtesy of an acknowledgment."

"God, what a scandal!" Gregory exclaimed. "It beats me why Civil Servants who bungle to the detriment of the nation shouldn't be publicly tried, and, if found guilty, dismissed from their posts with ignominy. After all, sailors, soldiers and airmen are court-martialled and disgraced if they fail in their duty or cause grievous loss of valuable war material through their own stupidity."

"By Jove, you're right!" Sir Pellinore banged the table with his weighty fist. "Unless they get suitable people into some of the Ministries soon the Government's going to lose the confidence of the country, and if they don't ease up on these absurd restrictions the effect on the *morale* of the nation is going to be utterly appalling. We're hoping to get the Germans down owing to the miserable lives they have to lead with rationed food, shortage of heat and light and the innumerable restraints placed on their individual liberty. Britain's trump card is that she has no need to inflict such a wretched existence on her people just because we're at war, but if we're not damned careful these unimaginative bureaucrats will make things as bad in Britain as they are in Nazi Germany."

"How are things going on the other side?" asked Gregory.

"As well as—possibly better than—could be expected, but it's unreasonable to imagine that the French stand any great chance of penetrating further for some considerable time to come, now that they're actually up against the Siegfried Line. You know that as well as I do. It looks now as though we've got to wait for Hitler's next move."

"Yes, that's just the trouble."

"The trouble is," said Sir Pellinore, "that the War House reckoned on Mussolini's coming in against us. That's why we had such a terrific naval concentration in the Mediterranean at the beginning of the war. Plan No. 1 was that while the French stood fast on the Maginot Line we should blast hell out of Italy;

sink everything they'd got in the Mediterranean, shell and bomb
their docks, oil dumps and railway junctions to blazes until
the poor old Italians wouldn't know which way to turn. Having
cleared the Adriatic, the B.E.F. was to sail up behind our fleet,
land in the neighbourhood of Trieste and drive through Austria
at the weak spot in Hitler's rear."

"I'm surprised that they ever seriously thought that Mussolini would come in," Gregory commented.

"Yes, but he's the cleverest diplomat of them all. Look
how he used that son-in-law of his, Ciano, as his stalking-horse
all through his *rapprochement* with Germany instead of acting
in person. When we were fools enough to alienate Italy through
sanctions he conceived the Axis with the idea of getting what
he could with Hitler's backing. He got Albania, but he was
much too clever to take the personal responsibility of hob-
nobbing with the Nazis. He went into a semi-retirement which
has left him perfectly free to pop up again and declare that he
always has felt that Britain was his best friend."

"We certainly don't hear much of Ciano these days."

"Naturally. Mussolini's come back into the ring himself—
though he was never really out of it. The fools who thought
that his son-in-law was getting the upper hand of him simply
didn't know anything at all about the two men."

"Well, what's the drill, then, since Italy is neutral, for the
moment, at all events ?"

"It's up to the house-painter feller to make the next move.
They say that next week-end will bring peace proposals. That's
evidently what von Ribbentrop is up to in Moscow now ; trying
to persuade the wily Stalin to give him back that huge chunk
of Poland the Russians have taken, so that Germany can offer
the Allies a new Poland, less the Corridor and Danzig, which
they will assert to be the only things they went to war
about."

"D'you think he'll get it ?"

"Some of it, but it's certain that Stalin will retain the Polish
Ukraine. After all, what's Russia had to fear these last few
years ? Not an attack from Britain or France, but one from
Germany. Everyone knows that Hitler's been itching to get
his claws on the Russian cornlands and oil wells but the attack
on Poland gave Stalin just the chance he wanted to pinch half
the country and advance his frontiers. Having locked his south-
eastern door so effectively he'd be mad to open it again. Still
I've no doubt that the Nazis will propose some form of peace

with the idea of throwing the guilt for any major war between the Great Powers on us, should we refuse to make a settlement."

"Which we shall do, of course."

"Exactly. They will then be faced with the alternatives of sitting down until we starve them into surrender—which would obviously suit us best—or using all their resources for some new, major move while they're still at the height of their power."

"Such as a drive through Holland and Belgium on the one hand and through Switzerland on the other in an attempt to encircle the French," supplemented Gregory.

"You have it. Or possibly a drive down through Hungary to Rumania."

"Mussolini wouldn't like that, nor would Jugoslavia ; and I gather that Russia has already said that she won't allow Germany to penetrate to the Black Sea."

"That is so. And the first principle of war is to destroy your enemy's main forces. No drive eastward can put France or Britain out of the war, which would have to occur before the Nazis could hope to win it ; so the logical conclusion is that they'll probably attempt a drive through Flanders and Switzerland accompanied by intensive air attacks on this country."

"Holland, Belgium and Switzerland all have pretty useful armies and they've had ample time to prepare themselves against an attack, so I shouldn't think the Germans would have it all their own way if they were to try that."

"The weight of the German army is enormous, so the results of such a move are quite unpredictable. The situation really hinges upon how far Russia is prepared to go."

"Apparently Maisky gave a very firm assurance that Russia didn't intend to infringe the neutrality of other countries."

Sir Pellinore drew his napkin over his white moustache. "True ; but Russia would like to see herself mistress of the Baltic. The main reason for the Anglo-Russian pact's breaking down was because we could not agree to give her a free hand with regard to the Baltic States. Germany did so, and secured a Russian pact in consequence. It doesn't follow, though, even if the Red Army moves into Estonia, Latvia and Lithuania, that they'll participate in the major conflict of the West."

"You don't think, then, that there are any real grounds for fearing a full, Russo-German military alliance, with Russian troops overrunning the Balkans or being brought to fight on the Western Front ?"

"God forbid !" exclaimed Sir Pellinore. "It might come to that, of course, but I don't believe it will and I have very good. grounds for supposing that it won't."

"Let's hear them," said Gregory with keen interest.

"When Voroshilov took over the command of the Red Armies on Trotsky's fall he reorganized the whole strategy of Russia. He believed then that Russia's future lay within her own boundaries, and there is no reason to suppose that he's materially altered his opinion since. He based his plans upon the supposition that Russia might possibly be attacked, but would never involve herself in a war necessitating her troops moving far beyond her own frontiers. Success in modern warfare depends almost entirely upon the availability of supplies. If Russia had had aggressive intentions Voroshilov would have established munition-factories, air-bases, supply-depôts and so on within a reasonable distance of Russia's frontiers so that he might the more readily feed an army advancing into Western or Southern Europe, but instead of this he did the very opposite.

"He marked a belt of territory two hundred miles wide inside the Russian frontiers, which he was prepared to regard as a sort of no-man's-land. Everything in it, including bridges, roads and railways, was to be destroyed as far as possible so that the enemy should exhaust himself while advancing through such difficult country and be an easy prey when he should suddenly come up against the main weight of the Red Army. He then scrapped nearly all the old munitions-plants in Moscow, Leningrad, Kiev, Kharkov and the other principal cities in European Russia and built new ones in a Forbidden Territory that lies behind the Urals, thereby securing himself against the destruction of his vital bases by enemy aerial attack.

"Up there on the borders of Asia he also established huge aerodromes holding literally thousands of planes, and as an enemy advanced into Russia these squadrons would be used to bomb their long lines of communication. From the nearest enemy frontier to Voroshilov's vast war-base behind the Urals is seventeen hundred miles. To go there and return means a journey of three thousand four hundred miles, and few modern bombers have such a range as yet. An enemy could invade Russia, therefore, but never defeat her, and any attempt to invade her territory would merely re-enact all over again the story of Napoleon's march to Moscow.

"On the other hand, Voroshilov's brilliant plan for the defence of Russia cuts the other way. If Russia turns aggressor her armies must move further and further from their bases. His great bases behind the Urals will therefore be useless to him, while the Russian railway system has still not improved sufficiently to make it easy to supply armies fighting upon such distant fronts from factories that are so far away. That's why I don't believe that the Russians will be fools enough to alter their whole strategy and come in up to the neck with Hitler in an attempt to overrun Europe."

The admirable dinner had run its course. The magnum stood empty on the sideboard in its silver filigree bottle-stand. Above the fine damask and cut-glass of the table swirled blue smoke from the cigars which Sir Pellinore and Gregory had lit just before they had pushed back their chairs and returned upstairs to the library.

"Now," said Sir Pellinore, closing the door behind them, "let's hear this idea of yours. It's some Mad Hatter's scheme, I'll bet a pony. But at all events I'm prepared to listen."

"I think I'd have chucked my hand in," Gregory said quietly, "if it hadn't been for that German girl I told you about ; the one whose car I pinched."

"Ha ! You young devil ! I send you out to do a job of work and all you think of is to have a necking-party with the first girl you meet. What's she got to do with it ?"

"A great deal. She had no idea what I was up to, of course, but like everyone who has kept their sanity she was all for an early peace. When I told her that my job was one which might have brought that about she begged me to see if I couldn't think up some new scheme by which I might succeed where I'd failed before, and I was rash enough to promise that I would."

"If I know you, you'd promise a woman anything if you thought you could get what you wanted out of her."

"You misjudge me," Gregory protested mildly, "and are speaking entirely for yourself. Everyone knows what a devil you were for the women in your younger days."

"Not so much of the 'younger days,' young man. I'm hale and hearty yet."

"I bet you are, you old ruffian ! And I wouldn't trust you near any woman I was interested in, for fear you might cut me out."

"Cut you out, eh ? Well, if this young woman's all you say she is, why, damn it ! I might have a shot at it when she comes over after the war, especially if you don't do your stuff better than you did outside Cologne."

"I don't think I did so badly, considering that she was proposing to have me shot only an hour earlier."

"Nonsense ! Getting kisses out of a woman is like getting olives out of a bottle ; the first may be devilish difficult but the rest come easy. You're not half the man I thought you, to content yourself with one."

"Unfortunately I lack your superb assurance and you may recall that the situation was not exactly the most perfect one for love-making. If I'd stayed much longer in that car I might have been deprived of the pleasure of taking a dinner off you to-night—or of taking any other dinner off anyone, for that matter. 'He who fights and runs away may live to fight another day' remember, and that old saying exactly describes the position at the time. In her car last Wednesday week I fought and ran, as it were, and here I am, still alive and preparing to fight again."

" 'A bird in the hand is worth two in the bush' might also apply," boomed Sir Pellinore, "but let's get back to business. You got all soulful about this delightful young thing—incidentally about the most stupid thing you could do, since I've never met a woman yet who didn't get bored with a man who got soulful about her—and you decided to be a hero for her sake. Is that the situation ?"

"Certainly not. I gave up being soulful about girls when I put away my Latin Grammar. But what she said did make me think ; and I had plenty of time to spare for thinking when I was sitting about in the concentration-camp at Nijmegen. Rheinhardt is out of it ; so is Erika von Epp. But Tom Archer is still a possibility and he's right here in London."

Sir Pellinore again brushed up his moustache. "My dear feller, I've told you a dozen times that Archer refuses to talk."

"Then we must make him."

"I don't see why you should imagine that you can succeed where the people in M.I.5 have failed."

"I do. Even in war-time the activities of M.I.5 are restrained to some extent. They may do a lot of funny things that nobody hears about, but this is still technically a free country and Archer is a public figure with an organization behind him which could kick up a pretty dust if the authorities went too far outside the law. I, on the other hand, am a free agent. I don't care two kicks about the law and I'm prepared to do any dirty business on the chance of getting what I want."

"You'll have to take the consequences if you're found out."

"Naturally. I'm quite prepared for that, but nothing they can do to me here in England is going to be half as bad as what the Germans would have done to me if they'd caught me snooping about along the Rhine."

"All right, then ; if you're prepared to land yourself in jug, have a cut at Archer—and good luck to you !"

"Thanks. I'm afraid, though, that I shall require your assistance."

"Sorry, my dear boy, but I can't give it to you. There'd be too much of a fuss if I were caught applying lighted matches to the soles of Mr. Archer's feet, and I imagine you're contemplating something of that kind."

"Possibly ; but I don't need your active help for anything like that. All I want from you is to get the right people to fake a photograph for me, because it's the sort of job I can't do myself or get any ordinary photographer to tackle."

"In that case I don't doubt that the matter can be arranged. Tell me a little more of the scheme you have in mind."

"It's like this. Before you put me on this job, Rudd was just as keen as I to get back into harness. When I told him that I'd been given a one-man job and couldn't possibly take him with me he was bitterly disappointed, so more to keep him happy than with any thought of practical results I put him on to finding out all he could about Archer while I was away. I'm thunderingly glad I did, now, because I think the good lad has got us something which will enable me to twist Mr. Archer's tail."

"Rudd was able to tell me a bit about what he'd been up to while we were changing clothes in the train last night, but you may remember that in the instructions I managed to smuggle out to you *via* that chap in the British Passport Control I particularly mentioned that when Rudd was given his orders about what to do when he arrived in Holland he was also to be told to write down every detail he could think of about his investigations and leave his notes in the top drawer of my desk. Directly I got home this evening I skimmed through them and they confirmed an impression I'd formed during our brief talk in the train—that he'd got us something pretty good."

"Let's hear it, then."

"Certainly," said Gregory, producing a fashion-plate from his pocket. "D'you think we might broach another bottle of that old Kümmel ? I'm sure it would be a great aid to perfecting my little plan while we're talking the matter over."

"Drat the boy!" exclaimed Sir Pellinore. "If I have you about the house often I soon won't have any decent liquor left to drink. Still, it was damn' clever of you to think of using the name of Mentzendorff for my imaginary valet in your inquiry that set the ball rolling. God! I laughed till I damn' near cried; and for that I suppose you deserve to be honoured. What's more, I could do with a spot myself."

He got up and pressed the bell.

Chapter XVII

BLACKMAIL

TEN days later Gregory received a small packet by special messenger. Having duly signed for it he examined its contents ; then sat back and roared with laughter. Sir Pellinore's people had needed time in which to secure various components of the photograph he required and had then had the extremely tricky job of blending them into one picture ; but there was not a thing about the finished article to suggest that it was a fake and Gregory felt that such a masterpiece of *photomontage* had been well worth waiting for.

Picking up his telephone he rang Tom Archer's house in Kennington, but learned that Mr. Archer was out and was not expected home until about six o'clock that evening. At half-past six Gregory rang the number again and got on to him at once.

"My name is Baird," he said ; "Joe Baird ; but I'm afraid that won't convey much to you, Mr. Archer. I'm very anxious to have a chat with you, though, about a matter that interests us both."

A deep, rumbling voice came back over the telephone. "I'm afraid I'm a very busy man, Mr. Baird. I couldn't spare the time to see you at present unless you care to state what your business is and it's very important."

"I'd rather not discuss it on the telephone," said Gregory.

"In that case you'd better write," said the voice, with an abruptness which suggested that the speaker was about to replace the receiver.

"Hang on a minute," Gregory said quickly. "I've only just got back to England from Budapest, where I've been living for the last three years. Some people out there particularly wished me to get in touch with you."

"What people ?" came the suspicious answer.

"Really, Mr. Archer," Gregory protested, "I'd rather not mention any names on the telephone, but I've some very important messages for you from my Hungarian friends which must be delivered by word of mouth. Surely you can guess the subject on which they want to communicate with you when I tell you that they live in Pest, on the *left* bank of the river."

"Oh ; all right, then," said the voice on a slightly different note. "Is the matter urgent?"

"Yes. I'd like to see you this evening if possible."

"Can you come down here?"

"Yes."

"All right then ; make it nine o'clock."

"Thanks." Gregory rang off.

At nine o'clock he was bowling along in a taxi a mile south of Westminster Bridge. The effect of the black-out was partially nullified by the moon, which was in its last quarter but shone in an almost clear sky, turning the few patches of low cloud a lightish-grey against which the blimps of the balloon barrage could be clearly seen in black silhouette. The taxi turned left from the main Kennington Road into a wide street of houses whose short gardens were fenced in on either side by iron palings.

In spite of the moonlight the taximan would have had some difficulty in finding No. 65 Walshingham Terrace, as the semi-circular fanlights above the doors of the houses, which carried their numbers, were now all curtained for the black-out, had it not been for a steel-helmeted A.R.P. Warden who gave them directions ; but having found the house Gregory got out, telling the man to wait.

The houses on either side of the street consisted of a solid block, but they were substantial, well-built affairs constructed in late Georgian or early Victorian times when Kennington was a well-to-do suburb, within easy reach of the City and Strand at a time when there were as yet no cars, tubes or motor-buses to enable business people to live further afield.

The district had gone down but the properties were well kept up, for Walshingham Terrace formed part of the London estate which is the patrimony of the Prince of Wales as Duke of Cornwall, and during his twenty years as holder of that title the Duke of Windsor had proved an exceptionally good landlord.

Striding up the short garden-path Gregory mounted a few steps and rang the bell. The door was opened to him by a thin-faced, intelligent-looking woman wearing heavy shoes and severe clothes, and having her grey hair smoothed flatly back. Gregory remembered vaguely that the Marxist leader had married an L.C.C. school-teacher, so this was evidently Mrs. Archer.

On his giving his name she said that her husband was expecting him and that if he would go right through he would find him in the back room ; and as she made way for Gregory to pass her she called out loudly : "Tom ! Here's Mr. Baird to see you."

A gruff voice called back through the door : "All right, Ellen ; tell him to come in," and advancing down the passage Gregory opened the door of a room that was evidently used as a study.

Archer was a big, burly man in his late fifties, who had probably been very strong in his youth but had now run to fat from lack of exercise. He was seated behind a small, square desk littered with papers, ash-trays, pipes and all sorts of other impedimenta.

The glance he threw at Gregory was not particularly amiable but Gregory liked the look of him for all that. There was something downright and honest about his big face with its powerful, jutting chin. He smiled in his most friendly fashion, therefore, and said :

"It's very nice of you to see me, Mr. Archer. May I sit down ?"

"Sure !" Archer pointed with his pipe-stem to a well-worn arm-chair. "So you're just back from Hungary, are you? Have much trouble in getting through ?"

"Trouble doesn't describe it," said Gregory with a grin, "because although I couldn't say so on the 'phone it's Germany I've just come back from."

Archer raised his heavy, black eyebrows and a glint of suspicion crept into his eyes as he inquired : "What about those friends of yours in Budapest, then ?"

Gregory shrugged. "I'm afraid they're just as mythical as my stay in Hungary, but that doesn't really affect the matter. Things are much more interesting in Germany at the moment, and it's there that I've been in touch with certain friends of yours."

"Indeed ? Who, may I ask ?"

"Herr Rheinhardt, at Traben-Trabach, for one."

"Never heard of him."

"Pastor Wachmuller, of Ems, for another."

"I've never heard of him either."

"Well ; that's not particularly surprising because, as you know, the three anti-Nazi groups in Germany have agreed to sink their differences and act together. Your friends would naturally be among the German Marxists, whereas Rheinhardt and Wachmuller were both Social Democrats. Still, it was they who gave me your name."

"For what purpose?"

"So that those of us here in England who sympathize with the anti-Nazi movement in Germany can get together and give them all the support we can."

Archer shook his head. "I'm afraid you've come to the wrong shop, Mr. Baird. I don't know anything about anti-Nazi movements."

Gregory smiled. "I can quite understand your reticence, Mr. Archer, but perhaps this will convince you of my *bona fides*." For fear that his pockets might be picked he had had the overlap at the thick end of his silk tie partially sewn up as a safe place in which to carry the precious swastika. Undoing his waistcoat he produced the swastika and held it out, hoping for an immediate reaction, but he was disappointed.

Archer glanced down at the symbol without betraying any sign of interest or recognition. "What's that thing got to do with it?" he asked. "It's a swastika turned the wrong way round, isn't it?"

"No; as a matter of fact it's the *right* way round—and the symbol of peace which opens all doors among the right-thinking." Gregory paused; he had used the phrase which he had heard from both Rheinhardt and Wachmuller, but still Archer remained entirely unmoved. He went on, therefore:

"You know as well as I do that certain high officers of the German Army are preparing a *putsch* against the Nazi leaders with a view to establishing a new German Government freely elected by the German people; their object being to bring about an honourable and speedy peace."

"Glad to hear it," said Archer.

"And it's up to us," Gregory continued, "to give them every support that we possibly can when the time comes."

"I see. But how d'you propose to give them any assistance now that we're at war with Germany? However much we may wish to help the honest German working-folk to turn out this gang of Nazi blackguards, our hands are tied."

"Not altogether," said Gregory, trying a new bluff. "When I was in Germany I was talking to General Gra . . . Damn it! What is the fellow's name?"

"Ask me another!" replied Archer unhelpfully.

"Good Lord! I'll forget my own name next! You must

G

know the man I mean ; he was a close friend of Baron von
Fritsch who died the other day. Why ; I had it right on the
tip of my tongue just now !"

"You did, eh ? Well, perhaps you're right, and you will
forget your own name next. At the present moment you call
yourself Joe Baird."

Gregory saw that he was right up against a stone wall, so
he did the only possible thing and said with a rueful grin :

"Mr. Archer, I congratulate you. You must forgive my
trying to pump you but it's my job to try to do so. My name
isn't Baird, and what it really is doesn't matter for the moment.
Nevertheless, it's quite true that I've been in Germany since
the war began and that I did meet there certain people who
were definitely plotting to bring about the downfall of the Nazi
Government. That is to your interest and to mine, so we ought
to work together."

"It remains to be seen what interests you represent."

"I represent the British Government, who are prepared not
only to give every aid in their power to any movement made
by the German Army in collaboration with the German people
to overthrow the Hitler régime, but also to guarantee a just
peace to Germany."

"A capitalist peace, huh ? A settlement which would enable
the bankers to make big loans to Germany on reasonable security
and place the German industrialists on the necks of the German
workers instead of the Nazis. No thanks !"

"You're wrong, Mr. Archer. It would be a peace made by
the freely-elected representatives of the German people."

Archer shook his head. "I'm having no truck with this
rotten, Imperialist Government of ours ; and they know it.
You're wasting your time, Mr. whatever-your-name-is, so I
think you'd better be getting along now. I've got a lot of work
to do."

"Now, wait a minute," Gregory pleaded. "You are an
Englishman, aren't you ?"

"No, sir. I was born in this country and I've lived here
most of my life, but I don't regard myself as an Englishman.
I'm a human being ; just like all the other human beings up and
down the world of whatever race or colour they may be. You
were about to appeal to my patriotism, weren't you ? Well,
you can save your breath because I'm not a patriot. It's because
people are wrongly brought up to get all hot under the collar
about the countries in which they were born and to take pride

in the fact that their forefathers have killed thousands of people born in other countries, that the world's in the rotten state that it is to-day. It's crazy, narrow nationalism and capitalist interests which are the sole cause of Germany, Poland, France and ourselves having once more been plunged into the hideous, legalized mass-murder we call war."

"All right," Gregory shrugged, "have it your own way. Personally, I honestly believe there's a lot in what you say, but unfortunately the world's not yet sufficiently educated to accept your doctrine of Internationalism and in the meantime we've got to make the best of a bad job. At least you'll admit that, life for the working-classes is infinitely better in every way in Britain and France than it is under Nazi rule, and our first job is to restore a reasonable degree of freedom to the German people. When we've done that, it'll be quite time enough to talk about abolishing Nationalism."

"Nothing," boomed Archer; "nothing can justify any Government's plunging its people into a new war."

"There I'm afraid we differ, but we've got to face cold hard facts. Four Governments *have* plunged their countries into war and it's up to you and me and every right-thinking person to try to stop the slaughter as soon as we possibly can. The Democracies will make no peace until the Nazis are destroyed. You're in possession of certain information which might help us to destroy them. I appeal to you once more, therefore, to tell me everything you know about this anti-Nazi conspiracy in order that the British Government may assist our friends abroad."

"It's no good. I've told you that I don't know anything, and if I did I wouldn't tell you."

Gregory's lean face went flinty. "In that case it's my unpleasant duty to remind you that the Government can take certain steps under the Emergency Powers Act. I am convinced that you are withholding information which might aid the Government in the successful prosecution of the war. Do you wish me to have a warrant issued for your arrest?"

Archer suddenly sat back, thrust his hands in his pockets and bellowed with laughter.

"Come off it, man! You can't frighten me. Putting me in gaol on a charge which couldn't be substantiated would cause much too much excitement in the Press. Even if you do, I don't mind. I've been in prison plenty of times for inciting to riot and the usual sorts of charges the capitalists use as bludgeons on any man who tries to secure a fair deal for the under-dog. You can do what you like but I'm not talking, and if it'd get rid of you any sooner I'd tell you why."

"Go ahead," said Gregory; "I'd be interested to hear."

"Well, it's this way. Supposing I *have* got friends among the German Marxists. There's no harm in admitting that; it's common knowledge. All right. I tell you who they are, and what do *you* do? Instruct some of your secret agents in Germany to get in touch with them. Your intentions may be all right, but what's the result? My friends are already watched night and day by the Gestapo. Some blundering fool of a British officer in a Tyrolese hat and plus-fours suddenly turns up in a slum street in Essen, Düsseldorf or Charlottenburg. The Gestapo sees him haw-hawing with my friends and what's the next thing that happens? They bung my friends in a concentration-camp, or worse. Nothing doing, thank you! You go and tell that to whoever sent you."

Gregory felt as guilty as though Archer had accused him personally of such unwitting betrayals. Both Rheinhardt and Wachmuller had paid the penalty of his rash indiscretion. The truth of Archer's argument could not be gainsaid and he felt sorry for the Marxist, but he had his job to do. It was a rotten job; a dirty piece of business; but nations were more important than individuals and Archer must be made to talk. Catching his eye Gregory held it as he said slowly:

"Pearl Wyburn's a pretty girl, isn't she?"

Archer stiffened perceptibly as he replied: "What's she got to do with this?"

"Quite a lot. She's the daughter of a very old friend of yours, isn't she? When she became an orphan you more or less adopted her and have treated her like your own child ever since. She was a bit difficult to handle because she was so darned good-looking and obviously not cut out for a job in a factory or an office. I've been at some pains to find out all about her, you see. She knew she was beautiful, too, and hard-headed little hussy that she is she was quite determined to use her beauty to get on in the world. Naturally she likes pretty clothes, and as she hasn't got much brain she did the obvious thing and got herself a job as a mannequin. But mannequins don't earn very much and in their private lives they're not allowed to wear the clothes that they display. In consequence she over-spends herself and you come to the rescue in order to keep her straight. If it weren't for you it's pretty certain that little gold-digging Pearl would have become the mistress of one of her rich admirers long before this, but you've fought that tooth and nail although she now costs you far more than you can afford. As her taste for luxury has grown you've had to ante-up more and more money, because the girl is a sort of obsession with you. I'm not going to state categorically that you've raided your Party funds, but since you've been paying the rent of that luxury flat of hers at Bryanston Court I should think it's highly probable. In any case, when the balloon goes up and the Party accounts are examined we shall find out whether you've been soaking the Party for her keep."

Archer's big face was suffused with colour. "What the hell d'you mean?" he roared.

"Simply this," Gregory replied with sudden, deliberate viciousness, "if you refuse to talk I'm going to see to it that your colleagues are informed that Pearl is your mistress and that you've been keeping her for years."

"That's a damned lie!"

"I know it is, my dear fellow, but what about it?"

"I'll have you for slander," Archer thundered. "It's one thing to make such accusations and another to prove them."

"Of course; but I shall succeed in doing both."

"You dirty, blackmailing swine! You know damned well she's a decent girl and that to suggest that a man of my age had been living with her would wreck her reputation. She'd never live it down."

"I know. And I'm very sorry for her. But it'll be your fault if she has to face this scandal, and it would be particularly inconvenient just now, wouldn't it? You see, I happen to know that she's got her hooks into Lord Bellingham's son, Ollie Travers, and looks like landing him."

"So you know that, do you? Then for God's sake give the girl a chance. He's a decent lad, even if he is an officer in the Guards. It's a filthy, lousy trick to threaten me with breaking up her prospects of a happy marriage."

"Oh, it's sheer, unadulterated blackmail, I quite agree."

"All right then; go ahead. By no possible means can you prove this damned lie so I'll get a judgment against you and clear her that way. Stink or no stink!"

"But I can prove it." Gregory quietly took the photograph from his pocket and passed it across the desk. "Have a look at that, Mr. Archer."

The photograph had been faked by an expert who knew his

job and although it had taken some days to procure the best possible results it had not been difficult to secure the necessary material. As Pearl Wyburn was a mannequin well known in the West End innumerable photographs of her in all sorts of costumes had been easily available from the fashion houses for which she worked. The one selected showed the attractive, long-limbed, fair-haired mannequin with very little on except some delightful undies. Archer himself was, of course, a public figure, so that it had been equally easy to obtain scores of photographs of him from the Fleet Street agencies, and one had been chosen in which he was seen relaxing, coatless and hatless, after addressing a big northern meeting on a hot day.

The two photographs had been skilfully blended into a specially-taken background with a bedroom setting. Pearl, in her undies, was standing near a tumbled bed, while Archer stood close by in his shirt-sleeves, smiling at her. On a side-table near-by stood an opened magnum of champagne, two half-filled glasses, cigarettes and chocolates. A valuable mink coat in which Pearl had once been photographed for a catalogue was thrown carelessly over an arm-chair. Altogether it was a most skilful and artistic production.

"Secret Life of Noted Marxist," murmured Gregory. "Man of Sixty Keeps Twenty-Two-Year-Old Glamour-Girl in Luxury Flat. How d'you like it?"

After one glance at the photograph Archer sprang to his feet, banged his fist on the desk and bawled: "You dirty, double-crossing crook! I'll have the law on you for this!"

"Oh, no, you won't," replied Gregory quite unperturbed. "You'd never dare to bring the case to court and you know it. We'd impound your passbooks and show the sums you've paid to and for Pearl, and no jury would give you a verdict. In addition I'd see that copies of this photograph were sent to all the Comrades and I'd have a special copy mounted for Captain the Honourable Oliphant Travers which would certainly put paid to Pearl's affair."

The burly figure behind the desk seemed to wilt and the age-lines suddenly showed more clearly in the big, determined face. Gregory felt an utter swine, but he had had to break Archer's will at any price and he knew now that he had succeeded.

"God blast you!" muttered Archer as he slumped down again into his chair. "I've known some dirty business in my time but this beats all. And you an Englishman!"

"I thought you were telling me just now that no race was

better than another ?" Gregory could not resist the gentle jibe.

"I was. But I didn't say that some weren't more developed than others. At all events we like to think that English people have reached a stage when they have more sense of what's just and decent than the rest. Our Government sneers at Hitler for making war on women and children, doesn't it ? The blasted hypocrites ! What's this but making war on an innocent man and a poor young girl ?"

"Don't be too hard on the Government," said Gregory. "I'm afraid you must blame me for this. No Government official has any idea of what I'm up to."

"I see," said Archer thoughtfully. "Then all that stuff about using the Emergency Powers Act was just a bit of bluff."

"More or less ; but that doesn't affect the present situation. I've got the negative of this photograph in a safe place, and I've plenty of dope about your interest in Pearl Wyburn which will quite definitely be construed as showing that she's your mistress. Either you talk, or much as I hate to have to do it I take steps to ensure the matter being made public."

Archer sighed, and drew a hand across his face. "All right. What d'you want to know ?"

"I want the names and addresses of the people with whom you've been in communication in Germany. I want particulars of any methods by which you're able to evade the censorship and communicate with them still, although we are at war. I want all the information you can give me about the anti-Nazi conspiracy. And before you start I may as well give you a warning ; it's no good giving me a lot of dope I can't check up on. I'm too old a bird to accept as gospel any yarn that you choose to spin me now that I've got you in a corner. I want to see your correspondence-files so that I can verify for myself most of what you tell me."

"I can tell you quite a lot ; but it's going to make things a bit difficult if you won't take my word for what I say. I don't keep dangerous correspondence like that here, in the house."

"Well, where do you keep it ?"

"I'm not going to tell you. It's with all the other confidential papers of the Party and you can't expect me to let anybody who's outside the Party know where we keep them. You know well enough that we're not tame Socialists who'd buy top-hats to go to Buckingham Palace in if they were asked there ; we'd rather burn the place. We're not hot-air Communists either ; we're even to the Left of the I.L.P. and if we lived in any other country we'd be called Anarchists. There's enough so-called treason in those files to make the lousy bourgeoisie take permanently to their beds and to keep the judges in permanent session for six months if the police got hold of them. You're plumb crazy to suggest that I should entrust the safety of all my friends to a police spy like you by telling you where our secret documents are kept."

"Then you must go and get the letters I want to see."

"Don't be silly ; they're among hundreds of others, all confidential stuff. If there were only one or two of them I could get hold of them when nobody was looking and bring them away for you to look at, but there're so many of them that it'd take me a good couple of hours to get them all out. The people who look after the files would never allow me to take a whole bundle of papers away like that, either ; big man in the Party as I am."

"Rotten game, politics, isn't it ?" said Gregory. "Especially when it means handling a lot of subversive literature. Naturally, you and your friends live in perpetual fear that you'll double-cross one another."

Archer shrugged. "That's beside the point ; the fact remains that once the letters have gone into the files there's no getting them out again."

"Then you'll have to take me to the place where the files are kept."

"That's a pretty idea," sneered Archer. "Who do I say you are ; Trotsky, or the King of Siam ?"

"You will say that I'm a German Comrade. I speak German very well, so you needn't be afraid I'll let you down on that score. We'll spin a yarn that I've just arrived here *via* Holland with the very perturbing news that I believe some of those letters you've received to be forgeries and that it's only by seeing them personally that I can ascertain whether this is a fact. You must explain that it's of the first importance that you should know one way or the other, because if they really are forgeries you're all being led up the garden-path, and that the only thing to do was to bring me down to see the letters in question so that you could find out."

Archer considered for a moment. "Yes. I suppose we could fix it that way, but I don't like it, all the same. We're talking turkey now, Mr. whoever-you-are, and between ourselves I wouldn't like to be in your shoes if the people down there find out that you're not what you pretend to be. To start with, the address at which the secret files of the Party are kept is one of the most jealously guarded secrets in the country ; Scotland Yard would give anyone a packet for it. The Party has got to protect its interests and its personnel. Honestly ; I wouldn't advise you to go there."

"I don't think you need be afraid that they'll find me out, and if there is a risk I'm quite prepared to take it. The point is that I've got to see those documents, and the sooner the better."

"All right," said Archer standing up. "You can't say you haven't been warned. I'll go and get on the telephone to see if there's anyone there now who can let us in. The place may be shut, as it's ten o'clock at night, but I think there's a chap sleeping on the premises."

He left the room and was away about five minutes. Gregory could hear him muttering down a telephone in the hall, but eventually he came back and nodded his massive head.

"It's O.K. We can go down there right away. It'll take us about twenty minutes in a taxi."

"Good," replied Gregory, standing up. "I've got one waiting. Let's go, shall we ?"

Outside, Gregory got straight into the cab and did not make any attempt to overhear the address which Archer gave the man but took the opportunity to slip the golden swastika back into the secret pocket in the end of his tie while unobserved. The moon was still up but the streets were not as light as they had been on Gregory's arrival, since heavier clouds had rolled up against which it was no longer possible to distinguish the balloons.

The cab ran eastward for a little way then north towards the river. Gregory recognized the big road-junction at the Elephant and Castle, after which they entered the New Kent Road, crossed the Old Kent Road and beyond it ran eastwards again through some twisting streets in the direction of Bermondsey.

The district was not a particularly salubrious one, but Gregory had hardly expected that the secret H.Q. at which the Marxists kept their highly dangerous plans for fomenting strikes and even revolution would be in the neighbourhood of Whitehall. It was much darker down here owing to the narrowness of the streets, and on the way he gave Archer an outline of what he proposed to do.

"Since a third person will be present," he said, "we'll spin the yarn I suggested about my being a German and I'll spend an hour or two going through the files with you pretending to identify most of the letters as genuine but picking out one or two as forgeries just to save face. As I examine them I can read their contents so I'll get a pretty good idea of what's going on ; enough, at all events, to enable me to check up on whatever you may tell me later when we fully discuss the whole position on our own. After we've done that I shan't trouble you again and I'll destroy that very unpleasant negative which shows you in such a compromising situation with little Pearl."

Archer seemed satisfied with this, and when the cab eventually pulled up at a cross-roads he said : "It isn't far now and we're going to walk from here."

Gregory quite understood that the Marxist leader was unwilling that their destination should be known even by the taximan, who might have recognized him from his photographs in the Press, so he got out and paid the man off.

Side by side they started to walk in silence down a gloomy street. Gregory thought that Archer would now take considerable pains to mislead him by dodging about for a quarter of an hour or so in the maze of squalid courts and alleys which surrounded them, but the Marxist did nothing of the sort, seeming not to care whether Gregory found the place again or not. They took the first to the right and the first to the left ; then Archer pointed to a small public-house that loomed up out of the shadows of what appeared to be a dark cul-de-sac, and muttered :

"That's the place."

As they approached Gregory peered into the murk of the side-turning. Not a light showed in any direction, but the faint moonlight made the clouds slightly lighter than the dead-black of the houses, over whose roofs Gregory saw some tall, slanting streaks of the same dead-blackness which he suddenly realized were the masts of ships. What he had taken for a cul-de-sac was evidently an alley-way leading down to the Bermondsey docks.

It was just past closing-time, so no sounds of talk or laughter issued from the bars of the public-house. Archer passed by the main entrance on the corner and walking twenty yards down the alley halted there, feeling about on the wall until he had located a side-door. Finding its bell he gave two short rings followed by a single very long one.

For a few minutes they waited there in the darkness ; then the door was opened and a man's voice said : "Hullo ! That you ?"

"Yes," came Archer's deep bass. "It's me, and I've brought the Comrade I was telling you about over the 'phone."

"Right-oh ; come in," replied the man, holding the door open for them to enter but shutting and bolting it behind them after they had passed inside. Gregory found himself in a narrow, dimly-lit hall ; he noticed with interest that there was a steel shutter above the door, which could be dropped in the event of a police raid, and that a large, electric alarm was affixed to a near-by wall-bracket.

Turning from the door the man who had let them in led the way up a flight of uncarpeted stairs. He was a small man with stooping shoulders and a shortage of breath which suggested middle-age. Gregory did not get a good chance to look at him until they reached the first floor and entered an office where bright lights were burning behind heavily-curtained windows.

Round the walls were ranged row upon row of steel filing-cabinets. Gregory had had a faint suspicion that as Archer had taken no particular pains to conceal the locality of the place he might have been trying to trick him, but this was certainly the Party H.Q. ; there could be no doubt of that.

"This is Comrade Chivers," said Archer, introducing the little man.

"Kröner," said Gregory in a guttural voice as he announced himself in the German fashion and bowed from the waist before extending his hand. "Gomrade Chivers, to meet you I am very bleased."

"I couldn't say so over the telephone, Chivers," Archer went on, "but Comrade Kröner here has just come from Germany with some very alarming news. He seems to think that some of the stuff we've had from the Comrades there are forgeries, so I thought the best thing to do was to bring him down at once so that we could find out."

Chivers, a grizzly-haired little man with pince-nez clipped to his long nose, seemed considerably perturbed at this announcement, and for some minutes he discussed with Archer the possible effects that forged letters containing misleading information might have upon their activities.

Gregory took in every word that they said. It was none of his business to concern himself with the affairs of the Marxists but he felt that he could not know too much about the men with whom he was dealing, as such knowledge might prove extremely useful later on, when he attempted to get into touch with their foreign colleagues. The trouble was, however, that

nothing they said conveyed very much to him ; they seemed
to be talking to some extent at cross-purposes. No names
were mentioned and there was nothing that he could get hold
of.

Suddenly it struck him that they were making conversation
solely for his benefit ; that Chivers and Archer were talking
only to delay his getting at the files. His senses suddenly alert,
he glanced at them and saw at once that they were talking at
random, unsuccessfully trying to disguise a nervous expectancy.
They were waiting for something to happen.

Instantly his suspicions were aroused, to be intensified a
moment later as he caught the sound of a footfall on the stairs.
Suddenly he realized that by insisting on coming down to this
secret filing-office he had given Archer a perfect opportunity to
lead him into a trap. Archer had been on the telephone for
quite a time before they left Walshingham Terrace. During
those minutes he might have given detailed instructions to
Chivers and other people in the house for the arrangement of
an extremely unpleasant reception for their unwelcome visitor.

Gregory cursed himself for not having brought a gun, for
that would have given him immediate mastery of the situation.
If he had known that he was coming to such a place he would
certainly have done so, for Sir Pellinore had years previously
secured for him a permit to carry fire-arms in Britain which
had never been revoked. But in London such a precaution had
seemed entirely unnecessary, particularly as he had originally
intended only to visit Archer's house in respectable Kennington.

The footfalls came again. At that instant Gregory caught
Archer's eyes fixed upon him with a curious expression and
something in the Marxist's glance told him with absolute certainty that his instinct had been right. Without hesitation
he acted.

Swinging his left fist in a vicious hook he took Chivers,
who was nearest to him, under the jaw. Lifting his right foot
sharply he aimed a savage kick at Archer's knee. When
Gregory went into battle against superior odds he never used
half-measures. He knew that it was only by being completely
unscrupulous that he had come out of so many tight corners alive.

As he moved he caught the sound of the footsteps on the
stairs once more ; closer now. They were heavy, and he could
tell that more than one person was descending from the top of
the house. If they were the guardians of the place and Archer
and Chivers had been waiting for them he was in for an

exceedingly bad time unless he could out the two Marxists and escape from the house before the others arrived.

Since Archer had been watching Gregory he was not taken by surprise. Dodging the kick he snatched up a heavy ledger and, with a loud shout, hurled it at Gregory's head.

Gregory side-stepped, but as he did so he heard the footfalls quicken as the men on the stairs broke into a run in response to Archer's yell.

"You rat !" snarled Gregory, leaping at the burly Marxist.

"Rat yourself !" bellowed Archer as they went down together in a heap.

With a crash the door was burst open, and out of the corner of his eye Gregory saw two big men who looked like ex-pugilists come plunging into the room.

Wriggling free of Archer he jumped to his feet, seized a chair and with its legs thrust out before him charged straight at the nearest thug. One of the chair-legs caught the big fellow right in the middle of his ugly mouth. With a howl of pain he fell backwards against the open door, but his companion grabbed another of the chair-legs and with one wrench jerked the chair from Gregory's grasp.

By now Archer was on his feet again and came lumbering heavily forward. Gregory stopped him with a punch like the kick of a mule that took him right over his heart. He grabbed the desk behind him and stood swaying there, half-dazed by the shock of the blow. The second thug had dodged round to Gregory's side and now sent a terrific right-hander to his head. Agile as a cat, he jumped backwards just in time to escape the full force of the blow, but the big man's fist grazed his head when he was off his balance and sent him spinning to the floor.

Gregory protected his face with his outstretched arm and the moment he had measured his length he rolled over and over of his own volition until he was brought up sharp by the line of files at the far end of the room. Wriggling to his knees he snatched up a large bottle of ink from a near-by desk and hurled it with all his force at the tough who had struck at him.

"Look out, Summers !" gasped Archer, but his warning came too late. The bottle caught the man full in the chest. It did not break as it hit him but its cork had come out and the ink spurted all over his suit ; a second later the bottle smashed to smithereens on the floor.

The force of the flying bottle brought Summers up short. With dismay on his face and blasphemies on his lips he stood for an instant staring down at the rivulets of ink running over his ruined clothes.

Chivers had staggered to his feet again ; but so had Gregory. He dived at the little man and grabbing him by one wrist and his coat-collar swung him round.

Shouting : "Come on, Ben !" to his companion with the bleeding mouth, Summers again came wading in.

Before the wretched Chivers knew what was happening Gregory had nearly broken his wrist with a violent wrench which pitched him forward under Summers' knees. The two of them fell in a tangled heap, and as the infuriated Ben came dashing in, his bullet-head well down and blood still dripping from his chin, Gregory dealt him a left upper-cut that made him reel, side-stepped adroitly, and jumping over Summers' kicking feet dashed for the door.

A wave of elation filled him as he leaped past his three attackers and raced across the room. If only he could gain the stairs before the two thugs had recovered he would have just time to wrench back the bolts of the street-door and plunge headlong into the darkness. Once he was out in the street he could yell for help, and it was hardly likely that Archer's men would risk police intervention by giving chase.

He was within a yard of the door when Archer, now partially recovered from the blow over his heart, heaved a chair at his legs. It caught him sideways-on ; he staggered, clutched wildly at the empty air and went crashing, flat out, in the open doorway.

Before he could rise Ben swung round and came at him yelling murder. Shooting out a hand Gregory grabbed his ankle, twisted like an eel and brought him down with a thud across his own body. Wriggling from under him he managed to scramble to his knees just as Summers, now up once more, came pounding across the floor with steps that shook the room.

To fend off Summers' attack Gregory threw his arms up in front of his face, but at that instant it seemed as though a ton of bricks had fallen on the back of his head. Unnoticed by him Comrade Chivers had picked himself up, secured a heavy, round ruler from the desk and slogged him with it on the back of the head.

For a moment Gregory swayed there on his knees, half-dazed. His arms slipped downwards, and Summers hit him in the face. As the blow came from above and was nowhere near his chin it did not knock him out, but it was sufficient to send him sprawling sideways. Before he could do anything to protect himself both the bruisers had flung themselves on top of him.

Ben, spitting curses from his bleeding mouth, gave him two vicious blows on the side of the face and knee'd him heavily in the ribs, driving the breath from his body. Then, as he twisted there in agony, doubled-up on the floor, the two of them threw him over on his face and secured his hands behind his back with a piece of stout cord, after which they lugged him to his feet and, panting, cursing and perspiring, pushed him into a chair.

With his head lolling forward on his chest he remained there, half-comatose for the moment. His brain felt as though attached to a large pair of pincers which were constantly opening and shutting, tearing at it every ten seconds as though to pull it out of the back of his skull where he had been hit. His right ear seemed to be twice its normal size from the blow that Summers had landed on it. His nose was bleeding freely from one of the vicious blows he had received while on the floor. His stomach ached intolerably from the effect of his having been winded and he swayed there weak as a rat, incapable of further thought or action.

As though through a mist he saw that Archer was waving the two thugs away from him ; then Archer's voice came to him as from a great distance.

"I warned you, didn't I ? You asked for it, and you've got it. I couldn't avoid bringing you here ; you forced me to."

Gregory tried to nod, but his brain seemed to slop forward as though it were loose inside his skull and the pain almost made him cry out. He bore no malice against Archer ; it was his own fault that he had landed himself in this wretched mess. He had made the unpardonable mistake of underrating his opponent, and it had been madness, even in England, to insist on being taken to such a place as this while unarmed.

Archer was speaking again. His voice came more clearly now. "You've only got yourself to blame. Now you know about this place what's to stop your coming down here again with the flatties from the Yard ? Our papers were safe here, but we can't shift all these hundreds of files to new quarters without running a big risk of something getting out, and their contents would send a score of our most trusted men to prison for the best years of their lives. That would wreck our organization and the game you tried to play on me shows that you yourself consider that national interests should be put before those of individuals. Our interests are international, so you've got to pay the price of having poked your nose into our affairs. Now we've got you we can't possibly afford to let you go."

Gregory slowly raised his head and looked at Archer. So they meant to keep him prisoner somewhere to prevent his having the place raided by Scotland Yard. That would be mighty inconvenient but he couldn't blame them, and to keep a man prisoner for any length of time is by no means easy. Sir Pellinore knew that he had gone down to see Archer that night, and when he failed to report the Baronet would set the giant organization of Scotland Yard in motion to trace him. The taximan who had brought him to within a quarter of a mile of this place would be questioned sooner or later, and that would narrow the area of the search. Special Branch men would keep Archer under observation from to-morrow onwards every time he moved out of his own house, so that he would never be able to come down to this place again without giving it away. Gregory knew, too, that even if the police failed to trace him the men who were set to guard him would sooner or later slacken in their vigilance, and he was prepared to back himself to think up some scheme whereby he could escape within a week from any private prison into which they might put him.

He suddenly noticed that Archer's face was very white and strained, as though he were about to do something which required an enormous effort of will, but upon which he was absolutely determined. Then the Marxist said distinctly :

"We can't keep you a prisoner here indefinitely, and now you've found out where we keep our papers you know too much for us to let you go. The London docks are only just round the corner and we're going to send you for a midnight swim."

Chapter XVIII

THE RATS GET THEIR PREY

SLOWLY the full horror of his situation percolated into Gregory's still half-dazed mind. Trussed up as he was, he was entirely at the mercy of Archer and the two gorilla-like morons, who were evidently the guardians of the place and would do anything that Archer told them.

The frightful thing about it was that Archer was being completely logical, and it was evident that the Marxist had made up his mind to murder him immediately he had won his point about being taken to the place where the secret files were kept. That, he saw now, was why Archer had not troubled to try to mislead him about the locality of the place after they had left the taxi ; he had already decided that once in the office Gregory must never be allowed to come out again, save for his short journey to the dock-side.

One of Gregory's gifts was his capacity for putting himself in other people's shoes and seeing their points of view. Archer was not an ordinary criminal and it was most unlikely that he had ever before contemplated murdering anyone, but this Marxian organization of his, consisting as it did of the Reddest of Red Communists, was the one thing for which he lived. He knew quite well that if he were to set Gregory free he could not possibly expect him to refrain from securing the assistance of the police and raiding the place to obtain the data he required about the German Communists, just as quickly as he could. He was wise enough to know also that it was an extremely difficult matter to keep any strong, active, intelligent man prisoner indefinitely. The only course open to him, therefore, was to eliminate Gregory entirely.

For all that, Gregory could not help feeling that the whole situation was utterly preposterous. The Gestapo might do this sort of thing ; you expected it from the Ogpu if you tried to monkey about with the diplomatic secrets of the Kremlin ; but damn it all, people did not commit murder for political reasons in Britain !

"You can't do that !" he choked out. "You can't ! This is England—London !"

"I can, and I mean to," said Archer firmly. "God knows, it's a frightful thing to have to soil one's hands with murder, but there's no other way out. You know too much to be allowed to live."

"I don't know anything yet." Gregory made an effort to pull himself together. "You never gave me a chance to see any of your files."

"You know where this place is."

"I'm not interested in your political activities. Supposing I were to give you a solemn undertaking to forget it ?"

"You wouldn't, or else you'd break it. You said yourself that you were completely unscrupulous in your methods providing you got what you wanted. Not an hour ago you utilized the most filthy blackmail to force my hand."

"I see," Gregory sneered, trying another tack, "at least you've got the decency to come into the open. It's not your high political conscience for which you propose to do me in at all ; it's just to save yourself from being found out by your own Party for the crook you are. You'd rather murder me than have it known that you've been embezzling the Party funds to keep that gold-digging little bitch, Pearl Wyburn."

"What's that ?" said Comrade Chivers suddenly.

"The truth," snapped Gregory. "Fish round in the inside pocket of my coat and you'll find a very interesting photograph of Comrade Archer and the glamour-girl he keeps in a luxury flat in the West End." Gregory thought he might be able to save himself yet, if only he could make his captors quarrel.

"It's a damnable lie," roared Archer, "and the photograph's a fake."

"Well, let's see it, anyway." Chivers took a step forward.

"No you don't !" Archer quickly barred his path. "It's not fit for any decent man to look at. As I told you on the telephone, this blackguard forced me into bringing him down here, and that's the way he did it."

"If there was nothing in this yarn of his, why didn't you refuse and hand him over to the police ?" asked Chivers sharply.

"Because he's faked the case so well that it might just hold water, and I wasn't going to risk a decent girl's life being wrecked that way. You've known me for twenty years, Joe Chivers. D'you trust me or not ? Come on ! Speak up, now !"

"Sure, Tom ; of course I trust you," Chivers said apologetically.

"It's only your being our treasurer that made me think a bit. The secret payments have been pretty heavy these last two years, and you're the only one who knows where all the money goes."

"Now look here," Archer turned and faced the smaller man, "Pearl Wyburn and the funds are nothing to do with this. I'm prepared to face the Committee any day with full explanations. In the meantime we've got a Government spy here who's succeeded in getting to know of these premises. It doesn't matter how ; that's beside the point. He has it in his power to wreck the whole Movement. Do we let him go, or do we take steps to close his mouth for good ?"

Gregory watched the smaller man with acute anxiety and his heart sank as Chivers slowly nodded his head. "That's sense, Tom. The one thing has nothing to do with the other. I'm afraid we'll have to do him in."

"Right," said Archer with sudden decision. "The sooner we're over with it the better, then. We'd best empty his pockets first, and remove any markings from his clothes so that the police won't find it easy to identify him when they recover his body. Get busy, you two, and strip him."

Summers and Ben lugged Gregory to his feet, undid the cords that bound him and began to pull off his clothes. As they were removed they were handed to Archer, who put the offending photograph in his breast-pocket, threw the rest of Gregory's belongings into a drawer and taking each of his garments in turn cut away their name-tabs or laundry-marks with a penknife. Within a few minutes he was standing naked in the middle of the floor with the two thugs still holding him firmly by the arms.

To enable him to dress again when the tabs had been removed they released him temporarily but stood by, one on either side, ready to knock him out at the first sign of renewed resistance.

He put on his clothes very slowly so that he might have as much time as possible in which to try to think out some plan by which he could save himself, but cudgel his wits as he would he could think of nothing but a sudden dash for the door, and he knew quite well that if he attempted such a thing the four of them would easily catch him before he could reach it, and that he would only be asking for another beating-up.

It seemed to him utterly fantastic that he might really be dressing himself for the last time. During his recent trip to Germany and at certain hectic times earlier in his career he had been near death over and over again, but he had generally had some weapon in his hand, while the settings of such escapades —usually some low den in a foreign city—had made the thought of death as the penalty of capture a not unnatural one.

Now, however, he was in the heart of London, the best-policed city in the world, and on the side of the law, yet here were two educated Englishmen calmly proposing to murder him with the aid of a couple of animal-like bullies because his activities had threatened their political organization.

As he pulled on his coat a mood of utter desperation seized him. It was now or never, since once his hands had been tied again they would not be freed until the cords were cut in the mortuary after his body had been dragged from the river. He stooped to tie the laces of his shoes ; then, as he stood upright, he twisted suddenly and jabbed his fist into the face of Ben, who was standing just behind him.

As Ben staggered back Gregory dived for the door, but instantly all four of them were on him. Before he had covered a couple of yards he crashed to the floor with Summers on his back, the tough's weight driving the breath out of his body. Ben kicked him revengefully in the ribs ; then he was held down on the floor while his wrists and ankles were once more tied.

Pulling him upright, Summers produced a grimy silk handkerchief from his pocket. Grabbing Gregory's nose he forced him to open his mouth, into which he thrust the handkerchief so that he could no longer make any sound but a low, incoherent gurgle.

"Quite certain you want us to put 'im in, Mister ?" Summers asked Archer suddenly.

"Yes ; he's got to go. Better take him through the ware-house and push him off the steps of the wharf," Archer replied.

"Orl right, Boss," said Ben, "but it's murder, yer know."

"The two of you have committed one murder already," said Archer coldly, "and rather than have us hand you over to the police you preferred to take this job and agree to do every-thing that you were told without question."

"Still, this ain't quite the same as doin' watch-dog 'ere an' sloggin' some of them blarsted Fascists on the 'ead when ordered," Summers protested.

A new hope began to flicker in Gregory's breast, but it was extinguished as soon as Archer spoke again.

"It's your lives or his," he said, "so you'd better make up your minds which it's to be. I expect Comrade Chivers has already told you that we're going to give you a bonus of a hundred pounds apiece to ease your consciences about this night's unpleasant work."

"O.K., Guv'nor," Ben nodded, "but let's see the 'undred."

Chivers walked over to a safe, unlocked it and took out some bundles of one-pound and ten-shilling notes from which he proceeded to count off two stacks of fifty pounds each.

"Here you are," he said, handing the money to the two men. "Fifty pounds apiece, and there'll be another fifty for each of you when you get back here."

Summers and Ben stuffed the bundles of notes into their pockets; then Summers said: "We'll be back 'ere orl right, under ten minutes, but I reckon Mr. Archer 'ad better come along wiv us."

"Why?" asked Archer, going a shade paler.

"'Case we're caught," replied Summers. "If a coupla rozzers 'appened along we'd be 'ad fer murder, wouldn't we? You'd swear you'd never seen us an' get orf scot-free. This 'ere's your job, not ours, so you gotter take the risk wiv us. That's fair, ain't it?"

"All right," Archer agreed. "It's pretty unlikely that there'll be any police about down here at this time of night, but I'll come if you wish. Let's get it over."

Summers stooped, threw his right arm behind Gregory's knees and picked him up bodily with a fireman's lift. With his head and chest dangling limply over Summers' shoulder he was carried downstairs, Ben and Archer stumping loudly on the uncarpeted treads behind them.

Outside in the alley it was pitch-black. Summers trudged heavily forward, jolting Gregory as he walked. With sudden, horrible distinctness the image of a hearse flashed into Gregory's mind. This was his own funeral procession; Summers was bearing him slowly but surely to the equivalent of the grave, while Ben and Archer were the mourners who had come to witness the last rites. A tag of verse recurred to him:

"The graveyard, the graveyard is a nasty old place;
They put you in the ground and throw dirt in your face."

There would be no dirt in his face, but slimy, stinking dock-water, polluted by the refuse of the ships. He would not have to swallow much of it, though, because they would not risk removing from his mouth the handkerchief which gagged him

in case he let out a shout for help before he went under, but for
all that the water would force its way up his nostrils and down
his throat. Nobody could ever say that Gregory Sallust was a
coward, but he shivered slightly at the thought. People may
say that drowning is not an unpleasant form of death, but he
wished now that the Nazis had caught him in Germany and put
him up against a brick wall. Shooting was at least a quicker
and cleaner way out.

He began to think of last-minute pleas he might make. Archer
was not a bad man, however misguided his political convictions
might be, and this horrible business must be going against all
his instincts. If only he could be persuaded to postpone execution Gregory felt quite certain that he would never carry it out.
He could beg the courtesy of a night's contemplation in which to
make his peace with God, or a last good meal with his favourite
dishes before he passed out. Such courtesies were always
granted to condemned prisoners, even to murderers for whom
the morrow would bring the hangman's noose about their necks.
Then he realized abruptly that with a gag in his mouth he could
no longer talk.

From the entrance of the dark alley to the wharfside was no
more than fifty yards, but although they had as yet covered
barely half that distance Gregory already felt that for a whole
lifetime he had been hanging over Summers' shoulder while
the thug plodded steadily on, bowed under the weight of his
heavy burden.

In his extremity all Gregory's senses had become hyperacute.
The rank smell of the garbage in the alleyway seemed to stink
to high Heaven ; his ears magnified Summers' heavy tread until
each step the thug took sounded like the knell of doom. He
could hear the footsteps of Archer and Ben, who followed close
behind. But there was yet another noise, slightly more distant.
It was a stealthy padding in the darkness behind Archer's back.

Suddenly a horrible, choking gurgle broke the stillness of the
night ; then came a cry of fear.

Halting in his tracks, Summers let Gregory slide to the ground
and swung round to face something that leaped at him out of
the darkness.

For the next few moments the alley was a scene of wild
confusion. Gregory was trampled on as men fought blindly in
the blackness. Someone screamed curses in an Asiatic tongue ;
another voice ordered silence in blasphemous English.

All at once the sounds of thumping blows and slithering

feet subsided. A torch with a shaded bulb shone out on the ground near-by, the spot of light flickering until it came to rest on Gregory.

"'Ere's the bhoy we're after," said a gruff voice. "Pick 'im up, now, and put 'im in the van. Jump to it, ye lazy spalpeens!"

Hands out of the darkness clutched at Gregory's limbs. He was hauled upright and half-carried, half-dragged back along the alley towards the street. What was going on he had no idea ; neither did he care. The only thing that mattered at the moment was that for reasons at which he could not even guess some gang of roughs had attacked Archer's party and had thus been the means of saving his life.

As he was dragged from the mouth of the dark passage the moonlight filtering through the heavy clouds made it just possible for him to discern the outline of a Ford van. Its doors were already open, and after pushing him inside the two men who had dragged him there scrambled in behind him.

When he pitched forward on the floor of the van his knees came into contact with the hard boards, but he fell with his face on something soft and yielding which was covered with what felt like cloth. As he turned his head his ear touched a cold, hard, uneven object like a small chain. Next moment one of the men who had attacked Archer's party struck a match to light his cigarette. Gregory saw then that his head was pillowed upon a man's middle, and he at once recognized the hard object against his ear as Archer's gold Albert.

Whether Archer was dead, unconscious, or only gagged and bound like himself he did not know, and in any case the Marxist's condition did not concern him ; he was more interested in the brief glimpse of the interior of the Ford that he was able to obtain before an angry voice barked : "Put that ruddy light out !"

It was empty save for Archer and himself on the floor and five men who occupied the seats running along either side. One of these looked like a Lascar, another like a Malay, while the others seemed to be Europeans.

As the smoker hurriedly put out his match the doors were slammed-to, someone ran round to the driver's seat and the van started off with a jolt.

Gregory was still half-suffocated by the gag and his first thought was to take advantage of the darkness to try and get the handkerchief out of his mouth. His hands were tied behind him, but he remembered that Archer had been wearing a horseshoe tie-pin and, wriggling his head a little higher, he felt about with his lips until he succeeded in finding the tie-pin and getting it caught up in a fold of the handkerchief. Fortunately the tie-pin was held in place by a safety-clip, so by jerking gently he was able to draw part of the handkerchief from between his teeth and loosen its pressure sufficiently to force the rest of it out with his tongue. But even when he was free of it he decided that his best policy was to suppress his curiosity and not to speak until he was spoken to.

For what seemed a long time the van ran through the darkness, twisting and turning down a score of streets until Gregory soon lost all sense of the direction in which they were going, but at length one of the men said to another :

"I 'ope Bill ain't forgot ter drop us orf at Euston."

"Don't you fret," came the reply ; "we ain't there yet, not by a long chalk."

This scrap of conversation told Gregory that they had crossed the Thames and were heading northwards, and it was obviously at Euston that the van pulled up five minutes later to let the two men get out.

Soon after the van had started off again it began to run uphill, so Gregory guessed that they were still going north towards Highgate or Hampstead. Some twenty minutes after the two men had been dropped at Euston the van slowed up, swung at right-angles on to gravel and pulled up. The doors were opened, Gregory was hauled out, lowered to his feet and held upright. By what little light there was he saw that they were in a private drive before the porch of a large house.

The driver and the man by his side, who appeared to be the leader of the party, got down and assisted the others to carry Gregory and Archer through the front door, past a black-out curtain and into a spacious, well-lighted hall where Gregory had a chance to look at all his captors for the first time.

The leader of the gang was a thick-set, red-headed man, and from the cut of his jib as well as from the slight brogue which blurred his Cockney accent Gregory was certain that he was an Irishman who had lived for a long time in London. The driver of the van was a crinkly-haired, hook-nosed individual ; probably a Levantine Jew. The other white man had untidy, ash-blond hair with very light eyebrows and blue eyes. He looked like a Nordic seaman, and the inclusion of the Lascar and the Malay in the party showed that it was composed of a gang of dock-rats.

Gregory asked himself what in the world these toughs could want with him. It seemed inexplicable, yet as the torch had been flashed on his face in the alley he had distinctly heard their leader say : "'Ere's the bhoy we're after ; pick 'im up, now, and put 'im in the van ;" words which showed clearly that he had been taken on this midnight ride by design and not by accident.

Archer was not gagged and was moaning now, but no wound showed on his body and no blood streaked his greying hair, so it looked as though he had been sandbagged and was just coming round. What sort of unguessed-at enemy could it conceivably be, Gregory wondered, who had put this bunch of dock-rats on to kidnap both Archer and himself ? And why had they been brought to this big house, which he was pretty sure was in Hampstead ? The thing did not make sense.

All he could do was to await enlightenment with an acute interest. Another man, a tall, long-chinned fellow with high cheek-bones, streaky, black hair plastered across a bald pate and the dark clothes of a servant, had just closed the front door and now appeared round the edge of the black-out curtain. He passed the group in the hall, opened a handsome, mahogany door on their right, and motioned them to go in. The Irishman led the way ; the others followed, supporting Gregory and Archer between them.

The room they entered was unusually lofty and of splendid proportions. Book-cases containing many rows of handsomely bound volumes lined the two longest walls, and at the far end a staircase at one corner led up to a minstrels' gallery beneath which was a huge table-desk inlaid with many rare woods. It was a flamboyant piece but obviously an antique, and Gregory estimated that it would fetch three figures at any auction-sale.

At the desk there sat a little, wizened man with a big, fleshy nose and a semi-bald head. He was dressed very neatly in smart, city clothes, and as he moved his head the lights glinted on the lenses of the pince-nez which were perched upon his obviously Semitic beak.

The other furnishings, including the Persian rugs scattered over the parquet floor, were all upon the same scale of opulence as the books and the desk, but Gregory had hardly time to take them in before he and Archer were dumped down in two chairs and the Irishman addressed the man at the desk.

"'Twas easy. We trailed 'im to Archer's 'ouse ; then down to a pub Bermondsey way. 'E was there 'arf an hour and they 'ad a bit of a disagreement. We 'eard 'em 'avin' a daisy of a quarrel upstairs, then out they come again with the boy-o trussed like a turkey, an' it's my belief they meant to chuck im in the river. There was two others with 'im then, as well as Archer, but we took on the lot an' 'twas a grand surprise we give 'em. The other lads were a pair of numskulls by the look of 'em, so we left 'em lying there, but these're the two you wanted an' 'twas no trouble at all."

The Jew nodded, and said : "You're quite sure that you were not followed by the police ?"

"Och ! Certain as I am of me own name. You've no need to worry."

Taking an envelope from a drawer of his desk, the Jew handed it across. "There you are, then. That was the sum agreed upon."

The Irishman ripped open the envelope with a dirty thumb, pulled out a wad of notes and counted them, then grinned and lifted a finger to his checked cap by way of acknowledgment. "Any other little jobs an' I'll be 'earing from you, Mr. Rosenbaum. You know where to find me and the bhoys."

"Thanks. You can take your men away now."

The Irishman signed to the rest of his gang, who had congregated by the doorway, and they all trooped out into the hall. The Jew took no further notice of his prisoners for the moment, but picking up his pen reverted to writing a letter on which he had been engaged when they had been brought into the room. Gregory heard the front door slam, and at the return of the repulsive-looking servant after seeing out the dock-rats Rosenbaum looked up and said :

"You had better go up and tell him that both of them have been brought in."

The man's extreme thinness, together with his bony face and abnormally long chin, gave him the appearance of a funeral mute, but his dangling, simian arms suggested a powerful grip. As he left them and went up the stairs to the minstrels' gallery Gregory wondered who was meant by the "him" he had been sent to fetch. What conceivable motive could anyone have for kidnapping two people of views and interests so divergent as Archer's and his own ?

He looked across at Archer and saw that his eyes were open. The Marxist was lying askew in an arm-chair with his hands bound behind his back, but he had raised his head a little and was looking stupidly about him, as yet hardly aware of what had happened and clearly every bit as puzzled as Gregory to find

himself in his present situation.   As he caught sight of Gregory
his mouth fell slightly open.   Evidently his first idea on coming
round had been that Gregory had finally turned the tables on
him and his two thugs by managing, through some means
unknown, to get some Government agents to lie in wait outside
the Bermondsey public-house and attack them.   The fact that
Gregory was still bound hand and foot obviously made him more
bewildered than ever.

Gregory was so elated at having escaped a watery grave that
he did not care very much what happened now, and on an impish
impulse he put out his tongue at the Marxist.   It was a gesture
of derision which he was to regret before he was an hour older.

Archer wriggled himself into a more comfortable position and
sat up.   Staring angrily at the little Jew, who was still writing
busily, he suddenly bellowed : "What the hell's the meaning of
this ?"

"Quiet, man, quiet !" said the Jew irritably.   "You'll know
in good time and it isn't the slightest use to make a fuss."

At that moment the attention of both prisoners was caught
by sounds from the minstrels' gallery, and they looked up to see
that a new figure had appeared upon the scene ; a plumpish man
of about forty, with his hair cut *en brosse*, who moved with a
curiously light, cat-like step in spite of his bulk.   He had a
heavy jowl, and from between small, light eyes set much too
close together there protruded a thin, sharp nose.   With the tall
servant behind him he padded almost soundlessly down the
stairs and stood for a moment at their foot, surveying the prisoners
while he puffed at an expensive-looking cigar.

Rosenbaum had risen immediately he had caught the faint
creak of the stairs, and vacating the chair behind the desk he
stepped aside.   With stooping shoulders and hands clasped in
front of him he stood in a deferential attitude, waiting for the
plump man to speak.

"So ! Rosenbaum, you've got them for me," said the newcomer, speaking German in a high-pitched, effeminate voice.
"Das ist gut, mein Kleiner Jacob, sehr gut."   With a self-satisfied
swagger the fat man padded forward and lowered himself carefully into the Jew's chair.

"Ja-wohl, Herr Grauber."   The Jew smiled blandly, 'washing
his hands with invisible soap' as he gave him the gist of the
Irishman's report.

Gregory thought with some satisfaction that the position
was at last becoming clearer.   Even had the plump man not

addressed the Jew in German, Gregory would have guessed his nationality from the cut of his hair and the shape of his head.

The Irishman had said that his gang had trailed Gregory to Archer's house before following them both down to Bermondsey. That must have been done on the instructions of the Jew, and the Jew was obviously the lieutenant of the German. Gregory realized that by some means which he could not even attempt to guess the German Secret Service agents in London had got on to him and for their own reasons had arranged for him to be kidnapped. That being so, the position did not look any too healthy, for if Archer had been willing to resort to murder to prevent Gregory's leaving the Marxist headquarters and reporting its whereabouts, the German espionage agents whose activities were covered by this house would be hardly likely to quibble at using equally desperate methods to prevent his going out of it now that he knew its situation and its secret.

As he reached this depressing conclusion Archer's voice boomed out again.

"What the hell d'you mean by bringing me here?" he roared. "Undo these cords, and let me out of this house at once."

"Silence!" snarled the German with sudden venom, but in English that betrayed not a trace of accent. "Speak only when you are spoken to, you Marxist scum."

"Scum yourself!" snapped back Archer, reduced to impotent *tu quoque*.

"Do you wish me to remain, Herr Grauber?" asked the elderly, round-shouldered Jew.

"*Ja*. Stay where you are, my little Jacob ; stay where you are," Grauber replied in a caressing voice, but he did not look at Rosenbaum as he spoke. He was studying Gregory intently with the pale eyes that peered out of his pink face from under silvery-blond eyebrows.

"So you are Gregory Sallust," he said suddenly, "alias General von Lettow, alias General von Heintisch, alias *Soldat* Johannes Heckt. I am most interested to meet you."

"Thanks," said Gregory. "I'd be better able to show my appreciation if I had the use of my limbs. It's a little difficult to get up and bow with one's hands and feet tied."

"I see no reason why we should have to carry either of you about." The German stabbed out his half-smoked cigar and casually picked up another from a large silver box on Rosenbaum's desk. "Karl, untie the feet of both of them, but leave their hands bound in case Mr. Sallust is tempted to give us an exhibition of heroics. Mr. Sallust is a very agile man, and stronger than you might think to look at him. He's dangerous, too, and we don't want any little parties like that to which he recently treated some of our people on the roofs of a block of houses in Ems."

"So you know about that?" said Gregory, with a grin, as the gaunt-faced servant untied his feet. The fact that his legs were being freed was not much, but it was something, and in any case he felt that he could not make matters worse by putting a cheerful face on things.

"Of course I know," the German replied in his high, staccato treble, "it is my business to know such things, and there is now very little that I do not know about how you employed your time during those few days during which you were in Germany."

"Good for you!" remarked Gregory, and when Karl had undone the cords that bound his feet he stood up, gave a formal bow, and asked: "May I have the honour to know with whom I am talking? I didn't quite catch the name. Was it Herr Glauber?"

"Grauber" the German corrected him, "*Gruppenführer* Grauber of the Gestapo, if you please. I am the chief of Department U.A.—1."

"I don't mind a bit," said Gregory amiably, "but I can imagine that there are plenty of other people in London whom it might not please at all."

"*Ach!* You choose to be funny, Mr. Sallust!"

"You won't find it funny if M.I.5 catch you here now there's a war on."

"Please do not concern yourself for me. I am very well placed for looking after my affairs. Do not think, either, that you English are the only people who can come and go between your own country and one with which you are at war without passing the frontier in an ordinary manner."

"So you're just over here for a day or two to get a few good square meals? Nice change, I should imagine."

"Not unpleasant. But the principal reason for my visit was an irrepressible desire to meet you."

"What's that got to do with bringing me here?" Archer cut in angrily.

"You," said Grauber icily, "are one of the lice which crawl

upon the bodies of carnivorous animals. Mr. Sallust has at least the courage of an animal, if not its cunning. Since you were with him when he was brought in you were brought in also. Be silent now, or I will have you gagged."

"May I hear how you got on to me?" Gregory inquired.

The Gestapo chief smiled; it evidently tickled his vanity to give details of the neat job of work he had supervised. Preening himself a little, he replied: "When Hecht was found in the car outside Cologne dressed in the uniform of a General—the nearest, I fear, that so undistinguished a man will ever get to achieving that rank—it was clear to us that the foreign agent whom we then knew to be masquerading as the worthy but defunct General von Lettow, and whom we later identified with yourself, had changed clothes with him. A few days later we received information from Holland that a deserter using Heckt's name and papers was in the concentration-camp at Nijmegen. Obviously that deserter was the same foreign agent; yourself, in other words; and you had succeeded in getting out of Germany. But the arm of the Gestapo is long. We knew that so active and foolhardy a person would not be content to remain in a concentration-camp for the duration of the war, so our agents in Holland were instructed to keep a careful watch. We learned of your transfer to the camp for British internees at Groningen within an hour of your setting out on the journey, but our agents at Groningen were much mystified because the prisoner delivered there had no resemblance whatever to the descriptions we had issued of you. Fortunately, however, we have good friends in the Dutch passport office to whom we put through an inquiry for any foreigner resembling yourself who had left Holland during the day following that on which you left Nijmegen. The number of travellers is now limited, and our friends were able to identify you for us without difficulty. A passport had been visa'd that morning, at the request of the British Consul at The Hague, for a man named Gregory Sallust, and a man answering to your true description had left Rotterdam that day by the midday boat.

"Our agents in London found your name in the telephone book—a very easy thing to do—and a watch was kept upon your flat in Gloucester Road. Once more the description of the Mr. Gregory Sallust who lived there tallied with your own. Having found our hare, it only remained for us to catch it and cook it. Had you not left your flat to-night in a taxicab you would have been sandbagged and brought in earlier. As it was your little trip down to the docks provided an admirable opportunity to bring you here without any fuss."

"Very neat," admitted Gregory, "very neat indeed. And now you've got me here what d'you propose to do with me?"

"Your ultimate fate is a matter of no importance. What concerns me is this little talk for which I have taken the trouble to come all the way from Germany. I am here to obtain from you particulars of the conspiracy which we both know to exist and which has as its object the destruction of the Government of the Third Reich."

"If you know about it, why ask me?" Gregory shrugged.

"I know quite a lot about it but I am anxious to know more."

"So am I. It sounds a most interesting and praiseworthy affair, but this is the first I've heard of any such conspiracy."

"You lie," said the German quietly. "You went to Germany with the definite object of getting in touch with these rats of Marxists and other disaffected elements which plot to stab us in the back. Papers found in the houses of both Rheinhardt and Wachmuller prove that they were interested in such a movement. It has no chance, of course; the rats will never dare to leave their holes and come out into the open; but it would be foolish to treat them with the contempt they deserve, because in petty ways they contaminate their immediate circles. Purely as a routine measure, and for the purification of the State, they must therefore be hunted out and eliminated."

Gregory heaved a mental sigh of relief. Evidently no papers connecting the movement with the Army chiefs had been found in the houses of Rheinhardt or Wachmuller. The Gestapo still believed that they had to deal merely with another crop of their hereditary enemies, the Communists and intellectuals. That, at least, was something.

"Of course," he said, "like everybody else I know that a quite considerable proportion of Germans hate your lousy Government. The secret broadcasting station of the People's Freedom Movement that you've failed to trace proves that, and while I was in Germany I certainly learned that the same old plots against the Government were going on, but they were only minor conspiracies. I found no trace of any concerted movement."

"So you won't talk, eh? That is very foolish. Unfortunately we lack the refinements here which we possess at Dachau and some other of our concentration-camps. . . ." Herr Grauber paused for a moment, then his dull, pale eyes seemed to light up in his face as he went on : ". . . but even without such aids to the loosening of unwilling tongues I can promise you, Mr. Sallust, that unless you provide me with the information for which I have come to England I will make you scream for mercy, courageous man though you may be, merely by the application to your eyeballs of the glowing end of this very excellent cigar."

Chapter XIX

MEN WITHOUT MERCY

GREGORY felt himself going moist under the collar. Nobody knew where he was, so there was no possibility whatever of his being rescued. Having had one unbelievably lucky break that night because Herr Grauber's plans had happened to run contrary to Tom Archer's he could hardly expect another. In this quiet house at Hampstead he was entirely at the mercy of the German.

He glanced up covertly, first at Rosenbaum and then at Karl. The eyes of the elderly, round-shouldered Jew were obscured by his pince-nez, but he appeared to be regarding Grauber with deferential attention, while Karl's dour, bony face was even more forbidding than that of his master. It was quite clear that no help could be expected from either of them, while however loud he might yell for help it was most unlikely that anyone outside would hear him, as the house was some distance from the road.

His racing brain flirted for a moment with the idea of making a bid for liberty, but he realized that as his hands were still tied behind his back it would be impossible for him to turn the knob of the door. The big windows behind him were heavily curtained. They were probably fitted with additional black-out curtains behind those he could see, and he had no idea which, if any, of them were open. It was equally hopeless, therefore, to contemplate making a dash for one of them in an attempt to throw himself out into the garden.

There are limits to human endurance, and although Gregory was more than normally stout-hearted he knew that a burning cigar-end placed against one of his eyeballs would make him scream and whimper like a child. Such agony, he felt sure, would reduce him to a state in which he would give anything away rather than continue to endure it and lose the sight of his other eye.

Grauber had been regarding him intently. After a moment he seemed to have summed up Gregory's reactions accurately, since he said: "*So!* You are prepared to talk?"

H

"Yes," Gregory admitted reluctantly. "I don't see the point of having my eyes burnt out if I can prevent it. You're quite right about there being an anti-Nazi movement in Germany; I was sent out to try to assess its strength and possibilities. The British Government are naturally anxious to encourage it as far as they can, even if it only leads to a certain amount of sabotage and necessitates reserved troops being kept from the Front to police the big cities. I was given Rheinhardt's name and that was all I had to go on.

"From Rheinhardt I learned of Wachmuller and I was just on the point of finding out a little more about the Movement from him when one of your idiot storm-troopers shot him dead. You know what happened after that. I was exceedingly lucky to escape from Germany, but I had to come home with my tail between my legs and I don't know a thing more about the business than when I started. That's the truth."

"Plausible, Mr. Sallust—but unsatisfactory. Even the British Government could not have been so stupid as to send you out to Germany on quite such a slender trail. There must have been other people besides Rheinhardt whom they intended you to contact if you had not had to make a bolt for it after enjoying our beautiful Rhineland scenery for only four days. Do you give me the names of these others, or do I apply the end of my cigar to one of your eyes?"

"Damn it! I'm speaking the truth, I tell you!" Gregory exclaimed. He knew how weak his statement must sound, and was sick with the thought of what the German might do to him in an effort to extract further information, which he would be utterly unable to give for the simple reason that he did not possess it.

Grauber stood up slowly and advanced with a mincing step until he was standing beside Gregory, who got a whiff of some sickly scent the German was using. For a full minute he said nothing, but gazed down into Gregory's face with his curiously light eyes while he significantly twiddled the cigar.

At last he spoke. "It is unfortunate, Mr. Sallust, that only by applying a very stringent test of your veracity can I ascertain whether or no you are speaking the truth. If you still maintain that you know nothing more when both your eyeballs are charred I shall have to accept your statement, but I should be failing in my duty were I to neglect any measure which might induce you to remember a little more."

With a swift, unexpected movement he jabbed the cigar

lightly at Gregory's right eye, brushing its ash off on the eyelid, so that although Gregory was not burnt he felt the heat of the glowing end as he jerked back in his chair.

"Stop that, you swine!" cried Archer in a sudden effort to intervene. "He's speaking the truth; he doesn't know a thing."

The Gestapo chief turned to stare at the Marxist. "I told you to remain silent," he commented icily.

"Is it likely that I'm going to sit here saying nothing while I watch you torturing a defenceless man? He's a secret agent, all right, but a damned bad one! And if you were to roast him alive over a slow fire he still couldn't tell you anything."

"You say that to try to save him."

"I say it because I know what I'm talking about. He came to see me with the idea that I might be able to put him on to something, but after mentioning the names of those two Germans you spoke of just now he petered out. If he'd known the names of any others, wouldn't he have mentioned them too, hoping to strike one with whom I might have had some dealings in the past? Of course he would. But he didn't. You won't get any more out of him whatever you do."

"*Warten Sie einen Augenblick!*" Grauber began to pace up and down as he went on thoughtfully: "I have not yet had time to consider what part you play in this. Let us think about that a little and put two and two together before depriving Mr. Sallust of his eyesight.

"When I heard that he had gone down to see you I naturally concluded that you were working together and that his visit was for the purpose of letting you know how some of your friends in Germany were getting on. Apparently I was wrong. You tell me now that, on the contrary, he came to you for the purpose of obtaining information about those Comrades of yours. Did he get it?"

"No, he didn't. I don't know any more than he does about this Movement you speak of."

"Yet Rosenbaum tells me that the gang of thugs he employed at my suggestion caught you carrying Mr. Sallust, gagged and bound, down to the dock-side with the evident intention of murdering him. Tell me, please; why should you suddenly decide to do that?"

"That's none of your business. It was purely a Party matter. We're on one side of the fence and since he's an agent of the Capitalist Government he's on the other. He'd have sabotaged our organization if we'd let him go, so we made up our minds to put him out of the way."

"Forgive me, Mr. Archer, if I say that I find your explanation rather thin. In Germany, in Russia, in many other countries Party hatreds are carried to such lengths, but in Britain—no. In this country people do not commit murder from political motives, however bitterly they may feel about their opponents." Grauber paused for a moment, while his pale eyes flickered from one to the other of his prisoners. "I wonder if either of you have any papers on you which might throw some light upon this interesting matter ? Rosenbaum, search them both."

While Grauber continued to pad softly up and down the elderly Jew ran through Gregory's pockets, drawing a complete blank. From Archer, however, he removed a miscellaneous collection of articles amongst which was the faked photograph.

Immediately Grauber saw the photograph he began to snigger. "What a pretty picture, and what a find ! I will see to it that this is reproduced and circulated so that the Marxist leaders in other countries can see how the English leaders of the working-class movement really live."

"It's a fake," growled Archer. "The girl's my ward and I've never set a finger on her in my life. She's a mannequin. That's how they got that picture of her in her underclothes, and the filthy skunks imposed it with one of me on that bedroom-scene background."

"The filthy skunks to whom you refer are, of course, Mr. Sallust and his friends ?"

"Yes. A pretty example of how the high-principled British Government goes to work. When all else fails they even stoop to blackmail."

"I begin to see daylight," murmured Grauber meditatively. "Mr. Sallust arrives at your house this evening and asks you for certain information regarding your friends abroad. When you refuse to give it he produces this very cleverly faked photograph and threatens to circulate it among your associates. That, of course, provides an adequate motive for your deciding to murder him. Let us suppose that you pretend to give way and promise to take him to some place where he will get the information that he requires. Thus you succeed in luring him down to the docks where you can have him quietly eliminated."

"One up to you," said Gregory. "Now you know exactly what happened and I hope you're satisfied."

"But I am not satisfied. Mr. Archer is an important figure in Britain's national life, so naturally our agents here took the trouble to collect a lot of data about him before the war. When one of Rosenbaum's people telephoned to say that you were at his house to-night I had his dossier turned up and found from it that, apart from his misguided political beliefs, Mr. Archer is a man of extremely high principles. I do not believe that he would soil his hands with murder from any purely personal motive. What, then, could his motive have been ? Was it, perhaps, that your blackmail succeeded ? That in a moment of weakness he gave you the information you required but later decided that he would murder you to prevent your making use of it ?"

"Nonsense," rumbled Archer. "I've told you already that I had no information to give."

Herr Grauber shook his head. "The more I think about it the less I am inclined to believe that. As an International Marxist of such extremely Left-Wing tendencies that even the official British Communists refuse to have anything to do with you, you must have connections with the leaders of subversive movements all over the world. Many of those in Germany would quite definitely be known to you. To protect yourself from the attentions of Scotland Yard you must have secret methods of communicating with your friends abroad ; you would need them even in normal times. It is therefore reasonable to suppose that although our countries are now at war such lines of communication are still open.

"Let us consider the situation a little further. Mr. Sallust is sent to Germany by the British Government to make any trouble that he can for the German Government. He tells us that he has, had to return without having fulfilled his mission. When he gets back, what does he do ? He says to himself : 'I have made a mess of things and I have blotted my copybook by getting Wachmuller—who was the only lead to this conspiracy that I had—killed. As I am a tenacious person, however, I am determined to have another go ; I must therefore get some more leads. Comrade Archer must be in touch with all the principal German Anarchists, so I will go and see him and I will either persuade or force him to give me some more names to work on.' "

Gregory lowered his eyes. It was extraordinarily interesting to follow Herr Grauber's mental processes, but the German was now getting too near the truth for comfort and Gregory had begun to fear that the outcome of his deliberations might prove most unpleasant for Archer and himself.

Still padding up and down Grauber went on in his high, piping voice : "Let us for a moment put ourselves in the place of Comrade Archer. When he learns Mr. Sallust's business with him he is anything but pleased and he stoutly refuses to give the information required, his reason for doing so being that he has no love for Government agents and is greatly alarmed for his German friends. He may or may not know that Mr. Sallust's first visit to Germany had had such disastrous consequences for those with whom he got into touch there, but he has in any case no confidence in the tact and discretion of British secret agents. He is afraid that if he tells Mr. Sallust the names of his friends in Berlin, Hamburg, the Ruhr and other manufacturing centres where the discontented are most numerous, Mr. Sallust will go blundering in like your proverbial bull in a china-shop and get those friends shot-up by my colleagues of the Gestapo.

"In the end, however, Comrade Archer is forced to give the names of certain of his friends by Mr. Sallust's threatening to use this pretty photograph, but a little later he regrets having been panicked into doing so and decides that rather than risk his friends being given away to the Gestapo through Mr. Sallust's stupidity he will eliminate Mr. Sallust. That, I think, is the real situation."

"The theory's sound enough," said Gregory, "but the facts are entirely wrong. I did exert pressure on Archer but he refused to tell me anything and convinced me that he could not do so only because there was nothing that he could tell."

Herr Grauber shook his head. "I do not believe that, but as it happens the point is quite immaterial. Whether he decided to murder you because he had given you information which he did not wish you to use or because he would stop at nothing to prevent your circulating this interesting photograph no longer interests me. One fact—one fact, Mr. Sallust—now emerges to me with perfect clarity. Such photographs as this cost time, trouble and money to make, for unless they are supremely well done it can easily be detected that they are faked. If you were only trying Comrade Archer as a shot in the dark you would never have undertaken such elaborate preparations in order to blackmail him. You did so only because you already *knew*, from facts which you had secured from some other source, that he could tell you what you wanted to know.

"Whether he actually told you anything or not does not now concern me at all. It is clear to me that Comrade Archer has information which it was worth your while to take a great deal of trouble to try to obtain. That being so he has information which it would—in other circumstances—be worth while for me also to go to a great deal of trouble to obtain. As it is, I am in the fortunate position of not having to bother to employ experts to fake photographs. Why should I waste my good cigar on your eyes, Mr. Sallust, when Comrade Archer's eyes are equally close at hand?"

"You swine!" said Gregory.

"You are ungrateful, Mr. Sallust. You owe it to my excellent reasoning powers that I do not propose to devote any more time to you now that I find I can tap the actual source of the information that you sought. After all, it is to that that you will owe the preservation of your sight—for a little while, at all events."

"What the hell d'you mean?"

"My friend, do not pretend to be more stupid than you are. Having caught you, is it likely that I would let you go? It is true that you committed many stupid blunders while you were in Germany, but even during your blundering you succeeded in killing quite a number of my subordinates; useful men who had considerable training in their work. If I released you you might be crazy enough to go back to Germany and kill others before you yourself were finally caught and shot. Besides, I would not like my charming host, the little Jacob here, who accommodates me so comfortably during my stays in London, to be inconvenienced by a visit from your police.

"And do you think that I would ever have told you of the method by which we traced you through the Dutch passport office if I had thought for one moment that you might live to use that information to make trouble for our Dutch friends? No, no. One of the advantages of my friend Rosenbaum's house is that it has a laboratory. In that laboratory there is an acid tank; a piece of equipment most useful to a scientist, but very useful also for disposing of bodies without trace. When I have done with you and Comrade Archer the acid bath will seal the lips of both you for good. Now, as I like to be alone when carrying out experiments to discover the amount of pain which a human being can bear before the will is broken down, I will excuse you for the time being.   Rosenbaum, I hope you have a good dinner for me. Go and see that nothing is lacking. Karl, take Mr. Sallust to the laboratory."

Karl advanced, took Gregory by his collar and hauled him to his feet ; then drew an automatic and signed with it for his prisoner to precede him towards a low door at the far end of the room, under the minstrels' gallery.

Gregory looked down at Archer. His big face had gone very white and little beads of perspiration already covered his brow.

"I'm terribly sorry for this, Archer," he said. "I don't bear any resentment now because you tried to do me in, and I only wish that I knew of some way to help you."

"Thanks," Archer muttered. "It wasn't your fault, I suppose. You were only doing your blasted job and trying to find out what you could. They—they can only kill us once, though."

Gregory turned to look at the Gestapo chief. "As for you," he said, "your turn will come, my friend ; you may be sure of that. Your boss has bitten off more than he can chew. Germany can't smash the British Empire, and sooner or later—it may be in one year or it may be in five—Germany's going to crack. When she does the German people are going to skin you and your kind alive. Just remember that."

Grauber smiled back quite pleasantly. "I'm afraid you have sadly neglected your opportunities of forming a true estimate of Nazi Germany, Mr. Sallust. The Third Reich is being rebuilt through the Nazi Youth Organizations and the purification of the race. To-day all that is best in my country is due to the spread of National Socialist ideology. It is a power greater than Christianity, and by it Germany will not only conquer but will go on to wider triumphs. For a long time past we have been laying the foundations of a Germany that will be the dominating force in Europe, and therefore in the world, for at least a thousand years. It is because you have so foolishly tried to obstruct the progress of this great world-force that you have to die. You must think of yourself as an insect, Mr. Sallust ; an insect vainly posturing in the path of a steam-roller. And now, if you will please walk in front of Karl, I will come when I have done with Comrade Archer and see you put in your last bath."

There was nothing for it. If Gregory used his legs he knew that Karl would use his gun, and to be shot like a rat at Grauber's feet could neither save Archer nor serve any other useful purpose. While there was life there was still hope, so he turned and walked towards the low door with the gunman-servant just behind him.

Gregory hoped that to reach the laboratory they would have to cross some part of the garden, where the darkness might once more serve as his friend. He would have to risk a bullet in the back, but that would be better than the certainty of a hideous death in the acid bath, and there was just a chance that he might be able to escape owing to the black-out. But he was doomed to disappointment. They went down a long passage and through a door on the right near its end into the laboratory. Karl shepherded him across it and into a further, cell-like room without windows or furniture, where he told him to sit on the floor.

"Look here !" said Gregory quickly, "if you go on with this game the British Intelligence people are certain to get you before long. When they do, you won't stand an earthly. They'll lead you out one cold morning down at the Tower of London just as they did Roger Casement and quite a number of other people during the last war. You'll have to face a firing-squad, and that's not a pleasant finish. I can protect you from that and guarantee that no harm shall come to you, if you'll put away that gun and let me out of here."

"Save your breath, man," Karl laughed grimly. "D'you think I want Herr Grauber to use the end of his cigar on me ?"

"You could come with me. In ten minutes we'd be back here with the police and it'd be Grauber, not you, who'd have to face the firing-squad at the Tower."

"You're wasting your breath, I tell you. Sit down, unless you want me to smash your face in with this gun."

"Why be a fool ?" urged Gregory.. "I tell you I could get you police protection. What's more,. I'll pay you a thousand pounds to compensate you for the loss of your job."

Karl's only reply was to hit him a sudden, vicious blow in the pit of the stomach which winded him and doubled him up. Next moment the German had kicked his legs from under him so that he fell backwards on the floor, bumping his head sharply on the concrete.

While he was still writhing in agony and half-dazed from the blow on the back of his head Karl pocketed his automatic, pulled out a length of whip-cord and tied his ankles together. Then, pulling the end of the cord up behind Gregory's legs, he tied it

to the other cord which bound his wrists behind his back, so that
he was bent almost double and could hardly move without
suffering acute pain.

Switching off the lights, Karl closed the door and left him.
As Gregory heard the key turn in the heavy lock he knew that
his last chance had gone, and he began to wonder whether
Grauber had sufficient mercy in his make-up to kill him before
plunging him into the burning acid.

Chapter XX

THE SILENT HOUSE

AS he lay there in the dark on the hard, concrete floor, his legs bent back behind him and the cords cutting into his . wrists and ankles at the smallest movement, he made a great effort to think coherently.

With the failure of his attempt to bribe Karl it really seemed that his number was up. There was, of course, always the chance of a raid by M.I.5. During the last hour he had been constantly having to remind himself that he was not in Germany but in London, his own home town. The British counter-espionage system was extraordinarily efficient, as Gregory knew from Sir Pellinore's frequent remarks on the subject. Nearly all the known secret agents of Germany in Britain had been caught and interned within forty-eight hours of the outbreak of war, and the spy-hunters had been at their work night and day ever since, raiding suspected premises, searching files, bringing in suspects for examination and following up the thousand-and-one suspicious circumstances reported by the police and the public.

Every week the meshes of their net became finer, making it ever more difficult for enemy agents to operate, or even to remain in hiding, without being detected. The National Register had been taken on the previous Friday, and the one thing that could be said in favour of an early introduction of the rationing-system based upon it was that it would be of tremendous help to the police in checking-up on the activities of the whole population, for enemy agents who had not succeeded in procuring ration-cards for themselves would not be able to live in hotels or lodging-houses. The keepers of such places would naturally become suspicious of any guest who refused to produce a card and had all meals outside, so that enemy agents would have to depend, for accommodation at least, upon householders who were also in the pay of the enemy.

Perhaps a squad of hefty fellows from the Special Branch was even now on its way through the darkened streets to Mr.

Jacob Rosenbaum's house in Hampstead. Grauber might be a very clever fellow and his English practically beyond reproach, but he could not altogether alter his very definitely Germanic appearance. Neighbours might have seen him leaving and entering the house and have reported their suspicions to the police ; the authorities had asked that every citizen should report any circumstances which might strike him as at all suspicious. During the last war Scotland Yard had received four hundred telephone-calls a day of such a nature. The great majority had concerned harmless neutrals and were due to spy-mania or excess of zeal, but a considerable percentage had led to arrests and finally to an almost complete black-out of enemy espionage in Great Britain. To bring that about once more the Yard men were perfectly willing to spend hundreds of hours investigating baseless rumours as a necessary corollary of the achievement of the desired end.

It was quite possible, therefore, that some zealous citizen might have reported Grauber as a suspect, or even if he came and went by night that they might have turned their attention to Karl, the German servant, who appeared to be Rosenbaum's man and a permanency.

Having got so far, Gregory groaned and eased his position by turning over on his side a little more. There was no doubt that Rosenbaum and Co. would be caught sooner or later, but the war was young yet and Britain's counter-espionage people were up against a problem with which they had never before had to deal : the thousands and tens of thousands of refugees from Germany, Austria, Czechoslovakia and Poland. Ninety-nine out of every hundred of these poor people were genuine victims of Nazi oppression to whom Britain, with generous hospitality, was giving the protection of her shores, but one in every hundred, if not considerably more, was an enemy agent who had been deliberately planted. It must have been the easiest thing in the world for the Gestapo to have picked certain of their own men, brought faked charges against them, raided their houses, confiscated their goods, thrown them into concentration-camps and apparently persecuted them unmercifully ; all with their own consent and in order to provide them with genuine histories against the time when their escape could be arranged for and they could take refuge in friendly Britain and begin their treacherous work. There must, moreover, be thousands among these refugees who had themselves escaped, but who still had relations and friends inside the Reich through whom the Gestapo could bring pressure to bear upon them to betray the country which was affording them hospitality.

North-West London, in particular, was now almost a foreign colony owing to this influx of refugees, so why should Rosenbaum's house be suspect, any more than a dozen others in the same road?

Gregory forced himself to face the facts. The chances of a police raid in the next half-hour were about as slender as those of Hitler's being assassinated within the same period. Things looked just as black as they could, he realized, and regretfully decided that he was for it this time.

At that moment he heard the first faint, whimpering cry. It came down the long passage, very thin but clear in the silence of the night, and the hair prickled upon Gregory's scalp as he heard it. That fiend Grauber was torturing poor Archer.

The sound came again; a long, wailing cry like that of an animal in pain. Gregory tried desperately to shut his ears to it and would have stopped them with his fingers had he been able, but as it was he had to lie there listening. It seemed a brutal thought, but for a moment he hoped that the frightful groaning which now came at regular intervals might grow loud enough to be heard by someone outside the house; an air-raid warden, perhaps, out on his rounds to see that all windows were properly curtained, or a late worker making his cautious way home through the black-out. But he knew that the house was big, solidly built and set well back from the road. The sounds of Archer's torment were carried to him under the cracks of the intervening doors and through their key-holes, but would never be heard outside.

He began to think again of the death which Grauber had planned for him. How like the thoroughgoing German mentality it was to choose a hide-out which had a laboratory containing an acid bath; the one perfect means of disposing entirely of human bodies. Even a big furnace would leave pieces of charred bone; but the acid would eat away bone as well as flesh, dissolving the body into its original components without leaving a single trace that it had ever existed.

How long he had been lying there Gregory did not know. It seemed to him that he had been in that black, cold cell for the whole night, but he knew that in such a situation every moment spun itself out interminably and that, in fact, he had probably been there no more than half an hour before those ghastly, sickening sounds faded into silence.

Straining his ears afresh he listened, knowing that the sands of his life were even now running out. Once Grauber had extorted from Archer the information he required there could remain no reason for his delaying further the elimination of his two prisoners.

Suddenly Gregory caught the sound of approaching footfalls ; faint at first as they came down the corridor ; louder as they entered the laboratory. A firm, heavy tread was interspersed by an uneven shuffling ; then a low moan penetrated to the cell.

Next moment the door was thrown open. By the light from the laboratory he caught one glimpse of Archer. Even in the shadow of the doorway he could see that his face was distorted with pain and covered with blood. Karl stood behind him, half-supporting him by a firm grip on his collar. As he released it Archer toppled forward and fell with a groan upon the concrete floor beside Gregory.

Gregory expected to see Grauber and the Jew behind Karl, but they were not with him. Karl stooped to examine Archer, who now lay upon the floor whimpering and only half-conscious. With quick fingers he tugged at the cords which still bound his hands behind his back, and finding them firm apparently decided that it was not worth while to re-tie his ankles. As he stood erect he said to Gregory :

"Herr Grauber told me to tell you that he now gives you a chance to learn from Mr. Archer all those things in which you are so interested. He himself now eats his evening meal. When he has finished he will come to watch me put an end to the two of you. *Heil Hitler !*" With a contemptuous snort the ghoulish German slammed and re-locked the door.

"Archer !" said Gregory as Karl's footsteps faded ; "Archer, can you hear me ?"

The only response was a low groan. Archer was evidently suffering too much agony or was too bemused to talk. He rocked himself gently backwards and forwards on the floor, moaning like a child. Trussed as he was, Gregory could do nothing but lie there and listen, his heart sick within him.

After a while Archer began to mutter incoherently to himself, and Gregory strained his ears in an attempt to catch the sense of what he was saying. It seemed that the unfortunate man was raving about the Nazis and praying to the God whom as a professed Atheist he had denied and scorned since his childhood, and had often described as a fiction invented by the priests for the enslavement of the workers, to bring the vengeance of Heaven upon his tormentors.

In the presence of so complete a breakdown Gregory temporarily forgot his own anxieties. "Archer ! Archer, old chap !" he said loudly, in an effort to comfort him, "it must have been hell, but as far as you're concerned the worst's over now. Try to fix your mind on your wife or count sheep or think of any damned thing except the pain you're feeling ; that may help just a little."

Evidently his words penetrated Archer's pain-racked mind, for the Marxist suddenly stopped his muttering and said slowly but distinctly : "You must get out of here. You must get out of here and warn them !"

Gregory knew only too well how impossible it was to do as Archer implored him, but he did not say so. Instead he inquired sharply, to concentrate the half-unconscious man's attention : "Warn whom ?"

"Warn Madame—Madame Dubois that . . ." Archer gasped ; then fell suddenly silent and rolled over.

At first Gregory thought he had fainted, but after he had waited some minutes for him to come round and Archer still made no movement he wriggled himself painfully across the floor and began to kick the Marxist gently with his bound feet in an effort to rouse him.

Archer neither stirred nor made the slightest sound. Gregory lay still again and listened intently for his breathing. There was no sound ; a strained, uncanny silence filled the cell. Gregory knew then that Archer was dead, killed by shock or a weak heart. Whatever the reason, the thing that lay there in the darkness was a still warm but lifeless corpse.

The advent of poor, tortured Archer had distracted Gregory's thoughts for a little while from his own desperate situation, but Archer was out of it now. Those fiends could inflict no more suffering upon him. Perhaps he was lucky ; he had at least escaped the additional torment of strangulation or worse. Gregory was torn by a dreadful fear that the sadistic Gestapo chief would not even afford him the mercy of a comparatively swift death, but would have him plunged alive into the burning acid. Grauber would not be able to use a pistol for fear that its report might attract the attention of someone outside the house, but if he had one streak of humanity in his make-up he would have Gregory either strangled or bramed with a pistol-butt rather than subject him to the unimaginable torment of being eaten away piecemeal by the corrosive fluid.

Sweating with fear and suspense Gregory lay there, wondering how long Grauber would take over his supper. Half an hour or less would probably suffice most people in such circumstances, but Grauber was not the man to be hurried when all the cards were in his hand. For all his sadistic beastliness he was not the coarse, rough-neck type of German that wolfs down a meal sufficient for six ordinary people in as many minutes. The feline step, the fastidiously chosen, well-cut clothes which concealed the powerful muscles of his big body, the scent he used and the mental gymnastics of which he was capable all proclaimed him to be that rare phenomenon, the cultured German who has all the instincts of the brute and is vicious to the core.

Cultured people do not as a rule wolf their food or swig vast quantities of beer, and Grauber was probably feeding on the best cold delicacies that Fortnum and Mason could produce and washing them down with a bottle of *Auslese* Hock which would not have disgraced the cellars of Sir Pellinore. He would doubtless linger deliberately over the excellent food and wine that Rosenbaum would certainly have provided for him, with the intention of inflicting as much mental torture as possible upon his victims before coming to see them murdered.

All at once the fluctuating wail of a siren pierced the silence. Instinctively Gregory tried to sit up, and at the jerk the cords binding his wrists and ankles cut sharply into his flesh. It was an air-raid warning ; there could be no doubt about that. The high note warbled insistently, urging the people of Hampstead to leave the streets or their beds and get down into the shelters.

The sound was like music to Gregory's ears. Anything might happen in an air-raid ; a bomb might even wreck the building in which he was lying and leave him, unharmed or only wounded, to be found by the rescue-squads. If there was no air-raid shelter in the house Grauber, Rosenbaum and Karl might leave it for the nearest public shelter, and if they did they might be delayed in returning or do something to arouse the suspicions of the A.R.P. wardens or of the others with whom they took shelter. At least the warning might afford him an hour or so's postponement of sentence, and every extra moment of life was precious in that it gave him just a fraction more hope of the occurrence of some miracle which might enable him to escape death.

The siren was still sounding when he heard fresh footsteps hastening along the corridor. Once more his heart sank. Many people were now openly declaring that they did not intend to take refuge in a shelter until they actually heard the anti-aircraft guns firing ; a crazy piece of foolishness since if, as was probable, the Germans were to come over very high they would be able to release their cargoes before the guns could locate them, so that the first indication of their presence over any particular area would be the bursting of the bombs.

Perhaps Grauber and Co. were of that school of thought. In any case it was reasonable to suppose that there would be some ten minutes' respite between the giving of the warning and the arrival over London of enemy aircraft, and no one knew better than Gregory the amazing amount that can be done by an active man in the comparatively short space of ten minutes. It would allow ample time for Grauber to have half-a-dozen helpless men put in an acid tank, if the tank were big enough, and to reach his dug-out afterwards well before the raiders came over.

His muscles tense, his nails digging into the palms of his bound hands, Gregory waited through seconds that seemed like ages. Someone outside was fumbling with the key ; then the lock clicked back and the door was flung open. Framed in the oblong of light there stood not Grauber or Karl, but the little Jew.

The light glinted on his pince-nez ; it glinted also on something else—a long carving-knife that he held in his hand. Gregory felt his gorge rise. The little brute was going to stick him like a pig, or cut his throat. That would be less horrible than being lowered alive into a tank of acid, but he shuddered at the thought of the knife's piercing him ; not to make a mere flesh-wound such as he might have received in a dock-side brawl, but thrust right home into his vital parts.

With extraordinary quickness for a man of his years Rosenbaum flung himself forward. Gregory squirmed away but the Jew seized him by the shoulder and thrust him over on his face. He waited, bracing himself to endure the vicious stab between the shoulder-blades that would send the blood spurting up into his mouth. The sweat was streaming in rivulets down his temples. He wanted to cry out, but no sound issued from his throat.

Suddenly the siren ceased its wailing and as from a great distance he heard Rosenbaum's voice. "The air-raid warning has saved you," he said. Then Gregory realized that he was hacking with the knife at the cords that bound him.

"That, and the fact that Grauber is terrified of bombs,"

Rosenbaum went on, panting as he worked. "He and Karl dashed out to the car. By now they will have run it into the big garage at the bottom of the road and will be taking refuge in the deep air-raid shelter on the corner there."

"Oh, thank God! Thank God!" Gregory breathed, almost unable to believe in his good luck. His limbs now freed he struggled to his feet and added : "But I owe my life to you."

"Yes. Grauber sent me to put you both in the tank while he fled to safety," Rosenbaum muttered, as he turned to cut the cords that bound Archer's still hands.

"It's useless to do that," said Gregory ; "the poor fellow's dead." Although he was quite certain of it he leaned over and verified his statement by feeling Archer's heart. It was absolutely still.

Rosenbaum groaned. "The horror of it ! The horror of it ! And in my own house. But what could I do ?"

"I suppose Grauber's got you under his thunb ?" asked Gregory quickly.

"Yes. My brother—my twin brother, who is my other self— is in Germany. He is in a concentration-camp, but as long as I serve them he lives in reasonable comfort. If I refuse, they have promised that he will have a lingering death. They say that they will beat him with flexible steel rods for two minutes every day until he dies." Suddenly the elderly Jew began to sob.

"Steady, now !" Gregory laid a comforting hand upon his shoulder, but the little man went on, sobbing out in gasping breaths :

"England is the country of my adoption. I was naturalized many years ago, and since then I have always thought of England as my country. I love her and would give every penny I possess to help her in her war against these brute beasts. But what could I do—what could I do ? At first I refused to help them, but they cut off my brother's little finger with his signet-ring upon it and brought it to me. Grauber brought it. 'A present for you, my little Jacob,' he said, and handed me a jeweller's box. I opened it, and there was my brother's finger, lying upon white velvet. I have no wife, no children. My brother is everything to me, and although we lived in different countries we have travelled thousands of miles in the last forty years so that we might be together for at least a few days in every month.

"That is why I have a laboratory here. He is an analytical chemist and I built it so that his visits to me should interfere as little as possible with his work. Even during the last war we used to meet quite frequently in Holland, for money talks, you know. How could I let him be beaten to death—how could I ? Yet not only have I been forced to become a traitor but I am also made an accessory to this poor man's death. If the police catch me now they will hang me for murder."

"Steady! Steady!" Gregory tried to check the spate of words. "I haven't the least idea what view the authorities would take of your case, but 'a life for a life' is a tenet in which I believe, and since you've saved mine you can rely upon me to do everything I can to save yours."

"You mean that ? You mean that ?" Rosenbaum seized his hand and pressed it between his own. "You will give me your protection ?"

"I'll do what I can, and I think it reasonable to suppose that a court might be lenient in view of the terrible form of mental compulsion that was brought to bear on you. The Law makes a very clear distinction in such cases between a willing accomplice and one who acts only under duress, and even if you'd tried you couldn't have prevented Archer's death ; Grauber would simply have shot you too. And incidentally you saved me from a pretty sticky finish. You'll have to come clean, though, and tell us everything you know about Grauber and his friends."

"But my brother—my brother !" Rosenbaum's voice rose again in an agonized wail.

"Have you any proof at all that he's still alive ?"

"No ; only that these devils tell me so and torture me with threats of what they could do to him."

Gregory shrugged. "What reliance can you place upon their word ? In innumerable cases, for months after a Nazi victim has been dead and buried in an unknown grave, they've told his widow and friends that he was still alive and have played upon their hopes for his eventual release. That's happened with thousands of people. Your brother may already have been dead for weeks. On the other hand, if he's still alive he may quite possibly survive until the war is over. Nothing that you can do will help him if he's dead and nothing that you can do for the Germans will ensure his better treatment. But if he *is* still alive you can shorten the length of his imprisonment by doing your best to help England win the war, because on the day she does so everyone in the German concentration-camps will be freed."

"It is true—it is true what you say, yet never before had I thought of it like that. All right, then ; tell me what I must do."

Suddenly the air-raid siren shrieked again with a long, steady blast, giving the all-clear signal. Apparently the raid had been merely a false alarm, or the raiders had been driven back before crossing the shore. Barely two minutes had elapsed since its first warbling note had ceased and the Jew had begun to babble out his confession.

"Quick !" cried Gregory. "Grauber will be coming back. Got a gun ?"

Rosenbaum shook his head. "No ; but there is no need for one."

"I'd give a packet to meet him with an automatic in my hand," Gregory snarled, "but as I'm not armed and he is I'm not going to chance running into him again just yet. We must get out of this !"

"He will not come back. It was to see you that he came over to London. He got what he wanted out of Archer and he had just finished his supper when the air-raid warning went. Karl packed his bag for him while he was feeding and it was all ready for him in the hall. Karl also telephoned after he had packed, making arrangements for him to leave England secretly to-night. As he left the house Grauber snatched up his bag and ran out with it. Now that the all-clear has gone he has nothing to come back here for and will by now be on his way to the coast."

Thrusting Rosenbaum before him Gregory strode into the laboratory, saying swiftly : "Nevertheless, I'm not taking any chances. If he's got half an hour to spare he may come back just to enjoy the fun of seeing me put into that acid bath. If you don't mind, we'll continue our conversation in the garden—near one of the doors to the street for preference—so that we can slip away into the darkness if necessary."

"Perhaps that would be best." Rosenbaum turned, locked the door of the cell and put the key in his pocket, did the same at the door of the laboratory and led Gregory out through a side-entrance into the open air.

It was very dark out there ; pitch-black after the bright lights of the laboratory. They stumbled forward, Rosenbaum leading, until they reached the even blacker shadows cast by a wall and the tall bushes on either side of a path running straight to it. Rosenbaum took out a cigarette-lighter and flicked it on, revealing a door in the wall which was evidently the tradesmen's entrance. He unlatched it and drew it a few inches open as he said :

"You can slip out of here to the street if Grauber does come back."

"That's better. And what about Karl? Is he returning to Germany with Grauber?"

"No, no. Karl is a permanent agent here. He is a German who took out British naturalization papers some two years ago. They forced me to sack my own servants and take him into my house three months before the war. He is supposed to be my butler-valet, but it is he who makes me clean his boots and make his bed while he sits about all day doing nothing. The house is in a shocking state, as they will only allow me to have a woman in twice a week to clean the big room you saw and my bedroom, in which Grauber sleeps when he stays here."

"Karl will be back for certain then, and he's got a gun."

"Not before morning; he will have to drive Grauber to the coast or wherever they go when Grauber leaves England secretly."

"You don't know where that is?"

"No. I only know that it used to take Karl about five hours whenever he went to meet Grauber or take him on the first part of his journey home. That was before the war, though; in this black-out the journey will take much longer."

"D'you mean that Grauber came and went in secret even before war was declared?" Gregory asked. "Why was that? He would have got into serious trouble if he'd been caught, and in any case it must have cost him a lot of unnecessary inconvenience."

"I think he preferred to do so to avoid becoming known by sight to the passport people at Dover and Harwich."

"I see. Of course, anyone could spot that he's a German. If I'd been a policeman in that A.R.P. dug-out he went to I'd certainly have asked to see his papers or some proof of his identity."

Rosenbaum shook his head. "That would not have done any good. He carries a Dutch passport and it is all in order. He speaks Dutch very fluently, too, so although the police might guess by his appearance that he was a foreigner they would find it very difficult to prove that he was a German. He is a marvellous linguist. You heard how he spoke English with less accent than myself, although I have lived here for over forty years, and he speaks French and Italian just as fluently."

"Altogether, a thoroughly dangerous customer," said Gregory. "Well, we'll see if we can't provide him with a nice little surprise next time he visits England—and you're going to help us."

"You really think, then, that the police will overlook my —my . . ."

"They'd be fools if they didn't, as you're the only person who can enable them to catch him."

"What am I to do?"

"How do you propose to account to Karl for the fact that my body's not in the acid tank when he gets back to-morrow?"

"That should not be difficult. As Grauber was running from the house he told me to put both you and Archer in the bath. It has a lid which clamps down, and as they are so sure of me Karl may not even take the trouble to unscrew it and look inside. The tank is narrow but deep, and if I had done as Grauber ordered I would have placed you in it one on top of the other. If I put Archer's body into the bath now Karl will see it if he looks in and will imagine you to be lying underneath."

The thought of allowing Archer's body to be eaten away by acid was a repellent one, but Gregory knew that he must not be squeamish over trifles. There was a war on in which thousands of people were dying every day. What did it matter what happened to a single corpse? The important thing was to catch Grauber, and in order to do so it was essential that Rosenbaum should not be suspected of having double-crossed the Gestapo. Archer had not served his country while he was alive, but he could do so now that he was dead, and it was upon this thought that Gregory said:

"That's right. Put him in the tank. Then you're to carry on here just as though nothing had happened. To-morrow I'll get in touch with you again."

"That would be most unwise. I am in any case almost a recluse, and for the last few months Karl has made me take steps to prevent even the few friends that I have coming here. A telephone-call would be certain to arouse his suspicions. It would be much safer for me to get into touch with you when I am away from the house."

"All right; you know my name and you'll find me in the 'phone book: Gregory Sallust, 272 Gloucester Road. We must try and fix a meeting as soon as possible, though, because I want to hear every detail that you can give me about Grauber and Karl. Could you manage anything to-morrow?"

"Yes. They have to let me go into the City every day, otherwise my absence from my office would excite comment. I dare not see you there because Grauber has planted a German refugee on my staff to watch me, but I have an appointment to see my lawyer at eleven-thirty to-morrow morning, and instead of going to his office I could meet you."

"Right. Where are your offices?"

"My firm is Rosenbaum and Schmelling, Tea Importers, of Mincing Lane."

"And where does your lawyer live?"

"His name is Reuben Sonnenschein and his office is in Norfolk Street, Strand."

"Good. In case they're watching you we'll meet in that neighbourhood; then they'll see that you start from your office in the right direction, at all events. Walk down to Mark Lane Underground station and take a ticket for the Temple, but as soon as you get into the station slip downstairs at a run and nip into the first east-bound train so as to lose anyone who may be trailing you. Get out at the first stop and change into a west-bound train which will bring you back to Mark Lane and on to the Temple. Get out there and take a taxi to the Strand Palace Hotel; there's nothing like doing one's business in a crowd if one wants to avoid observation. I'll meet you there at eleven-thirty sharp."

"All right, Mr. Sallust, I will do just as you say. Thank you—thank you a thousand times—for the way you have treated me. You have given me new hope; new life. In spite of all that I have done I feel that I may now hold up my head again."

"It's for me to thank you," replied Gregory, smiling in the darkness. "We'll meet to-morrow, then. Good night."

He had hardly stepped through the side-door when he suddenly pulled up short. "By-the-bye, I hate to bother you but could you lend me five bob for a taxi? Archer and his friends stripped me of every cent I had on me."

"Of course." Rosenbaum slipped his hand into his pocket and passed over two half-crowns. With a cheerful: "Thanks; I'll repay you in the morning," Gregory left him.

When he reached the road he realized that he had quite forgotten to ask where he was, but as the van which had brought him there had come uphill he turned downhill, knowing that Central London must lie in that direction. At the bottom of the hill he asked his way of a policeman and found that the next turning to the left would bring him into the Finchley Road, so he strode on in the hope of finding a taxi.

The increase of the petrol-ration from two to three gallons a day per cab had materially improved the situation for the taximen, but despite this most cabs were now out of petrol by ten o'clock at night, and between the great exodus from London and the black-out, which kept many people indoors, there was in any case little night-life to justify taxis remaining on the street after midnight. Thus every rank he passed was empty and he had a two-mile walk before he managed to pick up a cab just north of Baker Street.

By the time he got home he was feeling the strain of his long, amazingly hectic night. It was now four o'clock in the morning and it seemed unbelievable that only seven short hours before he had pulled up in a taxi outside Tom Archer's house in Kennington. So much had happened since. He had twice escaped death by the very narrowest of margins, and, as he realized when he looked at his haggard face in the bathroom mirror, the emotional strain had been tremendous.

Physically, too, he had suffered severely. His nose and upper lip were clotted with dried blood as the result of a blow that one of Archer's thugs had dealt him and he had a dozen other bruises on various parts of his body. His wrists and ankles were chafed and sore where the cords had bound them, his suit was torn and dirty and his hair dishevelled. Nevertheless he did not undress forthwith and flop into bed, for he had work to do later that day and experience had taught him that unless he did something to improve his state before going to sleep he would feel even worse when he awoke.

After turning on a hot bath he scribbled a note for Mrs. Cummins, a neighbour who had taken on the care of Rudd's lodgers in his absence, asking her to call him with breakfast at ten o'clock. Having pinned it outside his door he wearily pulled off his clothes, tipped a double ration of carnation bath-essence into the warm water, washed his face with tender care and lay soaking in the bath for twenty minutes, until the pain of his bruises was considerably eased. Not until then did he dry himself, get into bed and fall sound asleep.

Next morning at eleven twenty-five, as spruce and debonair as ever save for a slightly swollen nose and left ear, both of which were extremely tender but which were not particularly obvious to any casual observer, he entered the lounge of the Strand Palace Hotel and ordered himself a coffee. While reading the war news he kept a careful look-out round the corner of his paper for the arrival of Jacob Rosenbaum.

Twenty to twelve, ten to twelve, twelve o'clock came and went, yet the little man had not put in an appearance. Gregory waited for another thirty-five minutes to make quite certain that Rosenbaum had not thought he had said half-past twelve instead of half-past eleven ; then, both annoyed and worried, he gave it up.

He thought of going to see Sir Pellinore, but decided against it. He was miserably conscious that he had once again botched matters badly and that he was responsible for Tom Archer's death. Not that Archer was any great loss to his country, but his demise had cut off yet one more line of inquiry which might have provided profitable results had it been handled in some other manner. But for the life of him Gregory could think of no other approach which would have induced Archer to give anything away, and he had at least the consolation of knowing that he had failed only where some of the best men in M.I.5 had failed before him.

In spite of Archer's attempt to murder him Gregory respected the Marxist and regarded him as a political crank rather than as an evil entity, while the manner of his death had been so appalling that Gregory felt that any crimes he had committed against the Government of his country should certainly be overlooked. Although it was almost a foregone conclusion that his Party Benevolent Fund would take care of his widow Gregory meant to ask Sir Pellinore to institute tactful inquiries and to see that something was done for her if she was not decently provided for.

All that he had to show for his evening's work, therefore, was Archer's last phrase: "You must warn Madame Dubois. But who the devil was Madame Dubois? Certainly neither a German nor, apparently, an Englishwoman, so that this scrap of a clue —if clue it was—did not seem to be a very exciting item to hand Sir Pellinore upon a platter.

If, on the other hand, he could secure from Rosenbaum every single detail that the elderly Jew could give him about Grauber's visits, and about Karl and the man whom Grauber had planted in the tea-importer's office, these trails might enable M.I.5 to locate and corner a dozen other secret agents of the enemy linked up in the same chain, and there would also be a decent possibility of snaring Grauber himself next time he came to England. Gregory felt that if he could hand on all that information Sir Pellinore might consider that he had justified his night's work even though he was no further advanced with his own mission.

He therefore decided not to see Sir Pellinore for the time being, but he was exceedingly anxious as to what had become of Rosenbaum. Had he failed to keep his appointment only because Karl or the spy in his office had proved difficult, or had he slipped up somewhere? In an endeavour to find out Gregory, giving his name as Blystein, telephoned Rosenbaum's office, only to

learn that he had not been there that morning although he had
been expected and might still come in at any time.

He next telephoned Reuben Sonnenschein, Rosenbaum's
solicitor, but drew a blank there also. Rosenbaum had certainly
had an appointment there at eleven-thirty but had not kept it.
Turning up a telephone directory Gregory found that the house
to which he had been taken on the previous night was in Maresfield Gardens, Hampstead, but he did not dare to ring Rosenbaum's
number. Very perturbed indeed, he decided that he would think
matters over during a good lunch.

After more than twenty years as *maître d'hôtel* of the Berkeley
Restaurant his good friend Filippo Ferraro had left it some
months before the war and had gone to the Mayfair. This was
not one of Gregory's usual haunts, but as he liked the service of
his meals to be supervised by people who knew his tastes he
decided to go to see Ferraro.

Beaming as ever in his new setting, with numbers of his old
clientèle around him, Ferraro gave him a royal welcome and,
without Gregory's having to bother to think for himself, suggested
just the sort of luncheon he wanted ; a luncheon which was duly
served, and eaten with considerable enjoyment. After it was
over Gregory returned to his flat in Gloucester Road and went to
bed. It was only four o'clock in the afternoon, but he knew that
he would be wise to take any sleep that he could as and when he
could get it.

At eight o'clock he had a light supper in his dressing-gown,
then dressed and went out. Securing a taxi, he told the driver
to take him to the bottom of Maresfield Gardens.

He had decided that he must find out for himself about
Rosenbaum. Time pressed, and he must not delay longer than
he could help before reporting to Sir Pellinore. Perhaps Rosenbaum's non-appearance was due merely to the poor little Jew's
having got cold feet after his burst of renewed courage early that
morning and having decided that he dared not risk meeting
Gregory in a public place. But if that was the case, why hadn't
he telephoned during the afternoon, and why hadn't he been to
his office ?

On his second visit to Maresfield Gardens Gregory went
properly equipped. His favourite Mauser automatic was in his
hip-pocket. Another pocket contained a torch and a bunch of
skeleton keys. A jemmy was stuck in the top of his trousers and
he also carried about his person a pair of compasses, with a
diamond fitted to one point and a rubber sucker fitted to the

other, for removing rounds of glass from windows without their falling and crashing on the ground. In addition he wore rubber-soled shoes and was dressed in black from top to toe, which made him practically invisible in the London that had become a city of the shadows.

He paid off the taxi at the bottom of the hill and walked up it. Arriving before the house he tiptoed quietly up the drive and paused when he came to the narrow path which branched to the left, leading through some bushes to the tradesmen's entrance.

The house was in complete darkness, but so it had been on the previous night owing to the black-out restrictions which Gregory now had no reason to bless. If he could have found a chink of light he would have been to some extent reassured, for it would have given him reason to suppose that Rosenbaum was still in residence there, but that having become thoroughly scared at the thought of what might happen to him if he was discovered with Gregory he had not only failed to keep his appointment but had stayed indoors all day into the bargain to make quite sure that Gregory would not be able to waylay him on his way back from his office. If on the other hand the house was really in darkness it would suggest that Rosenbaum had panicked and fled, or that something had gone much more seriously wrong.

With cautious tread Gregory padded from window to window along the front of the house, but still could see no gleam of light. He then returned to the side-entrance, produced his bunch of skeleton keys and after a little patience found one that turned the lock. Very gently, so that its hinges should not creak, he eased open the door ; then closed it behind him with equal care and entered the garden at the back of the house.

Here too he examined every window with the utmost care both for signs of light and in the hope of finding one open, but in neither aim was he successful. He then tiptoed forward to a pair of bay windows which gave on to the garden. Like all the others they were closed and locked; but he thought that they would offer the easiest means of breaking into the house.

For a moment he waited there, undecided. It was essential that he should find out what had happened to Rosenbaum. If he had fled the police would have to be put on to him at once so that they could get any information that he might have at the earliest possible moment, while if he had been the victim of foul play and either made a prisoner in his own house or even murdered it would be urgently necessary to free him or deal with his murderer. As against these considerations, if he broke into the place and everything was all right Karl would be there. It was true that with luck he would have the drop on Karl this time, and unless Karl put his great, clumsy hands above his head within ten seconds Gregory meant to ensure him an extremely painful death by putting three bullets in rapid succession into his stomach ; but if he was forced to kill Karl or even capture him, bang would go any chance of catching Grauber on his next visit to England, and Grauber was the big fish.

There was of course always the chance that in breaking into the house he might alarm its inmates before he could catch them unawares, or that in the garden, where it was so dark that he could not see his own feet, he had broken some threads connected with a burglar alarm which had already warned Karl that some-one was snooping round the house. In either case it was he who would be caught napping, and within a few seconds of entering the house he would probably find *his* stomach full of lead.

Gregory was a brave man, but not a foolhardy one. In the days of the old war he had often walked round three miles of communication-trenches from his Company to his Battalion Headquarters rather than run across a hundred-yard dip in the ground over which a comparatively distant German sniper had a view. Most of the other officers ignored the danger, as the sniper's pot-shots scored a hit only once every week or so, but Gregory never crossed the open space during the ten weeks his Battalion was in that sector save when he was hurrying upon some really urgent matter, and then instead of walking across with nonchalant bravado he constantly altered his pace to confuse the sniper's aim, running ten yards and walking two or stopping dead for a moment before running on again. His men had ample proof of his courage in action, so there was no need for him to risk a bullet in an endeavour to impress them. He knew, too, that they would follow a cautious officer into all sorts of tough places far more readily than they would follow one who exposed himself to danger unnecessarily, knowing that such a man might risk their lives also where no risk need be taken.

In the present instance it was only the thought of poor little Rosenbaum that finally decided him to enter the house. It was just possible that he had slipped up somehow and that Karl was inflicting unmentionable brutalities upon him somewhere inside. Gregory knew that he would never be able to go home and sleep comfortably in his bed that night with such a possibility still in his mind.

Taking out his jemmy he inserted it in the crack between the French windows and pressed upon it gently. The flimsy lock gave with a snap but the leverage he had been compelled to exert forced the long windows open and, before he could prevent their moving farther, a stiff hinge had given a loud creak.

Gregory knew that death might be waiting for him on the other side of the curtains, but drawing his automatic he stepped inside.

Chapter XXI

DEATH AND KISSES

FOR a second he paused there holding his breath ; then he sank down on to his knees and gingerly lifted the bottom of the heavy curtain with the finger-tips of his left hand.

No light appeared. The room was in darkness, but if Karl was in the house and had heard the window creak as it had been forced open he might enter the room at any moment and switch on the lights. He would instantly spot the bulge in the curtains made by Gregory's body and fire at it, taking a chance as to whether the housebreaker was a police agent or an ordinary burglar. In either case he had the acid bath handy in which to dispose of his kill.

Turning sideways to present a smaller target Gregory crept on all-fours along the floor behind the curtain until he reached its edge and could pass round it into the room. Drawing himself upright again he listened intently. No sound broke the stillness of the darkened house.

Still holding his automatic, its safety-catch off, ready in his right hand, with his left he took out his spotlight torch and flashed it towards the end of the room. The beam flickered for a moment, then came to rest upon the door. Advancing cautiously between the pieces of heavy furniture which indicated by their shapes, shrouded in dust-sheets though they were, that the place was a drawing-room, he reached the door, pocketed his torch and put his hand on the door-handle. Firmly but gently he turned it right back, then cautiously began to open the door. There was no light in the hall either ; the eerie silence remained unbroken.

Opening the door to its full extent he passed into the hall, his automatic still gripped ready in his hand, his rubber-soled shoes making no sound on the polished parquet. A few steps took him to the bend of the stairs where, he remembered, they took a right-angled turn half-way to the floor above. Sheltering there so that he could not be shot in the back he flashed his torch again, first round the empty hall and then upward into the shadows of the staircase and the first-floor landing.

Pocketing his torch once more and treading with the utmost care he moved across to the door of the big library. Opening it a fraction he found that the library, too, was in darkness. It was still too early for Karl and Rosenbaum to have gone to bed, so unless they were in the kitchen quarters the house was presumably deserted. He pushed the door open ; then halted in his tracks. Something had stirred within the room.

A tiny yet distinct noise had unmistakably broken the eerie silence. Gregory grasped his gun more firmly and stared with straining eyes into the darkness, ready to pump lead into the impenetrable blackness of the room at the faintest indication of any movement. He waited for a full minute in tense silence ; not daring to breathe for fear of giving away his position to some unseen enemy.

He had just decided that the sound he had heard had been merely one of the nocturnal creakings natural to a deserted house containing old furniture, when it came again. It was not a creak, but could best be described as a prolonged click.

Again he waited. Another minute, and the sound came once more. It was exactly similar to that which he had heard before, and but for the fact that the intervals between the sounds were far too long it might have been the ticking of a clock.

For another three minutes he stood there, carefully controlling his breathing. The sounds continued at regular intervals, and after listening intently he decided that they could not be made by any human agency but must emanate from some piece of mechanism.

Very warily he moved forward into the room flashing his torch again. Its pale beam fell upon Rosenbaum's ornate desk. On it there lay open a large blotter, in the centre of which glistened a great, red patch of sticky-looking stuff. One glance was enough; Gregory knew that he was looking at a pool of congealed blood.

As he stood there staring at it there was a faint yet distinct "plop" as another drop of blood fell on to the blotter. This, then, was the sound which had broken the awful stillness of the room.

Slowly Gregory raised his torch. Its beam lit dangling, black shoes, a pair of legs, a body that appeared to have no arms, then a face fallen forward upon a narrow chest, its chin resting on a portrait of Adolf Hitler which had been hung about the skinny neck. It was Jacob Rosenbaum, and no closer inspection was needed to show that he was dead.

Something he had done or said must have given him away. Karl had exacted a terrible vengeance and by now had presumably fled. Turning, Gregory stepped back to the door and switched on the lights.

Then was revealed the full horror of the poor little Jew's end. His wrists were tied to the railings of the minstrels' gallery above the desk and he was hanging from them as though crucified, while protruding from his body and limbs were the hilts of a dozen knives. Gregory went forward and examined one of them. It was clear that at one stage of his career Karl had been a professional knife-thrower, earning his living by giving exhibitions of his art upon the stage, for the knives were unmistakably of the type used in such acts ; all of the same pattern, strong-bladed, with heavily-weighted handles and very sharp points so that they would easily embed themselves in a thick board.

The usual knife-throwing act, which Gregory had several times seen, necessitated the assistance of a pretty girl. Dressed in a loose robe she would take her stand in front of a thick wooden screen, when the knife-thrower would exhibit his skill by hurling his knives from a distance of some fifteen feet so that they would penetrate the board as near the girl as possible without actually touching her, gradually forming a palisade of steel around her body. A real ace knife-thrower could even plug his knives into the skirt, loose sleeves and puffed shoulders of the girl's garment so that she was pinned to the screen; unable to move at the conclusion of the exhibition without tearing her clothes.

Karl had exercised his skill on Rosenbaum, sending knife after knife into non-vital parts of the Jew's body with mathematical precision so that there were two in each of his arms, two in each leg, two just under his collar-bone, one in his stomach and a final blade in his heart. The two knives beneath the collar-bone each touched the wooden frame which held the unglazed photograph of Hitler ; the last blade, that which had ended the Jew's torment, had shorn through the stiff card of the photograph and pinned it to Rosenbaum's chest. For a moment Gregory was surprised at this act of apparent desecration by a Führer-worshipper, but he realized at once that a sadist such as Karl at the height of his frenzy would find the ultimate peak of perverted ecstasy in thus simultaneously slaughtering his victim and profaning that which he held most sacred. A wry half-smile twisted Gregory's lean face as he took in the grim symbolism of the scene. The same weapon, flung by the hand of a perverted fanatic, had transfixed both Führer and Jew. The forces of oppression, savagely wielded by Hitler's henchmen, would in due time destroy the man who had unleashed them.

As blood was still dripping from the body at intervals of about a minute Gregory felt certain that Rosenbaum could not have been dead very long ; Karl had probably been taking his time over the business, amusing himself by throwing one knife every half-hour or so during the day. He might even be still in the house.

Switching off the light again Gregory went cautiously back into the hall and investigated the dining-room at its far side and a small sitting-room next to the kitchen quarters at its rear, but all of them were dark and deserted.

He then proceeded upstairs and went through both floors of bedrooms. In one of these empty drawers and an empty wardrobe that had been left open suggested that Karl had occupied it and had recently made a hurried get-away.

When he had come downstairs again Gregory went through to the laboratory to make quite certain that the house was empty, and in the cell behind it he found the evidence which had given Jacob Rosenbaum away. On the floor there still lay the severed pieces of the cords which had bound his own wrists and ankles on the previous night. Karl, too, must have seen them, have become suspicious and on examining the acid bath have found only one body in it. Such a discovery would have been more than enough to have sealed the fate of the unfortunate little Jew.

Returning to the library Gregory took out his pocket-knife, cut poor Rosenbaum's body down, ripped the blood-stained portrait of Adolf Hitler from the knife which impaled it and flung it in the fireplace.

Hitler might stride about in his fine uniforms, pat little children on the head, listen to soulful German music, entertain acrobatic dancers while taking irreproachable care of their reputations and design magnificent new buildings for his State, but he was every bit as responsible as Karl for this foul, brutal murder.

It was his ideology which had inspired it ; it was his Gestapo chief, Heinrich Himmler, who had trained and paid men like Karl to carry out such hideous barbarities. Gregory sighed. What *could* one do with such people ? Shooting was too good for them. When Hitler's armies had been broken why should he expect the courtesies which were usually extended to defeated rulers on the supposition that they had gone to war only in what they had considered to be the best interests of their peoples ?

After the last war there had been a campaign to hang the Kaiser. But the Kaiser had not climbed to his throne by murder, treachery and graft ; he had inherited the sceptre of a Germany made strong and proud by Bismarck and a General Staff with a

I

tradition of victory behind it. He had undoubtedly been tempted to see his great military machine in action, yet the Great War, when it came, was not of his deliberate seeking. He had backed up his ally Austria-Hungary but had exercised a restraining influence at the last, refraining from ordering the mobilisation of the German Army until twenty-four hours after Russia had mobilised against him and he had received definite grounds for believing Germany to be threatened. After that he had been virtually in the hands of his Generals, and although by no means guiltless he had been no less so than several other hereditary monarchs who had loosed their legions in the old, imperialistic way during those fateful last days of July 1914.

Hitler was altogether different. He had been a man of the people, untrained in arms until he had been drawn into the last war as common cannon-fodder. What possible excuse had he for allowing his eyes to be blinded by the glitter of martial splendour when he must have known from his own experience the limitless misery that war brought to the masses? He knew, all right, but *he did not care.* He was utterly unscrupulous and had in effect been at war for years; not with England, France or Poland but with the whole human race. To glut his insatiable ambition he had plotted the murder of his political opponents, shot non-political but humanitarian Germans who had dared to raise their voices against him and butchered innumerable people among his own supporters because they had weakened in the ferocity of the campaign which was to lift him to unlimited power. Not content with that he had now betrayed the very masses which had raised him up by selling them to Russia and opening the gates to the Communism against which he had posed for years as their defence and sure shield.

Ten million Jews had groaned under his ordinances; millions of Czechs and Austrians had been scourged under his rule; the Polish cities had gone down in a chaos of fire and smoke and blood because the Polish people had dared to defy him. He had stolen millions of pounds' worth of property and goods from those who lived in the so-called German Protectorates and millions more from his own countrymen. Even Art had not been sacred to him. He had personally looted the finest Dürers, Rembrandts, Memlings, Van Eycks, Titians and Rubens from the public galleries of Germany and had sent them over the border to Switzerland to be stored with the intention of selling them in other countries if he were ever forced to get out.

He had broken his word, pledged in the name of his country

to the statesmen of the world.   He had lied in public about his intentions and in private to those who had befriended him in his early struggles.   Through his puppet Goebbels he had suborned the Press of a nation to stuff his fellow-countrymen with massed perversions of the truth.   Himself an Atheist, he had endeavoured to suppress Christianity and to substitute a new religion of which he was to be the God.   He was even the sort of rat that turns King's evidence, for at the trial which followed his ill-fated Munich *Putsch* he had betrayed his comrades, testifying against them so that he might get off with a lighter sentence.

Treachery, deceit, kidnapping, blackmail and assassination were the steps by which he had climbed to the highest peak of power ;   from it he had directed the casting of the German, Austrian, Czech, Slovenian and Polish peoples into abject slavery.

Every thrashing that the Gestapo had inflicted with their thin, steel rods ;   every death in the German concentration-camps from poor food and conditions unfit for humans ;   every rape committed by German soldiers who had got out of hand in Czechoslovakia and Poland ;   the agony of every little child that had died, crushed beneath falling masonry, burnt by incendiary bombs or torn by flying pieces of jagged steel in the Polish campaign ;   every open assassination in Germany or stealthy murder by night by German agents outside her borders ;   every one of these was Hitler's direct responsibility.

With another sigh Gregory picked up Rosenbaum's mutilated body, carried it upstairs to the principal bedroom of the house, laid it on the bed and drew up the counterpane over the poor, tortured face.

After this he spent half an hour in going cursorily but systematically through the house.   To have done the job with real thoroughness would, he knew, have taken several men at least twenty-four hours, but the police would attend to that in due course and would probably discover a concealed wall-safe, a *cache* under one of the floors, or perhaps even a secret wireless sending-apparatus hidden somewhere up under the roof.   All he could do for the moment was to run through drawers, cupboards and other likely places on the off-chance that the Germans might have left anti-British propaganda or other interesting material behind them, but he did not consider it likely and, as he had expected, his search proved unavailing.

Going out again through the drawing-room window into the garden, he walked round the side of the house, re-locked the

tradesmen's entrance behind him with his skeleton key and proceeded down the hill. In the Finchley Road he picked up a
taxi and told the man to drive him to his flat.

Upstairs in his sitting-room he considered the situation.
From his point of view it was even worse than it had been that
morning. Rosenbaum was now dead, so the experts could no
longer question him upon a thousand-and-one details of his association with Grauber ; details which, while perhaps seeming
trivial to him, might have linked up with other information and
have proved of considerable assistance to the counter-espionage
people. Karl could no longer be brought in at will, as he had
evidently abandoned the house and gone to ground elsewhere
immediately he had discovered that Rosenbaum had betrayed
them. Grauber was by now well on his way back to Germany.
There he would learn of Rosenbaum's treason through Karl or
other German agents, so although he might return to London
he would certainly never again visit the house in Hampstead.
Altogether the position seemed a pretty mess ; he would have a
failure to report to Sir Pellinore even grimmer than that of his
first effort.

Yet after a few moments Gregory's sense of humour came to
his assistance. Even though poor Rosenbaum had died a most
ghastly death only a few hours before, the world, life and the
war must go on. It was useless to give way to depression, and
to counteract the irritation and annoyance which Sir Pellinore
was almost certain to display he decided to give the grand old
chap a good laugh. Unlocking a cupboard, he made up a neat
brown-paper parcel ; then put on his hat and took a taxi up to
Carlton House Terrace.

It was still well before midnight, and when he jumped out
of the taxi he saw that a large car was waiting in front of Sir
Pellinore's house. One glance at the special number-plate
showed him that it belonged to a Cabinet Minister. In addition
to the policeman on the beat who was standing near-by an
Inspector was keeping a watchful eye on the street, and as he
rang the bell Gregory mused on the remarkable way in which
the police bobbed up from nowhere whenever anybody important
was about.

The man on the door informed him that Sir Pellinore was
engaged. Gregory said that he would wait, and was shown into
a downstairs sitting-room. His wait was a long one, as the
Cabinet Minister and Sir Pellinore remained closeted upstairs for
the better part of two hours ; but the footman asked if he might

bring Gregory a brandy-and-soda, and on returning with it brought all the evening papers, so while he waited he read them through from cover to cover, assimilating the latest war news.

Hitler's peace speech in the Reichstag and the world's reactions to it formed the most prominent items. It was much less conciliatory than Gregory had expected, but a very able piece of work. The facts had been marshalled—and distorted—with all the skill of a Machiavelli.

He referred once again to the injustice of Versailles ; a basic fact which every thinking man admitted. He had only righted that wrong done to the German people ; the last, the very last step had been forced upon him by the utter intractability of the Poles, who had flatly refused every appeal to reason once they had received guarantees from Britain. Colonies must be discussed, but this was no demand ; merely a reasonable request. They must all disband their armies and meet in an atmosphere free from threats. He was prepared to disarm, would be a good boy for evermore, and so on.

Gregory metaphorically stuck out his tongue ; a gesture which formed a rude but accurate interpretation of the reception with which the proposals were meeting in the French and British Press. He felt, nevertheless, that the speech was calculated to do the Allies considerable harm with the neutrals, but was cheered to see that most of the foreign commentators saw through it and that, most important of all, Mussolini did not intend to risk a rebuff by offering himself as a mediator.

Stalin had given up a large chunk of Poland, forming a new Russian frontier on the original Curzon line, but he had evidently done so only in consideration of a free hand in the Baltic, which meant that another of Germany's dreams had gone west. Hitler, however, was very firm on the point that Poland was now a Russo-German region and that he would permit no foreign interference there. He also threatened the Democracies with the most frightful things if they determined to wage war against him in earnest, but Gregory thought that a good sign. Von Ribbentrop had got Uncle Adolf into a pretty jam by having to surrender German interests in the Baltic, losing the Polish oil-wells and getting his master stalled off from the Ukraine and Rumania. One threatens only when one does not obviously hold the whip-hand. Stalin wasn't threatening anyone ; he was just quietly taking what he wanted.

The Turks who had been called to Moscow were in a bit of a fix, but as ever they were behaving like gentlemen. No one

could possibly expect them to quarrel with Russia, their
only friend at the settlement of Europe after the last Great
War.

When Lloyd George had backed that ruffian Venizelos in an
attempt to stamp out all that was left of the Turkish nation, it
had been to Russia that Turkey had turned. During the previous year Britain, France and Italy had sent vast stores of guns
and munitions to the Tsarist General, Baron Wrangel, who had
commanded the last stand of the Whites in the Crimea. After
Wrangel's defeat the Bolsheviks had *given* those millions of
pounds' worth of military equipment to Kemal Ataturk, the
great patriot, who was then the penniless leader of a ragged,
ill-equipped army which had been fighting almost continuously
since the beginning of the first Balkan War nearly twelve years
earlier, but which was still determined to fight on in order to
save Turkey as an independent nation. Those guns and shells,
given to Wrangel by the Allies, had enabled the brilliant Turkish
General to drive the armies of the Greeks, equipped by the Allies
though they were, back into the sea. They had had ignomini-
ously to re-embark for home while the British Fleet, ordered
there by Lloyd George, had impotently looked on.

The Turks could not be expected to forget what they had
owed to Russia's friendship in their hour of need, but even so
they appeared firm in their determination to honour their pact
with Britain. Gregory mentally thanked God for it, for a
German-Russian-Turkish *bloc* would have been no joke even if
it had brought in Mussolini on our side against his hereditary
enemies, the Turks, whom he certainly could not afford to have
in Egypt.

It seemed that this second week-end in October was merely
the lull before the storm. In the next fortnight anything might
happen and another half-dozen nations might be drawn into
the war.

It was nearly two o'clock when the servant returned to say
that Sir Pellinore would see Gregory, and with his parcel in his
hand he followed the man upstairs.

"Good evening," said Gregory as he entered the room, "I
see you've been advising the Government again."

Sir Pellinore was standing with his legs spread wide apart
and his back to a roaring fire, and his mind was evidently still
occupied with the discussion in which he had been engaged. He
waved Gregory towards a chair and did not reply for a moment ;
then he appeared suddenly to wake up.

"Eh ? What's that ? Nonsense ! I never advise anybody. No good at that sort of thing."

"Oh, no !" said Gregory with gentle sarcasm. "Everyone knows that you've an eye for a horse or a pretty woman and an infinite capacity for vintage port, but no brains—no brains at all."

"Impudent young devil !" Sir Pellinore growled. "Quite true, though. I suppose you saw his car outside ? A few of the older ones come to see me sometimes, but it's only for a little relaxation. They talk ; I listen. Gives 'em a chance to straighten out their ideas, that's all."

"Well, how are things going ?"

"Not at all badly. Our situation is at all events infinitely better than it was after the first five weeks of the last Great War. The way the B.E.F. has been transported to France with all those millions of tons of material is absolutely beyond praise, Churchill's dealing with the U-boat menace magnificently, and our Air Force, man for man and plane for plane, is proving itself streets ahead of the Germans'. Of course, it's Britain's luck that Hitler thought he could grab Poland and bully us into climbing down afterwards instead of loosing hell here right away. We'd have come through somehow—we always do—but the breathing space has been invaluable. Every day that passes without a major action is a gain to us and, if he continues to lie doggo, we'll be so strong by the spring that we'll have enough planes to blow every munition factory in Germany sky-high.

"And the home-front ?" prompted Gregory.

Sir Pellinore frowned. "The way the Ministry of Health has let down the doctors is a scandal, though. Over a thousand of the poor devils called up to stand by in the hospitals for air-raid casualties. Lots of 'em sold their houses, practices, everything. Then, after five weeks, they're told they're not wanted and dismissed without a cent of pay. The Ministry of Mines is behaving with even greater stupidity. They hold up the nation's coal supply because they fear that after an air raid it might be difficult to distribute to the comparatively few Government centres, forgetting how much more difficult it would then be to feed the thousands of ordinary depôts. People have got to have coal for the winter, haven't they ? Then why not fill every cellar in Britain while the going's good, and keep the few essential Government dumps supplied by an emergency service of lorries or any other damn' thing afterwards ? Much simpler."

Gregory knew that it was no good fishing for any special

items of information as Sir Pellinore was close as an oyster about anything which had been told him in confidence. That was precisely why all sorts of important people freely discussed State secrets with him. Producing his parcel without attempting to pump his host further, he said :

"I've brought you a little present."

Sir Pellinore gave him a quick look. "Really ? Very nice of you. What is it ?"

"Open it up and see."

Having cut the string and undone the paper, Sir Pellinore took out a dusty, long-necked bottle of Mentzendorff's pre-1914 Kümmel.

"By Jove ! Where did you get this ?" he exclaimed.

"I bought it when I was last in Paris, from the cellars of the *Tour d'Argent*, and I've been saving it up for an occasion."

"Ha ! *Tour d'Argent*. Marvellous cellars ; probably the best in Europe. I bet it cost you a packet, though, and it's very decent of you to bring it along to me, but what's the occasion ?"

"To celebrate my retirement into civilian life. I'm going to apply to my local Borough Council for an allotment and tend cabbages for the remainder of the war." Gregory had no intention whatever of doing any such thing, but the presentation of the precious bottle had enabled him to bring out that line of talk very neatly, and thus to prepare Sir Pellinore for the bad news that he was about to give him.

"I see," said Sir Pellinore noncommittally. "You've come another mucker, then ?"

"Yes. I've killed Tom Archer."

Sir Pellinore swung round. "You serious, Gregory ?"

"Perfectly. He's as dead as a door-nail, and his corpse is now rapidly dissolving in an acid tank."

"The devil it is ! But seriously, my boy, this is no joking matter. If the police get you you'll swing for murder. It's all very well to shoot these Nazi blackguards as you did in Ems, but to kill an Englishman in the heart of London is a very different matter."

"I didn't kill him with my own hands, though last night he damned nearly murdered me. I say that I killed him because it was owing to my going down to see him that he met his death."

"H'm ! That's a trifle better, but perturbing all the same. D'you realise that you've been responsible for the deaths of three innocent people in as many weeks ?"

"Four," said Gregory. "There was another chap called Rosenbaum who died to-day in peculiarly horrible circumstances entirely owing to my activities."

Sir Pellinore groaned. "You are a bird of ill-omen ! Damme ! If you're allowed to remain at large much longer you'll succeed in getting me killed next. Still, better tell me the facts and get it over."

Gregory gave a concise but extremely graphic account of his doings during the last thirty hours, and when he had done Sir Pellinore began to walk thoughtfully up and down.

"Only thing of importance that emerges from all this is that before he died Archer told you to warn Madame Dubois."

"Yes, but who *is* Madame Dubois ? Obviously a French-woman, but that doesn't get us any further. The name Dubois is about as common in France as Brown is in England."

"True. But I think I know the Madame Dubois to whom Archer referred. When that devil Grauber was torturing the poor feller he had to give away something. To protect his friends in Germany he probably swore that he knew very little about the movement there, but offered to give Grauber such information as he could about the French end of it."

"I don't see how that would have done Grauber much good."

"Don't you ? I do. The headquarters of the German People's Freedom Party are in Paris ; the great majority of the Germans who have escaped from concentration-camps and the intellectuals and Jews who have been thrown out are gathered there. They're very much tied up with the French Left Wing extremists, and Madame Dubois is one of the most able of the French Red leaders. The threads of this tangled skein evidently lead to Paris, and Archer gave away enough of the business to Grauber for him to be able to instruct his agents to get busy there. Best thing you can do is to catch the morning plane, see Madame Dubois and convey Archer's warning to her as quickly as you can."

Gregory suppressed a smile. That Sir Pellinore knew who Madame Dubois was had been a piece of specially good luck, but he had already made up his mind that he would go to Paris in any case and endeavour to sound anyone of that name who might be mixed up in revolutionary activities there. By so skil-fully breaking his bad news he had led Sir Pellinore into suggesting that he should go instead of telling him, as he had feared, that as his activities had now resulted in the deaths of four people he was to take no further hand in the affair.

"That seems the best line," he agreed quietly. "Of course, I'm not in a position to tell her exactly what Archer gave away because I don't know myself, but the knowledge that he was forced to split will at least put her on her guard so that she and her associates in Germany can change their methods of communication. Perhaps, too, as this will temporarily postpone my cabbage-fancying operations, we'd better postpone the drinking of that bottle of Kümmel until my return from Paris."

Sir Pellinore's blue eyes twinkled. "Congratulations, my dear boy, on handling a very tricky situation extremely well! But for goodness' sake don't get more people killed in France than is absolutely necessary. In any case, as it's getting on for three in the morning this is hardly the time to do justice to the contents of that lovely old bottle, but perhaps a tankard of champagne wouldn't do us any harm."

"Grand! I could do with that. Just about this time last night I honestly thought I'd never live to drink another."

As Sir Pellinore pressed the bell they began to discuss Rosenbaum's brutal murder in detail, and Gregory aired his views on Hitler.

"You're dead right," Sir Pellinore agreed, "the feller's personally responsible for every murder the Gestapo have committed. Because he's a smallish feller and has a pleasant sort of smile people are apt to underrate the power he wields. Fools believe he's an idealist who won the affections of the German people by lifting Germany from a state of destitution to one of reasonable prosperity. They believe that he's really in the hands of his advisers, who don't tell him very much of what's going on, and that it's they who're to blame for the persecutions and barbarities committed in his name.

"That's not the case. One couldn't have a clearer proof that he really rules the roost than the Blue Book upon the events leading up to the war. Neville Henderson contributed to it, and he states there that he put up a certain proposal to Goering. The Field-Marshal regarded it favourably, but said at once that because it was contrary to the Führer's views he positively dared not put it before him. Well, if Goering himself can't talk to the feller for fear he'll get a thick ear when reporting a conversation with the British Ambassador, who the devil can?"

Gregory nodded. "Hitler knows what's been going on, all right, and Himmler must have laid before him every one of his plans for intensifying the activities of the Gestapo before he would have dared to carry out his purges. It's extraordinary, though, the confidence he's managed to instil into his own followers. For instance, this Gestapo chief, Grauber, spoke last night with absolute conviction of Germany's winning the war, and said that they're planning the Nazi State to last for at least a thousand years."

"That is the idea. Every German child is reported on from the day it goes to a kindergarten. Only the best are sent on to the highest grades of prep. schools. The pick of those go on to the upper schools, then they're weeded out again and those with one hundred per cent. Aryan ancestry, proved physical fitness, and an outstanding record during their time in the Nazi Youth Movements are drafted to the universities or to the Führer Schools of the Third Reich.

"Male youth of the whole nation's shoved through a lot of sieves," Sir Pellinore went on. "Only those with an unblemished record through all stages can expect top jobs in after life. No-one who has not qualified through the Party organizations from the very beginning can hope to get anywhere in Nazi Germany. It's from the pick of the bunch that the S.S. are taken, and there are three hundred and fifty thousand of 'em—blond giants, all of whom can prove their Aryan ancestry back to the year 1750. They mayn't marry without Hitler's personal consent, and to gain that their fiancées must also prove their Aryan ancestries back to the same date. Have to be vetted, too, on their fitness for child-bearing, but these young men of Himmler's are not encouraged to marry. They're expected instead to sleep with every young woman they meet so that they can produce at least half-a-dozen children a year apiece, and it's no slur on a German girl to be the unmarried mother of an S.S. man's child. Think of that, my boy! Three hundred and fifty thousand multiplied by six—that means over two million new little Germans every year sired by the best human stallions of the nation. That's what your friend Grauber meant when he spoke of the Nazis creating a new Germany that would last at least a thousand years."

"What a thought!" Gregory murmured, "and every one of them brought up from the cradle, of course, to regard Himmler's boss as God. Deliberately taught that theft, arson, forgery, murder, and so forth are all praiseworthy things when done in the service of the Leader, and that to hear is to obey."

"Fortunately, we've caught the thing in time," said Sir Pellinore, with a grim smile. "Hitler hasn't been in power for six years yet, and it's much less since Himmler really got down to organizing his black-uniformed bravos. He's a most remark-able man, though, and between the S.S., the regular police and the Gestapo he's now got very nearly half a million picked men sworn to obey him. That's an enormous percentage of the population even in a country the size of Germany. What's more, he openly boasts that he's read every book on torture ever written that's obtainable in the German language, and he encourages his subordinates to do likewise. That's the type of man we're up against."

"In the long run it all goes back to Hitler. 'Like master, like man', you know."

"I agree, but it's a mistake to imagine that it would be enough to remove the Führer. He's the principal criminal, not a doubt of that, but one mustn't deceive oneself into thinking that everything would be all right if Hitler and his immediate followers were killed or imprisoned. War brings out the worst instincts in the Prussian, and there's no doubt at all that many of these men enjoy the dirty work they have to do.

"Take Rosenbaum's case. This feller Karl had to make his get-away and cover his tracks as far as possible, so from his point of view there was some justification for his killing the Jew, but the method by which he did it was a matter of deliberate, personal choice. He could have put a bullet into him from behind or slogged him over the head with a coal-hammer. Killed him quick. But what does he do? Strings the poor little devil up and chucks knives at him. That was an individual act of revolting cruelty, and when the war's over the little fish as well as the big have got to be made to answer for their crimes. We're not out against the German people, but by God we're out against the Nazi Party root and branch, and every fibre of that poisonous growth has got to be destroyed."

"I don't think you need worry," Gregory remarked, "the German people will attend to the little Hitlers when the balloon goes up, even if there are half a million of them."

For a while they talked on about the Gestapo, and when they had finished the bottle of champagne that had arrived some time before Gregory rose to say good-night. It was four o'clock by the time he got back to his flat, but as he had slept for several hours between mid-afternoon and early evening he was not particularly tired. He left a note instructing Mrs. Cummins to call him at seven, snatched two hours' sleep, bathed, dressed, packed a bag and caught the nine-o'clock plane from Croydon. By mid-morning he was in Paris.

Whenever he stayed in the French capital he put up at the St. Regis, in the *Rue Jean Goujon*, just off the *Champs Elysees*. It was a quiet hotel and Gregory preferred it to the larger places, although it was quite as expensive, because each of the rooms was furnished with individual pieces instead of the usual standardised bedroom-suites. Many of them were valuable antiques, giving the place the atmosphere of a beautifully-furnished private house rather than of an hotel and Gregory liked luxury and comfort whenever he could get it.

On his drive to the hotel he noted many stacks of sandbags and specially protected shop windows as in London, but there were plenty of people about, so he assumed that now the war was five weeks old and there had been no air-raids, a good proportion of the evacuees had returned to take up their old activities. Many men in horizon-blue mingled with the crowds, and here and there, near the centre of the city, a khaki-clad British officer.

As soon as he had settled in at the St. Regis he telephoned a French journalist whom he knew and succeeded in securing from him the address of the Madame Dubois who was prominent in French Marxist circles.

After luncheon he took a taxi to her apartment, which was in one of the better streets of the Montparnasse quarter. The sight of the block of flats in which she lived told him at once that she was not the type of Marxist that considered it necessary to live in a slum. A smartly-uniformed, one-armed porter took him up in a lift and he rang the bell of Flat No. 14. The door was opened by a pretty, plump little maid, but on Gregory's inquiring for Madame Dubois the girl shook her dark head. Madame was not at home.

"When will she be back?" Gregory asked in his best French, which was very nearly as good as his German.

The girl made a grimace. "Poor Madame is here no longer. She met with an accident. Three nights ago she was knocked down by a car right outside the flats and she was taken straight to a nursing-home."

Gregory had a sort of hunch that he could guess how the 'accident' had been caused. Only that morning, in the early hours, Sir Pellinore had told him that the Gestapo's foreign department, U.A.–1, consisted of no less than 5,000 picked men who were all still outside Germany, either in belligerent or neutral countries. It was their business to engineer accidents to anyone who might be counted an inveterate enemy of the

Nazis, and therefore likely to use their influence against the acceptance of the peace proposals designed to let Hitler get away with the rape of Poland. Cabinet Ministers and other important folk in France and Britain were most carefully guarded by their own Secret Service people, but Madame Dubois held no official position and Sir Pellinore had said that her influence among the French working classes was immense. He thought it more than probable that the men of U.A.–1 had done their best to eliminate Madame Dubois and had succeeded in doing so, temporarily at least.

Having secured the address of the nursing-home he went there to make a personal inquiry as to the extent of Madame Dubois' injuries. After waiting for a quarter of an hour he saw a portly, grey-haired matron who, while very voluble, was by no means cheerful about the condition of her patient. Her description of the circumstances in which Madame Dubois had been injured confirmed Gregory's theory that she had been deliberately run down, for she had apparently been knocked down in the black-out not twenty yards from her apartment, which she had just left, by a car which had been stationary outside the block but which suddenly started up and charged right into her as she crossed the road. The driver had not even waited to ascertain the extent of her injuries and the car had disappeared into the darkness.

The matron went on to say that Madame Dubois' left arm had been broken in two places, her collar-bone fractured and her head badly cut, besides which she had sustained severe concussion. Although she was now out of danger it would be quite out of the question for her to see anybody, even her closest relatives, for at least ten days or possibly a fortnight. Stymied again, Gregory thanked the matron and went disconsolately out into the October sunshine of the Paris street.

Taking a taxi to the *Taverne Royale*, near the Madeleine, he ordered himself a *Vermouth Cassis* and sat down to review the situation. As he would be unable to interview Madame Dubois for the best part of a fortnight it seemed that the only thing to do was to return to London, there to possess his soul in such patience as he could muster, though it was galling to remember that every day during which he kicked his heels in enforced idleness hundreds of people were being killed and wounded in the battle areas, while his mission was the one factor which might bring the slaughter to a swift conclusion.

It seemed intolerable that he should be compelled to sit

still and do nothing when somewhere in Paris there must be people who could place him in possession of the very facts which would justify his taking the risk of entering Germany again in a new attempt to deliver the list of the Inner Gestapo, together with the letter signed by the Allied statesmen, to the unknown German general who was plotting Hitler's downfall. Even though he was unable to talk to Madame Dubois in person there must be some way in which he could discover and get in touch with her associates, who would doubtless be as well informed as she.

It next occurred to him that as Madame Dubois had been taken straight to the nursing-home after her accident she would have had no opportunity to remove, conceal or destroy any correspondence that might have been in her flat at the time. It was hardly likely that she would have left any secret documents lying about, but on the other hand it was quite possible that her desk would contain letters which would act as pointers to the identities of some of her associates. The more he flirted with the idea the more certain he became that it was now up to him to obtain access to Madame Dubois' apartment by hook or by crook and to go through her papers.

The charming vision of the pretty little maid who had opened the door to him flashed back into his mind. Perhaps something could be managed in that direction ; at all events, he would return to see. He paid for his drink and took a taxi back to the block of flats in Montparnasse.

The same attractive girl opened the door again, and greeting her with his most charming smile he said :

"I've been to the nursing-home and I'm sorry to say that Madame is even worse than I had feared."

"Yes, poor Madame is very ill indeed," the girl agreed.

"It's extraordinarily unfortunate that she should have met with an accident just at this time," said Gregory, "I wanted to see her on most important business. I've come all the way from London to do so, in fact."

The maid shrugged. "I'm afraid that Monsieur has had his journey for nothing. They say that it will be at least ten days before Madame is able to receive anybody."

"I know," Gregory nodded, "so I suppose I'll have to kick my heels in Paris all that time. I must see her before I go back, but I shall be horribly bored waiting here ; the only men I know in Paris are all away serving with their Regiments."

A dimple showed just below the left corner of the girl's mouth as she replied demurely : "Even in war-time, Monsieur,

Paris is not altogether a dead city, and with the men at the Front there are even more ladies than usual with time on their hands."

"That's true," agreed Gregory, as though the thought of ladies had never even occurred to him.

"I do not think that Monsieur need be bored for very long," she went on, lowering her dark eyes until her lashes were like fans upon her cheeks, "unless, of course, he finds the company of ladies boring."

Things were going in just the way that Gregory wanted, and he hastened to rebut the implication. "Good Lord, no! There's no companion like a pretty girl for cheering one up, but unfortunately the only girls I know in Paris are all doing war work, and I'm afraid they won't be able to get much time off. It can be terribly lonely in a big city, you know, when you've nobody to talk to."

"Poor Monsieur, that is very sad." A mocking note crept into the girl's voice as she fiddled demurely with the handle of the door. "But not all the girls in Paris are doing war work, and some of them are perhaps lonely too. A gentleman of Monsieur's distinguished appearance should not have to remain lonely for very long unless he chooses."

"I certainly wouldn't do so from choice," said Gregory, "but the devil of it is I'm rather a shy person. I'd hate to be ticked off through trying to scrape acquaintance with a decent girl, and picking up the sort of woman one finds in the bars and dance-halls doesn't amuse me."

"That is understandable, but if one does not take a chance one doesn't get anywhere in this life," said the girl with true French realism.

"In that case I—er—wonder," Gregory murmured hesitantly, stimulating acute nervousness, "I suppose you have to work terribly hard looking after the flat—Madame's family— and all that sort of thing?"

"*Mais non!* Madame has no family, and now she is away the place is never untidy, so I have very little to do."

"But—er—I mean, a pretty girl like you must have plenty of boy-friends to occupy any free time that she has?"

She shook her head with a sad little grimace. "*Mon cher ami* is a Sergeant of the *Chasseurs Alpins* and like the rest he is with his Regiment."

"Then—in that case—perhaps you too feel a little lonely and bored, now that you've got hardly anything to do?"

"Very lonely! Very bored!" she agreed, flashing him a sudden smile.

"Then—er—couldn't we do something about it? I do hope you won't think I'm the sort of chap who wants to force himself on you, I mean. But for the next ten days I'm going to be absolutely at a loose end. Could you—would you—er, take pity on me, sort of thing, and come out and have a spot of dinner with me somewhere this evening?"

"But what a long time you took to ask me that!" she smiled. "Of course we must console one another. Our loneliness is due to this awful war, and we are allies, are we not?"

"*Vive la France!*" cried Gregory with sudden enthusiasm.

"*Vive l'Angleterre!*" replied the young minx gaily. "What is your name? I cannot call you 'Monsieur' all the time."

"My name's Gregory—Gregory Sallust. And yours?"

"Collette Pichon."

"I say, that's nice. Well, look here Collette, it's most awfully decent of you to say you'll spend the evening with me. Shall I come back for you in an hour, or what?"

"If you wish, *Grégoire*. But it is nearly seven o'clock already and in war-time all the restaurants close so early. It will not take me long to change; you can come and wait for me if you like."

"Grand!" Gregory seized her hand and kissed it.

"How gallant for an Englishman!" she laughed.

"It's catching. Paris, you know. Just the sight of you standing there, looking so jolly attractive. But, by Jove, if I knew you better it wouldn't be your hand I'd kiss!"

"*Méchant! Méchant!*" she exclaimed in mock reproof. "But in ten days anything might happen, might it not? And after all, there is a war on."

"Anything might happen in ten hours," Gregory grinned, "or in ten seconds, for that matter," and dropping his rôle of the dumb Englishman he suddenly put his arm round her shoulders and kissed her on the lips.

She drew back quickly and lifting a small, plump hand smacked his face, but it was a friendly slap and he knew that she was not really displeased as she said: "You go too fast, Monsieur. I do not permit such things on so short an acquaintance."

Gregory reverted at once to the bashful idiot, and looking at his feet, mumbled: "I'm terribly sorry; just couldn't resist it, you know. Not like me at all. But you won't let it make any difference to this evening, will you, if I promise to be terribly good and not do it again?"

"This time I forgive," she replied with conscious graciousness, "as to the future, we will see. Perhaps I will let you kiss me good-night in the taxi on the way home, but I am not certain that I like you enough yet. Come in now and have a cigarette while I change my dress."

With restored gaiety Gregory followed her into the sitting-room of the flat. It was a well-furnished apartment with a modern *décor*. It was evident that Madame Dubois had an artistic eye and that in spite of her work for the down-trodden she herself believed in living in considerable comfort. He seated himself in an arm-chair near a big, glass-and-steel desk that was covered with letters and books. As he took out his cigarette-case Collette gave him a paper to read ; then with a wave of her hand and a gay smile she left him, closing the door behind her.

Gregory puffed cheerfully at his cigarette while he gave her a couple of minutes to reach her room. Collette was a nice little soul and he congratulated himself upon the approach that he had made to her ; a skilful mixture of awkward Englishman and "I'm a devil when I once get going." It was just the line to appeal to a girl of her type. The 'humble suppliant' touch from a well-dressed foreigner was probably quite new to her and rather intriguing, whereas she would have been bored by a man who, although he appeared to be well-off, did not suggest by the twinkle in his eye that he liked his bit of fun.

It might take a few days to get Collette just where he wanted her, but after to-night he would have ready access to the flat and she was evidently alone in it. Sooner or later there would arise an occasion when she had to go out to do some shopping. He would pretend that he didn't feel very well as an excuse for not accompanying her and she would leave him there with his feet up on the sofa and an aspirin in his hand. Given an hour alone in the place he would back himself to find any secret wall-safe that there might be, and later he would be able to devise some scheme for getting her out of the flat long enough for him to attempt to open it. In the meantime, as she was going out to dine with a smartly-dressed man it was quite certain that she would put on her best clothes and make up her face with special care, so he could count on a good half-hour before she rejoined him. Standing up, he began to examine the letters and papers that strewed the glass top of the big desk-table.

They had been tidied, presumably by Collette, into two piles. He soon saw that the left-hand one consisted solely of bills, but that on the right seemed more promising as it comprised letters nearly all of which were hand-written. There were about twenty of them and from their headings Gregory saw that they came from places scattered all over France.

The first that he read came from Abbeville and contained a long, rambling account, written in an uneducated hand, of the death of a French miner who had been killed by accident on his company's premises at a time when he had no right to be there. It appeared that his widow had claimed compensation but that the company had refused to pay on the grounds that although he had met his death on their premises he had not been there at their request nor had he been engaged on work for them at the time.

The next came from a silk-operative in Lyons who had been dismissed by his employers for circulating revolutionary literature among his fellow-workers. He had not been able to find other employment and was now destitute. Would Madame Dubois help ?

A third was from a prison outside Marseilles. The writer had been arrested in a riot and sentenced to a term of imprisonment for injuring a *Gendarme*. The prisoner was a widower with two children aged eight and ten, and their sole support. Neighbours were looking after them for the moment but they were poor people who could not afford to do so without some assistance. Would Madame Dubois contribute ?

It soon became clear to Gregory that Madame Dubois was the trustee of a fund to be utilised for Communists or their families who found themselves in financial difficulties owing to their participation in subversive activities. None of the writers appeared to be even local leaders, but men and women of the rank and file whose names and addresses were quite useless to him.

It had taken him some twenty minutes to go through the letters and he had also spent a little time in examining the bills, but as he reckoned that he had still a few minutes before Collette was likely to return he looked round the room for any other place where papers might be kept.

In one corner there was a tall, narrow bureau with deep drawers ; it had been painted a duck-egg blue so that it should harmonize with the colour-scheme of the room. It was thus made comparatively inconspicuous, and it was for this reason that he had not at first noticed that it was really an ordinary office filing-cabinet. He felt at once that the material he was after was much more likely to be found here than among the papers on the desk.

Tiptoeing across to it he tried the top drawer and found to his delight that it was unlocked. He had just pulled it out for about a foot when he heard the tapping of high heels in the corridor and swiftly pushed it back again. But the wretched thing jammed when it was still not closed by a quarter of an inch. He had no time to pull it out again and ease it home so he had to leave it as it was, thanking his stars that it had not jammed further out. As it was, only a careful observer would have noticed that it had been opened at all.

In two quick strides he had put a couple of yards between the cabinet and himself and when Collette entered the room she found him idly gazing at a Surrealist painting which appeared to depict a number of herrings growing from the branches of a tree planted in a bath-tub.

As he turned, took Collette's hand and kissed it again, he thought she looked prettier than ever. A gay little hat from which a stiff, gauzy veil stood out in all directions was perched on her head, partially concealing her dark hair, and the curves of her trim figure were admirably displayed in a smart, black coat and skirt. Not for the first time Gregory gave full marks to those young women of France who were not too well blessed with this world's goods yet always managed to present a delight-fully *chic* appearance owing to their skilful planning and their natural flair for clothes.

He wondered where to take her for dinner. The *Tour d'Argent*, the *Café de Paris* or any other of the *de luxe* places would be overdoing it. She was so pretty and smart that he would not have been ashamed to have been seen with her at the Ritz, but if he were to take her to one of the haunts of the *haute monde* she might run into some previous employer and feel rather awkward.

Then there was Pocardi's, the huge Italian restaurant off the *Boulevard des Italiens*, where large and appetising meals were to be had at comparatively moderate prices. It was a favourite spot with the French *bourgeois* when they wished to hold a little celebration ; the sort of place to which a well-paid clerk might take his girl as a treat. Gregory had often fed there in his earlier years when in Paris and not so well off as now. For a moment he considered it, but it was quite possible that Mademoiselle Collette Pichon had been taken to Pocardi's by other boy-friends from time to time and he wished to strike a fresh note if he could.

Suddenly the thought of the *Vert Galant*, down by the river on the right bank, flashed into his mind. Quiet and unostentatious, it was yet one of the oldest-established restaurants in Paris, and the cooking there was excellent. From the plumpness of her trim figure Gregory felt certain that Collette enjoyed her food, and when he suggested it she beamed with delight.

"How lovely ! It is very good, the *Vert Galant*. Real French cooking—not the sort of messed-up things they make for you English and the Americans in the smart places—so I have been told. I have never been there and I'd love to go, but I'm afraid you will find it very expensive."

"I don't think we need worry about that," Gregory smiled. "I want to give you the very best dinner we can get. That's the least I can do, since you've been kind enough to take pity on me."

She shrugged. "Ah, well, I suppose you can afford it. Some of my friends have to be careful of their money even when they wish to give me a good time, but you look very rich. All Englishmen have lots and lots of money, haven't they ?"

"I'm afraid that's rather an old-fashioned idea," he laughed. "It's lingered on in France from the days when every Englishman who travelled was a *milord* and went about with bags of golden guineas. I'm certainly no millionaire, if that's what you mean, but I think I've got enough to take you to most of the places you'd like to visit in Paris while I'm waiting for Madame Dubois to get well enough to see me. Come on ; let's go, shall we ?"

Opening the door for her to pass, Gregory closed it behind them, then drew her hand through his arm as they set off gaily down the corridor. Out in the street he found that the Paris black-out was not as bad as that in London, as a system of blue-shaded lights had been established, and they had no difficulty in getting a taxi.

The *Vert Galant* came up to their expectations. Gregory had a way with waiters ; a quiet, authoritative manner that never failed to impress from the moment he entered a restaurant. They sensed that he was the sort of client who knew exactly what he wanted and was prepared to pay for it and to tip well into the bargain. So silent-footed minions came and went for a couple of hours while little Collette tucked in to her heart's content and Gregory encouraged her to have all the good things she fancied.

She was an amusing small person, and he decided that he

could not have found a more entertaining companion with whom to pass an evening if he had combed all Paris with that aim. She was attractive to look at across a table, she smoked her cigar-ette and drank her after-dinner *fine* with an air. She had no trace of false shame about being a maid, and between gusts of laughter she related many amusing episodes concerning people with whom she had been in service, while her shrewd, sound commonsense made her comments upon the war and the general situation very well worth listening to.

Gregory did not attempt to pump her about the Marxist friends of Madame Dubois. She might assume, if she liked, that he had come to Paris to see Madame Dubois upon that sort of business, but he had made up his mind to make her forget it as soon as possible. With her mind free of such speculations she would be much more inclined to leave him alone in the flat for which she was responsible. She showed no curiosity about his affairs and appeared to be entirely absorbed in enjoy-ing herself.

While she was away powdering her nose after dinner he bought her a huge bunch of roses from the restaurant flower-seller, and on her return she hugged them to her with the delight of a child who seldom sees sweets at all but has just been given a box of candies.

Soon afterwards the restaurant closed and they had to leave it for the darkened street. Owing to the curfew there was no possibility of their going on anywhere else, so Gregory gave the taximan the address of Madame Dubois' flat.

Collette climbed in with her arms full of roses, while he clutched a parcel containing two bottles of champagne. He had instructed the waiter to put this up for him with the idea in the back of his mind that as there was nowhere else to go and the night was still young Mademoiselle Collette might extend to him the hospitality of the delightful flat of which she was the sole custodian.

Gregory would not normally have attempted to kiss her in the taxi because that was not his technique, but as she had raised the matter herself he thought he might expect it. When the cab was well under way, crawling steadily along the river-bank, he accordingly slipped his arm round her and drew her to him. But she quickly used the roses as a screen and turned away her head.

"Oh, come !" he protested in a hurt voice. "You did promise me another kiss in the taxi going home."

"I did not *promise* anything," she dissented.

"You said you'd let me kiss you when you knew me better if you found that you liked me. Don't you like me?"

"Oh, I like you lots and lots, *Grégoire*," she replied with a mocking note in her voice. "You make me laugh and I like that. You're very generous, too. I like that also in a man."

"Well, then . . ." said Gregory.

"Why be so impatient?" she shrugged. "Let us drive round for a little."

Gregory promptly ordered the cabby to crawl round for a bit, and the man complied. He was used to such orders at that hour of the night.

For the next twenty minutes Gregory tried small-talk, badinage and even a little playful rough-housing, but still Collette used her roses as a barrier and would not let him kiss her. At length he got fed up with her refusals and, deciding that he had advanced as far as she was prepared to go on a first evening, he ordered the taximan to drive to the address he had first given.

She laughed as she heard him give the order, and declared: "So you are going to drive me home now. And then, all on your own, you'll go back to your hotel and dream of me. Think how nice that will be!"

"I'll certainly do that," he agreed, "but I wish I hadn't to go to bed so early. You're not tired either, are you? You don't look it."

"No, *Grégoire*, I'm not tired. I don't intend to go to sleep for hours yet."

"Can't we go on laughing and talking for a bit, then?" he asked, renewing his attack.

"But where? There is nowhere to go—and you have told the man to take me home."

"Exactly! Why not there?"

"But what would Madame say?"

"I don't see why Madame should ever know anything about it."

"I don't expect she would if neither of us told her."

"Then—why not?"

"All right," she said with sudden decision, "you shall come in and have a cigarette."

Having arrived at the flat Gregory paid off the taxi. They went straight up in the lift and along the corridor to Madame Dubois' flat. Collette fished a key out of her bag and opened the door. The lights in the corridor had been dimmed as an air-raid precaution and the flat was unlit.

"We'll go through to the sitting-room," Collette said, and walked inside without bothering to switch on the light in the hall. Gregory closed the door behind him and for a moment they were in pitch-darkness.

Suddenly the lights clicked on and Gregory saw that two men were sitting in the hall. One of them had an automatic ready in his hand. Collette had turned at the sitting-room door and, pointing at him, said swiftly :

"Messieurs, this is the man who endeavoured to rifle Madame's papers. I am convinced that he is a spy."

Chapter XXII

BEHIND THE BARS

COLLETTE'S reference to Madame Dubois' papers instantly told Gregory what had given him away. It had been that accursed filing-cabinet, which had jammed before he had had time to close it properly. Ill-luck must have caused her glance to fall on the cabinet just before they had gone out to dinner. She must have noticed at once that the top drawer was not quite closed and have realised that Gregory was the only person who could have tampered with it. That had been quite enough to enable a quick brain like hers to jump to the conclusion that the nice Englishman who was going to take her out to dinner and who pretended that he was so lonely had in reality a very different motive for cultivating her acquaintance.

Gregory had learned at dinner that she had been in Madame Dubois' service for the past eighteen months, which would have been ample time for anyone of her intelligence to gather that although Madame lived in a pleasant, well-furnished flat she was anything but an ordinary, well-to-do widow. All sorts of queer people doubtless came to see Madame, and Collette had probably been specially chosen for her discretion. He remembered now that while she had talked most freely that evening of her previous employers she had not let slip a single fact about either Madame Dubois or her acquaintances. Collette evidently liked her absent mistress, and having found him out had taken drastic steps to protect her interests.

Gregory gave her full marks for the way in which she had handled the situation. Instead of panicking when she had noticed that the cabinet had been tampered with and trying to turn him out of the flat, or betraying any of the humiliation she must have felt on the sudden discovery that her visitor was really interested not in her own charms but in her mistress's affairs, she had kept her head and at once laid her plans for trapping him. Having taken an excellent dinner off him she had then gone calmly to the cloak-room and telephoned these men to lie in wait for him, afterwards making him run her round in a taxi for twenty

minutes to give them ample time to get there and prepare their
ambush.

But who were the men ? That was the question which principally agitated Gregory's violently disturbed mind as he gazed
down the nearest fellow's gun-barrel. Were they a couple of
Marxist thugs ? For all he knew Collette might be in Madame's
confidence and herself a member of the Paris organisation, in
which case she would have known whom to 'phone up for
assistance. The fact that she had accused him of being a spy
pointed to that, while if she was in the game she probably suspected also that Madame Dubois was not suffering from injuries
received in any normal accident but had been intentionally run
down, and that Gregory was one of the people who had attempted
to murder her in this way.

On the other hand, the two men might be detectives ; it
would have been to the police that a maid would normally have
telephoned had she suspected that a plausible young man who
was making up to her intended to try to burgle her mistress's
flat.

Whichever solution of the problem was correct he had certainly landed himself once again in a damnable mess. If the
two men were Marxists it was hardly likely that they would
accept his word for it, after Collette's accusation, that he had
come over to see Madame with the most friendly of intentions,
while—worse still—if they were detectives they would probably
hold him as a suspect and he would have to swallow the bitter
pill of calling on Sir Pellinore to get him out of jail.

He was not left long in doubt. While these thoughts had been
flashing through his mind the two men had stood up and stepped
towards him. The one with the gun was short and stout, with
a plump face and round, innocent, baby-blue eyes ; the other
was a much younger fellow, of the dark, *Provençal* type, and
walked with a limp.

While the fat man continued to cover him with the gun the
other walked round behind him, frisked him and removed the
pistol from his hip-pocket. The manner of the frisking was so
slickly expert that after it was over Gregory had little doubt
where he stood. He was in the hands of the French police.

The fat man spoke with a swift, clipped accent.

"Monsieur, I am Police Lieutenant Ribaud, of the *Sûreté-
Générale*. It has been reported to us that you visited this apartment under suspicious circumstances. I require you to accompany us to Headquarters for questioning. Here is my authority."

He flashed a cellophane-covered pasteboard under Gregory's nose for a second and slipped it back into his waistcoat-pocket.

"I'm delighted to meet you, Lieutenant Ribaud," said Gregory, regaining his *savoir-faire*, "but I can't imagine that anything I've done here is in any way illegal, and what can have given Mademoiselle Pichon the extraordinary idea that I'm a spy simply passes my comprehension."

"You came here to inquire for Madame," Collette stormed. "Two hours later you returned, told a plausible story that you were alone in Paris, and induced me to go out to dinner with you. My evenings are my own, so why should I not accept? I did so, but while I was changing my clothes you took the opportunity of going through Madame's filing-cabinet. Whether you have stolen anything from it I do not yet know, but you may have done so.

"Madame has many political enemies. She is more hated by the Nazis than any other woman in France. We cannot prove it, but both the police and her friends believe that she was deliberately run down by German agents last week. Those devils would stop at nothing to put her out of the way now that Germany has made a peace move, for they know that all her influence would be brought to bear against its acceptance. You pretend that you are an Englishman. I cannot tell whether that is true or not, but you are certainly a foreigner and it is quite clear that you meant to make friends with me so that you could have the run of this apartment. Why should you do that if you are not one of Madame's enemies? I repeat, I believe you to be a Nazi spy."

Little Collette had become a changed woman. Her dark eyes were flashing with a hatred which she did not attempt to conceal and she spoke with extraordinary venom.

"*Chérie*, you're quite mistaken," Gregory assured her. "Look, here's my English passport."

As he produced it from his pocket she waved it contemptuously aside. "Passports can be faked. You went to Madame's filing-cabinet. If you look you will see that the drawer still remains a centimetre open. I dust the room every day and I will swear that the drawer was flush with the cabinet this morning. No one else has been in this flat since Madame left it except yourself."

"Well, well. Curiosity killed the cat," said Gregory amiably. "I had half an hour to pass while you were beautifying yourself for my delight. What if I *was* at a loose end after I'd finished the paper, and *did* pull that drawer open out of idle curiosity? Very reprehensible conduct on the part of any guest, no doubt, but hardly grounds for accusing him of being a Nazi spy."

"It is enough, in view of the activities of the owner of this apartment, for us to desire your presence at the *Sûreté-Générale*, Monsieur," said Ribaud. "What have you in that parcel?"

"A couple of bottles of champagne," Gregory laughed. "I had hoped to persuade Mademoiselle to share them with me. Surely that proves the—er—innocence of my intentions?"

The Frenchman caught the point and smiled with quick humour, but Collette was not amused.

"You think you are very clever, Monsieur, do you not? But let me tell you that after I found you out I only encouraged you for my own purposes. I would not drink with you now if it were my last chance to drink on this earth."

"Isn't life strange?" murmured Gregory with a wicked twinkle in his eye. "Just think of it; you won't even drink with me now, whereas if you hadn't happened to notice that the drawer of that cabinet was open you'd probably have had your head pillowed on my manly chest by this time and be deriving considerable pleasure from the thought that in due course you were going to give way to my persuasive powers and let me sleep with you."

To his delight, Collette flushed deep pink with rage and, stamping her little foot, cried angrily: "Monsieur! How dare you! I . . ."

Ribaud intervened abruptly. "We waste time. Mademoiselle, I regret it exceedingly, but we shall have to trouble you also to accompany us to the *Sûreté* so that you can sign a statement. Will you be good enough to lead the way? You, Corbin, will follow; Monsieur will go next, and I will bring up the rear so that Monsieur may not be tempted into any foolishness on the way downstairs."

They filed out in that order, went down in the lift and crossed the hall of the block as though they were four acquaintances going off somewhere together, but immediately they had stepped out into the darkness of the pavement Gregory felt his right wrist grabbed and the limping Corbin snapped a single handcuff on to it, the other of the pair being attached to his own left wrist. The gentlemen of the *Sûreté* were evidently taking no chances of his getting away in the black-out. Round the corner a police-car was waiting for them, and a few minutes later they were at Police Headquarters.

In a small room on the ground floor a uniformed Sergeant took particulars of Gregory's passport and details of the arrest. Mademoiselle Collette Pichon wrote out a full statement, signed it, and ignoring Gregory's courteous "good-night" accepted the offer of the gallant French police that one of their cars should take her home.

Gregory was then led to a cell, and when he had reached it Ribaud turned to him and said: "It is our business to search you, Monsieur. I trust that you will raise no objections, for it would be completely useless to do so."

Gregory shrugged. "All right, go ahead. The last thing I wish to do is to obstruct you in the execution of your duties."

He partially undressed at their request and they not only emptied his pockets but also ran over his garments, feeling every seam to make sure that nothing was sewn inside it. On his removing his shoes they found under the thin, inner soles the balance of the 5,000 *Reichmarks* which he had brought out of Germany.

Before leaving for Paris that morning it had occurred to him that Madame Dubois might just possibly give him information which would make him wish to attempt an immediate return into Germany without waiting for the money to be sent out from England, and he had replaced the *Reichmarks* in his shoes simply because he did not consider it wise to carry so large a sum loose about his person.

The two French detectives made no comment whatever on this interesting find and placed the notes with the other belongings which they had taken from his pockets, but Gregory knew that his carrying a big wad of German notes in so unusual a manner was going to take some pretty skilful explaining away, and he was quick to realize that his prospects of getting the French police to release him after a cursory examination were more than halved by this unfortunate discovery. When they finally left him with a brief "good-night" they took all his possessions except his clothes, shoes, cigarettes and lighter. Lighting a cigarette he had a look round his cell.

It was a quite comfortable cell, but that was little consolation to him. He thought with regret of the lawn sheets and rich hangings of the room which he had expected to occupy that night at the Saint Regis, and cursed his folly in having been so impatient to get at Madame Dubois' secrets instead of having waited a while until an opportunity had arisen on which he could have arranged to have remained alone at her flat.

Sitting down on the edge of the bed he realized suddenly that he was very tired. He had had only two hours' sleep very early that morning, and the amount which he had managed to get in on the previous day had hardly made up for the tremendous strain through which he had passed the night before. It was no good crying over spilt milk, however, and there would be time enough in the morning to consider the repercussions of this new muddle in which he had landed himself. Pulling off his shirt and socks he crawled into the narrow, iron bed and almost immediately drifted off to sleep.

It had been only about a quarter-past twelve when he had turned in, so although he was wakened at seven by a warder he felt considerably better for his good night's rest. His cheerfulness was not further restored, however, by having to content himself with a cold wash in a microscopic basin instead of luxuriating in a hot bath.

Gregory was a born night-bird and never at his best in the morning. Unshaven, and according to his own standards unwashed, his humour was abominable, particularly as he knew that though he had been roused at the regulation hour it was unlikely that he would be taken from his cell for examination until much later in the morning ; but a breakfast of excellent hot coffee and a huge chunk of new French bread put more life into him and his brain gradually began to turn over.

As far as he could see the French police had very little on which they could hold him ; the statement of a maid that he had been prying into her mistress's papers was hardly enough, while it was no crime to be in possession of foreign currency. His passport, too, was perfectly in order, as the authorities could soon ascertain by telephoning the Passport Office in Whitehall, and the English manager at the Saint Regis, who had known him for years, could be called on to come forward and give evidence as to his identity. On the other hand, it was a damnable nuisance that they had found those *Reichmarks* in his shoes. Owing to the war the ordinary laws for the protection of individual liberty had been entirely washed out by special emergency powers granted to the police, and if he could not satisfy them upon every point there was nothing to prevent their detaining him as a suspect for as long as they liked.

If they decided to hold him on suspicion his position would become a very difficult one, for he would have to appeal to Sir Pellinore to extricate him—the very last thing that he wanted to do But he felt reasonably confident that he would not have to do so.

Just after half-past ten little Ribaud arrived and took him up to the top floor of the building, where they entered a fine room with a lovely view over the roof-tops to the spires and domes of Paris.

At a big desk near the wide windows was sitting a tiny, grey-haired man whose lined face rather resembled that of a monkey; his hands were clasped over his stomach and his eyes cast down in an attitude of Buddhistic contemplation. The desk was remarkable only for the fact that it had not a single paper on it.

"This is the prisoner, *mon Colonel*," announced Ribaud briefly.

The little man looked up and Gregory saw that the resemblance of his wizened face to that of a monkey was heightened by a pair of remarkably quick, dark eyes.

"Be seated, Monsieur," he requested in a gentle voice, "and you, Ribaud, sit down."

"Thanks." Gregory took a chair, crossed his legs and produced his cigarettes. "D'you mind if I smoke, sir?"

"Not at all. It is soothing for the nerves and you are probably not feeling your best at this hour of the morning. Although it's not particularly early I expect you miss the comforts of the Saint Regis, of which we were unfortunately compelled to deprive you. Would you be good enough to tell me, Monsieur Sallust, what business brought you to Paris?"

"I came to see Madame Dubois," replied Gregory, "upon a private matter which I can assure you to be in no way inimicable to the interests of the French Republic; quite the contrary, in fact."

"However private this matter may be I feel sure that you will not object to telling me about it. My position here necessitates my acting as Father Confessor to a great many people and you can entirely rely upon my discretion."

"Madame Dubois is interested in the International Workers' Movement, and so am I," Gregory explained briefly.

"International!" repeated the little man. "May I help you out by suggesting that it is the German end of this organization in which you are interested?"

Gregory smiled. "You're quite right—but only as a means to bring about a speedy conclusion of the war."

"Monsieur Sallust; you are probably aware that the Communists, Marxists and Anarchists, all those in fact who are commonly termed 'Reds', have recently found themselves in a very difficult situation. On the one hand is their intense hatred of the present German Government and all it stands for ; on the other it is part of their basic creed that all wars are engineered by the capitalist interests and that it is the inarticulate masses who principally suffer from them. Certain of the Red leaders have suddenly become greater fire-eaters than your delightful Colonel Blimp himself—as witness the pro-war declarations of the British Communist Harry Pollitt which have just caused his Comrades to retire him from a key position in the Party—while others still cling uneasily to the doctrines of their God, Karl Marx. You, perhaps, have convictions of that type and are yourself a pacifist ?"

"No, no, Colonel," Gregory laughed. "I held a commission in the last war and was even lucky enough to be given the Military Cross. I'd have joined up again in this one if the British Government hadn't developed rather curious ideas about the unsuitability for service of old soldiers, however fit, if they happen to be over a certain age."

"My compliments !" The monkey-faced Colonel inclined his head. "I am always happy to meet a gallant officer. I only wish that I had been able to welcome you to France in more pleasant circumstances. Permit me to introduce myself. I am Raoul Lacroix."

Gregory knew then that the man opposite him was one of the greatest brains in Europe, an officer whose name rarely appeared in the papers but was known to every Cabinet Minister in the world and to everyone who, like Gregory himself, lived on the fringes of high politics. Colonel Lacroix was the supreme head of the famous *Deuxième Bureau*, whose agents relentlessly tracked down the enemies of France from Martinique to Assam and from the heart of Paris to the most desolate outposts of the great French Empire.

"I am honoured, sir," he said, bowing from his chair. "By reputation you are well known to me."

The Colonel bowed in return, and continued : "I am glad, Monsieur Sallust, that you are not a pacifist. As you know, the Red extremists who still cling to their old creed are fomenting a dangerous 'peace at any price' movement. It was for this reason that my Government found it desirable a week or so ago officially to dissolve the French Communist Party. Over sixty Communist Mayors were then placed by us in a situation where they could amuse themselves by playing dominoes as a change from politics, and I have formed the opinion that you are not the type of man that would care to be restricted to the game of dominoes for the duration of the war. Since you are not a pacifist, will you please explain the nature of your interest in the International Workers' Movement ?"

"As you've pointed out yourself, sir, this war has split the Movement from top to bottom. Some of its members consider that nothing can possibly justify the horrors of a fresh war; others, intensely anti-Nazi and anti-Fascist, are all in favour of a war provided that it brings about the collapse of the Dictator countries. It is in the latter group that I am interested."

"You wished, then, to contact Madame Dubois for the purpose of getting in touch with the German Labour people who are plotting to overthrow the German Government. Finding that she had met with an accident and could not be interviewed you decided that you would try to get the information you required by going through her papers without her knowledge, and attempted to seduce her servant in order to further this plan."

"That is the situation exactly, sir."

"Good. We progress. You are not a British Secret Service Agent. We of the *Deuxième Bureau* have the closest possible relations with our good friends in your Military Intelligence. If you had been acting for that department you would not have been in this room for one minute before giving me an indication of that fact. For whom, therefore, are you working ?"

"For myself. Since I couldn't get into the Army again I decided to try to serve my country in some other way, and fomenting trouble in Germany seemed to offer possibilities."

"I fear that either you are not telling me the truth, Monsieur Sallust, or that you have a very great opinion of your own abilities. How is it possible for an individual Englishman to influence the course of events in an enemy country unless he has certain data given him to work upon by somebody who is on the inside of high politics ? Are you quite sure that you were not sent by some statesman or other person of importance to operate privately on their behalf ? Politicians, you know, are not always in agreement with their Governments and quite frequently indulge in a little private enterprise. I think you'd better tell me the truth."

Gregory shook his head. "I'm afraid you've missed the mark there, sir, but you're right in implying that no individual can do as I intended without influential backing. I'm rather a vain chap, but you've made it quite clear to me that I've bitten off more than I can chew. I've been very stupid and given your people a lot of trouble, but as I certainly haven't done any

K

damage to the Allied cause I hope you'll treat my case leniently and let me go home with my tail between my legs."

"If only I were quite certain in my mind nothing would give me greater pleasure," the little man purred, "but there are just one or two points upon which I would like you to satisfy me first. Four thousand, two hundred and twenty *Reichmarks* in notes were found in your shoes. What was your object in carrying this considerable sum in enemy currency concealed upon your person ?"

"I had hoped, sir, that if I could get the information I wanted from Madame Dubois I might be able to smuggle myself into Germany and stir up some trouble there for the Nazis. I put the notes in my shoes only because I didn't like to risk losing the money by carrying it loose in one of my pockets."

"Quite understandable. A wise precaution and a very laudable idea. And now that you have made me quite happy on that score perhaps you will tell me why you were carrying this pretty thing ?"

With a sudden jerk of his hand the Colonel threw the golden swastika on to his desk, where it gleamed solitary and potent in the wide, empty space.

"Oh, that !" Gregory laughed. "It's just a charm—the Nazi symbol reversed. I carry it for luck."

The Colonel shook his head. "Unfortunately I am one of those very practical people, Monsieur Sallust. I do not believe in luck and this, I understand, was found in a secret pocket in the end of your tie."

"Well, sir, if you must know the truth it once belonged to a very beautiful woman and I carry it for sentimental reasons."

"Indeed ! And of what nationality was this lady ?"

"She was a German."

"Her name ?"

"No, really, sir !" Gregory's only refuge was to imply that he had had an affair with the young woman. "It isn't fair to ask me to disclose that ; she—er—used to wear the little token tied on to her undies."

"Her status, then ?"

"Oh, she was just a wealthy German girl whom I met while she was staying in London."

"Wealthy ?" repeated the Colonel quizzically, a faint smile lighting his monkey-like face for the first time. "You do not confine yourself, then, to your interest in the German Workers' Movement ?"

Gregory saw that he had blundered. He should never have given away the true status of the original owner of the swastika. To his distress the little Colonel sat up abruptly and said :

"I have much to do, Monsieur Sallust, so you will forgive me if I terminate this interview now. On your own confession you were seeking to get into touch with Madame Dubois, a person with dangerous political antecedents and connections. You attempted to gain access to her private papers. You were carrying over four thousand *Reichmarks* concealed about you, also an emblem similar to that which is generally associated with the Nazi Government. You state furthermore that the reason for your carrying this symbol is an intimate association with a German lady of good standing. I fear therefore that we must detain you until further investigations have been made into your real reasons for this visit to Paris. Good morning."

Gregory shrugged his shoulders but made no protest. The little man's manner was so decisive that he knew he would only be wasting his breath. Bowing to the Colonel he allowed Ribaud to shepherd him from the room and back to his cell.

On thinking things over he was not unduly depressed. Apart from the facts they had already obtained the French Secret Service could bring nothing against him. The French would of course apply to the British Secret Service for information concerning him and the British, having disclaimed all knowledge of his activities in Paris, would furnish them with a dossier substantiating the fact that he was a law-abiding British subject.

Eventually, therefore, his captors must come to the conclusion that he was just one of the notoriously mad English who, barred from the Army by his age but still extremely active and patriotic, had decided to see what he could do to help win the war on his own without any authority from anyone ; just a harmless lunatic, in fact, who had had his head turned by reading too many spy stories late at night.

It would probably take them several days to arrive at these conclusions, but when they had done so they would hardly be able to find any reason for detaining him further and would presumably release him, though possibly keep him under supervision should they allow him to remain in France.

Resigning himself to face another spell in prison he asked his warder if he could see Lieutenant Ribaud. When Ribaud came to his cell Gregory requested that somebody might be allowed to buy him some books and that his suitcase with his toilet articles and other necessaries should be collected from the Saint

Regis. Ribaud took the list of books that Gregory produced and promised to see to the matter.

His things arrived during the afternoon so that he was at last able to shave, after which he settled down to the routine of prison life. The food was quite passable and as he was an omnivorous reader he did not mind his confinement very much, finding that he got all the air and exercise he required in the two hours each day for which he was paraded round an inner courtyard with a number of other prisoners.

For the first few days he did not expect anything further to happen, but the life was unlike that which he had led in the Dutch internment-camp in that here he was kept in solitary confinement and was not allowed even to exchange pleasantries with the warders, let alone to converse freely with the other prisoners whom he saw at excerise. It was irritating not to be able to discuss the developments of the war with anyone, although he kept abreast of them through the papers that he was allowed to buy.

On the 14th the Royal Oak was torpedoed at Scapa but her loss was more than offset by the news that the Turks had settled their differences with the Russians without jeopardising their pact with the Allies. Two days later the Germans attempted to bomb the Forth bridge but massed air attacks on Britain still failed to mature. It was a strange war. Except that Britain held the Seas practically nothing had come about as had been anticipated and during his enforced inactivity Gregory found his thoughts turning more and more from it to the Lady of the Limousine. It was now over a month since he had met her but her face still haunted him.

By the end of the week he had still not been re-examined and was beginning to become decidedly impatient, and with the passing of the eighth and ninth days his impatience grew. Surely they could have satisfied themselves about him by this time ? The question was, were they bothering to do so ? Now that there was a war on the *Deuxième Bureau* would be absolutely over- whelmed with work. Since they already had him inside they would be devoting all their energies to the catching of other spies. Doubtless a routine inquiry had been put through about him but they would certainly not be troubling to expedite it.

On the tenth day of his imprisonment Gregory realized that by this time Madame Dubois might be well enough to see him, which meant that from now on every day during which he remained in prison delayed the furtherance of a remote yet definite possibility of bringing the war to a speedy conclusion. However faint its prospects of success nothing could possibly exceed such an aim in importance. It had now become imperative that he must somehow regain his liberty, yet puzzle his wits as he would he could see no way out save that of eating humble pie and calling Sir Pellinore to his assistance.

All through the eleventh day and most of the following night he wrestled with the problem. Nothing in his life had ever caused him humiliation as bitter as that which he experienced when, on on the twelfth morning, he asked his warder for pen and paper and wrote a note for Colonel Lacroix in which he said that if the Colonel would get in touch with Sir Pellinore Gwaine-Cust he thought that the British Government might arrange for his release.

During the thirteenth and fourteenth days he fretted impatiently, desperately anxious to be free. The cell seemed to have become smaller and he could no longer enjoy reading even his favourite authors. On the morning of the fifteenth day Ribaud appeared once more and took him upstairs again to the Colonel's room.

Lacroix was seated as before, in Buddhistic beatitude behind his bare, spotless desk, contemplating his small hands as they lay folded on his middle.

"Good morning, sir," said Gregory. "As you've gathered, I've had to throw in the sponge."

The little man looked up and smiled. "Why didn't you do so earlier? It would have saved you a very dreary fortnight."

"I thought you'd find out for yourselves that I was a quite harmless person and release me without my having to obtain outside help and confessing what a fool I'd made of myself."

The Colonel nodded. "I understand that very well. But which of us in this great game we are playing has not at one time or another had to confess to making a blunder? If it is any consolation let me tell you that I twice narrowly escaped being cashiered when I was a younger officer and through over-keenness had failed to go about my work with the requisite caution."

Gregory smiled. "That is certainly a consolation, coming from a man like yourself, sir. I'm very grateful to you."

Colonel Lacroix waved aside the compliment and opening a drawer in his desk produced a telegram which he handed across.

Gregory picked it up, saw that it was addressed to him and read :

"HAVE DRUNK KUMMEL MYSELF AND APPLIED TO KENSINGTON
BOROUGH COUNCIL FOR ALLOTMENT TO GROW CABBAGES ON
YOUR BEHALF GWAINE-CUST."

He gave a rueful grin and said : "Well, there it is ; I've got
the sack."

"I, too, have had the sack," said the little Colonel. "More
times than I care to remember. But I'm still here, you see, and
now they give me the best room in the building to sit in. We
have a charming view from here, don't you think ?"

"Are you implying that I should tear this telegram up ?"
said Gregory quietly.

Colonel Lacroix shrugged eloquently. "Telegrams do not
always reach their destination. If I am questioned in a few
weeks' time I shall have to admit handing it you. If, however,
you care to give it back to me now I might leave it in the drawer
of my desk and forget to give it to you for the time being. There
are times when my memory for details is not very good."

Gregory turned in his chair and looked straight into the
shrewd, dark eyes in the humorous, wizened face. "May I ask
why you propose to do this for me, sir ?"

"Monsieur Sallust, I am qualified to occupy this chair only
because I have the gift of judging men. Your record in the last
war is enough to show that you are courageous. Our previous
conversation showed me that you are no fool. The British
authorities now vouch for your patriotism. I have formed the
opinion that if you were to be entrusted with any mission you
would do everything in your power to carry it through successfully. If my superiors had not given me another chance when
I was a young man I would not be sitting where I am to-day.
I would like to give *you* another chance."

Gregory inclined his head. "I accept your offer very gratefully, sir."

"In that case do you feel that you would be justified in
telling me what you have been trying to do ? If you could confide
in me I might be able to render you some assistance."

"Certainly," Gregory replied with rising elation, "I'm sure
that neither Sir Pellinore Gwaine-Cust nor the people for whom
he's acting would have the least objection to my giving anyone
in your position full particulars of my mission."

He then gave a quick résumé of Sir Pellinore's original
instructions to him, his visit to Germany and his subsequent
activities. When he had done Colonel Lacroix nodded ·

"I know, of course, of the letter from the Allied Statesmen that you mention and of the list of the Inner Gestapo, both of which are with our friends in Berlin. A British agent secured the latter just before the war broke out, so it was agreed that it should be left to the British to get both of these documents to the proper person if possible. But even if you succeed in performing this extraordinary difficult task I am not altogether sanguine about the ultimate result of the anti-Nazi conspiracy."

"Why?" asked Gregory. "Don't you believe that if the German Generals could once be persuaded to act they would be capable of pulling off the proposed coup?"

"I'm decidedly doubtful about it. While such a conspiracy lies dormant it is always difficult for the secret police to secure particulars of it, but once the conspirators become active there is a much greater risk of leakage. Every man of importance in Germany is watched day and night by the Gestapo, so the success of such a venture lies on the knees of the gods. If it is as powerfully supported as you suppose such a *putsch* might succeed; if on the other hand the Gestapo are forewarned it might well be crushed before it could even start."

"You agree, though, that it *might* succeed?"

"Certainly."

"And that if it did it would result in a speedy end to the war?"

"I'm not sure about that. It is possible, of course."

"But you admit the possibility of success, and surely even the slenderest chance is worth any conceivable trouble or sacrifice."

"I'm not certain whether I agree with you there, either. I spoke just now of the ultimate result of your scheme, and it is of that which I am thinking now. In the long run it might be better for Europe and the world that this war should be fought to a finish."

"But, good God, Colonel! Think of the appalling sacrifice of human life involved! Such a sacrifice would be utterly pointless if, as an alternative to it, we could overthrow the Nazi Government. After all, this war is different from other wars in that we are fighting a political party, not a whole people."

Colonel Lacroix sighed. "There you are wrong, my friend. Listen to me for a moment, please. You British are a sentimental people. You like to think of the typical German as a fat, good-hearted fellow who likes his beer and his music. You have now persuaded yourselves that he has been led astray by that big, bad wolf, Adolf Hitler, but that is not the case at all.

"There are, I admit, good, honest, intelligent and kindly Germans. No race is all bad. But however pleasant the average German may appear in peace-time, you will find that he is no longer a good, kindly fellow when he goes to war. Underneath his harmless exterior he has a cruel, barbaric streak, a love of regimentation, a lust for fighting and an inborn desire to dominate. The English always make the mistake of believing that the Germans are like themselves, but that is not true.

"Most English people prefer the Germans to the French. No, please do not protest ; I know quite well of what I speak. You consider that we are mean, egoistical and selfish—out for ourselves first, last and all the time. Those of your women who are romanticists disapprove of the realism which most Frenchmen bring to their love-affairs, while those who are more staid consider that there is something not quite nice about the amount of time which the average Frenchman devotes to his amours.

"Nevertheless, although you say you do not like us there is a great deal in common between our two races. It would be difficult to say which of the two has contributed more in the spheres of literature and art, in both of which we lead all the other nations of the world. Both races have developed to a point at which they hold their women in high respect and treat them as equals. Both have brought civilization to vast, overseas territories and both, above all, have a positively fanatical belief in the necessity of the freedom of the individual.

"It is for these reasons that although you must have heard innumerable English people say that they did not like the French I doubt whether you have ever heard one say that he did not like France. Between us we lead the world in an orderly, civilized way of life and deep down each race knows that the two peoples stand for the same ideals of toleration, justice and liberty.

"Now regard the Germans. You have a superficial liking for them because you are allied to their Saxon element by distant ties of blood. Your women prefer Germans to Frenchmen because they are also romanticists to a certain extent and are much more reticent than the French ; but what has Germany contributed towards the civilization of the world compared with ourselves ? Their art and literature cannot approach ours either in quality or in abundance. The average German despises his women, relegating them to child-bearing and household drudgery. The Germans can drive subject peoples to work for them by using the whip and the bayonet, but because they do not believe in, and are basically opposed to, the freedom of the individual they have proved themselves incapable of colonizing successfully.

"The German *likes* to be regimented, drilled and ordered about. He has no personal conscience and believes that any act, however brutal or despicable, is justified if carried out as part of a plan to enable Germany to enslave other races. That is why Germans of all classes demand a leader who will place the interests of Germany before those of humanity, before their own solemn pledge given in treaties and before the rights of neutrals, and the more unscrupulous that leader is the more they admire him."

As the Colonel paused Gregory said : "You consider, then, that Hitler and his crew are no better and no worse than other Germans ?"

"I do not say that, but I do say that Hitler achieved power only because he was the type of man that the German people wanted. His theories of Aryanism appealed to their narrow race-consciousness. Whereas France and Britain have always given their hospitality and protection to reputable folk of every race and colour the Germans *enjoyed* suppressing the Jews and other non-Aryan peoples. The easy, bloodless victories which Hitler gave them over the Saar, Austria and Czechoslovakia appealed to their vanity and stimulated their ambition to dominate other races. Their campaign against Poland has been carried out with a ruthlessness scarcely believable in an allegedly civilized people. It is true that Hitler ordered the attack but it was the German people, representatives of every class and community dressed in field-grey uniforms, who performed the individual acts of violence against Polish civilians, including women and children."

"What's the solution, then ?" Gregory inquired. "You say that it won't be sufficient to overthrow the Nazis when we're victorious, but we can't butcher or imprison a nation of eighty-five million people."

Colonel Lacroix smiled. "No. That would be both inhuman and unnecessary. The root of the trouble is that as a race the Germans are very backward.

"In England you had your revolution in the seventeenth century. Out of it there arose Oliver Cromwell, who suppressed individual liberty far more ruthlessly than had any of your kings, created a great Army and very nearly made you bankrupt in the process. You were very glad when your King Charles II came home to take over again. You had your revolution, but

afterwards things readjusted themselves and as a nation of free
people England has never looked back from that moment.

"In France we had our revolution at the end of the eighteenth
century. Out of it there arose Napoleon." Lacroix made a
gesture of salute. "The greatest military genius the world has
ever known. But he, too, suppressed individual liberty in a most
ruthless way, created a vast Army and nearly sent France bankrupt in the process. We were very glad when our king, Charles X,
came home to take over again. We had had our revolution ;
afterwards things readjusted themselves and as a nation of free
people France has never looked back from that moment.

"The Germans had their revolution only at the conclusion of
the Great War, early in the twentieth century. Out of it there
arose Hitler, who has suppressed individual liberty far more
ruthlessly than any of the German Emperors, has created a vast
Army and has very nearly made Germany bankrupt in the process.
We have therefore good historical precedents for hoping that
when Hitler's day is done things may readjust themselves in
Germany and that the German people will at last develop a true
appreciation of the value of individual liberty. Such an appreciation will alone make it possible for them to live happily and
prosperously within their own borders, no longer desiring to
threaten the freedom of their neighbours."

"Surely, then, the sooner we can get rid of Hitler the better ?"

"Of that I am not certain. As I have said, he has achieved
his present position only because he symbolizes the lust for power
and desire for domination which are still inherent in the German
masses. If he is too easily overthrown that spirit may not be
killed at his fall and another Hitler may arise in a dozen years'
time. Britain and France would then have to fight yet a third
Great War for the preservation of their ideals. Germany has
already had one lesson ; her defeat of 1914-18. It may be
necessary to give her several such lessons before her people come
to realise that our code of 'live and let live' is better than their
own crazy ambition to force their will upon others.

"It is my business to look into the future of France, and I
am inclined to think, therefore, that if only we had some means
of preventing its spreading to other countries it might be better
not to conclude this war too speedily but to carry it on until
Germany is beaten to her knees and every single German of this
generation is forced to realize that bullying does not pay, and to
teach that doctrine to his children. There would then be a real
hope that the rising generations of Germans might choose for

their rulers men of a different type—men sharing a greater, saner and more human outlook."

"Am I to take it, then," Gregory asked uneasily, "that you prefer not to give me your assistance now that you know the nature of my mission ?"

Lacroix shrugged. "First things must come first, and none of us can foresee the future. I was speaking only of possibilities. A long war might weaken both Germany and the Allies to such an extent that both sides would be in danger of falling an easy prey to the Bolsheviks afterwards. In any case it is our duty to spare our own generation all the suffering we can, so we should do our best to bring the war to a successful termination at the earliest possible moment. If you succeeded in your task it might bring about an internal upheaval causing Germany's collapse and the setting up of a new Government with which the Allies would feel justified in discussing peace terms, and I will therefore do all in my power to help you. Tell me, what is the first move that you intend to make ?"

"I shall see Madame Dubois if she's well enough, give her Archer's warning for what it's worth and try to persuade her to give me the names of some of the leaders of the Movement inside Germany."

"Good. As Madame Dubois is of the extreme Left she has no particular reason to be fond of the police. At times we have to check her activities, so I don't think I can help you in persuading her to give you the information your require. If you succeed in getting anything of interest, though, ring up my secretary, Jules Villebonne, at this office, and he will give you an appointment to come and see me again. We shall then be able to decide whether I can help you on the next steps of your campaign."

Gregory stood up and shook the diminutive, monkey-faced Colonel warmly by the hand. "I can never say how grateful I am to you, sir, for giving me this chance," he said fervently. "I only hope that I shan't disappoint you. May I take it that I'm discharged ?"

Colonel Lacroix smiled. "Without a stain upon your character. You will find Ribaud in Room 101 on the floor below this. He will attend to the necessary formalities and you will be able to establish yourself again in the comfort of the Saint Regis before luncheon."

Gregory found Ribaud, and the formalities of his release were soon concluded. As he drove back to the hotel after a fifteen-days' absence he felt a new man. The latter days of his confinement had irked him sadly and liberty was doubly good now that he had the support of the little Colonel and the prospect of going straight into action again.

Immediately he reached the Saint Regis he telephoned Madame Dubois' flat. Collette answered the call but did not appear to recognize his voice, and as he did not wish to waste time by entering into long explanations he gave a false name and inquired whether Madame Dubois had yet returned home. Collette told him that Madame was still in the nursing-home but was expected back at the end of the week.

He then rang up the nursing-home and asked if he might speak to Madame Dubois. The operator said that he could not, but that she would take a message. Gregory gave his proper name and put through an inquiry as to whether Madame Dubois would see him for a short time that afternoon on very important business. After a brief wait the reply came back. Madame would see him at four o'clock.

Having settled himself again in the Saint Regis he considered for a moment whether he should telephone Collette and surprise her by asking her out to luncheon, but decided against it. She was a delightful and amusing little person but she lacked the qualities which would have aroused real interest in him.

For Gregory beauty and gaiety were not enough. He demanded that any woman to whom he devoted himself should possess intellect in addition to these basic essentials. He thought, as he had often done during the past five weeks of the beautiful Lady of the Limousine. Now there was a woman to lunch with whom he would have crossed Europe, and if there had not been a war on he would have taken the afternoon plane into Germany to try to find her.

He wondered rather sadly if they would ever meet again, and had to confess to himself that it was very unlikely. Now that Hitler's impossible proposal that he should be allowed to get away with the murder of Poland and should be granted a cessation of hostilities until he might decide that the time was ripe to demand something else had been definitely rejected by the Allies there seemed to be every possibility that the war would drag on for two or three years at least, and Gregory knew himself too well to believe that the fleeting though extremely strong impression she had made upon him would last as long as that. By the time peace came he would have forgotten the way she had looked and the things she had said on their strange journey from Coblenz to Cologne, and even if he should chance to recall the memory of her, more recent matters would by then be absorbing his attention.

Instead of telephoning Collette, he went to a florist's and ordered a huge bunch of roses to be sent to her. On a card which was to go with them he wrote :

"I'm just as English as you are French, although the authorities took a fortnight to satisfy themselves about me. But I'd hate you to think that I bore you any grudge for being the cause of my spending a rather dreary couple of weeks, and you showed extraordinary cleverness in protecting your mistress's interests. I admire loyalty above everything, and so, *chère* Collette, I salute you. *Grégoire*."

Having lingered until half-past three over a luncheon at the *Cheval Pie*, which was in most pleasant contrast to prison fare, he bought himself a few new ties at Sulka's and then proceeded to Madame Dubois' nursing-home, arriving there punctually at four o'clock.

When he had given his name and Madame's room had been telephoned he was asked to go straight up. As he knocked on the door a rich, deep voice called : *"Entrez !"* He entered, to find that Madame Dubois was now out of bed and was lying, propped up with pillows, on a long sofa.

A bandage still covered a portion of her head, partially concealing her silver hair, but the cuts on her face could not have been serious as they were now perfectly healed. Gregory saw at once that he had to deal with a woman of very strongly marked personality. Her eyes were black and intelligent, her nose imperiously arched, her chin jutting and her mouth firm.

As he entered, instead of greeting him as he had expected, she raised her eyebrows in blank surprise and said swiftly : "Monsieur, you have made a mistake, I think. You must have been directed to the wrong room."

He hesitated on the threshold. "But aren't you Madame Dubois, then ?"

"I am."

"Well, I'm Gregory Sallust, and they told me downstairs that you'd see me. You gave me an appointment for this time, if you remember."

"What ?" she queried sharply, sitting up amongst her pillows. "You say you are Gregory Sallust ? But you cannot be—at least, you are not the Gregory Sallust that I know."

The smile on Gregory's lips faded. He shut the door behind him and advanced quickly into the room. "Madame," he said, "would you be kind enough to tell me how long you have been receiving visitors here?"

"I have been seeing members of my family for some days, but it was not until the day before yesterday that they would allow me to receive some representatives of the Press. I was allowed to interview business visitors yesterday for the first time."

"Then you saw a man yesterday who called himself Gregory Sallust?"

"I did." Her look of doubt and alarm suddenly deepened. "Do you insist that you are the real Gregory Sallust and that he was using your name?"

"I do, Madame. Could you describe him to me?"

"He was bigger than you; not exactly fat but plump-looking, with fair hair cut *en brosse* and a rather effeminate voice."

"God's death!" exclaimed Gregory. "Pardon me, Madame, but this is intensely serious. Do you know if he's still in Paris?"

"No. But you can find out; he was staying at the Hotel Crillon. I know that because he 'phoned up several times asking for an interview and was eventually persuaded to leave his address so that the people here could telephone when I was well enough to see him."

"Thanks. Permit me." Gregory snatched up a telephone connected to a wall-plug by a long flex and snapped out : "Police ! Urgent. *Sûreté-Générale, Deuxième Bureau.*"

He was connected almost instantly and asked at once for Jules Villebonne, secretary to Colonel Lacroix. A moment later Villebonne was on the line. Gregory gave his name and said :

"Whatever Colonel Lacroix is doing, please interrupt him at once to tell him that Grauber, the Gestapo chief, is in Paris. He has been here for some days and has used my name to obtain an interview with Madame Dubois. He saw her yesterday, and was then staying at the Crillon. Will Colonel Lacroix send some of his men to the Crillon immediately. I'm going straight there and will meet them in the hall."

While he was speaking Madame Dubois had risen to her feet. He turned to see her standing behind him, swaying weakly, her face suddenly old and haggard.

"What is this?" she stammered. "A Gestapo man? Merciful God ! What have I done? What have I done? I have been tricked, and people will pay with their lives for my stupidity."

Gregory put out a hand to steady her, and eased her down on to the sofa again. "Calm yourself, Madame, I beg," he soothed her. "The worst hasn't happened yet. I can identify him whatever name he's using there, and we shall be able to prevent his getting back to Germany with any information you gave him. I'll let you know the moment I have any definite news for you."

Snatching up his hat, he dashed from the room. Out in the street he hailed a taxi and promised the driver a hundred francs if he would get him to the Crillon in ten minutes. The cab started with a violent jerk almost before he could leap in, but as he was jolted back into his seat he was already feeling for his gun. He took it out and clicked a bullet up from the magazine into the chamber. Grauber would certainly be armed and Gregory did not mean to give him a chance to shoot first. He did not mean the French police to shoot him, either. Grauber was his pigeon.

Chapter XXIII

"THE BEST LAID PLANS O' MICE AND MEN"

DETERMINED as the taximan was to earn the hundred francs even at the risk of his own and his passengers' necks, and nobly though he succeeded, the agents from the *Sûreté* reached the Crillon before Gregory. As he entered the lounge of the hotel Ribaud broke away from a little group of men standing there and came up to him.

"I have men on the other entrances, Monsieur," he said in a low voice, "so if he's in the hotel we'll have him within the next five minutes. Let us make an inquiry at the porter's desk."

Ribaud flashed his card of authority in front of the hall porter and Gregory asked if a Mr. Sallust was staying there. The porter replied that no-one of that name had registered, but Gregory was not at all surprised at this as in order to do so Grauber would have had to fake a British passport in his name. Evidently Grauber had used it only when getting in touch with Madame Dubois' nursing-home and had told the hotel people that he was expecting a telephone message from a friend of that name who had not yet arrived.

On Gregory's describing Grauber the porter's face brightened at once. "It is Monsieur van Zelden that you mean, sir. He is a Dutch gentleman and has been staying in the hotel for the past week."

"Is he in?" asked Ribaud.

"No, Monsieur. He went out just after lunch, and has not returned yet. I have not been off duty since then so I would have seen him if he had come in again, but I'll ring his room if you wish to make quite certain."

"No, no." Ribaud promptly held up his hand. "Don't do that. I wish to speak with a representative of the management. But first I must telephone."

He got on to the *Sûreté*, and in order that the frontiers could be watched if Grauber should slip through their fingers, Ribaud gave Gregory's description of the German Grauber and the information that he was using a Dutch passport in the name of van Zelden.

An under-manager was then fetched and the business in hand explained to him, upon which he produced a set of pass-keys and at Ribaud's request took the party up in the lift.

Grauber, with the ample funds of the German Secret Service at his disposal, was evidently doing himself well. He had a suite consisting, so the manager informed them, of a bedroom, a bath-room and a private sitting-room.

On arriving at the sitting-room door Ribaud took the pass-key from the manager, inserted it noiselessly in the lock, turned it with his left hand and, drawing his gun with his right, flung open the door. Beside him Gregory also had his gun ready in his hand, but for the moment he had no occasion to use it. The hall porter had been right ; Grauber had not yet returned and the suite was empty.

"To save the possibility of trouble down in the hall we will wait for him here," Ribaud told the manager, and swiftly began to place his men. One he sent to the pickets on the entrances of the hotel with Grauber's description and instructions that they were to remain at their posts until further orders ; he was then to wait outside the main entrance and stop the German if, having once come in, he should attempt to leave again that way. A second man was to join the first at the main hotel entrance. A third was to take up his position in the floor-waiter's pantry further down the corridor so that he could cut off Grauber's retreat if he should try to escape. A fourth was to be provided by the manager with some window-cleaning utensils and make a show of cleaning a window at the other end of the corridor so that he could cut off Grauber's retreat in that direction, while Ribaud, his assistant Corbin and Gregory would remain in the suite to tackle Grauber when he appeared.

As the others went off to take up their positions Ribaud, Corbin and Gregory began to make an examination of Grauber's belongings. He had only one large suitcase, but practically every article of his in the suite showed the extraordinary care with which he had built up his identity as Heer van Zelden, a Dutch neutral.

A two-days'-old Dutch newspaper and some Dutch magazines littered the table in the sitting-room, a box of Dutch cheroots lay on the writing-desk and in one of its drawers were several correspondence files containing letters and invoices, all evidently faked or stolen, which would have at once satisfied any curious person that Heer van Zelden was undoubtedly the prosperous Dutch business man he seemed. Several of Grauber's ties had the tag of a haberdasher in Amsterdam and even his suitcase bore the mark of a Dutch manufacturer. There was nothing whatever to connect him with Germany or with his recent visit to England.

Having examined everything with considerable care they sat down to wait, but it was a dreary business. At five o'clock they were all keyed up in anticipation of his arrival. By six they had settled down, realizing that he might not be back until dinner-time. By seven they were anxious to get the job over. By eight they were keyed up again, but by nine they realized with irritation that he must be dining out.

Gregory and his companions were now both hungry and thirsty, so Ribaud telephoned down to the manager and asked him if he would be good enough to bring them up some sandwiches and a bottle of wine himself, as he did not want a waiter to know that there were detectives in Grauber's room or possibly to run into Grauber himself in the corridor, having just deposited the tray.

The manager appeared shortly afterwards with a good snack meal which whiled away the time until ten. They expected that Grauber might appear shortly after this hour owing to the curfew, but eleven came without his having done so and they decided that he must be visiting somebody in a private apartment.

By midnight they were thoroughly tired of waiting, but nevertheless had not the least intention of leaving without getting their man. At half-past twelve the manager appeared again, this time of his own volition, with a fresh supply of drinks. One o'clock came and two, but still no Grauber, so they began to think that he had succumbed to the attractions of Paris and having acquired a girl-friend had gone off to spend the night with her at her flat.

It seemed pointless for all three of them to spend sleepless nights, so they divided the remaining hours of darkness into watches, two of them remaining ready and alert in case Grauber should come in while the third snatched a couple of hours' sleep on Grauber's bed.

Corbin was given the first spell of sleep and Gregory the second. When they aroused him to relieve Ribaud it occurred to him to pass the time by making a more thorough examination of Grauber's belongings. He knew that every item would be scrutinized with microscopic care when it arrived at the *Sûreté* in case it might conceal a list of telephone-numbers or addresses or possibly the key to a cipher, but he saw no reason why he should not anticipate this scientific examination by a few hours.

Corbin agreed with him that it would be a good idea, so they set to work. The detective began to look through the Dutch newspaper and magazines for any advertisement or small paragraph amongst their letterpress referring to van Zelden or to the firm for which he was supposed to work, as any such item would be certain to contain some hidden meaning.

In the meantime Gregory took Grauber's razor and carefully cut in half each of the long Dutch cheroots in case one of them contained something written on a tissue-paper spill. Having cut Grauber's shaving-stick in pieces without result, he then ran the razor along the seams of the stiffer parts of Grauber's clothes, such as the collar of a spare lounge-suit, and took out the buckram, afterwards removing the soles of the German's bedroom slippers ; but in every case he drew a blank. His next procedure was to examine each item of Grauber's clothing to see whether it was evenly stitched throughout, as it is possible to conceal the key to a cipher in the irregularities of the stitching of some specially-sewn garment such as a tie, but here again he could find nothing out of the ordinary.

Corbin was still carefully scrutinising the pages of the magazines in the hope of finding some message which one of Grauber's colleagues in Holland might have inserted in the guise of an advertisement when Gregory began to tackle the big suitcase. When he had ripped out the lining of its bottom he found that beneath it, instead of leather, was a thin sheet of steel at one side of which there was a small nick. Inserting his nail in the nick, he pulled, and a portion of the plate slid back to reveal a shallow recess. This was only about an eighth of an inch in depth, but quite deep enough to hold the several sheets of paper which, to his joy, he found concealed there.

Corbin came over to help him examine them, but the papers contained only long lists of numbers which conveyed nothing at all to them. They were considerably elated by their find, however, as they had every reason to hope that they had found the key to one of the Gestapo's secret codes which the deciphering office of the *Deuxième Bureau* would be able to apply with valuable results.

There was one other item in the false bottom of the suitcase ; an oblong of cardboard, waistcoat-pocket size, in a cellophane cover. It had a certain similarity to the warrant of authority which Ribaud had flashed under Gregory's nose when he had arrested him, and Gregory saw that it was Grauber's identity-card as Chief of the Gestapo Foreign Department U.A.—1, giving him absolute power over every German and German agent outside Germany and powers almost as great in the Reich itself.

At eight o'clock they aroused Ribaud and told him of their find, which consoled him considerably for the otherwise fruitless night that they had spent. All three of them were unshaven, tired and irritable after their long vigil, but now that morning had come they began once more to hope that Grauber would put in an appearance. It was possible that he was breakfasting in bed with some young woman or had passed the night at the apartment of a friend, but as his baggage was still at the Crillon it was certain that he would return there during the course of the morning unless he had somehow learned of their presence at the hotel.

The manager brought them a *petit déjeuner* of rolls and welcome hot coffee, together with the morning's papers. As Ribaud's men had been on duty all night he telephoned the *Sûreté* and had them relieved, but as the morning wore on the three watchers began to feel despondent again.

It was possible that Grauber had an associate upon the hotel staff who had seen Ribaud and his men take up their positions and had promptly telephoned a warning. As Grauber was such a big shot there was good reason to suppose that he would employ subordinate agents to watch his quarters for his own protection. It was quite certain that he would not have left Paris without collecting his luggage and paying his hotel-bill unless he had had some extremely good reason for doing so, and by midday the conviction had grown upon Gregory and Ribaud that the German had been warned in time and had slipped through their fingers.

As there was still a faint hope that he might return to the hotel round about lunch-time they sat on doggedly until two o'clock, but they then finally decided that it would be useless to remain there any longer.

Ribaud left three of the relief men downstairs in the manager's office so that if Grauber should chance to come back that afternoon two of them could close the corridor to his room, once he was in it, and see that he should not get out again until the third man had telephoned the *Sûreté*. He then went off to report to his chief while Gregory returned to the Saint Regis.

He ordered a luncheon-tray to be sent up to his room and

ate a snack meal while bathing, shaving and changing, after which he went straight out again and took a taxi to the nursing-home.

Directly he sent up his name Madame Dubois said that she would see him, but he found her in an irritable mood which he knew would not be improved by the news he had to give her.

"Well?" she inquired sharply as soon as they had greeted each other. "Why did you not telephone as you promised?"

"I had no news to give you. Ever since I left you yesterday I've been with the *Sûreté* people in Grauber's suite waiting for him to return to the hotel. His baggage is still there but he hasn't turned up, so it now looks pretty certain that somebody tipped him off and that he's given us the slip."

A long sigh of relief escaped her. "You say that his baggage was still in the hotel when you got there at half-past four yester-day afternoon. That means he was still in Paris then, and could not have received any warning of your presence until later. Unless he left France by plane from some secret landing-ground he will not yet have got back to Germany. Therefore, the warning I have sent to the Comrades there will arrive in time."

"You've managed to get to work very quickly."

"That was not difficult ; such emergencies are arranged for. Immediately you left me I sent birthday greetings by telegram to friends in Belgium who will dispatch similar telegrams to my friends in Germany."

"You think, then, that they will be able to evade the Gestapo even when Grauber returns? Everything possible is being done to stop him on the French frontier, but he probably has a dozen aliases with passports to match and may succeed in getting through *via* Belgium or Switzerland."

Madame Dubois took out a compact and began to powder her beaky nose as she replied : "It would normally be very difficult for Germans to disappear from their ordinary occupations and move to other towns without the Gestapo's getting to hear of it, but the war has made a big difference. Quite early in the war the Saar area was evacuated and a fortnight ago the Ger-mans evacuated the whole of their civilian population for a depth of sixteen miles behind the Siegfried Line. The evacuations were carried out very hurriedly and they have lost trace of thousands of evacuees. They gave special broadcasts issuing the names of over ten thousand people on whom they were trying to check up. In such a state of confusion my friends stand a reasonable chance of moving from their homes to other parts of the country and passing themselves off as evacuees without arousing suspicion."

"That's good," said Gregory, "but what about the Army officers? They can't disappear like that."

"Army officers?" Madame Dubois repeated, looking at him in surprise. "What have they to do with this?"

"Surely you are aware," Gregory replied, "that the anti-Nazi politicals, the Intellectuals and certain high officers of the Army have sunk their differences, temporarily at all events, with the idea of taking concerted measures to overthrow Hitler?"

"I have heard rumours of that," she admitted, "and I hope that it is so, since one prominent Army chief would be worth a thousand poor, helpless working-people in any revolt against the Nazi régime. My friends, however, are the leaders of the German Freedom Movement which, as you know, consists almost entirely of the most resolute among the anti-Nazi working-classes."

"Would you mind telling me," Gregory requested, "just what took place when you saw this man Grauber who impersonated me?"

"He said that he came from Tom Archer who is a good friend of mine, and from the way he spoke of Archer he convinced me that he knew him well. He then went on to talk of the work we are doing, and he mentioned the names of a number of German refugees who are assisting to direct the Movement from Paris. I was naturally suspicious of him at first, but he produced a letter from a German who is still in Germany, speaking of him as entirely to be trusted. That convinced me of his *bona fides*, so I spoke openly of the Movement, and while he gave me what appeared to be a lot of information as to what was going on underground inside Germany I also mentioned the work that various other Comrades were doing."

"It was this letter he produced which persuaded you to talk, I suppose?"

"Yes. Without that he would have got nothing from me. It was an introduction from a well-known winegrower whom I had known for years and whom I trust implicitly."

"Was it by any chance from Julius Rheinhardt?" Gregory asked quietly.

She gave him a sharp glance. "Yes; how did you know?"

"I guessed it because Rheinhardt was arrested over five weeks ago. I thought they would have killed him long since, but evidently they decided to put him in a concentration-camp and make use of him instead. I'm afraid that letter must have been extracted from poor Rheinhardt under torture."

"*Mon Dieu!* These fiends!" With a violent gesture Madame Dubois stubbed out the cigarette which she was smoking. "Is there nothing they will stop at?"

"Nothing," said Gregory. "I suppose you don't know that poor Archer is dead and that he died from shock or a heart-attack after Grauber had had him kidnapped and had played the devil's game on him?"

She closed her eyes for a moment. "Poor Tom, poor Tom. So that's how Grauber got to know so much about me and the Movement here in Paris."

Gregory nodded. "It is clear, Madame, that you feel as I do about these people. I'm going to ask you now to give me all the help in your power."

"To what end?" she inquired.

"So that I may go to Germany and take certain steps which will be of enormous assistance to the anti-Nazis."

"How can I help you in that?"

"By giving me the names of the people you mentioned to Grauber so that I can get in touch with them when I arrive in Germany."

"But they will have had my warning by this time and will have left their homes to conceal themselves from the Gestapo, so even if I were willing to do so I could not now tell you where you would be able to find any of them."

"I see that," Gregory agreed, "but there must be others whom you know and whose names you didn't mention to Grauber?"

She gave him a swift, suspicious glance. "That is true, but I am afraid that I cannot give them to you either."

"Why? We are working for the same cause."

"As far as the overthrow of the Nazi régime is concerned, yes, but upon other matters we find ourselves in opposite camps. Grauber represented himself to me as a friend of Rheinhardt's, who is a capitalist but a man of very liberal views. He also represented himself as a friend of Archer, and as a man who shared the same political views as those held by Archer and myself. Those ideals are shared by most of my friends in Germany, but they are by no means the ideals of the French and British Governments. In fact, as you've no doubt heard, the French Government recently dissolved the French Communist

Party. You are an Englishman of good class and you are also associated with the *Sûreté-Générale*. I have therefore every reason to regard you as a political enemy."

Gregory began to speak, but Madame Dubois cut him short and hurried on.

"Let us suppose that there is a revolution in Germany. You have mentioned that certain Army chiefs might lead it. Do you think that if the revolution is successful the Prussian *Junkers* will give the German working-people a fair deal? No, no! That is too much to hope. They may combine to settle Hitler's business, but afterwards they will begin to quarrel. The Army chiefs will try to arrest the Marxist leaders and unless the common soldiers side with us the Generals will come out on top. The British and French Governments will not wish Germany to go Communist, and I know, my friend, how these things are done. Your Scotland Yard and the *Sûreté-Générale* will send lists of those German Marxists about whom they have information to the German Generals. If I give you the names of my friends their names will be on those lists and their situation will be no better than it is under Hitler."

"Listen, Madame." Gregory leaned forward and used his most persuasive tone. "You are a Red. I have always believed that a fair deal could be secured for the workers without their resorting to desperate measures, but you are quite justified in considering me as a White. Nevertheless, in this business we have got to sink our differences and combine. Whatever happens, the German workers' situation could not be worse than it is under Hitler. Let the future take care of itself. If only the war can be brought to a successful conclusion I think we may rest assured that the democratic Governments of France and Britain will insist that a democratic Government be set up in Germany, and that will curb the power of the Generals. Under a true Democracy the majority of the people will decide which form of Government they prefer and . . ."

"Under a true Democracy." Madame Dubois cut him short. "And you consider, I suppose, that France and England are true Democracies, although Chamberlain and Daladier have been ruling for months past with all the power of self-appointed Dictators?"

"I know for a fact, Madame, that the man in the street in both Britain and France has infinitely more freedom than his counterpart in Germany."

"Perhaps. But it is not enough—it is not enough. Private

ownership, the banks, hereditary privilege of every description must all go."

Gregory shrugged. "Madame, it can serve no useful purpose for us to discuss such problems now. The French and British Governments are out to destroy the Nazi system, which we both agree to be utterly evil. Surely, therefore, you will not let party politics sway your judgment and prevent your giving me your co-operation."

She shook her head. "I do not know. There is much in what you say, but we have worked for so long, for so many years, to bring real freedom to the peoples of Europe and the world. Many of my friends in Germany are entirely unsuspected. Even in the event of revolution they would remain behind the scenes and a new Government formed under the ægis of the Generals would know nothing of them. If I give you their names I jeopardise their whole future and the great work for humanity which they may do when things have settled down again."

She hesitated for a moment, then went on in a tired voice : "For me it is unusual not to see clearly the line that I should follow, but this injury to my head has robbed me of my powers of concentration. Perhaps, after all, we should attend to first things first, as you say, and bend all our energies to getting rid of the Nazis, whatever price we have to pay for it later. But I can give no decision now. I must think it out quietly. Yes ; when I am alone. I must think. Come to see me again to-morrow."

With that Gregory had to be content for the time being, as he saw that it was useless to press her further at the moment, so, making his adieux, he went downstairs and took a taxi to the *Sûreté*.

On the way he thought over his recent interview. Had he been able to approach Madame Dubois according to his plan, as a friend of Archer's and a Marxist sympathiser, he might have got the information he wanted. On the other hand, he might have failed to do so, since he had no letter such as that extorted from Rheinhardt by Grauber with which to convince her of his good faith.

Two thoughts, however, remained to console him : first, that as she evidently knew nothing of any Army chiefs involved in the conspiracy she could not have given away anything about them to Grauber, so at all events they were safe ; second, that as far as the German Freedom Party was concerned she held all the threads in her hands—threads which would certainly lead him somewhere if only he could lay hold of them. From

her last words, too, he felt that there would be a very good chance
of persuading her to line up with him at the interview arranged
for the following day.

On arriving at the *Sûreté* he sent up his name to Colonel
Lacroix, and after a wait of some twenty minutes he was taken
up to the big room on the sixth floor.

"So our bird escaped us," the Colonel said at once.

Gregory nodded. "Yes, sir. He must have had someone
planted in the hotel to watch his room, but the things I found
in the false bottom of his suitcase will, I hope, prove a lucky
haul."

"They have been handed to the deciphering office, and I
had word only a few minutes ago that the sheets of figures form
the key to a new code which had so far defeated our experts.
That is extremely valuable, and I am happy to offer you my
congratulations."

"Thank you, sir," Gregory smiled. "Our failure to catch
Grauber was damnably disappointing, though."

"We may get him yet. Unless he has a secret landing-ground
somewhere and can fly to and from Germany as he wishes he
will find it extremely difficult to leave France. The moment
you telephoned yesterday I gave instructions for a special
watch to be kept on the frontiers for a Heer van Zelden and his
description has been widely circulated in case he has several
passports and tries to get out under a different alias. I take
it you've been to see Madame Dubois again this afternoon?
What luck have you had with that troublesome lady?"

Gregory gave particulars of his interview with Madame,
and said he felt almost certain that with a little more persuasion
she could be induced to see reason.

"If your interview with her to-morrow is successful, what
d'you propose to do afterwards?"

"Go back into Germany, sir."

"How?"

Gregory smiled. "That, sir, is where I'd like to avail myself
of the assistance which you so kindly offered me yesterday."

Lacroix nodded. "I have no doubt that we can arrange
matters, but the choice of an identity suitable for the work
you have to do must lie with yourself. The Army did not prove
a very happy experiment as far as you were concerned, either
in the commissioned or non-commissioned ranks, but unfortunately every fit man of your years in Germany will be in some
kind of uniform by this time.

"We could, of course, give you a false hump which would demonstrate to all who saw you the reason for your not being in any of the fighting services, and you could carry the papers of a commercial traveller, which would justify your moving freely about from town to town, but the objection to providing you with any such marked deformity is that it would make you very easily traceable if some act of yours arouses their suspicions and they wish to rope you in for questioning."

"If you don't mind, sir, I'd like to think the matter over very carefully before coming to a decision."

"But certainly! Your life will depend upon your choice, my friend, so I hope that you will take as much time as you need. - I . . ."

The Colonel was interrupted by the gentle burring of a telephone. He picked up the receiver, listened for several minutes, saying *"Bon! Bon!"* at intervals, and replacing it, smiled across his desk at Gregory.

"Good news. We've got Grauber!"

"By Jove!" exclaimed Gregory. "What a grand surprise! A big man like that has so many underlings he can utilize that I felt quite convinced he'd get away. Did he come back to the hotel, after all, or did they pick him up at one of the frontiers?"

"Neither. He managed to get out of France, but the *Deuxième Bureau* knows no frontiers when it is after enemy spies. He left on the Amsterdam plane this morning, dressed as a woman. You mentioned, I think, that he has a high-pitched, effeminate voice, so he is probably used to playing such a part. He fooled the airport police here, at all events, but as several of the air services are now operating again, I warned our agents in Belgium, Holland, Switzerland, and Italy to keep a look-out for him when any planes arrived from France.

"You told me also that he had friends in the Dutch Passport Office, but he is not the only one to have friends there. Knowing that he had been staying here as a Dutchman I requested my friends in that office to make a particularly careful examination of any people purporting to be their own nationals who might come in by plane during the next twenty-four hours. Grauber was carrying the passport of a Vrouw Gotwinder of Haarlem and it was all in order, but one of the Dutch passport officials happened to come from Haarlem and to know that Vrouw Gotwinder died a few weeks ago. An examination by police matrons revealed that the lady carrying her passport was not a lady at all."

"Grand !" murmured Gregory. "But I suppose you can't extradite him ?"

The Colonel shook his head. "No. That we cannot do, but he will be charged with carrying a false passport and sentenced to a term of imprisonment. The Dutch are extremely anxious to preserve their neutrality, and the activities of people like Grauber are apt to jeopardise it. As we shall be able to provide them with particulars of his true identity I think we may rest assured that the sentence will be a heavy one, putting our friend Grauber out of the game for some time to come."

"Hang on, sir !" Gregory suddenly slapped his knee. "That's given me an idea. As Grauber has been knocked out of the ring and we've got his Gestapo chief's identity-card, why shouldn't I go into Germany as Grauber ?"

Colonel Lacroix's dark eyes twinkled in quick appreciation of the idea. "Why not ?" he murmured. "He stole your identity so why should you not borrow his for a little ? His offence makes him liable to imprisonment, not internment, so the German Legation will not be informed of his presence in Holland, and his associates in Germany will believe him to be still in France."

"How about his trial, though ?" Gregory asked, with sudden doubt. "If that's reported in the papers, the Germans are certain to see it. The people in the German Legation at The Hague are bound to hear about it, at all events."

"Perhaps the French Minister might be able to arrange for the case to be censored. He's on very good terms with the Dutch Government, and as a courtesy to him they would probably agree to Grauber's name not being mentioned at his trial. There would be nothing contrary to precedent in their trying him as an alien who had attempted to enter Holland with a stolen passport. The passport could not possibly have been issued to him owing to his sex, which makes the case a very simple one, and I see no reason at all for his real name to be given during the hearing."

"If you could arrange that," Gregory said, "I'd have a clear run. I'd have to chance coming up against some other Gestapo man who knew Grauber personally, of course, but that risk would be altogether outweighed by the enormous advantages I'd gain by assuming his status and privileges. I'd be able to travel on any train I wished merely by showing my pass, to commandeer cars and to lord it over everybody without one chance in ten thousand of meeting a man bigger than myself

in the Nazi hierarchy who would dare to challenge me. I suppose
you can get me the right kind of uniform ?"

"Oh yes, there'll be no difficulty about that, but while I could
smuggle you into Germany as a civilian by a dozen different
methods I don't see for the moment how I could do so if you were
dressed as a Group Leader of Black Guards."

"That is the snag," Gregory admitted. "They never wear
their uniforms outside Germany. How about landing me behind
the lines at night from an aeroplane ?"

"Perhaps that could be done, but it would be very risky.
When you made your first trip the war was only a week old,
Germany's eyes were fixed on Poland and it was no very difficult
matter for the British to land you unobserved in the flat country
north-east of Cologne, but the situation has changed a lot since
then."

"Over fifty Divisions have now been moved from the Eastern
to the Western Front to support the twelve already there. The
whole country for miles behind the Siegfried Line swarms with
troops, and that applies also to the country further north,
between Cologne and Aachen, as there are very heavy concentrations of enemy forces on the Dutch border. You would now
stand a much graver risk of landing in a field which, unknown
to us, had been occupied perhaps only a few hours before as a
bivouac for troops on the march.

"More important still, there is now ten times the aerial
activity over Western Germany that there was six weeks ago.
The British planes still fly over very high at night, but any
unidentified aircraft would certainly be challenged if it flew at
less than twenty thousand feet, so you would probably find
yourself being escorted down by a flight of Messerschmitts.
No. Such a project would be doomed to almost certain failure
and I cannot advise it."

"Say I took the uniform through in my luggage ?" Gregory
suggested.

Lacroix grimaced. "I don't like that either. All luggage is
now most carefully examined, not only for contraband but also
for newspapers and documents. They turn everything out of
the trunks and the Customs people go through them with a
fine-toothed comb. If you attempted to enter Germany either
as a neutral or as a German civilian the discovery of a S.S. chief's
uniform in your baggage would lead to your immediate arrest.
If on the other hand I had a passport and other documents faked
up for you purporting to show that you were actually Grauber,

the news of your arrival in Germany would get back *via* the frontier people to Gestapo headquarters in Berlin. When you failed to report they would immediately become suspicious and send out a broadcast call for you. When you still failed to turn up you would find yourself once again a hunted man."

"Supposing I had an outside suit of civilian clothes made and wore the Gestapo uniform under it ; then stripped off the civilian things when I had passed the frontier. How about that ?"

"No, my friend, no. Now that Germany is in a state of war she treats all visitors from outside her frontiers most unceremoniously. They have to strip in the Customs sheds and are searched to their skins, so if you tried that dodge you would be a dead man before you had been in the country twenty-four hours."

"I have it !" Gregory exclaimed suddenly. "I've been wanting to compare a bit of the Maginot Line with a bit of the Siegfried Line for a long time now."

"Ha, ha !" cried the Colonel. "I get you. It is an old trick and a good one. If you had been going over dressed as a German officer or private I would have suggested it myself. But you must remember that Gestapo chiefs are far too careful of their skins to go wandering about in the battle-zone, and since the Army detest the S.S. they would jump at the chance of hauling you up if they found you in their own territory."

"No, wait. You provide me with the uniform of a German soldier taken from one of your most recently captured prisoners so that it is that of a man belonging to a Division which is still in the Line. We pack my S.S. uniform into a knapsack and with a big mackintosh covering the whole caboodle one of your Military Intelligence people takes me up into the French trenches.

"During a night-attack I slip out into no-man's-land, shed the mackintosh and get across into the Boche front line looking like an ordinary Jerry with a two-days' growth of beard, then make my way back through the communication-trenches to the rear of the German battle-zone. Once I'm out of the military area I find a quiet spot where I can shed my soldier's uniform unobserved and put on that of a Gestapo chief, after which I can set about my business and use Grauber's card of authority without running any immediate risk of his apparent return from abroad being reported to Berlin."

The Colonel nodded. "That is good, my friend, really good. But you will have to risk being killed or wounded by a shell when you cross no-man's-land and you must not minimise the danger of running into somebody who knows Grauber even if you succeed in entering Germany."

"The first risk is no worse than any soldier has to face in a night-attack and the second can't be avoided. As an enemy agent inside Germany I'd be liable to be challenged at any moment whatever identity I might assume, and going as Grauber at least gives me a tremendous pull in that I can move about the country as quickly as trains and cars can take me and with absolute freedom, which is more than one out of a hundred thousand Germans can do at the present moment."

"Yes, that advantage is immense. So be it, then. See Ribaud on your way out and ask him to have you measured for an S.S. uniform. The S.S. are vain fellows and very smart, so it must fit you perfectly. The fit of the captured soldier's uniform is not so important and it will be best to have one which has been soiled in battle taken from an actual prisoner. I will get in touch with our Military Intelligence people about that."

Gregory smiled as he stood up. "I hope we're not trying to run before we can walk, sir, because it'll be no good my going back into Germany like a blindfold man, without a single clue to work on—and that'll be the position if Madame Dubois makes up her mind that she's not going to tell me anything to-morrow. If she does I'm afraid we'll have to wash the whole thing up and consider the game played out."

"But I thought you felt reasonably certain that you could persuade her to talk ?"

"I do, sir. She struck me as being a fine woman, but if I can't do it any other way I propose that with your permission we issue a warrant for her arrest."

"H'm," the Colonel grunted. "I fear that won't do much good. Madame Dubois is a woman of great character. Owing to her subversive activities she has been in prison on numerous occasions already, so if she makes up her mind not to talk I don't think for one moment that you'll succeed in opening her mouth by trying to bully her."

"I don't intend to, sir. The warrant would only be to give me the power to take her out of that nursing-home when she's well enough—which should be in a day or two now—but I don't propose to cart her off to prison. I shall take her instead to the biggest hospital in Paris to see the young men of France wounded and dying. She is a woman, *mon Colonel*, she will help us to stop the war after that."

The Colonel's face was wrinkled by one of his rare,

illuminating smiles. *"Bon garçon! Bon garçon!* How right I was to give you another chance!"

It was nearly seven o'clock when Gregory got back once more to the Saint Regis. Having had only two hours' sleep on the previous night he was feeling distinctly jaded, and as he wanted to be as fresh as possible for his all-important interview with Madame Dubois on the following day he decided to have something sent up to his room and get a long night's rest by turning in very early. When he had ordered his meal he undressed and went to bed.

The floor-waiter brought his dinner, with which he treated himself to a bottle of champagne as a good pick-me-up. Afterwards, relaxing between the cool sheets, he felt considerably better.

The plan for his return into Germany was a good one. He would spend a dangerous hour in crossing no-man's-land but he had been out on many a night-patrol in the last Great War and had no reason to suppose that conditions had altered very much. There would be the same old snags, such as barbed wire through which he would have to cut his way and Very lights which would reveal him to the enemy if he were not careful to conceal himself as he crept forward, but there would also be the same old muddy shell-holes and abandoned sectors of blown-in trench in which to hide.

Once he was inside Germany the chance of meeting anyone who knew Grauber personally would be really very slender. Say Grauber had even as many as one thousand personal acquaintances—a very high number for any man to have—there were still some eighty-five millions of Germans, so that only one German out of every eighty-five thousand would be capable of declaring on sight that he was not Grauber. Actually, too, the odds were enormously greater, for even if one of Grauber's acquaintances passed him in the street they would have no means of telling that the S.S. officer whom they saw was an impostor posing as Grauber, so the only real risks that he would be taking were those of registering at some hotel where Grauber was known or having to announce himself as Grauber to someone who knew the Gestapo chief by sight.

About Madame Dubois he was now reasonably sanguine. By one means or another he felt certain that he would be able to persuade her to talk. But, of course, everything depended on that.

At nine o'clock he put out his bed-side light and turned over to go to sleep. He was just dropping off when a gentle tapping on his bedroom door aroused him. Sitting up, he switched on the light again and called: *"Entrez!"* The door opened and Ribaud walked in, carefully closing it behind him.

"Hullo!" said Gregory, "You're looking a bit glum; what's the matter?"

The plump Frenchman nodded slowly. "I have reason to be, *mon vieux*. Colonel Lacroix has sent me to tell you that an explosion wrecked the nursing-home half an hour ago. Madame Dubois is dead."

Chapter XXIV

THE SCARLET IMPOSTOR

GREGORY groaned. "Poor woman! That's sunk us though; put paid to the whole caboodle. How did it happen?"

Ribaud shrugged. "It is impossible to say for certain as yet, but I can give a good guess. Madame Dubois' nurse was injured, but when she recovered consciousness she was able to make a statement. It seems that a parcel arrived for Madame by the evening post. It was a long box bearing the name of a florist, and the nurse remembers that at the time she took it upstairs she thought it curious that a florist should send flowers through the post instead of delivering them. She gave the parcel to Madame and the moment she had left Madame's room there was a violent explosion. She herself would have been killed had she not been on the far side of the door. It looks as though the parcel contained a bomb, concealed among the flowers, which was exploded by some mechanism or other as Madame opened it."

Picking up a cigarette Gregory threw the box down the bed to the Frenchman as he asked: "Have you any idea what time this parcel would have had to be posted to be delivered with the evening mail?"

"Yes. Parcels take longer than letters, especially in war-time. Even if it was posted in Paris it must have been handed in before the post-offices closed last night."

"That would have been Grauber's work then. If he'd learned obout our being at the Crillon soon after a quarter-past four, which was about the time we arrived, he'd have had ample time to prepare and post the box before six. Does the nurse remember the name of the florist?"

"Unfortunately, no. She noticed only that the address was in Clichy, but that gets us nowhere. I'd bet a cask of Bordeaux to a whisky-soda that the florist was an innocent party to the crime. As I reconstruct it, Grauber bought some flowers from the nearest florist directly he'd been warned and took them back to the apartment at which he had received the warning—which might be anywhere in the Clichy district. He inserted the bomb, then either went out himself to post the parcel or sent one of the occupants of the apartments, who must be his agents."

"Then it looks as though my trip to Germany is off."

"I fear so. There's no sense in risking your neck to no purpose, and that's what you would be doing if you went with nothing to work on."

"All right ; there it is. I've had some narrow escapes in this affair so I mustn't grumble at Fate, but she's certainly played some dirty tricks on us so far as the business itself is concerned. One way and another we've had filthy luck. Will you thank Colonel Lacroix for letting me know so promptly and say that I'm entirely at his disposal if he can spare time to see me and thinks there's anything else I can do ? Frankly, though, I can't see any possible opening at the moment."

"*Certainement*. I'll give the Colonel your message. At all events it looks as though you'll have a more comfortable time to-night than we did last night. I'm just going off duty and I'll be glad to get to bed myself."

"Well, a jolly good night to you ! You've earned it."

Gregory managed to raise a smile and Ribaud smiled back as he left the room.

Though Gregory lay awake for some time puzzling his wits to find some fresh way in which to tackle his problem he could not for the life of him think of one, so his elation of half an hour before having sadly evaporated he put out the light once more and went to sleep.

By late the following afternoon he had heard nothing from Colonel Lacroix so he began to ring the numbers of a few of his old friends who normally lived in Paris. It was a forlorn hope to try his best friend, the gay and debonair Jean de Brissac, but all the same he rang up the Invalides and found as he had expected that Captain de Brissac was away with his Regiment.

Gregory soon found that nearly all the people he knew were out of Paris employed on some form of war work or other but he managed to locate Paul Desvoeux, a prominent journalist who was also an expert on foreign affairs, and arranged to lunch with him on the following day. Later that evening he ran into a Royal Flying Corps officer in the Ritz bar who was a friend of his and the two of them spent as hectic an evening together as war-time Paris could provide.

No word came from Colonel Lacroix either on the Wednesday or Thursday so Gregory killed time as well as he could, but on the Friday morning he received a telephone message asking him to call at the *Sûreté-Générale* at six o'clock.

When he was shown into the Colonel's room the little man said : "I regret that I've had to keep you doing nothing for these last few days when you probably wished to return to England, but I have had many other affairs to attend to and I wished to see you again for a last talk before you left France. I also have a telegram for you."

"The original one, I suppose ?" Gregory smiled ruefully.

"No, another. It came in yesterday."

Taking the flimsy, Gregory read :

"RUDD SAFE HOME BUT YOU STILL GALLIVANTING WITH THE GIRLS IN PARIS I SUPPOSE STOP WONDER IF HAVE ANY MONEY LEFT AFTER WHAT YOU MUST HAVE HAD TO SPEND ON WREATHS STOP HAVE THROWN KUMMEL BOTTLE IN DUSTBIN STOP CANCELLED ALLOTMENT AND BESPOKE PADDED CELL FOR YOU INSTEAD STOP GWAINE-CUST."

"Evidently he has heard about Madame Dubois' death," supplemented the Colonel.

"That's about it, and I'm afraid I've let the old chap down pretty badly."

"No fresh line of attack has occurred to you since our last talk ?"

Gregory shook his head. "I'm sorry, sir ; I've puzzled my wits with the problem until they're half-silly but now Madame Dubois is dead I'm afraid we're up against a blank wall once more."

"That is regrettable, because if only you could have succeeded in your mission you might have performed a great service to humanity. An internal revolution in Germany might well have put an end to the conflict in its early stages, whereas there is now a grave danger of its spreading."

The Colonel was in a talkative mood, and went on to give Gregory an outline of the situation.

"The Turks have behaved splendidly, and their check to Russia has temporarily relieved us of grave anxieties in the Near East, but I fear that Stalin's appetite has been whetted by his easy conquests. It may be that he has only seized this opportunity to lock his gateways more firmly against possible future aggression in the West, but there are sinister indications that he is reviving all the old, imperialistic aims of the Tsars.

"Ever since the Russian troops marched into Poland they have been hard at it Bolshevising that part of the country which they took over. Estonia, Latvia and Lithuania, though retaining a nominal independence, must now be regarded as forming part of Russia.

"Finland may succeed in maintaining her independence with the backing of the Scandinavian kings and the United States. Field-Marshal Mannerheim will fight if necessary. He is a great soldier and a great patriot. In 1918 he ignored his Government's order to sue for peace, and with an army of 12,000 peasants he drove 90,000 Russian Red Guards out of his country. Unfortunately, however, the Finnish Air Force is almost negligible, and how can the Scandinavian countries hope to defend themselves against the terrific weight of the Red Army if Stalin once sets it in motion?"

"Still," Gregory smiled, "it's the Germans who have suffered most through the reshuffle in the Baltic."

"True. The new situation there does not affect the Allies very seriously, save as a grim indication of possible eventualities in other areas. We've always regarded it as a Russo-German sphere of influence and can only hope that these two strange bedfellows will sooner or later cut each other's throats over Sweden. But will Stalin be content with his gains in the North? The Turks may succeed in persuading the Rumanians to come to some arrangement with the Russians over Bessarabia and with the Bulgarians over the Dobruja, but immense Russian forces are now massing further east on the borders of Turkey, Iraq and Afghanistan."

Gregory shook his head. "I think it most unlikely that the Turko-Russian friendship will be broken, and the Turks are a very brave people. Surely Stalin will only be playing our game if he has any idea of expanding his native Georgia and coming down from the Caucasian Mountains into the Turkish plain?"

"Perhaps. But Iraq and the oil-wells must be a temptation to him, and Afghanistan is in no position to resist Russian aggression. The British are confident that they could hold the north-west frontier, but a war in India would automatically divert a considerable portion of their main war effort from Germany, and as a certain section of the Indian population has been clamouring for self-determination for many years they might seize the opportunity to stage another Indian mutiny."

"In that case, perhaps the best solution would be to go the

whole hog and give India her independence," Gregory remarked. "We had a packet of trouble in Egypt up to a few years ago, but once the decision was taken that the British were to withdraw the attitude of the Egyptians changed entirely. Instead of throwing stones at the British police and Tommies, they said that as long as they were allowed to rule themselves they were only too pleased, for us to remain and train their own army. It was a case, I think, of 'Better the devil you know than the devil you don't', and they infinitely preferred the British staying there to the possibility of Mussolini's walking in one fine day over the Libyan border. Consequently, we are now in the happy situation of being able to regard Egypt as one of our most loyal allies."

Colonel Lacroix shook his head. "The two problems are entirely different. The people who do the talking in India are drawn almost entirely from one class, that of the educated Babus, who inhabit the great cities. They do not voice the opinions of the Princes who still controlled huge States, neither do they speak for the inarticulate masses of the south-east. These people would much prefer a continuance of the British Raj to being ruled by Babus who are every bit as foreign to them as are the English."

"That's always been my view," Gregory agreed, "and I was speaking only of a measure which might be very bad in the long run, but the only sound one to take in a possible eventuality."

"Exactly. And it is just such possible eventualities which are keeping the Allied Statesmen awake at night. Take Holland. Personally, I do not believe that Hitler will invade the Low Countries until the spring, and our main danger there is the possibility of his invading Holland, but not Belgium. If, in that case, the Belgians did not voluntarily go to the assistance of the Dutch it would be impossible for us to send military support to the Dutchmen without infringing Belgian neutrality."

"And once he had overrun Holland he'd be in an infinitely better position to start the big *strafe* on Britain," added Gregory.

"Not only that," the Colonel went on. "He could offer the Dutch East Indies to the Japanese. Relations between Britain and Japan have greatly improved of late, but the Japanese have little scruple about taking other people's territory, as we have seen from their endeavour to subdue China. With a major war on their hands in the West, could Britain and France give sufficient support to Australia and New Zealand right at the other end of the world to enable them to prevent the Japanese acquiring a vast new Empire throughout the whole of the Australasian continent ?"

"There's always the United States," Gregory murmured.

"They did not go to war to protect their own interests in China, so why should they go to war to protect our interests in the Pacific ?"

"How about Mussolini ?" Gregory suggested. "Italy is a first-class Power these days, and Mussolini's very ambitious to increase his Empire. If the Dutch would agree to give him a good slice of their East Indian possessions he might be induced to send the whole of his fleet and the best part of his Air Force out there to get them.

Colonel Lacroix smiled. "A most interesting idea, and the one good thing which has come out of the reshuffle is the excellent *rapprochement* between Britain and France and Italy. Short-sighted people blamed Chamberlain and Daladier for Munich, but it gave us time to press on with our rearmament and time to weaken the Berlin-Rome Axis sufficiently for Hitler's scrapping of the anti-Comintern Pact to wreck it entirely. Through that we have regained the invaluable friendship of Italy and Spain.

"But to sum up, you will see that although there is a lull at the moment the whole world is now a tinder-box, and sparks may cause it to burst into flame at any moment in a dozen new directions. It has therefore become more vitally important than ever that the war in the West shall be brought to a successful conclusion before that happens. Once Germany's out of the ring there'll be little likelihood of Russia's moving, or the drawing in of Holland, Belgium, Switzerland, Hungary the Balkans, Finland, Turkey, India, Japan and half a dozen other nations. That is why I felt that I had to talk to you again to find out if there was any conceivable way in which you could endeavour to make a new start on your mission."

"The only thing I can suggest, sir, is that since I've got nowhere with the subversive elements, I should attempt to get right to the heart of the matter by tackling somebody high up in the German Army. But whom to tackle ? That's the question. If you can give me the name of a really important Army leader whose past history leads you to suppose that he may be involved in this affair, I'm willing to go back into Germany and take the big gamble of going direct to him and laying my cards on the table."

The Colonel nodded. "That is a very gallant offer, Monsieur Sallust, as to do as you propose would be tantamount to walking blindfold to your own death. If the General you approached were not involved in the conspiracy you would be led straight out and shot, while even if he were, and you could not persuade him of your *bona fides*, he might have you executed for his own protection."

"The risk isn't really greater, sir, than those which thousands of our own men are facing every day at the Front, or that which the British pilots took when they dived flat out to within a hundred feet of the mastheads of the German battleship they bombed at Kiel."

Colonel Lacroix shrugged noncommittally. "If only General Baron von Fritsch had not been murdered I'd have let you go to him. Prince Rupprecht of Bavaria would also have been a worthwhile bet, but I hear that he, too, has been assassinated by the Gestapo on Hitler's orders because it was feared that in the event of a rising he might proclaim himself Regent of Bavaria. Field-Marshal von Blomberg, who had the confidence of the Army before his disastrous marriage, is now a prisoner in the fortress of Landsberg. With him are Generals Pogrell, Niehot and Lang, all good men, but rendered powerless. Then there was a new purge only last week. Von Hammerstein, a former Chief of the General Staff, and von Stulprangel, with several others, were all removed from their commands because they were suspected of Monarchist tendencies. They were all probably involved in this conspiracy, but it is useless to think of them now.

"Of those who remain, von Brauchchitsch is an unknown quantity and von Keitel is so very anti-British that I think he is almost certainly hand-in-glove with von Ribbentrop."

"What about a really bold stroke?" Gregory suggested. "Say I went to Goering?"

The Colonel did not say that Gregory was mad, but considered for a moment before replying. "I see how your mind is working. Evidently you appreciate, as I do, that Goering is in a class apart from the other Nazis. He is no soap-box orator, but an ace airman of the last War, with many powerful connections. He owes his rise almost entirely to that, and to his really magnificent organising ability. It was he who won over the *Reichswehr* for Hitler, who still uses him as his main go-between with the Army leaders. The other Nazis would have pulled him down long ago if it hadn't been that Hitler is the master of them all, and knows very well that Goering is really more important to him than any of his other supporters because he is respected by the Army and is the one Nazi in whom the upper classes have any faith.

"How the Allied Governments would view a new German Government purged of the Nazis and headed by 'Iron Hermann' I can't say, but Goering keeps his word and the one thing that they would demand of any new German Government is trustworthiness. I have no doubt at all, though, that the Army chiefs would follow him if he decided to throw Hitler and the rest overboard."

"Well, I'm prepared to have a shot at getting to him if you wish it, sir."

"No. I'm afraid I can't allow that. You see, we have as yet not one atom of proof that Goering is disloyal to Hitler or that he could be tempted to become so, and I'm not going to send you on a mission which has so fantastically small a chance of success."

"D'you think it's any good my trying those Generals whose names begin with 'Gra . . .' ? The ones Sir Pellinore Gwaine-Cust turned up, I mean. They were Generals Grabenhoff, Grauwitz, and Gröner."

"No. None of them is of sufficient importance to be the man we're after. But wait a minute ! Tell me again exactly what Pastor Wachmuller said just before he was shot."

"He said, 'When you see General Gra . . .' "

"Ha ! Then I don't believe he meant that 'Gra . . . as the first syllable of any surname at all. I believe he was going to say 'General *Graf* von something-or-other.' There are many Counts in the German Army, and that would have been much more likely."

"By Jove, you're right !" Gregory exclaimed. "Now, who is there that's both a General and a Count, and might be our man ?"

The Colonel pressed a bell-push and had a German Army List brought. They went through it very carefully, but it conveyed little to them ; so many of the high officers of the German Army had come from noble families and had succeeded to their titles by the time they had reached the rank of General. There were General Count von Arnhem, General Count von Blauwitz, General Count von Braunberg, General Count von Busfeld and dozens of others. Most of them held comparatively unimportant posts, and though a few were on the Great General Staff or commanding Army Corps it was utterly impossible to decide which of these titled Generals might be the head of the conspiracy.

In the end Gregory realized that the search was hopeless. "What filthy luck it was," he murmured, "that we lost the best lead of all before I had a chance to use it."

"What was that ?"

"Why, the woman who was the mistress of Hugo Falkenstein, the armaments millionaire ; the beautiful aristocrat who holds in her hands the threads of every Army intrigue and has known all the German Generals since she was in her cradle—Erika von Epp."

"Erika von Epp ! What has she to do with this ?"

"I thought I'd told you. It was she to whom that little reversed swastika belonged, and when she was in London just before the war she drank to the time when her own friends would be back again at the head of affairs in Germany. Unfortunately, she was on the high seas on her way to New York when war was declared, and none of our people have been able to trace her in the United States, so it looks as though she's gone down to Mexico or South America on some mission for the Germans."

"*Parbleu !* You're wrong there," exclaimed the Colonel, "she was back in Germany a week after war was declared. The day the Nazis marched into Poland she changed ships in mid-Atlantic, presumably on instructions from her Government. The ship to which she transferred was one of those which eluded the British Navy in the first days of the war by sailing round the North Cape ; it landed her at the Russian White Sea port of Murmansk, and she flew home from there."

"Your agents serve you well, *mon Colonel*," said Gregory with rising excitement.

"Erika von Epp has always been worth watching. She is one of the most dangerous, as well as one of the most beautiful, women in Europe."

"And I haven't a doubt that it's she who holds the key to this riddle. I'd never have dreamed of wasting my time on people like Rheinhardt and Archer if I'd thought there was the least chance of getting in touch with her. And she's back in Germany, eh ? D'you happen to know where she is at the present time ?"

"That I cannot say, as she moves about the country a great deal. She has an apartment in Berlin, but her home is in Munich.

You knew, of course, that she married about a year ago ? She's now the Countess von Osterberg."

Gregory smiled. "Her conduct in London just before the war didn't indicate that she took her marriage very seriously. She takes it so lightly, in fact, that she doesn't even use her title, but continues to be known by her maiden name."

"She's a mysterious woman, if ever there was one : rich, beautiful, clever and with a finger in every international pie. If you were willing to gamble your life there'd be some real justification for risking it on the chance of opening communications with the German Army leaders through her."

"I'll start for Germany just as soon as that S.S. uniform you were going to have made for me is ready."

"Good boy ! Good boy !" said the Colonel, with a smile. "I don't think the order for it was cancelled, so find out from Ribaud about a fitting. The uniform will take a few days to complete, but I'll get in touch with our Military Intelligence people at once and discuss with them which will be the best sector in which to operate when you make your attempt to cross no-man's-land. Have you any personal preference ? If you know one sector of the Front better than the rest you may have less difficulty in finding your bearings when you arrive behind the German lines."

"I don't think it matters much. I've motored through most of the country between Luxemburg and Basle at one time or another, and on both sides of the frontier, but I don't know any particular part well enough for it to make any difference. Still, there is one thing I'd like if it could be arranged. I've a great friend, Captain Jean de Brissac, and if his Regiment happens to be anywhere near the Front, I'd like to take the opportunity of seeing him again. If he could be detailed to act as my liaison officer to shepherd me through the Army zone to your front line—unless, of course, he's engaged on especially important work—I'd be grateful."

"De Brissac—yes, I know him. A very promising young officer to whom we owe the invention of our new machine-gun. He was the man who had such extraordinary adventures in the South Atlantic, wasn't he ? Didn't he get marooned for several months on some unknown islands in the uncharted seas ?"*

"That's the fellow, sir."

"Well, he's a Major now, and he left his Regiment only a

*UNCHARTED SEAS (Hutchinson & Co.), 16th Impression.

day or two ago to take up a Staff appointment. I'll find out about him and see what can be arranged."

Colonel Lacroix stood up, and Gregory realized that the interview was over. Downstairs he met Ribaud, and arranged for a fitting of his S.S. uniform that afternoon, then, with a lighter heart than he had had for some days, he left the Sûreté to turn over the new plan in his mind and make preparations for it.

There were actually very few preparations that he could make, save to get some large-scale maps and study them with a view to obtaining a thorough knowledge of the topography of the country behind the German battle-front and to buy a Baedeker's *Germany*, in order to refresh his mind about the lay-outs of Munich and Berlin.

He wrote a brief note to Sir Pellinore saying that he would not yet require the padded cell as he proposed to remain on the continent and a long letter to his old friend Rudd, thanking him for the part he had played in Holland and enclosing a cheque for a substantial amount which would ensure his not having to worry about the uncertain rents of his other tenants for some time to come.

It was Tuesday, just a week after Madame Dubois' death, and the last day of October, before he heard from the Sûreté again. Ribaud telephoned him after luncheon to come for a final fitting of his S.S. uniform. With its white tabs and silver braid on the dead black, its high-crowned cap, its swastika armlet and its silver eagle it was a tremendously impressive affair. The tailor who had measured him for it had done a good job of work, and declared that he could carry out the one or two very minor alterations necessary that evening, and have it finished by the following morning.

Gregory's original idea had been to carry this uniform through the German lines in a knapsack, but when he thought the matter over more carefully he soon realised that no soldier would go out on a trench raid carrying a heavily-loaded knapsack on his back and he therefore asked Ribaud to arrange for him to be provided with a wooden box of some kind, bearing German lettering, which had contained ammunition or stores.

They then discussed what he should take into Germany with him and went carefully through Grauber's belongings. Except for the soap his shaving-kit was still intact, so Gregory selected this, a set of his enemy's underclothes to wear and a few other small items which he could stow away in the wooden box which he would receive at the same time as the German private's uniform in which he was to cross no-man's-land. When this had been arranged Ribaud told him to report again at ten o'clock on the following morning and to be ready to leave Paris forthwith.

On the Wednesday, having packed up his own belongings and deposited them with the manager of the Saint Regis, he paid his bill and went to the *Sûreté*. He was shown straight up to Colonel Lacroix, who proceeded to give him his final instructions.

"The S.S. uniform and the oddments of Grauber's you are taking have been packed in a suitcase for you," he said. "Here is a first-class railway voucher. You will catch the midday express for Nancy. The train services from there are now irregular, of course, but your friend Major de Brissac will meet you on the station and motor you to the headquarters of a Division near Saarbrücken. We selected that sector because it is a quiet one, yet not so quiet that a small, local action will arouse undue comment, and because the houses of the evacuated town will give you good cover for the first stage of your journey through the enemy lines.

"At the Divisional Headquarters they will give you dinner and provide you with facilities for changing into the soldier's uniform. The Divisional Intelligence Officer will then accompany you as far as the front-line trenches, where a Company Commander will give you particulars of the local terrain. We have arranged for a trench raid to be made at about 11.30, as with the exception of their sentries the Germans will by then have settled down for the night, but you will thus have the maximum number of hours of darkness in which to work and with good luck you should be far enough behind the lines to change into your S.S. uniform before dawn. As your *Reichmarks* were returned to you on your release together with Erika von Epp's swastika I assume that you have ample funds."

Gregory nodded, and the Colonel went on :

"Here is Grauber's card of authority and here are a few letters purporting to have been written to him which I have had faked up as an additional means of establishing your identity as Grauber should it prove necessary. On this slip of paper I have put Erika von Epp's two addresses : Apartment 64, the *Eitel Haus*, Unter den Linden, Berlin, and *Das Kleine Schloss*, Prinz Ludwig's Höhe, Munich. Prinz Ludwig's Höhe, as you are probably aware, is a suburb of Munich some fifteen minutes' run by car from the centre of the city, where there are many big houses, each with its own grounds and gardens. You'd better memorize these addresses and then destroy the paper. I have also one piece of good news for you. Grauber was brought before a Dutch court yesterday and sentenced to six months' imprisonment. His real name wasn't mentioned so as far as he's concerned you have an absolutely clear run."

"Well, that *is* good news," Gregory grinned. "I hope he doesn't miss the revolution, though, because I'll have murder on my hands if he doesn't get what's coming to him and the rest of his gang of cut-throats from the German people."

"I also have a telegram for you." The Colonel stooped to his desk, which still had not a single sign of activity upon its top, and opened a drawer. "Here it is."

"What, another?" laughed Gregory as he took the slip. It read :

"HAVE REPLACED BOTTLE AND AM ADDING ELEVEN MORE BOUGHT TO-DAY BY TELEPHONE FROM THE TOUR D'ARGENT STOP BUT WILL NEVER TOUCH THE STUFF AGAIN UNLESS WE CAN DRINK TO YOUR SUCCESS IN IT STOP GWAINE-CUST."

"Why this change of heart, I wonder?" Gregory murmured.

"I took the trouble to inform him," said Lacroix quietly, "of the considerable service you rendered us in getting the key of that Gestapo code, and that you were returning into Germany with a new line on the old affair."

"That was very good of you. You see, I value his opinion of me enormously and it's grand to have this telegram from him before I start. I value your opinion too, sir, and you may be sure that I'll do my damnedest to pull this thing off."

"I know you will." The bright-eyed Colonel stood up and extended his hand. "If you succeed you will have earned the gratitude not only of Britain and France but also of the whole world. May *le bon Dieu* have you in his keeping and grant you wisdom, courage and resource."

On leaving the strange little man who was the custodian of so many secrets Gregory went downstairs, collected the suit-case from Ribaud and took a taxi straight to the station.

His reservations were all in order and the train steamed out punctually at midday. As it gathered speed a phrase in Sir Pellinore's second telegram recurred to his mind : "*Wonder you have any money left after what you must have had to spend on wreaths.*"

A horrible truth lay behind the half-humorous gibe. He was indeed a bird of ill-omen. Rheinhardt was probably dead by now. Pastor Wachmuller had been shot before his eyes. Archer, Rosenbaum, Madame Dubois—all were dead, and it was he who, through his impostures, had brought death—agonizing, bloody, scarlet death upon them.

Now that he was once more to become an impostor and plunge headlong into the deadly game how many more unfortunates were to be blotted out through this terrible scarlet hoodoo that seemed to be upon him? It was a horrible thought and he forced it from his mind, knowing that he should snatch what sleep he could while the train roared on towards the now ever-moving frontier where night and day the advance troops of the mighty French and German armies were at deadly grips.

Chapter XXV

BEYOND THE MAGINOT LINE

IMMEDIATELY he stepped out on to the platform at Nancy Gregory heard a joyful shout, and his old friend, the dark, dashing de Brissac, gay in his smart uniform of horizon-blue and his scarlet, gold-braided *képi*, came hurrying to meet him.

De Brissac piloted him to a closed car and they were soon heading for the battle-front. A chill wind was blowing and it was raining, but the weather did not seem to depress the Frenchman, who gave free rein to his delight at this unlooked-for reunion that the war had brought about. He asked no questions, however ; it was his job to convey Gregory through the French military area, not to inquire as to what work he might be engaged upon.

They took the road to Château Salins, where they first heard the mutter of guns, then bore north-east *via* Baronweiler and Faulquemont. From Baronweiler onwards signs of military activity increased, and soon they were threading their way in and out of the long, twin processions of lorries and mechanized units moving to and from the Front. Every village through which they passed was crowded with French troops in khaki, while here and there they picked out the uniform of an English officer on some special duty or the blue of British Air Force detachments. Long lines of tanks were drawn up on special metalled sidings by the roadside, batteries of artillery, ambulance units and engineer companies seemed to be parked in nearly every field, while on the fringes of every wood they passed infantry or airmen were cooking their suppers, and they could make out the shapes of planes lightly concealed by branches broken from the trees.

Owing to the patterns with which everything was camouflaged it was impossible to see much of the war equipment until they were quite close to it but it was obvious to Gregory that enormous reserves of troops and material had been concentrated there in readiness for the great battle which had been preparing for weeks, and which might still be launched at any moment if Hitler were mad enough to override the counsels of those of his Generals who were urging him to be patient until the Spring.

Between Faulquemont and St. Avold they passed through the Maginot Line, but by that time the evening light was failing and Gregory could see little of it except occasional rows of concrete and steel tank obstacles winding away on either side of the road and huge, grass-covered mounds which had low doorways in their rear showing that they were forts and gun emplacements.

The booming of the guns was much louder now and individual reports could be clearly distinguished against the background of their dull, distant rumbling. Occasionally there came a sharp explosion and a great cloud of black smoke billowed up across the evening skyline as the Boche *strafed* the French back areas, or with a sound like the crack of a giant whip one of the French big guns sent a great shell rumbling overhead towards the Siegfried Loop.

It was dark by the time they reached Forbach, a small town some five miles from Saarbrücken, which was still in German hands, and only about three from the frontier. In this sector the French had neither advanced nor retreated very far as the outworks of the Siegfried Line ran nearer to the frontier here than at any other point along the whole battle zone. A bow had, in fact, been thrown out from the Loop of the Siegfried Line to protect Saarbrücken, and it was within this, right on the frontier itself, that sporadic fighting had been taking place ever since the war had broken out two months before.

Even the dimmed lights of the car showed a little of the damage that had been done by the constant shelling of the German heavies, but they turned right on reaching Forbach's ruined market-place and ran out of the wrecked town to a small *château* that was being used as a Divisional Headquarters. One wing of the building had been shattered and as Gregory followed de Brissac out of the car he saw a lot of the fallen rubble in the courtyard, but the rooms in the rest of the house had remained untouched and great activity was going on within.

De Brissac led Gregory into the anteroom of the Officers' Mess and introduced him to a Staff Colonel who in his turn introduced both of them to a number of other officers, and soon they were all having drinks together.

No-one inquired what a civilian was doing there. The presence of de Brissac, now attached to the staff of the Fifth French

Army, as Gregory's sponsor was enough, and the Divisional Commander greeted them both with warm handshakes. After this dinner was announced and they all moved into the Mess.

It was a simple but good meal, washed down with an excellent though not outstanding claret, and Gregory would dearly have loved to have lingered there exchanging jokes and reminiscences of the last war with these genial Frenchmen, but he had work to do. Immediately after dinner, therefore, de Brissac asked the General to excuse them both and they were taken by an orderly to the office of the Divisional Intelligence Officer, a grey-moustached Captain named Laurent whom they found eating sandwiches as he had arrived back too late for dinner after questioning German prisoners in one of the advance cages.

Having already received his instructions about Gregory he led him and de Brissac upstairs to his own room, where Gregory found the uniform of a German soldier of the 147th Infantry Regiment laid ready for him on a chair. It formed a strange contrast to the smart, black S.S. uniform which he carried in his bag, as the soldier's uniform was of thin, poor-quality stuff containing only a small proportion of genuine wool. Its field-grey was muddied from service on the battle-field and a large splash of blood on one trouser-leg indicated that one of the companions of the prisoner from whom it had been taken had been killed or wounded just beside him.

As Gregory picked it up he gave a sniff of disgust. Judging by the smell of his clothes the German who had worn it had not had a bath for a fortnight. Captain Laurent laughed at Gregory's squeamishness and said that he must not mind the smell, as to ensure his having the uniform of a regiment that was still in the German line this one had been taken off a man captured only that morning. He assured Gregory that he had at least taken the precaution of having it put through the de-lousing plant that afternoon.

While Gregory put on the dirty, grey garments and tried on a selection of captured German boots until he found a pair to fit him de Brissac changed from his smart Staff uniform into easy, khaki battle-dress which he had brought in a bag. Gregory protested that he did not want his friend to come right up to the front line with him but de Brissac only laughed.

"As though I would allow you to go alone, *mon vieux*! Why, all sorts of things might happen to you. But nevertheless I do not wish to get my nice tunic and breeches all covered in mud through crawling about in the shell-holes our splendid guns have been making by the thousand up there."

Knowing that it would be useless, Gregory protested no further and began to pack his S.S. uniform into the wooden box that Laurent had secured for him. The black stencilling on its sides showed that it had originally contained German canned-fruit and it took the uniform, high-crowned cap and shining, black field-boots quite comfortably.

In the last war Gregory had never shirked a necessary danger or an urgent duty, but he had an absolute loathing of routine and most violently disagreed with the ruling in King's Regulations which laid it down that whenever a party of twenty or more men was sent out on a job, even if it were only to collect hay or to march a mile to the divisional baths, an officer should be sent with them, especially as in all armies except that of Britain such parties were left in charge of their perfectly competent N.C.O.s.

As a result of his views he had soon developed all the cunning of the old soldier in the gentle art of swinging the lead, and he had found that the best way of escaping tiresome duties was to give the impression that he was already engaged on some other work. A man who is walking quickly and carrying something is obviously not at a loose end, so whenever Gregory had had occasion to leave his hut or tent behind the lines he invariably used to set off as though in a hurry to get somewhere, carrying with him a large sheaf of papers.

This little trick had saved him endless hours of dreary, pointless duties, and applying the same psychology now he hoped that by carrying the tinned-fruit box he would immediately be put down as a fatigue man by anyone he bumped into behind the German lines, and would thus escape much awkward questioning.

Donning their steel helmets and slinging their gas-masks over their shoulders the three of them went downstairs and got into de Brissac's car, which began to crawl slowly along the road through the dead black-out.

The rain had ceased, but it was very cold. Although it was only November the 1st snow had already fallen in that area a few days before. From overhead there came the noise of an occasional plane to mingle with the constant drumming of the guns, which could now be heard very plainly and which recalled to Gregory old memories of the Somme and Passchendaele.

Now and again a shell exploded some distance to right or

left of the road as the German gunners searched for the French batteries. Once there was a series of bright flashes and deafening reports as a French battery concealed in the darkness suddenly came into action near the roadside without the slightest warning, the blast from the cordite of the shell charges making the windows of the car rattle.

About a mile further on the car halted by a row of faint red lights, and on Laurent's· saying "We must walk from here," they stepped out into the blackness. They were challenged by a sentry at the red lights, but Laurent gave the password of the night while de Brissac used some straps they had brought for the purpose to adjust the box containing the S.S. uniform firmly upon Gregory's back so that he should have his hands free for his crawl across no-man's-land. They then proceeded up the road on foot.

It seemed to Gregory that they walked for a long time, and once they had to fling themselves flat at the warning wail of an approaching shell which passed close over their heads to explode some fifty yards behind them. Now and then they heard the muttering of voices in the darkness and glimpsed shadowy figures belonging to infantry detachments that had been relieved or stretcher-bearers coming down the line.

At last, after they had been challenged for the fourth time, Laurent said : "Here we leave the road. In daylight this point is visible from the German lines." He led the way between low walls of sandbags, down a flight of wooden steps and into a broad, duck-boarded trench.

The trench zig-zagged from side to side and they blundered along it in an inky blackness which was now and again dispersed by the glare of a Verey light sent up from the advance trenches. After a time they were challenged yet once more and a crack of light appeared in the side of the trench from a dugout that was being used as a Battalion Headquarters.

From that point on the communication-trench grew narrower as they plodded steadily onwards and cut across several others, but owing to the darkness they sensed rather than saw these intersections except when an occasional Very light went up or Captain Laurent flashed his shaded torch for a second to make sure that they had not taken a wrong turning in the maze. Another challenge, this time in a low voice, halted them again. They had reached the headquarters of one of the Companies actually holding the front line.

Having given the password for the night Laurent stooped

and fumbled at the side of the trench until his fingers closed upon a heavy anti-gas blanket. Lifting it a little, he flashed his torch and the others followed him inside, down a few steps and past a second gas curtain into the dugout, a low, boarded, underground room about twelve feet square, lit only by a couple of candles stuck in the necks of bottles.

As Gregory glanced round he felt as though the past twenty-one years had been merely a dream. This was no Maginot Line with lifts, bathrooms, dining-halls and electrical equipment. They were now in territory twenty miles beyond the outermost of those great underground barracks, but as there had been no advance on this sector since the third week of the war the French had had time to dig themselves in and to create the same sort of rough-and-ready, underground living accommodation that Gregory had known in the great trench systems of the last war.

The dugout was blue with cigarette smoke and held a fuggy warmth for which they were grateful after the bitter cold outside. Nearly a third of it was occupied by two beds made of wire netting, on one of which there lay snoring a young officer, unwashed, grimy and fully dressed except for his boots and overcoat. Revolvers, steel helmets, binoculars, water-bottles, gas-masks and map-cases were strewn about where they had been thrown down, or dangled from nails hammered into stout posts. The board walls were adorned with a few artistic, coloured prints of nude girls, torn from the pages of *Esquire* and *La Vie Parisienne*. Another third of the floor space was taken up by a good-sized table at one end of which were piled dirty plates and mugs while at the other the Company Commander was scribbling away with an indelible pencil, making up returns.

He glanced up as they entered and nodded to Laurent. Then, noticing de Brissac's rank-badges, he stood up and saluted. Laurent made the introductions, during which Gregory learned that the Company Commander's name was Moreau, but Gregory himself was introduced merely as *"notre ami* about whom you have received instructions."

"We're all ready for you, Monsieur," Moreau informed him. "A raiding party is to be sent out to stir up a little activity so that in the ensuing confusion you may have a chance of getting into the enemy front line unobserved."

"Thanks," replied Gregory. "I'm sorry that you should have to expose your men on my account, but unless we give their sentries something to occupy them I may be spotted coming in from no-man's-land. If that occurred when none of them had been out they'd probably think I was one of their men who'd been trying to desert, and it's very important that I should avoid being questioned until I get well behind their lines."

Moreau nodded his agreement. "If only the enemy artillery doesn't become too active we'll be all right," he said, "but they've been much more restive on this front lately and last week they made quite a big push further north. Will you have a drink before we start?"

"I'd love one," Gregory smiled, and picking up a bottle of brandy Moreau poured stiff tots into four enamel mugs.

"*Bonne chance, mon ami!*" De Brissac raised his mug to Gregory, and the others followed suit. The brandy was fiery stuff but it warmed Gregory up for the dangerous business that he knew lay ahead of him.

"Shall we go?" asked Moreau, stubbing out his cigarette, and as Gregory nodded Laurent said: "Well, I leave you here. Good going, and a safe return!"

Gregory shook hands with him and then extended his hand to de Brissac, but the dark, good-looking Major shook his head.

"Don't be a fool, Gregory. Naturally I am going with you as far as I can."

"Nonsense!" Gregory growled. "We can't afford to risk the absolutely unnecessary loss of brilliant young Staff Wallahs."

De Brissac's smile broadened into a grin. "You forget, my friend, that you are under my orders and I have instructions to see you safely on your way. No arguments, now. Every moment of darkness is precious to you now that the enemy has settled down for the night. We must not waste time in talking."

Gregory knew his friend too well to protest any further, so he followed Moreau out through the anti-gas lock and up into the darkness.

They traversed several more trenches before they came to a deeper one which Gregory guessed to be the front line. Sentries were standing at intervals along the fire-step above them and in one of the bays Moreau held a whispered conversation with another officer after which he turned, fumbled for Gregory's hand and shook it, saying:

"This is Lieutenant Gautier, who is to lead the raid. Stick

close to him and he will take you through our advance posts and wire. Good luck to you."

"This way!" said another voice, and taking Gregory by the arm Lieutenant Gautier guided him along the trench to a place where a small sap made it easy to climb from the fire-step on to the parapet. As Gregory went up the N.C.O.s were already passing the whispered word along the line and other men were scrambling up on to the parapet on either side of him. Gautier came round in front and de Brissac took up his position by Gregory's side.

"The enemy trenches are about half a kilometre away," whispered Gautier. "A rise in the ground ahead partially covers us from here so we can walk the first hundred metres, but if they send up a Verey light fling yourselves flat."

Slipping and stumbling they went forward over the uneven ground. Suddenly Gautier pitched forward with a muffled curse and it was only just in time that Gregory stopped himself from following the Lieutenant head-foremost into a freshly-made shell-hole that had been concealed by the darkness.

Gautier crawled out on the far side and again they advanced. No sound broke the stillness save the squelching of their boots in the mud and the dull mutter of the guns. The distant sky was faintly lit by a constant flickering, like summer lightning, as the forts in the Siegfried Line shelled the French rear, but immediately ahead there was unrelieved darkness.

All at once a flash of bright light appeared only a quarter of a mile distant. Soaring upwards until it was about eighty feet above the ground it turned in a graceful curve and sank slowly earthwards, lighting up the whole scene almost as vividly as daylight.

The instant that the Verey light burst Gregory and his party flung themselves flat in the mud, but by its light he saw figures just ahead of them.

"One of our advance machine-gun posts," muttered Gautier. "We don't run to concrete pill-boxes here."

The men ahead were crouching on the foremost lip of a big crater, protected only by a few sandbags over which their gun was sighted.

As the Verey light went out the raiding party advanced again. Passing the machine-gun nest they plodded up a broken slope on the crest of which they came to barbed-wire. Gautier told them to remain where they were for a moment and meanwhile he crawled about on his hands and knees until he found the passage through the belt. At his whispered order they followed him, now squirming on their bellies in the muck and slime.

Gregory knew that at any moment after they had passed the wire they might come upon an enemy patrol or raiding party, so he took from his pocket the automatic he had brought with him and went forward with it at the ready, now crouching as low as he could.

A shell whined loudly over their heads, to burst with a roar in the trenches behind them as they flung themselves face down on the wet earth, and for seconds after the explosion they could hear the sods which it had thrown up falling around them.

They had now covered half the distance and were going forward with the utmost caution, advancing for a few steps at a shuffling run, then pausing for a moment to listen. At last they reached the enemy wire and the worst part of the business began. While Gregory and de Brissac lay still on the waterlogged ground Gautier produced a pair of wire-cutters and started to cut his way through the wire ahead of them.

As each strand snapped it emitted a faint "ping", quite loud enough to alarm anyone who might be within thirty yards or so. They expected a Boche machine-gun to open fire upon them at any second. The cold was intense, and to remain inactive was a horribly nerve-racking business.

It took Gautier a quarter of an hour to cut his way through, and even when he had succeeded the barbs on the loose strands of wire clawed at their clothes and their naked hands as the three of them struggled through the narrow passage he had made. On their bellies the whole time now they squirmed forward through squelching, clinging mud that smothered their clothes and weighed them down.

Suddenly a shot rang out a little way to their right.

"Come on !" growled Gautier hoarsely, and jumping to his feet he began to run towards the enemy trench system.

The shot was followed by another ; then a machine-gun came into action and made the night hideous with its staccato clatter. Over the German trenches, now only a hundred yards away, a Verey light burst, then another and another, throwing the uneven ground into sharp relief. Gregory caught a glimpse of the French soldiers who had cut their way through the wire on either side of his own party at the same time as Gautier. They were all in the act of scrambling for cover, and the next second he himself had sprung down into a waterlogged shell-hole and was standing knee-deep in icy water beside Gautier and de Brissac. Several machine-guns came into action before the Verey lights sank and faded.

With the return of darkness the three scrambled from the shell-hole and dashed forward again. A blinding flash cleft the blackness ahead of them, and with a sharp cry Gautier stumbled and fell. De Brissac's automatic barked twice as Gregory threw himself down beside the fallen Lieutenant. They dragged him back into the shell-hole and when they were under cover de Brissac switched on his shaded torch.

Blood was streaming from Gautier's mouth. A big fragment of a hand grenade had shattered his chest and lung just above the heart ; he was already dead.

Shouts, curses and shots now sounded from every side. Gregory and de Brissac left the dead Lieutenant, crawled out of the crater and staggered on, clearly visible now in the flashes of the rifles and machine-guns and of the grenades which were exploding all about them.

Suddenly a series of louder explosions added to the din. The enemy had called for artillery support and shells were bursting among the French troops as they strove to cover the last hundred yards to the German trenches.

Gregory was running on when de Brissac grabbed his shoulder and pulled him down. "It's no good," he muttered. "You'll never make their trenches while this is going on. We must wait until it's died down."

The French artillery had now come into action. Lurid bursts of flame splashed the blackness of the German trenches, and acrid clouds of smoke half-obscured the hideous scene. For ten minutes the artillery duel and machine-gun fire continued unabated while Gregory and de Brissac cowered, shivering where they lay, their faces pressed against the cold, wet earth and their fingers clawing the mud, knowing that at any instant they might be blown sky-high or feel their flesh rent by a shell splinter. Both were brave men but both were sweating, not with the fear of death but with the fear of being transformed in a flash from conscious human beings to screaming imbeciles by some insupportable agony of pain.

Gradually the hellish din grew fainter as the shelling ceased. The Germans knew that the French attack had been broken and that there was no need to expend further ammunition. The French fire ceased shortly afterwards. The machine-gunners of both sides kept it up for a while, then they too fell silent.

The German Verey lights flared less frequently and once more darkness closed down over no-man's-land, hiding the dead and the dying. Apart from the never-ceasing rumble of the distant guns the only sound was the shrieking of some poor wounded wretch further along the line who had probably got caught up in the German wire while trying to drag himself back to the French trenches.

"They're on the alert now," whispered de Brissac, "so you'll have to be mighty careful, but you haven't far to go and with luck you'll be able to slip into one of their saps unobserved."

"Right. Then I'll leave you," Gregory whispered back. "No sense in your coming any further. Thanks, old friend, for having seen me so far."

De Brissac fumbled for Gregory's hand in the darkness and wrung it. "Good luck, *mon vieux*, good luck ! We'll drink a bottle of Chambertin together yet when this filthy war is over."

Gregory left his friend and crawled forward. He was now a little uncertain of his direction as he had lost his bearings in the excitement of the attack, but after he had covered about thirty yards a Verey light from the German trenches showed him that he was heading too far to the right. As it burst he wriggled forward and slid down into a shell-hole. The light was a dud and fizzled out almost as soon as it had exploded.

Crouching there in the darkness he became suddenly aware that someone else was beside him in the shell-hole. He could hear the man's faint breathing.

Was it a Frenchman or a German ?

Next second he knew. Another Verey light burst high above him, revealing a soldier in khaki.

Gregory was ready with his pistol, but so was the Frenchman with his rifle. Gregory saw mingled fear and intent to kill dawn in the man's eyes.

Momentarily Gregory had forgotten that he was in German uniform. With sudden horror he realized that he was in a most ghastly fix. He could not kill the Frenchman who was glaring at him and in the split second that it would have taken to pistol the fellow had he been a German he saw the man's finger crook itself around the trigger of his rifle.

Gregory's mouth fell open. His eyes started from his head. He was staring straight down the rifle-barrel and the point of the bayonet attached to it was only two inches from his gaping mouth.

Chapter XXVI

A QUIET NIGHT AT THE FRONT

IN a violent effort to save himself Gregory threw up his arm, knocking the rifle aside just as it went off, and his steel helmet rang like a gong as the bullet struck it. Fortunately he had knocked the man's rifle up so far that the bullet merely grazed the top of the helmet and glanced off without penetrating, yet the blow almost stunned him, knocking him backwards against the side of the shell-hole.

The bullet ricochetted away with a loud whine. As he staggered backwards his feet slipped from under him. He fell, dropping his pistol as he clutched at the wet earth to save himself. As he lay spread-eagled and half dazed in the icy water at the bottom of the shell-hole he heard the splashing of his attacker's feet as he came charging forward. Just as the Verey light sank from view Gregory glimpsed the Frenchman towering above him, his rifle now raised and pointed downwards. The man was about to bayonet him in the stomach.

"*Kamerad !*" he gasped, "*Kamerad !*"

"Think I'm going to risk my life taking you back ?" cried the *Poilu* with a blasphemous oath. "Your number's up, Boche. Take this !"

As Gregory strove to hurl himself aside from under the downward-plunging bayonet, a voice from above him rapped out "*Attention !* No prisoners are to be killed. We require them for questioning."

Between Gregory's desperate wriggle and the darkness the man's stab had missed Gregory's body, but the bayonet had pierced the loose part of his tunic and pinned him to the ground.

The newcomer scrambled down into the crater and flashed his torch on Gregory's face.

"I'll take charge of this man," he said swiftly to the *Poilu*. "Get back now as quickly as you can and rejoin your company."

With a feeling of incredible relief Gregory recognized de Brissac's voice.

"Who's that ?" asked the man doubtfully.

"I am Major de Brissac. I was with your Lieutenant Gautier, who has just been killed. Sharp, now! Do as I have said!"

"*Oui, mon Major*," muttered the man. "It's a pity, though, that you turned up just then. Another minute and the swine would have been dead." Then, placing his heavy boot firmly on Gregory's stomach, he gave a sharp heave and pulled his bayonet out of the ground.

When the man was out of earshot de Brissac gave a low laugh. "That was a near one! What a good thing it was that I'd made up my mind before you started to follow you and see you safely right up to the Boche trenches!"

"Thank God you did!" murmured Gregory fervently, as he struggled into a sitting position and readjusted the box, which had been wrenched sideways across his back in the fall. "I doubt if I've ever been nearer to cashing in my checks. But why the hell didn't you do something sooner, if you were just behind me?"

"I dived into the next shell-hole when that Verey light went up. It wasn't till I heard him fire his rifle that I realized you were in any trouble, and after that the whole thing was over in a couple of seconds."

"Well, thanks again. God! It's cold, isn't it? I'm wet through and half-frozen."

"Here, have a pull at this." De Brissac extended his flask, and Gregory took two large swallows.

"Ha!" he exclaimed as he handed it back. "That's better. I'll go ahead again now," and picking himself up he climbed out of the crater with de Brissac behind him.

Once more they wormed their way forward on their bellies. As each Verey light went up they lay dead still, not daring to lift a finger, their faces flattened against the earth and their bodies forming a portion of the scarred and tortured landscape.

Ten minutes later Gregory heard the mutter of voices. They were speaking in German and he knew that the enemy's front-line trench lay just ahead of him. Wriggling along the parapet he covered another twenty yards and then lay silent for a minute, listening with his ear to the ground.

There was no sound now except the dull booming of the guns shelling the back areas and the occasional crack of a distant rifle-shot. He dared wait no longer as another Verey light was due to go up soon. Turning in the darkness he felt for de Brissac's head and silently patted him on the shoulder, then dragged himself forward for another couple of yards and slid down over the parapet.

An even more perilous part of his programme had now begun. As long as he had been able to shelter in shell-holes he had been moderately safe except from shell-fire, trench-mortar bombs or hand-grenades, and even when crawling in the open he had had de Brissac to support him, but he was alone now, and he did not know the German password for the night.

As he would be unable to give it the first sentry to challenge him would place him under arrest and take him to the German Company or Battalion Headquarters for questioning. It would soon be discovered that he was not one of their own men although he was wearing the numerical badges of their regiment. They would then examine the canned-fruit box he was carrying and directly they found the S.S. uniform in it the game would be up.

In consequence he dared not make his way through the enemy trench-system but had to risk being seen crawling over the ground above as well as the possibility of being killed or wounded by a French shell. Wasting not a moment he fumbled round in the darkness against the parados of the trench until he found a foothold, and heaving himself up climbed out of it on the far side.

There were shell-holes here, too. The ground was pitted with them where the French barrage had checked the reserve troops that the Germans had sent up to support an attack launched in this sector during the previous week. Warily he crawled forward from hole to hole until he reached another trench. Here he paused again to listen, straining his ears for some sound of talking or breathing which would indicate the presence of German troops, but he could hear nothing. Another Verey light splashed up into the blackness above him, and as he crouched there holding his breath he saw that the trench below was empty.

The instant that the light went out he jumped down into the trench, clambered up its far side and, crouching low, stumbled on again as quickly as he could, knowing that he must attempt to cover several miles while the darkness lasted. Twenty yards further on the feel of the ground changed and he suddenly realised that he was crawling over rubble. He had reached the ruined houses on the south-eastern outskirts of Saarbrücken.

After taking a swig of brandy from his flask to warm himself up he went forward again, going even more cautiously now for fear of falling head-first into some cellar exposed by the blasting-down of the houses under eight weeks of French bombardment.

As he crept from one heap of rubble to another he occasionally heard voices. Now and again a Verey light illuminated the scene of ruin and desolation, showing roofless houses and crumbling walls with shallow communication-trenches running between them. Once he glimpsed the steel helmets of two soldiers protruding from a trench no more than four feet away from him, but the men did not suspect his presence and he was able to make a détour round them in the darkness.

Although he was making his way not through the centre of the town but through its eastern outskirts, the cross-sections of trench among the ruins seemed endless, and he began to fear that he had lost his way when the flash of a bursting shell some distance to his right lit for a second a sluggish stretch of water directly in front of him and he knew that he had reached the Saar river.

This, as he had known from the beginning, was the worst obstacle that he had to face. In summer he could have swum it, with his boots tied round his neck and the canned-fruit box into which he could have pushed his soldier's tunic and trousers supported with one hand on his head ; but now with the bitter cold numbing him where he crouched beside the river-bank he knew that he dared not risk it. To plunge naked into the icy water might affect his heart and send him to the bottom before he could reach the other bank. Even if he succeeded in doing so the effect of the cold upon him would be so terrible that he would be near collapse when he got to the other side and quite incapable of facing the additional strain of the miles he had yet to cover before dawn. The only alternatives were to find a derelict boat or a bridge which would enable him to cross the river while keeping his clothes dry.

With chattering teeth he made his way along the bank stumbling across the uneven ground and ruined wharfs until ten minutes later he caught sight of a faint glow which came from a partially-concealed brazier where several soldiers were sitting in a wooden lean-to. Approaching with the utmost caution he found that they were a picket posted at the head of a pontoon bridge which had been flung across the turgid river. To cross the bridge without being seen by the men on duty there was impossible, so he unstrapped the box from off his back and waited.

Presently voices caught his ear and a little squad of about a dozen Germans appeared out of the shadows, heading for the bridge. Silently Gregory rose, and putting his box on his shoulder so that he would look like an officer's servant or a fatigue man carrying stores from one place to another he waited until the squad had passed him and then fell in about twenty yards behind them.

At the bridge-head the leader of the squad was challenged by the picket, but evidently gave the password as the straggling bunch of shadowy figures trudged forward on to the bridge of boats. With his heart in his mouth Gregory hastened his step a little, and looking neither to right nor to left plodded boldly on towards the picket.

The man on duty there thought, as Gregory had hoped, that he was a straggler in the squad that had just gone by, and allowed him to pass without a challenge. Two minutes later he was across the river.

On the far bank he struck a road which led in the direction for which he was heading. There would be patrols and sentries along that too, he knew, so he dared not take it. Even if he were to follow the ditch at its side he would be running the risk of being challenged greater than that which he had run while crawling through the ruins, but on the other hand he might get hopelessly lost unless he stuck to the road now that he had found it, so he crossed the ditch. The time that he had spent in crossing the outskirts of the ruined town and crouching by the bridge-head seemed endless, but on looking at the luminous dial of his watch he found that it was only an hour and twenty minutes since he had entered the first German trench, and cheered a little by the thought that dawn was still a long way off he pressed on along the border of the grassland and ploughed fields on the far side of the ditch.

The road seemed quite deserted, but after half an hour he came to a group of colliery buildings, the tall shafts of which stood out against the night sky, and the sudden opening of a side-door in one of them disclosed the silhouettes of soldiers carrying stretchers.

Almost as soon as the door was opened a loud voice cried from the road: "Screen that light, damn you! D'you want us all to be blown to hell?" Someone inside the building drew a heavy curtain across the doorway but Gregory had seen enough to realize that it was a field dressing-station from which ambulances would collect the wounded, so this was evidently the

furthest point to which the Germans were still using the road
for motor transport.

Moving round the backs of the buildings he found the road
again, but a little further on his path was barred by other cottages
and a factory. He knew that he was now in the highly-industrial-
ized Saar basin with its iron foundries and coal mines and he
was reasonably confident that he had reached St. Johann, a
biggish village which, he knew, lay just to the north-east of
Saarbrücken and contained the railway junction that served the
town.

This impression was confirmed when, having climbed several
fences in the course of a détour of the village, he came out of a
backyard to find a railway track cutting right across his route.
After crawling over the metals he turned left and went on until
he struck the road again, finding that another railway lay on its
far side and ran north-east parallel with it.

The road sloped gradually upwards and at its side a long
line of vehicles was parked. In the darkness it was impossible
for Gregory to identify them individually as small tanks, motor-
tractors or cars but a murmur of voices told him that there were
troops among them, probably halted for a spell before making
their last trek forward to some concealed position nearer the
battle-front. Gregory knew that owing to the constant aerial
activity of the Allies all German troop movements were taking
place as far as possible under cover of night, so that from this
point on the road would now probably be as crowded as Oxford
Street at its busiest, whereas had he been there in daylight he
would have found it naked and empty.

He could see the glow of the men's cigarettes as they had a
last smoke before advancing through the village and would
himself have given anything for a cigarette, but he dared not
have one as long as there was still any risk of his being challenged.

The road was easy to follow now as there was constant
movement on it but he kept about twenty yards to its right and
trudged on, his boots now heavy with clay, across the fields,
occasionally stumbling into a ditch or being brought up short
by the edge of a slag heap near one of the coal mines. A short
distance further on he came to wooded country and knew that
he had entered the Kollerth Wald.

The trees in his path now made the going even more difficult
and although it seemed to him that he had been crawling,
scrambling and trudging for the whole night long he doubted
whether he had as yet put more than three miles between himself

and the Boche front line. A glance at the luminous dial of the German wrist-watch which had been given him with his kit showed him that it was a quarter-past two in the morning, so it was now about two and three-quarter hours since he had gone over the top with Lieutenant Gautier.

The wood ended abruptly. He crossed an open field and scrambled over the hedge that bounded its far side. Suddenly a challenge rang out directly in front of him.

From faint noises in the darkness ahead he realized that he had stumbled into a field which was being used as a bivouac, and knowing that if he answered the challenge his game would almost certainly be up he ducked down beside the hedge and began to make his way towards the road on all fours.

The challenge came again but this time the voice held an uncertain note. The sentry had probably seen his head and shoulders faintly outlined against the skyline as he had climbed the hedge but had decided, on receiving no answer to his shout, that his imagination had played him a trick.

Gregory headed for the road, knowing that if he turned the other way he might strike another section of the forest and lose himself in it ; he had now no alternative to crawling over the ditch and up on to the highway although, once there, he would be compelled to mingle with the troops which were constantly moving along it to front or rear.

Once on the metalled surface he drew himself upright, waited until a column of infantry had passed on its way down from the line and crossed it as quickly as he could with the intention of taking to the fields beyond the railway on its far side. These, however, were also occupied by reserve troops bivouacking for the night so he had to return to the road once more.

The going was easier here, but against that was the constant fear that at any moment he might run into a barrier at which an Area Commandant's Military Police were controlling the troops going up and down the road. The Germans had such a system, he knew, because they were faced with the problem of preventing the many desertions that were always taking place from Regiments in the line, and by this means they could check up on everybody entering or leaving any given area.

He had proceeded for about half a mile along the road, the sides of which had now become wooded again, but so thickly that he could not have moved at any pace among the trees, when he heard the drone of planes overhead. Somewhere in front of him a whistle blew, and the shadowy figures near-by ran

M

for cover, disappearing into the darkness. Gregory jumped into the nearest ditch. He did not need to be told what was happening. Neither side was yet using its Air Force to bomb munition-plants or back areas where civilians might be injured, but both were supplementing their artillery bombardments by occasional bombing-raids on points actually within the battle zone. These were French or British planes overhead and they were about to *strafe* some German strong point or road junction.

He lay there listening to the threatening hum that beat down from the dark clouds above but after a minute it grew fainter. The planes evidently intended to drop their deadly cargoes further inside the German lines. The whistle blew again—two blasts this time—and the shadowy figures emerged once more from their hiding-places to climb into their light lorries and tractors.

Dodging in and out among them he started off again along the road, which was now quite straight and sloped upwards, but he had not gone twenty yards before a bright flash, closely followed by a loud explosion, pierced the darkness about a mile ahead of him. The night-bombers were flying on a carefully-calculated course, their objective some cross-roads, bridge or railway siding up there in the distance. For about five minutes the bombs rained down, blotting out the drumming of the more distant gun-fire as they crashed on to the hillside. The flames which sprang up from fires started by the bombs showed him that there were factory buildings there on which the airmen had secured some direct hits, and he could see their tall chimneys against the light of the flames.

Gregory trudged on with more confidence now, since he had not yet encountered one of the expected Military Police barriers. He had constantly to dodge in and out among the traffic, but he nevertheless kept a wary eye upon any halted groups ahead in case they were troops that were being passed by the Area Commandant's people, although he now considered that if there were such a post on this road it would be up in the burning village.

It was close on three o'clock when he reached the first house of the village, which showed up in silhouette against the fires which were still burning. He was just debating with himself whether to take to the fields again and work round the village or to go boldly forward with his box on his shoulder in his guise of a fatigue carrying a case of stores when he suddenly heard once again the ominous droning of aeroplanes.

A second later the whistle blew and running to the side of the house he flung himself down under the shelter of one of its walls. For what seemed an eternity the Allies' planes droned round and round overhead. They were searching by the light of the flames for the near-by railway-station or bridge which formed the bulls-eye of their target, but to Gregory, waiting there in the darkness, it seemed as though they were searching for him.

Suddenly there was an ear-splitting roar, then another and another until the very ground seemed to quiver. There was the sound of falling masonry followed by a scream of pain, and an anti-aircraft battery blazed into action close at hand.

In the few minutes that followed it seemed to Gregory that no-one but himself could have remained alive in that hell of monstrous detonations; then they ceased as abruptly as they had begun. The house by the side of which he had sheltered was still standing and apart from being half-deafened by the noise he found himself quite unharmed.

Realising that he now had at least a chance of getting through the village unchallenged during the confusion following the raid, he humped his box on his shoulder again and plunged forward on to the road.

Other men, also unharmed, were emerging with him from the shadows and as he advanced he was amazed to find how little harm the bombs had done. The tanks and tractors began to move again, and although he saw another fire that had been started, a tank turned turtle by the violence of the explosions and several dead and wounded men who were being picked up by their comrades the raid did not seem otherwise to have had very much effect.

Nobody took the least notice of him as he pressed on as quickly as he could. Within ten minutes he had left the village behind and had discovered that the raid had been to some purpose after all. There was a huge gap in the road where a bomb had fallen exactly in its centre and further on a good half of its metalled surface was destroyed for several yards where two bombs had fallen in the ditch beside it. The columns of mechanized units going up and down had been compelled to halt but some of the men were already busy with their shovels, filling the craters with stones from heaps that had been dumped at the roadside for that purpose.

As he went on the traffic diminished and Gregory realised that the village through which he had passed must have been the German advanced rail-head for that sector and he was almost certain that it was Dudweiler. If he was right in this assumption he knew from his recent, intensive study of the maps he had bought in Paris that he must be on the Saarbrücken-Neunkirchen road and that the next place along it of any importance was Sulzbach.

A few minutes later his deduction was confirmed by the puffing of an engine and the chugging past him of a train on the railway to his left. He had passed through the Loop of the Siegfried Line at St. Johann and was now approaching the two-mile-deep belt of field-fortifications which formed the Line itself and which had Sulzbach a little more than half-way along the road through it.

Satisfied with his progress so far he walked a little way down the road, sat down, took a gulp of brandy and lit a cigarette.

Fortunately the night was fine so the mud on his clothes was rapidly drying, but it had caked into a crust on his face and hands and he knew that the next problem was to find water in which he might wash unobserved. He dared not risk going to any inn as long as he was in the uniform of a private as he would be certain to be questioned by some N.C.O., while on the other he could not transform himself into a smart officer of the S.S. as long as his face and hands were still filthy with the dirt of the battle-field.

Having had a very welcome rest he got back on to the road and pressed on as fast as he dared without exhausting himself. Now and again a great shell passed overhead, making a noise like a flying tram-car as it ploughed its way through the air to crash on one of the forts of the Siegfried Line. Sometimes the shells fell to his rear or on either side of him, detonating with a terrific roar that echoed down the dark valley, but none of them came near enough to necessitate his flinging himself flat to avoid splinters.

He endeavoured to accustom himself to the surprises of the night, but try as he might he was unable to repress a start every time the darkness to one side or the other was stabbed by a huge flash which momentarily threw the trees into sharp silhouette as one of the great Krupp guns which reared their ugly nozzles to the sky from their concealed emplacements in the woods roared defiance at the French.

At no time during his tramp was he alone upon the highway. Always there were moving shadows either in front of or or just behind him ; figures and forms thrown up by the flickering in the sky as ambulances, Staff cars, tractors, lorries, road repair parties, water-carts, motor-cycle dispatch-riders and all the other components of the immense paraphernalia of a vast army in the field came and went.

It was four o'clock in the morning when he saw some red and green lights ahead and slowed his pace until he had ascertained that they were situated at the near end of a small bridge over which traffic was allowed to pass only in one direction at a time. Here was another place at which an Area Commandant's police might be on the watch for deserters, and muddied all over as he was it was quite certain that he would arouse their immediate suspicions. But the bridge suggested water, so moving off the road once more he slithered down a steep bank and found, as he had expected, a shallow stream.

Following its bank for a couple of hundred yards he tested the river-bed with one foot and finding it to be stony plunged boldly in. It was horribly cold but only about thirty feet across and at no point deeper than his knees, so he waded through it, knelt down on the opposite bank, and removing his soldier's tunic steeled himself to wash his face, hands and head thoroughly in its clear, chill waters.

As it was now over seven weeks since he had had his head shaved his hair had grown a couple of inches, but he had had it trimmed in Paris so that it now stood up almost straight in front in similar fashion to Grauber's. Gregory's hair was dark and Grauber's fair, but so dissimilar were the two men in face and figure that he had not thought it worth while to attempt any further resemblance by having it bleached with peroxide. However, cut *en brosse* as it now was it tallied with a prevalent German fashion and it was still not long enough to cause him any difficulty in drying it, an operation which he performed on the inside of the tunic. Then, shivering so violently that his teeth chattered, he stripped to Grauber's under-garments, opened the canned-fruit case and dressed himself in the smart, black S.S. uniform.

He would have preferred to have penetrated further behind the German line before changing, and did so now only because he might not find another equally suitable spot before he was caught by the approach of dawn. In any case, he reckoned that he must now be a good six miles behind the German front-line trenches so although he was still deep in the battle zone he thought that the presence of an S.S. man on special duty would probably not be considered strange at that distance from the Front.

Folding up the soldier's uniform he put it in the box together.

with the steel helmet, the boots and some loose stones, then flung the lot in the river. Two more big swallows of brandy and the violent flapping of his arms restored his circulation a little, and within a few minutes he was back on the road again.

After covering another mile and a half he entered a small town which he felt certain was Sulzbach. It was evidently being used as a Divisional, or more probably a Corps, Head-quarters as there were many cars about and great activity was going on while the darkness lasted. Here too the blast-furnaces were still in operation and the glow from them gave enough light for him to see quite distinctly the dreary rows of workers' dwellings which lined the streets. Making no further effort to conceal himself he strode boldly forward until he reached a small square in the centre of the town, where he halted a soldier and gruffly asked the way to the railway-station. The man directed him without comment ; five minutes later he found the station-yard and entered a small booking-office.

Although it was 4.40 a.m. and still pitch-dark the place was as crowded as it would normally have been on a market-day morning. No civilians were to be seen ; the travellers were all officers or soldiers dressed in uniform field-grey. Even the man behind the *guichet* in the ticket-office was a soldier, but ignoring him Gregory walked straight to the barrier and produced his Gestapo pass.

He had accomplished the first part of his journey, but owing to cold and tiredness his spirits were low. Yet he must now face the first real test. Would he be halted by the Military Police and questioned as to what he was doing in the battle zone, or would Grauber's pass enable him to make his way unchallenged across south-eastern Germany? Drawing himself up he gave the man on the barrier a haughty stare and waited with a beating heart.

Chapter XXVII

BACK INTO GERMANY

IT was an anxious moment for Gregory as the Sergeant of
Military Police on duty there looked at him. He was by no
means certain that the Gestapo did not have a special voucher
for travelling just like Army officers, but he had pinned his
hopes to the belief that they were so powerful in Germany that
every door was open to them and they could go where they would
without let or hindrance.

To his infinite relief the Sergeant merely glanced at Grauber's
card of authority, then drew back immediately and gave him a
smart salute. Half-lifting his hand in acknowledgment he
strutted through the barrier and walked along the platform to
the R.T.O.'s office, where he asked the military clerk on duty what
time the next train left for Carlsruhe. The man replied apologetically that he could not say for certain but that any train
going westwards would take him to Kaiserslautern whence he
would be able to get a connection without difficulty.

Swaggering out again Gregory strode up and down the
platform for the next quarter of an hour, smoking cigarettes until
a train rumbled in. A crowd of officers and men was waiting for
it but Gregory pushed his way in among them, making straight
for a first-class carriage. The train was empty, evidently having
been just made up outside the station, but every seat in his
compartment was instantly taken.

The blinds were all drawn, rims of black were painted round
the edges of the windows as an air-raid precaution and only a
dim, blue light burned in the roof of the carriage. No heat was
on and it was very cold. Three of the officers who had got in
with Gregory obviously knew each other as they were talking
together with the air of old friends ; the remaining three
seats in the compartment were occupied by himself and two
others.

As the train chugged out of the station the conversation
became general, the two other officers introducing themselves
to the group of three. In spite of the cold they made a jolly

party, as they were all leaving the battle-front on short leave
or to be posted on special duties elsewhere, but they all eyed
Gregory askance and were extremely careful to keep off both
politics and the progress of the war. That suited him very well
as he did not want to give his name or to enter into conversation,
and closing his eyes he snuggled himself down in his corner to
get some sleep.

Like all trains behind battle-fronts this one was running to
no fixed schedule and was intolerably slow. It would run on
for a while at about twenty miles an hour, halt for ten minutes,
run on for another stretch, halt again and so on.

After Gregory's eyes had been closed for some twenty minutes
two of the officers began to talk in cautious whispers, but he
was not interested in their probably adverse comments upon the
mess that Ribbentrop had made of German interests in the
Baltic or the unexpectedly heavy losses that they had suffered
before they had succeeded in dislodging the French from captured
territory, and soon afterwards he fell into a doze.

When he awoke it was broad daylight. The officers were
all tumbling out of the carriage and on glancing out of the window
he saw that the train had reached Kaiserslautern. Pulling
himself together he followed the officers out on to the platform,
went to the booking-office and inquired for the next train to
Carlsruhe. The clerk informed him that it left number four
platform at eight-fifteen and a glance at the clock had already
shown him that it was twenty minutes to the hour.

His two-hours' nap, broken by the constant jolting of the train,
had done little to refresh him. He was still tired after his
long hours of exertion and now had a filthy taste in his mouth
into the bargain, so he made his way to the buffet. The girl
behind the counter gave him a quick : *"Heil Hitler !"* and
although the selection of food was indifferent he was glad enough
to secure a cup of *Ersatz* coffee and a packet of biscuits. Just
as he had finished his coffee he noticed a pile of *Schinkenbrötchen*
at the back of the counter and signed to the girl to pass them
across.

"I must punch your ration-card if you want one of those,
Herr Gruppenführer," she said hesitantly, but he gave her one
sharp glance and she nervously grabbed the stand of ham rolls
and passed it across without more ado.

Gregory ate a couple, stuffed two more in his pockets, flung
a five-mark note to the girl, who beamed at him with sudden,
astonished pleasure, and with a wave of his hand swaggered out

of the buffet as though he had been a Gestapo chief all his life,

The train for Carlsruhe was also crowded and at first he could not find a seat, but he spoke to the ticket-collector and with a swift *"Heil Hitler !"* the man dived into the nearest first-class smoker and ejected an elderly civilian from a corner seat.

Gregory felt horribly ashamed of taking the now vacant place as he knew that the old gentleman would have to stand in the corridor for the whole of the journey, but he dared not show it. Nodding haughtily to the collector he passed the old man without a glance and flung himself down in the corner of the smoker.

During the journey he dozed again, rousing up only when the train ran into Carlsruhe at half-past nine. He had decided to break his journey there instead of proceeding direct to Munich because he felt it would be wise to get a really sound sleep to refresh him after his great exertions, once he could reach a town well outside the battle-area.

With head held high and a swinging step he left the station and proceeded towards the Hotel Krönen.

As he strode along everybody made way for him, and although the pavement bordering the old streets of the town was narrow even the women got off it into the gutter lest he should have to deviate by a hair's-breadth from his course.

The Germans had not changed much, he reflected, since the Kaiser's day. He remembered how astonished he had been on his visits to Germany as a boy, before the last Great War, to see smartly-dressed women step off the pavements at the approach of Prussian Army Officers. It was not that the Germans were an ill-mannered race as a whole, but just a part of the centuries-old psychological plan by which the nation had been brought to regard its warrior caste as a race of demigods. It appeared that the same respect was now held to be due to the black-uniformed Storm-Trooper officers, who had been selected from the flower of Germany's manhood.

On reaching the hotel he marched straight up to the *Bureau* and flashing his Gestapo card in front of the small, elderly man who stood there he demanded a room.

"Sofort, Herr Gruppenführer !" The little man positively jumped in his eagerness to oblige. "The best ! The best !" he exclaimed, hurrying round from behind his counter. "The hotel is full. It is the war, you know—so many officers—but they have all gone out. I will have the belongings of one of them

moved—a beautiful room with a private bath, on the first floor."

With a nod unaccompanied even by a smile of appreciation, Gregory followed the elderly clerk to the lift and went up with him to the first floor. Chambermaids and pages came running at the desk-clerk's call. *"Heil Hitler! Heil Hitler!"* they cried at the sight of Gregory, and within three minutes the offending garments and belongings of the German Colonel who had occupied the room the night before had been hastily thrown into his bags and carried out.

Gregory would have laughed had not so much depended upon his playing his new part realistically. Even he was surprised at the power which a mere change of clothes had suddenly conferred upon him and the evident fear which his presence inspired in everyone whom he encountered. He knew that he must continue to look severe if he wished to maintain this ascendancy, so he stood there frowning, dark-faced and saturnine, until the servants had left the room. Then he asked the clerk : "How do the trains run for Munich this evening?"

"There is one at six o'clock which gets in just after midnight, *Herr Gruppenführer*, or there is one at eleven-thirty which will get you there by half-past seven in the morning," the little man replied quickly.

"I will take the eleven-thirty," declared Gregory. "I wish to be called at eight o'clock this evening. At nine o'clock you will send me up a meal, as I wish to eat quietly in my room, and at a quarter to eleven you will have a car ready to take me to the station."

"Jawohl, Herr Gruppenführer, jawohl. What do you wish for dinner?"

For the first time Gregory allowed his face to relax slightly into a smile. "Food is a little difficult these days, is it not? But we must not mind that ; we must economise our stocks because we have a long war to fight. What do you suggest?"

"I will see the head-waiter, *Herr Gruppenführer*, but I know that he had some Rhine trout in this morning and we could offer you a duck."

"That will do," nodded Gregory, "and send up a bottle of hock with it ; a good Pfalz wine for preference."

"Jawohl, Herr Gruppenführer, jawohl!" Washing his hands in the air, the little man bowed himself out.

Immediately he had gone Gregory drew the curtains of the windows, pulled off his clothes and tumbled into bed. In Nazi

Germany it was evidently a far better proposition to be a Group-Leader of the Black Guards than a General called out of retirement, and Grauber's card of identification had certainly proved as potent as a magic wand. Musing on these pleasant thoughts Gregory fell asleep.

He slept on right through the day until he was called at eight o'clock. His only baggage consisted of his shaving-tackle and a piece of soap distributed among the various pockets of his clothes. He spent the next hour in bathing, shaving and re-dressing himself so that when his dinner-tray arrived he presented the immaculate appearance that was essential to the maintenance of his rank.

With considerable pleasure he noted that the management had added a large champagne cocktail and a selection of vegetable and sausage *hors-d'oeuvres* as a fillip to his meal. In due course a cheerful-looking, plump little waitress brought him his Rhine trout and the duck, together with an excellent bottle of Deidesheimer, a water ice which he did not eat and some mushrooms on toast which he dispatched with relish.

Having finished his late dinner, he sent for the evening papers and amused himself by reading the latest war news as seen through the distorting spectacles of *Herr Doktor* Goebbels. At half-past ten he went downstairs and asked for his bill.

The desk-clerk muttered something about the manager, and a portly man of about sixty came forward, bowing and clicking his heels, to say that the hotel had been honoured by the *Herr Gruppenführer's* presence, and he hoped that he would do them the honour to regard himself as their guest. The hotel and everything in it was always at the *Herr Gruppenführer's* disposal. He begged the *Herr Gruppenführer* to speak well of it to his distinguished colleagues. *Heil Hitler !*

Gregory also "heiled Hitler" with extreme promptness, and with a word of thanks assured the manager of a good mark in the Party records. He was then ushered out to a waiting car by the manager, the little clerk, the head-waiter and a number of other menials, all of whom wished him a good journey and, standing in a row on the pavement with raised arms, "heiled Hitler" lustily as the car drove off.

At the station he had no difficulty whatever. It was all too easy. Civilians scattered before him, every Brown-Shirt emitted an explosive "*Heil Hitler !*" as he passed. Even the black-clad S.S., recognizing his high rank-badges, came swiftly to attention at the sight of him. Railway officials ran to do his bidding, and finally some unfortunate upon the train was deprived of his first-class sleeper to accommodate the lean-faced Nazi chief.

As he had slept all day he was feeling very fit again, so for an hour or so he read a book that he had bought on the station, while the train rumbled on through the night. But sleep was a precious thing to anyone carrying out the kind of work upon which he was engaged, and Gregory could always do with a lot of it when other matters did not require his attention, so at two o'clock he put out the light, turned over and slept once more, waking only when the guard came to inform him that they would reach Munich in another fifteen minutes.

He was now faced with a problem similar to that which had confronted him on his arrival at Cologne—the acquisition of a suitcase, night-things and so on in order that his lack of them should not be considered strange by the management of any hotel at which he stayed. The shops were not yet open, however, so he was compelled to postpone his shopping until later in the day.

His status as Group-Leader Grauber, dread chief of the Gestapo Foreign Department U.A.—1, was making everything fantastically easy, and the few hours during which he had played the rôle had convinced him that he had no need to fear questioning by the police, Army pickets or hotel staffs, whatever he cared to demand or wherever he chose to go. His only dangers were that he might run into some other Nazi chief who knew Grauber personally or register at some hotel at which the real Grauber had stayed.

For that reason he would much have preferred to have stayed at some small, unpretentious hotel, but by virtue of his position he dared not do so. Reckoning Hitler as an Emperor, which in all but name he was, Gregory knew that in Grauber's shoes he must rank as a Prince, or at least a Duke, in that new Nazi aristocracy for which the best was evidently barely good enough. To stay at any small place would be certain to provoke the sort of comment that he was most anxious to avoid, so taking the bull by the horns he made straight for the Regina Palast, the most luxurious hotel in Munich.

Here again the production of Grauber's card at the *Bureau* worked wonders. The hotel was full, but—of course—a bedroom with private bath would very shortly be at the disposal of the *Herr Gruppenführer*. In all the best bedrooms, one of which they would be honoured to give him, people were still dressing, as it was only eight o'clock, but would not the *Herr Gruppen-führer* deign to take breakfast while arrangements were being made?

Gregory signified his agreement to this proposition. Amidst a chorus of "Heil Hitlers" and without anybody mentioning the word "ration-card" he was provided with a chicken-liver omelette, coffee and fruit in the grill-room.

Afterwards he acquired the morning papers and took possession of a room out of which somebody had been turned for his accommodation. By the time he had bathed, shaved and assimilated the latest war news it was half-past ten, so he thought that he would get down to his real business and pay a call at *Das Kleine Schloss* out at Prinz Ludwig's Höhe to ascertain whether Erika von Epp was in Munich.

He felt quite sure that the hotel would have accommodated him with a car had he asked for one, just as the Hotel Krönen had done the previous night. There were plenty of cars in Germany that had not been commandeered, and the only difficulty with which the ordinary person met when trying to secure one was the petrol ration. It seemed clear, however, that either the hotel managers or the members of their staffs had to sacrifice a portion of their own rations without any argument if people like Nazi Group Leaders had not got their own cars with them and urgently required means of transport.

Gregory could have had a car, or anything else for that matter, without the least difficulty ; there was no doubt about that ; but in case he slipped up anywhere he thought it a wise precaution to leave no traceable link between the Regina Palast and Erika von Epp's house, and in consequence he decided to go out there by some other means.

Leaving the hotel, he bought some cigarettes at a tobacconist's and inquired of the woman who served him the best way to reach Prinz Ludwig's Höhe. She told him that it was about five miles from the centre of Munich, but that he could take a local electric train from the left-hand side of the *Mittelbahnhof* which would get him there in about fifteen minutes.

At the station he found that he had about twenty minutes to wait but he simply walked to the barrier, as had now become his habit, and boarded the electric train when it came in. It stopped at every station and ran for part of the way through pleasant, open country. By twenty-past eleven it had deposited him at the Prinz Ludwig's Höhe halt.

He made no inquiries at the station, but walked away from

it for nearly five minutes before stopping a postman and asking him if he knew the whereabout of *Das Kleine Schloss*. The man directed him upon what proved to be quite a long walk, but at about twenty to twelve he arrived in a road bordered only by large, private houses, each of which was surrounded by trees, wide lawns and well-tended gardens. He found that of Erika von Epp nearly at its far end.

A gravel drive led up to a long, low, two-storeyed building which was battlemented and constructed in imitation of a mediæval fortified manor-house—hence, obviously, its name : "The Little Castle." Gregory marched up the front-door steps and rang the bell.

It was answered by a trim maid in black-and-white uniform of whom Gregory inquired whether the Countess von Osterberg were at home.

The girl shook her head. Unfortunately he had missed the *Frau Gräfin* by ten minutes. She had just gone into Munich in her car.

"When do you expect her back ?" Gregory asked.

"Not until this evening," the girl replied. "She is both lunching and dining out."

"In that case," said Gregory, "at what time do you think she will get in after dinner ?"

"I can't say for certain," replied the maid, "but I should think at about eleven o'clock."

Gregory considered for a moment. He thought it important that the Countess should not learn of his visit and that he intended to come out again to see her. If she did, she might get wind-up at the news that an S.S. officer was looking for her and call in one of her high Army-officer friends to be present at the interview. It was most essential that he should see her on her own, so he produced his Gestapo card and said to the girl :

"Now look here, there's no need to be frightened. Nobody's going to harm your mistress, but I wish to question her on a certain affair and I'm coming back this evening at about eleven o'clock. If she comes in first on no account are you to say that I've been inquiring for her and that I'm coming back to-night. If you fail to obey me and the *Frau Gräfin* learns, through you or through any of the other servants here, that I've called this morning the Gestapo will have something to say to you about it, and what they say will not be at all pleasant. Do you understand ?"

"*Ja, ja, Herr Gruppenführer,*" said the girl meekly, a

frightened look coming into her dark eyes. "I won't breathe a word about Your Excellency's visit."

"That's right," Gregory nodded. "You just forget it and I'll be along about eleven." Upon which he turned away and set off towards the station.

Shortly after one o'clock he was back in Central Munich. He lunched at Humplemeyer's, a restaurant of international repute which had been the favourite resort of Munich's gourmets in the old days, because he thought it would be interesting to see what sort of a meal one could get in war-time Germany if one had money but refrained from using either a ration-card or blackmail. Butcher's meat and butter were unobtainable, he found, but the restaurant had an ample supply of fish, game, tinned luxuries, forced vegetables and fruit. Prices had risen appallingly—about three hundred per cent. in two months—but if one could afford to pay one could still feed as well there as at most places in Europe.

After luncheon he went out to do his shopping, purchasing a suitcase, night-things, underclothes and so forth and ordering them all to be sent to the hotel. Back there once more he read for a while up in his room, had an hour's nap, rang for the floor-waiter to bring him a couple of champagne cocktails and, having consumed them, went down to dinner.

The hotel was crowded. Nearly all the male guests were in one uniform or another, and as Hitler had ordered that no mourning was to be worn for the war dead most of the women present had on colourful day-clothes, so the dining-room provided a gay and interesting scene.

As he ate his meal Gregory wondered how to fill in his time until ten o'clock, for it would be pointless to set off for Prinz Ludwig's Höhe before that time. He had slept a great deal in the last forty-eight hours and having finished his book, did not feel very much like starting another, as he was now all keyed-up by the knowledge that unless anything very unforeseen happened he was to see Erika von Epp that night. After all these weeks of desperate endeavour he was at last likely really to get somewhere with his mission.

On strolling out of the restaurant he saw a number of officers and girls going down a broad staircase to the basement, so he followed them and found that underneath the restaurant there was a big ballroom. Many couples were already seated at tables round the walls and in the centre of the room there was a railed-off, oval dancing-space which was slightly lower than the rest of the floor, so that the heads of the dancers were just about on a level with those of the people sitting at the tables outside the railing. A band was playing swing music at the far end of the room and it seemed that the officers and women who represented the more fortunate classes among the Munich population were forgetting, for a time at least, the strain and uncertainty of the war.

A waiter led Gregory at once to a small table, so having ordered a liqueur he thought that he might just as well sit there listening to the band and watching the dancers until it should be time for him to go out to *Das Kleine Schloss*.

The men had the very clean, almost polished appearance common to German officers and, by and large, they were a fine-looking lot. But the women were disappointing. Most of them were dowdy by the standards of London or Paris and their figures were not good. The best among them were a few blondes with china-blue eyes and pink, doll-like faces, but their hair was not well coiffured and although they appeared healthy enough they had a drab, untidy look. Little Collette, Gregory reflected, could have given them all points in general smartness of appearance.

He had been there about twenty minutes when two officers at the table next to his muttered something and turned right round in their seats to look towards the door. Gregory turned to follow their glance, then he suddenly stiffened where he sat.

A strikingly beautiful girl had just come in. Her pale, oval face was framed in an aureole of rich, curling golden hair. Her figure was a poem in living grace, and her clothes had a quiet, impeccable distinction. She carried herself with the hauteur of a Princess and made all the other women in the place look like scullery-maids by comparison. He recognized her instantly. It was his Lady of the Limousine.

Almost at the same instant she glanced in his direction, and as their eyes met he saw first astonishment and then fear dawn in hers. But she was unaccompanied and as he rose slowly to his feet she gave him a sudden smile.

Taking a couple of steps forward he clicked his heels in the approved manner and bowed. "If you're alone," he said, "may I have this dance?"

"I'm afraid I'm not alone," she answered quickly. "The friend I'm with was called to the telephone, but he asked me to come down and secure a table. He'll be joining me at any minute."

"Never mind," Gregory smiled. "Let's dance until he does come down. I'm more thrilled than I can possibly tell you to see you again."

"All right, then ; just a few turns." She laid her hand lightly on his arm and allowed him to lead her down on to the dance-floor. The band had just struck up one of the old Viennese waltzes, and a hundred couples were already swaying to its infectious rhythm. As they glided off together she whispered :

"You say you're thrilled to see me again, but that's nothing to what I feel. My heart nearly came up into my mouth when I saw you sitting there."

"You were glad, though ?" Gregory murmured.

"I don't know whether I was glad or sorry. Glad to see you —yes, but oh, my God ! The risk you're running by coming back into Germany !"

"I came at your special invitation," Gregory smiled down into her eyes.

"You found a new road, then ; a new hope of succeeding in your mission to bring us all peace ?"

"Yes, I think so. Given a little luck I may pull it off this time."

"But this uniform you're wearing. The uniform of a Group Leader of the S.S.—how did you get it ? It's stolen, I suppose ?"

"No. Made for me in Paris. I stole the papers of the man who's entitled to wear it, though."

"Even so, you should never have come to a place like this. It's in just such a crowd that you might meet someone who knows the man you're impersonating."

Their whispered conversation was carried on under cover of the music. Had they been sitting at a table scraps of it might perhaps have been caught by someone listening intently, but there was no danger of their being heard as they revolved among the constantly shifting crowd. It was for this reason that Gregory had at once asked her to dance with him, but even so he knew what a terribly dangerous game he was playing.

So many of the other men were staring at his lovely partner with open admiration and at himself with envy. One indiscreet phrase drifting to the ears of any of them would betray the fact that he was not entitled to the uniform he was wearing, and the results of such a slip, not only to himself now but also to the beautiful girl with whom he was dancing, would be too terrible to contemplate.

The ease with which, lightly pressed against him and resting

her long, slender hand upon his shoulder, she followed his steps
was a poem in movement. He was filled with an insane desire
to let Erika von Epp and his mission go hang. After all that he
had been through he was entitled to a few hours' uninterrupted
enjoyment. He could go out to Prinz Ludwig's Höhe to-morrow
instead of to-night. Now that he had run his lovely Lady of the
Limousine to earth, a few hours were neither here nor there, if
only he could persuade her to remain with him for the rest of the
evening.

With his lips almost touching her ear as they swayed together
he murmured : "I've simply got to talk to you. During all these
weeks since I left you outside Cologne there hasn't been a day
when I haven't dreamed of seeing you again. Somehow or other
you've got to get rid of the man you're with and spend the
evening with me."

Her scented cheek brushed his lightly as a butterfly's wing
as she very slightly shook her head. "Not this evening ; it's
impossible."

"Why ? Is it somebody with whom you're in love ?"

"No."

"Somebody who's in love with you, then ? But that's a foregone conclusion. Is it some officer home on short leave from the
Front on whom you're taking pity ?"

"No ; not even that. But it's somebody very important."

"If you're not in love with him and it's not someone who's
going back to the Front and may never see you again, he can't
possibly be as important as I am. You know that I love you,
don't you ?"

"Yes," she whispered. "I saw it in your eyes as you greeted
me just now."

"And you love me. I saw it in your eyes, too. There
was fear in them as well as surprise when you recognised
me."

"This is wrong—wrong." She dug the nails of her right hand
sharply into his palm. "Our countries are at war ; no happiness
can come of it."

"One day there will be peace, and it is my work to bring that
day nearer."

"I know. But until then it's madness for us two to talk of
love."

"Maybe, but it's the sort of madness that's worth all the
sanity that's left in this rotten world. Make any excuse you
like, but somehow you've got to get away from your friend and

let me love you for this little hour before my work drags me away from you again—perhaps for ever."

"I can't—I can't ! I've told you the man I'm with is important. I'd get rid of him willingly, but it's my work, too . . ."

"Oh—work !" he cut her short. "Surely you can let work go hang for once. Just for to-night let's imagine ourselves in some fairer, happier world where there's no war, and think only of each other."

As they swayed to the rhythm of the waltz he began to sing its refrain softly in her ear :

> *"Dream on, Beautiful Lady ; dream and forget,*
> *Dream on, Beautiful Lady, in love's sweet net ;*
> *Waking brings but regret,*
> *Dream on, dream and forget,*
> *Dream on, Beautiful Lady, in my arms yet."*

"No !" she exclaimed ; no, please ! The work I'm doing is desperately urgent. I'm trying to do the same thing as you. Everything that I have, every moment of my time, must be given to my attempt to secure an honourable peace for my country. The man I'm with is one of the key-men. If I play him properly to-night I may be able to persuade him to do something which will help the cause of peace immensely."

A sudden thrill of excitement caused Gregory's grip on her to tighten. The lovely girl he was holding in his arms was so obviously a *Hochwohlgeboren* that it was quite certain that nearly all her male relatives would be Army officers. Her car had been driven by a military chauffeur when he had first met her so one of her friends, at least, must be an officer of high rank. Was it possible that in her, by pure chance, he had stumbled upon somebody who could give him the key to the anti-Nazi conspiracy ? He bent his head and whispered swiftly : "Is the man with whom you must spend the evening one of the Army leaders ?"

The perfume of her hair filled his nostrils as she shook her head and whispered back : "No, he is a high official of the Nazi Party."

Gregory felt a sharp stab of disappointment. She was evidently working on lines quite different from his own although with the same object ; trying, perhaps, to foment a split among the Nazi chiefs or to organize a Peace Party among them through which some of them might hope to save their necks by throwing Hitler, Himmler and von Ribbentrop overboard.

While he was speculating on the point she spoke again,

sharply this time : "Look ! He's just come in. He's sitting down at that ·table near the door—next to the one where there's a girl with blue flowers in her hat."

They were at the other end of the room, right on the edge of the dance-floor near the band. As she spoke she pulled herself away from him and added in a quick, frightened whisper : "I must leave you now ! He mustn't see us together in case he questions me about you. *Aufweidersehen !*"

The second before she had drawn away from him to step off the floor Gregory had turned his head to look over his shoulder. Between the moving forms of the dancers he caught sight of the girl with the blue flowers in her hat, at the far end of the room, and on the instant his heart seemed to stand still.

The man sitting down at the next table was Grauber.

Chapter XXVIII

ONCE MORE A FUGITIVE

FOR an instant Gregory stood there almost paralysed ; then he realized that the lovely Lady of the Limousine had already left him and that they had made no plan to meet again.

He took one swift step off the dance-floor after her, but her back was now turned to him and she was walking down a gangway between the tables. Her walk was graceful and unhurried, her head held high, as she accepted as only her due the glances of admiration which were cast at her from every side. In half-a-dozen strides he could easily have caught up with her, but he knew that it would be as much as his life was worth to attempt to do so.

As the dance-floor was sunk like an oval pool two feet below the level of the rest of the room, the faces of the dancers were visible only to the people seated at the tables round its rim. It was that which had rendered Gregory practically immune from being spotted almost at once by anyone entering the room. He felt certain that Grauber had not seen, or at least recognized him, otherwise the Gestapo chief would not have sat down at a table but would promptly given the alarm to the other S.S. officers who were present and ordered his arrest. But if he followed the girl he would be visible to everyone in the place. The odds were at least ten to one that Grauber had caught sight of her by now and if Gregory ran after her he would attract instant attention to himself, the result being a speedy end to his mission and probably to hers as well.

All he could hope for after this second brief meeting was that fate might ordain that their paths should cross yet again. His immediate concern must be to get out of the place as quickly as he possibly could, since now that he had left the dance-floor Grauber might recognize him from the far end of the room. It would be the height of folly even to approach the few yards necessary to regain his own table and linger there the couple of minutes requisite to pay his bill. Keeping his face turned sideways as though he was looking for somebody he walked quickly behind the band to a second exit from the ballroom and slipped outside.

In the passage-way he paused to light a cigarette and steady his nerves. How in thunder Grauber could have appeared in Munich when he was supposed to be a prisoner in Holland was past Gregory's comprehension. He had certainly been in a Dutch gaol four days earlier. Colonel Lacroix was not the man to make mistakes about that sort of thing. However, the manner in which he had escaped or secured his release was of no importance for the moment. The thing that was causing Gregory's brain to rev. like a dynamo was the disastrous effect that Grauber's unexpected return to Germany might have on his own situation.

Although the one glimpse that Gregory had caught of him had hardly lasted more than a second he was absolutely certain that this was no case of mistaken identity. The lovely Lady of the Limousine had specifically said that she could not spend the evening with him because her work demanded that she should devote it to a high official of the Nazi Party, and if that hadn't been enough the man to whom she had drawn his attention was wearing a uniform identical with his own. There was no doubt whatever that the Nazi whom his lovely lady had gone to join back there in the ballroom *was* Grauber ; and not Grauber the secret agent slinking about in a London black-out or on the run in the Clichy district of Paris, but Grauber back in his own country, in his own native Germany and vested with the almost limitless authority wielded by the real chief of Gestapo Department U.A.-1.

Was Grauber staying in the hotel ? If he were, Gregory considered that his own number was as good as up already. When the Gestapo chief had first entered the place the people at the desk would have been amazed to learn that a second *Herr Gruppenführer* Grauber existed. Explanations would have ensued and a squad of Black Guards was probably waiting in the hall upstairs to arrest him immediately he appeared.

On the other hand, if Grauber were staying at the almost equally luxurious Bayerischehoff, a few doors away down the Square, and had only come into the Regina Palast for a few hours' amusement, there was a chance that he might get away.

But for how long could he hope to remain at liberty ? Nazi Group Leaders were of even more importance than he had assumed, as was clearly demonstrated by the servile manner with which he had been received everywhere in the country since he had donned his S.S. uniform.

The managers, hall-porters, head waiters and all sorts of people at the Bayerischehoff were certain to know their opposite numbers at the Regina Palast. Even as he stood there puffing heavily upon his straw-filled cigarette—which was already nearly consumed—two such members of the staffs might be comparing notes, each boasting that his hotel had received the patronage of a powerful Gestapo official, and the result of any such exchange of information was quite certain to be catastrophic as far as he was concerned.

Now that the real Grauber had arrived in Munich it could only be a matter of hours—or, at most, the night—before his own impersonation was discovered. In any case, every minute was vital if he hoped to save his skin, and the sooner he made his attempt to get out of the hotel the better.

He would never even have considered wasting precious moments in going up to his room to fetch any of his belongings if it had not been for the fact that his cap and greatcoat were still there, but he could not possibly walk about the streets in an S.S. uniform without them. If Grauber were staying at the Regina Palast a squad of S.S. men might already be up in the bedroom, but Gregory felt he must risk that. If he could find some way to alter his rank-badges and so make himself a less conspicuous personage he might be able to remain at liberty for some days, given his cap ; without it, once his description had been circulated, he would easily be identified by any policeman.

Having made his decision he walked to the lift and told the one-armed liftman to take him up to the third floor. Leaving the lift there he came cautiously down the backstairs to the first floor, on which his room was situated, thus avoiding any Nazis who might have been posted in the hall or on the lower staircase to watch for him.

Peering round a corner along the main corridor, which ran the whole length of the hotel, he saw that it was empty except for an elderly woman in a quilted dressing-gown. Immediately she had disappeared into her room he undid his pistol holster, put his hand on the butt of his automatic and tiptoed forward along the passage.

Pausing outside the door of his room he threw a quick glance in the direction of the landing. To his relief, no Storm-Troopers were posted there. For a minute he listened with his ear pressed to the panel of the door. No sound came from inside it. Drawing his gun, he unlocked the door and boldly flung it open.

The room was in darkness, and flicking on the light with his free hand he saw that it was empty. He saw, too, how it was that he had so far remained unsuspected.

On a small table there were several parcels ; they were the things he had ordered from various shops that afternoon. But at the foot of the bed there were two large, pig-skin suitcases and these were marked with black initials which showed that they belonged to Grauber.

He must have sent his luggage straight from the station to the hotel without bothering to telephone for a room. Doubtless he knew that however full the place was accommodation would be provided for him. On closer inspection Gregory saw that a printed label was tied to the handle of each suitcase giving the Group Leader's name in full. When the bags arrived the hotel porters had naturally imagined them to be Gregory's luggage and taken them straight up to his room. Grauber, meanwhile, had probably had some business to transact, or a private dinner-party, to which he had gone direct from the station ; and arriving late for his appointment with the Lady of the Limousine at the Regina Palast he had not yet spoken to anyone at the desk but had gone straight into the lounge where he knew she would be waiting for him.

Dearly as Gregory would have loved to examine the contents of those two bags he knew that he would be insane to attempt it. With swift, sound reasoning he saw at once that if he left the bags alone there was just a chance that Grauber might not learn anything about him until the morning, as he would assume that the other things in the bedroom belonged to some ordinary German citizen who had been turned out of it ; whereas if he found that his suitcases had been tampered with he would send for the management right away. The cat would be out of the bag and a description of the man who had posed as him would be winging its way over the telephones and wireless five minutes later.

For Gregory deliberately to have robbed himself of the few hours' start he might get would have been sheer craziness. Seizing his cap and greatcoat he dashed into the bathroom for his shaving things, stuffed them in his pocket, switched out the lights and cautiously emerged into the corridor again.

The sight of Grauber's bags in his room had assured him that he was reasonably safe for the moment. If the management already suspected him there would have been Black Guards there and others on the staircase. He did not know of any side-entrance to the hotel but he felt certain that he could count upon his lovely lady detaining Grauber down in the ballroom upon her business for some time yet, so bracing his shoulders he strode downstairs and across the main hall as though he owned it.

Except to step aside for him as usual nobody took any particular notice of him, and two minutes after leaving his bedroom he was out in the street.

"What the hell does A. do now?" he thought desperately. "I dare not go to another hotel, in this town at all events. I suppose my best plan is to make straight for the station and take the first train out for anywhere; then head once more, with my tail between my legs, for the nearest neutral frontier. But that means abandoning any hope of seeing Erika von Epp. Hell and damnation! What infernal, god-forsaken luck!"

He was already moving in the direction of the *Mittlebahnhof* but with every step he took his bitter despondency became more deeply coloured with obstinate rebellion. What a tale to have to tell Colonel Lacroix who had put such faith in him! How could he face Sir Pellinore after bringing about so many deaths and then abandoning his mission when having come so near to achieving his objective? Rheinhardt, Wachmuller, Archer, Rosenbaum and Madame Dubois had all paid the penalty of having known him. That had not been altogether his fault, but only two days before Lieutenant Gautier and other French soldiers had laid down their lives to ensure him a fresh start. How, with the thought of that in his mind could he ever again look at himself in a mirror unless he returned to France with something to show for their sacrifice? He was damned if he was going to turn tail and run this time!

It was aready half-past nine. Erika von Epp's maid had said that her mistress would probably be home by eleven. In another two hours, if only he stuck to his guns, he might at last be in possession of the vital information which he had sought for so many weeks.

By remaining in the neighbourhood of Munich for the night he enormously lessened his chances of getting away safely the next day. Erika von Epp might be willing to help him, but he had brought disaster upon too many people to be willing to accept assistance from her which might lead to her arrest. If he stayed in Munich he must depend upon his own wits to get him out of the city the following morning. But stay he would. He was now determined to do so, and to hear what Erika von Epp had to say, even if he were afterwards caught and shot before he had had an opportunity to use anything he had got out of her and to bring his mission to a successful conclusion.

In this state of cussed-mindedness he reached the station and instead of turning into the main hall he walked to the barrier beyond which the local trains ran out. Owing to the war evening services had been restricted and he found that he would have to wait twenty-five minutes before a train was due to depart. The platform was almost deserted, and walking to its extreme end, where there were no lights at all, he sat down on the last seat, secure there from the casual glances of any passengers who might gather later on the platform near its barrier end.

His thoughts reverted to the lovely girl he had just left. How strange that he should run into her again ! And yet, per-haps, not so strange after all. Outside their private houses the rich move in a very limited circle, frequenting only half a dozen or so great hotels in each capital or pleasure-resort, and one or two, at most, in other large towns. He had often noticed when travelling abroad that it was almost impossible to walk into a luxury hotel without meeting somebody that he knew, or at least recognized from having run up against them some-where else, so as the Lady of the Limousine was now in Munich it was not really a very startling coincidence that he should have encountered her in the smartest public centre of Munich's social life.

He realised now that he had been thinking of her much more frequently during these past weeks than he had admitted to himself. Perhaps that was partly due to the strange circum-stances in which they had first met, but it was not altogether that. The lovely lines of her face rose again, clearly now before his mental vision, and she was even more beautiful than he had pictured her when dropping off to sleep or in dreamy reverie before getting up each morning during the inactive periods that he had spent in the concentration-camp at Nijmegen and in prison in Paris.

He always considered himself extremely hardboiled about women, and although he had had many affairs it was a long time since he had been in love, yet he admitted to himself that he was in love again now. Curious, he thought, how one never really grows out of that sort of thing, and in fact, how one's longing is intensified by age and experience. In the late thirties one can so easily become a callow youth again, and positively long for the touch of one woman's hand. He knew the symptoms well enough and they were all there. Somehow

or other he had got to find her again, and hold her in his arms
once more. But there was little chance of a third fortuitous
meeting, and although, owing to her beauty, she should not be
difficult to trace, any attempt to run her to earth was absolutely
out of the question at the moment. He dared not linger in
Munich a single second longer than was absolutely necessary, or
even return at any time while the war lasted to the Regina Palast
where his inquiry must start without grave risk. But immediately
the war was over it would be safe for him to do so. Therefore
a personal reason was added to his urge to complete his mission
at the earliest possible moment. The electric train ran smoothly
in, and by twenty past ten he was out at Prinz
Ludwig's Höhe.

The October moon had waxed and waned while he was in
Paris, so this first week of November found the warring nations
plunged in nightly darkness once again. Munich had already
had a leaflet raid, and now that all hope of peace had faded
the folk of the Bavarian capital were in constant fear that
next time the British came over they might drop bombs. In
consequence, the black-out restrictions were very severe.

In the main streets of the city traffic signals and dimmed
motor headlights still gave pedestrians enough light to find
their way about without difficulty, but here in this wealthy
residential suburb it was a very different matter. Only the
blacker outline of tall trees against the dark sky indicated the
walls of the gardens where they ended at the side of the road.
Not a chink of light showed from any of the houses and the
few cars that were about crawled along with their lights heavily
hooded.

Gregory's sense of locality was normally excellent, and
having walked to the house only that morning he had felt
certain that he could find his way there again, but the black-
out defeated him. It was only after he had lost his way twice
and had had to inquire of other pedestrians whom he passed
groping their way through the shadows, that he eventually
found *Das Kleine Schloss* and realized that he had not set out
any too early after all, as it was now past eleven.

The same trim maid opened the door to him, and said at
once that her mistress had not yet returned.

"All right," said Gregory, stepping past her into a tiled
vestibule, "I'll wait for her."

"As you wish, *Herr Gruppenführer*," replied the girl timidly,
and led him across a big, richly-furnished hall, from which a

broad staircase ran up to the floor above, to a lounge-room
with book-lined walls and comfortable sofas.

When Gregory had seated himself in an arm-chair she said,
"I am afraid you may have to wait some time, *Herr Gruppenführer*, because the *Frau Gräfin* telephoned a little after ten to
say that she was going on somewhere and would not be back
until late, so we were not to wait up for her. The other servants
have already gone up to bed, but as I knew you were coming
I stayed downstairs to let you in."

"I see," said Gregory thoughtfully. "Well, you'd better
run off to bed now. But wait a minute; I suppose the *Frau
Gräfin* will return alone?"

"It's impossible to say, *Herr Gruppenführer*. Sometimes
the gentlemen who see her back come in for a few minutes
and sometimes she brings several friends in for a last drink on
their way home. Drinks and sandwiches are always left out for
her when she's returning late."

The possibility that Erika von Epp might bring back a
crowd of friends, or even a single male companion did not suit
Gregory's book at all. If she had been in when he arrived he
had intended to tell the maid to inform her that he wished to
see her alone on urgent private business, so that even if people
had been with her she would have left them to receive him in
some other room. Now, however, believing all her servants to
be in bed, the Countess Erika would let herself in with her
own key, and anybody who was with her would almost certainly
come on him sitting there at the same time as she did.

Standing up again, he said abruptly: "It's most important
that I should see the *Frau Gräfin* alone, and that none of her
friends should suspect my presence here. I suppose I may take
it that, even if she does return with an escort, having given him
a drink she'll be alone when she goes up to her bedroom?"

The maid looked slightly embarrassed. "It has not always
been so, *Herr Gruppenführer*. The *Frau Gräfin* is a good mistress
and it is not for us servants to criticize what she does, but it's
some time since any gentleman except the *Herr Graf* has stayed
here, and he's away at the Krupp factories in Essen
now."

Gregory smiled. "Well, I'll have to chance it. You can
put the lights out here, and take me up to her room."

The girl was obviously terrified of him, and she replied
with immediate submissiveness: "*Jawohl, Herr Gruppenführer,*
if you will please to follow me."

Switching out the lights in the lounge and leaving only one burning in the hall, she led him up the broad staircase and along a thickly-carpeted corridor to a huge room at the back of the house.

In an alcove at the far end of it there was a vast, low bed with rose-satin draperies that fell gracefully round its head from a big gilt coronet supported by two golden cupids. The ceiling was washed with pale pink, which gave the room warmth, and it was furnished with every luxury that limitless money and rich taste could devise. There were two other doors at the far end of the room, one either side of the great bed. Walking over he found that the nearer door led to a bathroom. It was almost as big as a good-sized best bedroom. The walls were painted sea-green with brightly-coloured tropical fish, coral fans and waving seaweeds, so that the whole formed an undersea scene, and at one end of the room there was a huge, tiled, sunken bath. He admired Erika's taste and her love of luxury. The other door gave on to a clothes-closet, a long, narrow room where rows and rows of dresses, tweeds and furs—at least a hundred in number—hung shrouded in transparent, dust-proof coverings. After a glance inside he stepped back into the bedroom.

A subtle perfume lingered in the hangings of the bed, and as he brushed past them it was wafted to him. He stood there a moment recalling all he had heard of the room's owner. She was said to be beautiful, dangerous and unscrupulous. She had been the mistress of Hugo Falkenstein, the armaments million-aire, and had a reputation for gallantry. This Countess was a woman of birth and breeding who had gone wrong. She had taste, as the room showed, but it was a taste for luxury over-done. It was the room of a Princess who had become a great courtesan.

Returning to the maid, he said: "I shall wait here. You go to bed now, and remember, if you leave a note or take any other steps to warn the *Frau Gräfin* of my presence, you will see the inside of a concentration-camp."

The girl went very pale and stuttered: *"Nein, nein, Herr Gruppenführer.* I've said nothing, and I will do exactly as you say."

"Good. You can go, then."

As the maid left him Gregory arranged the door so that it was about a foot ajar and he would be able to hear the Countess when she let herself in and crossed the hall below. He then selected the most comfortable chair and pulled it into position opposite the door. After a moment it occurred to him that when the Countess came upstairs she would see through the partly-open doorway that there was a light in her room, and would realize that somebody was in there. That might lead her to rouse her household before advancing further for fear it was a burglar; so he switched out the light before he sat down.

It was a dreary business waiting there in the darkness. He tried to concentrate his thoughts on the best way of leaving Munich the following day and to think up some scheme by which he could obtain lower rank badges for his S.S. uniform so that he should not arouse so much comment wherever he went, but his thoughts for once refused to collect themselves in order. Anxious as he now was about the difficulties of retaining his freedom for more than a few hours—or, at the most, days— he was extraordinarily keyed up at the thought that before morning came he would at least have succeeded in making contact with the mysterious and sinister Countess.

If, as he believed, she held the key to the anti-Hitler conspiracy the worst part of his mission would by then have been accomplished, and even if he were caught afterwards they might in the meantime have arranged some way in which she could complete the job which he had set out to do.

He heard midnight strike on a grandfather clock down in the hall; one o'clock; two o'clock. He was not tired, because he had had ample sleep in the last few days, but every moment of darkness was precious to him, and if the Countess returned home very late, by the time he had had his conversation with her there might not be very much of the night left in which he might slip away into the friendly shadows for the first steps of his flight from Munich, before his description was issued and the hunt was up in earnest. It was about a quarter-past two when he heard the click of the latch and then the closing of the front door down in the hall.

Drawing his gun he slipped back the safety-catch and listened intently. If by chance the gallant Erika had any thought of entertaining a boy-friend upstairs in her room that night, Gregory did not mean to be caught napping.

There was no sound of voices and only one set of light footsteps coming up the stairs. Evidently she had returned unaccompanied or had dismissed her escort on the doorstep without offering him a drink.

Firm, brisk steps were coming along the short corridor. The door swung open. Gregory sat there holding his breath. The lights flashed on. Erika von Epp stood there framed in the doorway. Gregory gave a gasp of surprise and came slowly to his feet. Erika von Epp was the lovely Lady of the Limousine.

Chapter XXIX

SATAN'S CHILDREN

HER eyes opened wide in blank surprise ; then she smiled. "So you decided to play burglar, or bribed your way in, and came up here to wait for me ? How very clever of you !"

Gregory had hardly recovered from his astonishment. He stammered, "You—you *are* the Countess von Osterberg— aren't you ?"

"Of course, although I prefer to be known by my maiden name, Erika von Epp." She closed the door behind her and walked slowly towards him. "But why d'you look so surprised ? You knew my name, you must have known it, to connect me with this house."

He shook his head. "No. You never told me what it was, and I've had to leave you so suddenly after both our meetings that each time I've forgotten to ask you. I know quite a lot about Erika von Epp, though."

"Indeed ; and what have you heard about her ?"

His lips twitched into a smile. "People who should know say that she is the most dangerous woman in Europe."

She pulled off the short, dark fur coat that threw up the halo of her golden hair to such perfection, and cast it on a near-by chair. "Perhaps I am. My enemies certainly believe me to be a modern Lucretia Borgia. But what do *you* think, having known me without knowing anything about my terrifying reputation ?"

"Dear Erika." He took her hand and kissed it lightly. "Quite a number of people have had good cause to regard me, too, as one of Satan's children."

"Satan's children," she repeated with a low laugh. "What a lovely phrase ! And birds of a feather, eh ? Yes. We're the type who have no illusions, and no scruples about the way we get anything we've fixed our hearts upon, so we're evil people to come up against."

"Yet we can be loyal and gentle to those we love."

There was nothing of the round, doll-like china-blue about

her eyes. They were deep in colour and oval in shape. For a moment they held his fixedly as she said :

"You told me to-night that you were in love with me. Was that true ?"

"Of course. Why should you doubt it ? I had no axe to grind, no earthly reason in the world to tell you so except that for these last seven weeks two glimpses of your face, the sound of your voice and the touch of your lips have haunted me."

She shrugged "Why, after all, should I not believe that ? You're not the first ; you won't be the last. Men have been falling for me ever since I was seventeen. It was only that I thought, just for a moment, that you *did* perhaps know all the time who I was and had taken that line as a British Secret Service agent."

"I swear to you I didn't know ; and I'm glad of that now, because I might not have fallen for you so readily if I had."

"It makes no difference to you, then, that instead of being, as you probably supposed, a nice young girl, I am a woman— yes, let us be frank—a woman with a very shady reputation ?"

"Not an iota. Haven't I told you already that I'm one of Satan's children ? I've always held life up at the end of a pistol and taken the best it could give me regardless of the consequences."

"So you, too, are a conscious hedonist ? Ah well, it would be a dreary world if there weren't a few pagans like us left to defy the conventions with which the timid herd would like to shackle us. But, if you didn't know my name, what are you doing here ? And how did you get upstairs into my room ?"

"Getting up here wasn't difficult. I called this morning just after you'd gone out and I threatened your poor maid with the direst penalties the Gestapo could inflict if she told you any-thing about it. When I came back this evening I made her bring me up here because I didn't want to be seen by anyone you might, perhaps, have brought in for a drink when you got home. Then I packed her off to bed. As for the reason of my seeking out the famous Erika von Epp—" Gregory produced the golden swastika with a flourish—"I wished to return this to her."

"The symbol of peace opens all doors among the right think-ing," she murmured, turning the little charm over curiously in her long fingers. "Tell me ; where did you find it ?"

"I didn't. A good-looking young Guards officer found it caught in his sock when he undressed to go to bed early one summer morning. It was the only concrete thing by which he

N

could convince himself that he had just returned from a night in Paradise."

"Dear Jimmy!" she smiled reminiscently. "He was a very sweet person and damnably good-looking. It was fun for the little time it lasted. 'Ships that pass in the night,' you know, and the wireless spark that unites them for a moment before they draw apart again on their paths across the desolate ocean. I was right, then, in thinking that he was not such a fool as he looked. I didn't dare let a word drop to anybody who mattered while I was in London; there are too many Nazi spies there. But I felt certain he wasn't covered—he wasn't important enough—yet he evidently had the sense to turn in that toast which we drank together to the Army and the speedy return of the old days. It was a line thrown out almost at random but I hoped that someone would pick it up and use it to communicate with me. How strange that person should be you!"

"Yes. And if only I'd known who you were weeks ago, when we first met outside Coblenz! Still, the line's established now. What can you tell me of the German Army leaders who are conspiring to overthrow Hitler?"

"*Achtung!*" she put a finger to her lips and cast a nervous glance round. "Since we're to talk of such things we must do so in whispers. One never knows who is watching and listening, even in the privacy of one's own bedroom."

He smiled. "I've been waiting for you here for over two hours so I think I should know if anyone was lurking behind the curtains."

All this time they had been standing face-to-face, but now she moved away from him and pointed to the doors at the far end of the room near her bed.

"Just make certain that there's no one in the bathroom or in the clothes-closet. You must be hungry and thirsty after your long wait. I'll slip downstairs and get some wine and *Brötchen*, then we will talk. Here!" She thrust the swastika into his hand. "As you have carried this for so long, you may keep it."

He thanked her with a smile, and although he had already examined the other rooms he knew that in Nazi Germany one could not be too careful. There might be a Gestapo spy among her servants who had taken up a position there on hearing her enter the house, so as she left the room he drew his gun and walked towards the bathroom. Flinging open the door and switching on the light he found it as he had expected—empty.

He also made a swift re-examination of the clothes-closet, but there was no one there.

Returning to the bedroom he waited patiently until Erika reappeared, carrying a heavy tray with fruit, glasses, two bottles of champagne and a selection of cold delicacies spread on half-rolls.

Gregory smiled as he took it from her and set it on a low table. "Two bottles, eh? You must have guessed, I think, that half a bottle only increases my thirst."

"And mine," she said quietly. "It is French, too. I've always believed in keeping a good cellar and I added a hundred cases of Veuve Cliquot to it just before the war, as a precaution."

He laughed. "With the German tax on French wines, that must have cost you a packet.'

"Not as much as you might suppose. My good friend, Hermann Goering, arranged the matter for me."

"Goering?" he repeated, lowering his voice. "Is he in this? I had an idea that he might be."

"No—at least I don't think so. But he's the only decent one among the Nazi leaders and I have known Hermann since I was a little girl."

While Gregory opened one of the bottles she picked up a *Brötchen* and bit into it with her strong white teeth.

"Is that smoked salmon you're eating there?" he exclaimed. "And by Jove! By the colour of it I believe that's real butter!"

"Of course," she nodded, still chewing her mouthful. "It's all tinned. But what would you? Anyone who remembers the last Great War is a fool if during peace he could afford to do so, yet did not lay in adequate stocks for this one. Because Hitler goes crazy I see no reason why one should starve."

"You can't remember the last Great War, though."

"Can't I? How old do you think I am?"

"You probably expect me to say twenty-three, but you have no need of flattery and I'm not going to give it to you. When I first saw you I put you down as twenty-six."

She smiled. "I believe you. But I was born in 1911 so you see I'm twenty-eight. I was already going to my first school at the time of the Armistice and in Germany the years that followed the war were even worse than the years of the war itself. It was the ghastly time we went through then that made me what I am."

Gregory had filled two goblets with champagne. He handed one to her and lifted the other, smiling into her eyes. "Well, anyway, here's to us—Satan's children!"

"Satan's children !" she repeated, smiling back and drinking a long draught of the golden wine.

"I know how grim things were in Germany after the last Great War," he went on, "and since you speak of that time so bitterly, I take it that you haven't always had so much money ?"

She nodded. "Those years were terrible beyond belief. Half the men of the aristocracy, many of our best and bravest, had been killed in the war. Even those who survived were nearly all suffering from war wounds, and the hatred of the whole people was our portion. As Germany had lost the war and could not take her suffering out on her enemies she blamed the officer caste for having led her into it. Our estates were seized, and our investments were no longer worth the paper they were written on once the mark had gone tumbling into the abyss. They would not even give us jobs if they could find other people to do the work. The Jews got their claws into us and stole all that we had left : our jewels, our furs, our antiques, our cellars of wine and everything we had managed to save that was of any value. They all went for a few marks which were barely sufficient to keep us for a week or two in bread.

"I, Erika von Epp, who as a child had known every care and comfort, even during the war years, grew up in a little Munich flat that was hardly better than a tenement. We hadn't even the facilities to wash ourselves properly, our clothes were of such poor quality that I was half-frozen by the cold each winter and for weeks on end I suffered virtual starvation.

"Friends of my elder sister—married women as well as girls —were forced to haunt the big hotels and become prostitutes in order to keep their helpless old parents, or their husbands and brothers—gallant officers, whose war wounds deprived them of any possible hope of employment.

"I didn't have to do that, because I was pretty enough to get a man for myself. At seventeen, within a week of having managed to land a job in a Munich store, I became the mistress of one of the departmental heads. What a come-down for the proud Erika von Epp, eh ? But he wasn't a bad fellow, and it meant security, and that was what mattered ; warmth and at least enough food to eat for my family and myself. And, young as I was, I was shrewd enough to know that the tiny flat he gave me was a better proposition than hawking myself to casual foreign visitors and rich men, by which I might have made more money for the time being but would certainly have lost my looks through sitting drinking half the night in the dubious dance-places. D'you blame me ?"

Gregory shook his head. "No. Since the whole of your own caste was down and out and there was no hope of your making a decent marriage, you were very wise to save yourself for better times. I bet you didn't remain the mistress of that departmental head for long, though."

She laughed. "No. Poor Otto only lasted for a few months. One night he was fool enough to bring one of his Directors back to dinner, and of course the inevitable happened. That was, I think, the worst thing I ever did, because he was old and I had to set my teeth to prevent myself from screaming every time he touched me. But he was rich, and he had many influential friends. By that time Otto was willing to marry me, so I could have become respectable if I'd wished, but I deliberately took on that old beast, Horsfelich, because I knew that through him I'd secure the things I'd always longed for—the things that were my right by birth and beauty.

"There were a lot of men after Horsfelich ; some I liked, some I didn't, but by that time I'd become completely cynical and each of them was a new milestone on the road to power and wealth. When I was twenty I met Hugo Falkenstein, the Jewish armaments millionaire. I'd been brought up to detest the Jews and all they stood for ; to consider them a race apart, unclean, only to be tolerated because some of them had brains and could be made useful—as was the attitude of all well-born Germans in the Kaiser's day. Cynical as I was it had never even entered my head that I might one day become the mistress of a Jew. Yet I did ; and not, as you might suppose, because I was greedy for a share of his millions. I already had plenty of money, expensive clothes and even quite good jewels by the time I met Hugo. I became his mistress because I loved him. But why am I telling you all this ?"

Gregory smiled across at her, drinking in the perfection of her beauty. Except for the little wrinkles round the corners of her eyes, caused by laughter, there were no lines upon her face. It seemed impossible that she had been through so much because she appeared so fresh and unspoilt. But he knew that that must be because of the spirit that animated her ; unquestionably she must be a girl of enormous courage to have lived as she had done and yet not to have allowed those sordid early years to get her down. In answer to her question he said :

"You're telling me about yourself because you know that every single thing about you interests me intensely."

She shook her head. "No ; it's not exactly that. It's because I want you to know the real me, I think. With most men I hide the skeletons of my dead affaires. They're nothing to be proud of, and generally I try to avoid anything which reminds me even vaguely of those nightmare years of my early youth. Except to Hugo I've never before confessed to any man that I sold myself to get on in the world, because it's almost impossible to do that and keep a man's respect. But with you, somehow, I felt that I could. Perhaps that's because, although this is only the third time that we've met, our meetings have been in such extraordinary circumstances that they've brought us together much more intimately than ordinary meetings would have done. I've thought about you a lot in these last weeks, although it seemed quite pointless, and I've kicked myself for a fool for doing so. You're gay and brave and I'm sure you know that you're horribly attractive. If I hadn't let you kiss me when we were in the car together things might have been different, but that seemed to do something to me, and night after night I've hardly been able to get to sleep through wondering if you got away safely and what had happened to you. Perhaps I'm a fool to tell you that, but I don't think so because I do believe you love me, and although I'm proud as Lucifer with most people I've got no pride at all where anyone I really like is concerned."

"Nor I," murmured Gregory, taking her hand and carrying it to his lips. "You've done something to me that no woman has done for years. I'd walk through fire for you. Nothing that you could tell me about your past would make one iota of difference to the present. Tell me about Hugo."

"He had the soul of an artist, the brain of a great statesman and the generosity of an Emperor. He was an extraordinary mixture. I've never known a man who was at the same time so kind, so considerate, so thoughtful for his friends, yet so utterly ruthless with his enemies. He saw at once that I was not just a beautiful doll to be kept in a luxury flat for the amusement of his leisure hours but that I was his equal intellectually, and we formed an amazing partnership. Sometimes we travelled together, sometimes he sent me alone as his ambassador, to negotiate with diplomats and Ministers. I travelled all over Europe and several times to America. He wanted me to marry him, but I wouldn't, as that would have altered my status and made me less useful to him.

"It's a curious psychological fact that if I'd become Frau Falkenstein, the wife of a Jew, many of my old friends among the best families would have ceased to receive me ; while as long as I remained Erika von Epp—although most of them knew of my association with Hugo—my position was rarely brought into question."

Gregory nodded. "Yes, I understand that. By refraining from marrying him you enabled them to keep face."

"Exactly. And during those years brains, blood and guts had begun to count again the remnants of the German nobility were gradually struggling back to positions of importance. Captains and Majors who had had their epaulettes torn from their shoulders by the Reds after the war had become Colonels and Generals in the reconstituted *Reichswehr*. Some of their women were a little difficult to start with, but with the men I had no trouble at all. In my house here in Munich and in my apartment in Berlin all the most promising elements of the new Army began to congregate, and as soon as they began to appreciate the power that I wielded even the most sticky of their women came too.

"With Goering I had an excellent understanding and I was often able to be of great assistance to him on matters concerning my Army friends. Europe had given Germany a rotten deal, and in those days many of us thought that the Nazis would not only prevent Germany from going Communist but would also make her strong and respected again.

"Then the Jewish persecutions began. At first I was able to protect Hugo and many of his friends, although I could do nothing for the masses. Hugo might have saved himself. He was too important a man for the Nazis to quarrel with if they could possibly avoid it, but he refused to stand by and see the poorer people of his race robbed and maltreated. Goering tried to persuade him to leave Germany and even promised to protect his interests, but he would not go.

"As the persecutions got worse and worse the gulf widened. Eventually Hugo wrote to Hitler pleading for the reasonable treatment of his race, and threatening that if the Führer remained adamant in his refusal to change his policy he would withdraw his financial support from the Government. The reply was his arrest, and he died six months later from the brutalities inflicted on him in the concentration-camp at Dachau."

"So that's why you're so bitterly anti-Nazi," Gregory said

softly. "If you loved him, I can understand just how you must have felt. But why did you marry von Osterberg?"

She shrugged. "That was to please my father. He was of the old school and had very high moral principles. The life I was leading nearly broke his heart. He tried not to show how glad he was when Hugo died, but in spite of all my faults he was always terribly fond of me and his one craving was to see me respectably married into one of the good old German families before he died himself.

"Last winter he became very ill and it was obvious that he couldn't last more than a few weeks. I could have married a dozen different men, but Kurt von Osterberg suited me best because I wished to please my father and yet remain my own mistress.

"Kurt is a scientist, but he was always short of money to carry out his experiments. He's a charming fellow, already in the early fifties, and although he is devoted to me, he's not in the least possessive. He's very proud to be known as my husband, content to remain my friend and more than grateful that I'm able to keep him in funds for the scientific experiments which mean so much to him. In that way I managed to retain my personal freedom and make my father's last hours happy. But since Hugo died, although I've tried hard to interest myself in one or two nice men like Jimmy, I have been like a dead person, until . . . ."

"Yes, until . . ." Gregory prompted her.

She laughed "Oh, until one night in September when a lean-faced ruffian held up my car, very nearly lost his life in taking my pistol from me and then made me kiss him. But it's your turn to tell me about yourself now."

Slowly Gregory shook his head. "I think I've been dead too, or half-dead anyway, for a long time until that night in September. My own career of crime hasn't been half so spectacular, but I'll tell you later about some of the high spots which might amuse you. In the meantime, what in the world were you doing this evening in the company of that swine, Grauber?"

She sat forward quickly. "You know him, then?"

"Do I not, my dear!" Gregory produced Grauber's Gestapo card and showed it to her. "I pinched this off him in Paris ten days ago, and for the last forty-eight hours I've been posing as *Herr Gruppenführer* Grauber myself."

"*Lieber Gott!* What rashness! He's such a big shot that the Gestapo know of his presence in every town he visits. If he is here and you turn up in Frankfurt or Cologne as him, it's quite certain that your imposture will be discovered within a few hours."

"I know," Gregory agreed with a rueful smile. "And for that reason my impersonation of him ceased from the second I set eyes on him this evening. But I was under the impression he was tucked away in prison in Holland and that I should be reasonably safe in using his name anywhere in Germany as long as he was out of the country."

"He *was* a prisoner in Holland. He returned to Germany only last night."

"I wonder how the devil he managed to do that. He slipped through our fingers in Paris, but we warned the Dutch that he might be coming through Holland and they arrested him—dressed in women's clothes—for using a forged passport. I was informed that they'd given him six months."

"They did, but Grauber is too big a fish for the Nazis to resign themselves to losing his services for that length of time. As soon as he could let Himmler know where he was the Nazis made a deal with the Dutch Government."

"How could they do that without causing the Dutch to contravene international law?"

"Quite simply. Grauber was not in the same situation as a German airman or a soldier who had penetrated into Holland in uniform during war-time. He had done nothing to infringe Dutch neutrality, but was simply arrested on a civil charge for using a forged passport—just as a Jewish refugee or anybody else might have been. A few weeks ago an ace Dutch press photographer, Hendrik Brederode, blotted his copybook very badly on the Polish front. He managed to get away from a bunch of pressmen who were being shepherded round the battlefields. With a telescopic lens he took some photographs of Hitler looking at the mutilated bodies of the Polish women and children his airmen had killed. The photographs were discovered, so Brederode was arrested and imprisoned. When the Nazis wanted to get Grauber back they simply arranged with the Dutch Government to exchange Grauber for Brederode."

"I see," Gregory nodded. "So that's the way it was. But what on earth induced you to spend the evening with a brute like that?"

She yawned, showing her even white teeth and the tip of a little red tongue. She looked much younger than she was but rather tired, which made Gregory feel a positive ache to take her in his arms and kiss her. With a shrug of her shoulders she replied : "I've often spent evenings with people that I have disliked intensely if I thought that I could get something out of them that I wanted very badly."

"I suppose the swine's in love with you, and you're playing him for what he's worth to you. God ! What a horrible business ! The very thought of his laying a finger on you makes me go all queer inside."

"You foolish darling !" She laughed indulgently. "I thought you considered yourself hardboiled. Surely you know that when a woman like myself uses her best weapons she expunges such episodes from her mind immediately afterwards, and that they don't really mean a thing to her."

"All the same, it makes me more eager than ever to get my hands round Grauber's fat neck. It's as though he had added sacrilege to his other crimes."

She rested a hand on his shoulder for a moment. "It's nice that you should feel like that about me, but in this case you've no cause to worry. Grauber is not interested in women. Like a lot of his colleagues, he is a pervert."

"I thought he might be, but in that case what was he after with you ?"

"I'm not quite certain, but I think that he's now playing a double game. For a long time he cultivated my acquaintance solely to find out all he could about my friends in the Army, and he was too important a man for me to refuse to have anything to do with him. He was then made chief of the Foreign Department of the Gestapo, U.A.-1. Other work occupied him, I suppose, and he ceased to bother me, so for many months I never saw him except through chance meetings. But immediately after von Ribbentrop signed the death-warrant of the Nazi Party this summer by making the pact with Russia, Grauber began to interest himself in me again.

"Many of the Nazi leaders—men like Hess and Deutsch—are incredibly stupid ; just strong-arm men, thugs out of the gutter who have managed to elbow their way to high positions through having attached themselves to Hitler in the old days. But not all the Nazis are fools, and the more intelligent of them are shrewd enough to realize that Hitler stabbed his strongest champions—the German lower middle classes—in the back when he consented to an alliance with the Bolsheviks. It was the German "little man's" fear and hatred of Communism that brought Hitler to power, and his deliberate betrayal of the anti-Comintern front has robbed him of millions of supporters."

Gregory was craving to make love to her, yet he knew that if he once started he would never be able to stop, and it was absolutely essential that he should learn exactly where Grauber stood in this affair. With an enormous effort he resisted the temptation to take this poem of graceful curves crowned by the delicate, aristocratic face and burnished golden hair into his arms as she stood up and beginning to pace restlessly up and down, went on :

"The price of Russia's support was the surrender of Germany's rights in the Baltic and the withdrawal of German communities which had been established in the Baltic cities for many hundred years. Think what a blow that was to every patriotic German, whatever his politics or station. The shrewder Nazis began to see that if Hitler could not secure a favourable peace with the Democracies which left him in possession of his Polish gains as an offset to the Baltic losses, his day was done.

"If Germany could not defeat the Allies in 1914–1918, it is quite certain that she cannot defeat the Allies in 1939–1943. By a series of swift blows while at the height of his strength Hitler may succeed in renewing his prestige for a while and postponing a decision. If he overruns Holland and Belgium it may add a year to the length of the war. If he can persuade Stalin to let him overrun Hungary, on the understanding that they carve up Rumania between them, it may add two or three years to the length of the war. But Russia is not really behind Hitler, and even if she were her mineral wealth and agriculture are not developed enough for her to have surpluses sufficient to maintain German munition-factories at full blast and to keep German larders filled with essential foodstuffs. So Hitler's ultimate defeat is inevitable.

"That's quite certain," Gregory agreed.

"And afterwards Britain and France may have to come to Germany's aid against Russia."

"I doubt if that will be necessary, at all events in our time, but many long-sighted people in England think that's the way things will pan out. But . . ." as he caught a whiff of her perfume he drew in a sharp breath, and hurried on, ". . . let's get back to Grauber. The sooner we've done with him the sooner we can talk again about ourselves."

"Grauber and people like him are now asking themselves what will happen after Hitler's fall," she replied, with an understanding smile, "and they see a Communist revolution sweeping

Germany which would mean a certain and probably extremely painful death for every one of them. Is there any way in which that could be prevented ? Yes ; one way, and one way only. We Germans are fundamentally a law-abiding people. We proved that by emerging from our last revolution instead of going Bolshevik. A new revolution could be prevented if the Army took over in time, because the great majority of the people would prefer to accept an Army dictatorship rather than allow their cities to be looted by criminal mobs and permit their country to plunge headlong into a state of anarchy."

"I see," said Gregory. "So friend Grauber is planning to rat on his boss and the more stupid of his colleagues ?"

She shook her head. "I don't say that, but I think he's preparing the ground for such a move should it become necessary. As I've already said, he's playing a double game at the moment, trying to get anything he can from me which he can use for the benefit of the Nazis as long as they look like remaining in power and there is some chance that Hitler may get himself out of the mess he's in. Personally I'm convinced that the Allies can't be bought off at any price now, but Hitler has brought off some absolutely staggering diplomatic coups in his time. One must give him that, and Grauber and Co. believe that he may still succeed in securing a settlement by holding up Stalin as a bogey, playing on the fears of the neutrals and persuading President Roosevelt, on humanitarian grounds, to lend himself to negotiations. Hitler would come out of it, of course, with lowered prestige, but without entire loss of face. He would still be the master, and as diplomacy is his long suit he'd probably scrap von Ribentrop, throw over Russia and re-establish himself by fresh diplomatic triumphs.

'As long as there is any hope of that, Grauber will continue to do his job with complete ruthlessness. He could never hope to achieve such a high position as he has at present under any other Government, so he'll do everything he can to keep Hitler in power until he is quite certain that Hitler's goose is cooked. On the other hand, he would like to keep on good terms with me so that he could use me as a bridge over which to escape if need be, and he thinks that I could save his neck with the Army leaders should they decide to take over."

"And what do you get out of all this ?" Gregory inquired.

"Nothing so far, except the added security from Nazi interference which I derive through his colleagues knowing that I'm on good terms with him. But when the time is ripe Grauber may prove a key man to the whole situation. Before he was appointed chief of Gestapo Department U.A.-1 he was on other work which placed him in possession of very jealously guarded Nazi secrets.

"The Army leaders dare not act until they're much better informed where they stand than they are at present. It's vital that they should know whom they can trust and which among the officers round them are Gestapo spies that must first be eliminated. Grauber could tell me that if he chose to do so. When the danger-signals begin to flash Grauber will come to me. He will say that he has always been my friend and ask me to put in a good word for him with my friends among the Army people. He and I will then have a show-down, and I shall say 'Give me what I require and your life shall be spared. I could do without it, but it would make things easier for us. You know what is about to happen, so talk or I will throw you to the dogs. Take your choice about it, and be quick now !' "

Gregory poured himself out another glass of wine and beamed with satisfaction. "That's grand ! We'll go now to my end of the business. We've each learned where the other stands, by pure chance and without any need for fencing. We've both been playing the same game for weeks past, and the only pity is that we didn't realise it sooner.

"As far as Grauber's concerned I don't think it will be necessary for you to offer him his life, because I believe I can give you the thing you've been hoping to get from him. It is the list of the Inner Gestapo who are all Army officers that have been placed in positions where they can keep a constant watch on the Generals. Am I right ?"

"*So !*" she breathed, "you have that ? You can really give me absolutely trustworthy information as to who they are ?"

"Yes. The list was secured by a British agent just before the war, and is at present in safe keeping in Berlin. With it there is a letter, signed by responsible Allied statesmen, stating that if the German Generals will depose the Nazis the Democracies will guarantee a round-table conference and a new deal for Germany. The whole object of my mission is to secure those two documents and place them in the hands of the General who is the secret head of the anti-Nazi movement."

"But this is marvellous—*kolossal !*" She clasped her hands and her eyes were shining. "And how glad I am now that I decided to leave that trail in London just on the chance that

I might be used if it were desired to open communications with the Generals !"

"It was a grave risk you took. If your words to Jimmy whatever-his-name-is had been reported to a Nazi agent you would have been for it."

"Perhaps. But I felt reasonably sure that if Jimmy passed on my apparent indiscretion at all it would be to your Intelligence people and to no one else."

"If that was your intention, why didn't you speak more plainly—give him something more definite and impress upon him the importance of turning it in ?"

"I had no authority to do so ; and as I didn't know that war would break out so soon I had planned a short trip to America. If the Gestapo had learned of my remarks and questioned any members of the General Staff about me, there was nothing concrete in what I had said and they could have laughed it off as the tipsy blathering of a reactionary *Hochwohlgeboren*. Then they would have let me know in secret that I had better remain in the States."

"Then as long as the Nazis were in power you'd never have been able to return to Germany."

"True ; but what was that in comparison with even the slenderest chance of becoming the channel for setting in motion the one plan that may save Germany from untold suffering ?"

"What is even more marvellous is that you should be the one person who can ensure my carrying out my mission successfully."

"Yes. Now you can no longer go about as Grauber you'll need help to get to Berlin, other clothes and a new personality so that when Grauber discovers that somebody has been impersonating him here, his impersonator will have disappeared from Munich without a trace. Naturally I will help you. Before morning we will make a plan, and between us it should be a good one."

"I felt sure I could count on you there the moment you entered this room," Gregory smiled, "and without your help I'd be hard put to it even to get out of Munich now I'm on the run again. But I didn't mean that. I can't complete my job until I know to whom I must hand those papers when I've collected them from Berlin. That's why I came to see you, as Erika von Epp."

She drew back suddenly. "I'm sorry, but I'm afraid I can't tell you that."

"What ?" exclaimed Gregory. "But you *must* know ! To whom would you have handed the list of Inner Gestapo yourself if you'd succeeded in getting it from Grauber ? If you don't know the actual head of the conspiracy you must know somebody who's in it pretty high up, and that will serve my purpose."

She shrugged. "Oh, I know myself, of course ; but I can't tell *you*."

"D'you mean that you don't trust me ?" Gregory frowned and the old scar on his forehead went white.

"Please don't put it that way." She made a little grimace. "If it were a question of my own life I would trust you—I swear that—but this is a question of the whole destiny of Germany ; the future of eighty-five million people hangs upon it. You have returned to me my golden swastika. When you didn't know who I was you told me the broad outlines of the work upon which you were engaged. Everything that you've said since convinces me that you're heart and soul with us ; but that is not enough. When I was working with Hugo I learned that one must trust nobody. What proof have I that, instead of being a British Secret Service agent, you are not working for Russia with a view to sabotaging Germany ? Smash the Army first and let Hitler smash himself afterwards ! That would suit Stalin's game. No, the risk is too great ; I cannot possibly give you the information that you require."

Gregory stood up. "But don't you see that if you refuse to do so I'm stymied—I can't do a thing ? You've *got* to believe that I'm playing straight with you in this ; or if you won't at least tell me how I can convince you that I am. Hang it all ! What was the point of your leaving a trail in London if when we picked it up and followed it to you we were only to come up against a blank wall ?"

"Ah ! That is a very different matter," she said quickly. "All I did was to leave a pointer to myself as a suitable post-box if your Government wished to open negotiations with the anti-Nazi Generals. If you will produce these documents I will gladly pass them on to the right quarter."

"No," said Gregory, "I'm afraid that won't do. I would trust *you* with *my* life but I'm not trusting anyone with those papers. What proof have I, apart from my personal belief in you, that the Gestapo didn't suspect this plot months ago and get you, when you were in London, to plant a trail that might bring back to them vital information about its possible development ? The fact that you spent the evening with Grauber is quite enough to suggest that you're hand-in-glove with him. For that matter, since you're a notorious adventuress, you might be in the pay of Stalin yourself."

"Yes, you're right." She lit a cigarette. "We may trust each other personally, but we can't take each other's words when the future of Europe lies in the balance. But I think I see a way. I shall not tell you the name of the head of the anti-Nazi conspiracy, but I can arrange for you to meet him in secret."

"Ah, if you can do that—enable me to hand the two papers to him personally after he has satisfied me as to his identity so that I'm sure he really is a high-up General and not a Nazi spy—the trick is done."

She nodded. "I can do it, but if I do you'll know who he is once you've met him, and the papers might be forgeries. Therefore, after the meeting you will have to become his prisoner while the documents are checked and the *Putsch* prepared, so that it will be impossible for you to betray him before it is carried out. Are you prepared to become a hostage for your own integrity?"

"Good God, yes !" Gregory exclaimed. "That's fair enough. I don't care what happens afterwards if only I can get those papers to the right man."

She smiled into his eyes. "Then, that's settled. To-morrow we leave for Berlin. I suppose you're quite sure that you were not followed here ?"

"Quite. And fortunately I took special precautions when I came out here this morning, so even if they're after me already they won't have the faintest idea where I've got to. What's more, I didn't actually let your maid read my Gestapo card or give any name, so there's no possibility of any leakage through your servants of the fact that Group Leader Grauber is supposed to be here. I'm, er—afraid, though—" Gregory's lips twitched suddenly—"that you'll have to put up with me as your guest until the morning."

Her very blue eyes held amusement and mockery as she said quietly, "I can offer you a very nice room just along the corridor."

Gregory took her hand and kissed it. "Even walls have ears, it's rude to shout, and I want to go on talking to you."

"Yes," she murmured, "and I want to go on talking to you, so I suppose if we were only characters in a spy story this chapter would finish with the words, 'and they talked until the dawn.' "

"That's it; and the book would end up with a convenient fatal accident to your husband, after which you would shyly accept me as Number Two and we should live happily ever after. But as it is, we're real people—just Satan's children."

She nodded. "Perhaps it's better so. There are no lost illusions afterwards, anyway. Let's drink a toast to the Devil's brew that was animated by a spark of pagan godliness and made us what we are."

He waited until she had refilled the champagne goblets, then put his arm gently round her and smiled down into her eyes as he said: "I don't see why we shouldn't talk until the dawn, do you? But that's no reason why we should remain standing up all the time!"

Chapter XXX

ARREST

WHEN all unknown to them dawn stole upon the world outside the heavy curtains of the quiet, dimly-lit room Erika stirred drowsily beside him, her golden head pillowed on his chest. Gregory lay on his back and he was staring upwards at the two gilt cherubs which supported the coronet above her bed.

For three hours he had been as near to heaven as any mortal man can reach, but now a new terror was clutching at his heart-strings. The thoughts that had haunted him in the train from Paris a few days before had returned with redoubled force, and added to them was a far grimmer dread of the future.

He had brought death by now to Julius Rheinhardt. He had brought death to Pastor Wachmuller; death to Tom Archer; death to Jacob Rosenbaum; death to Madame Dubois. Would his scarlet trail now bring death to this wonderful girl he had found in the enemy land ?

Gregory had no grounds whatsoever on which to justify any immediate fears for Erika. The fate which he dreaded might overtake her could only come to her through him, and as he lay there listening to her gentle breathing he knew that he was safe for the next few hours.

She had told him that unless she left special instructions she was never called but rang for her breakfast after she had wakened naturally each morning, and as an additional precaution he had locked the bedroom door. Nobody in Munich could possibly know where he had got to, and providing that he was not seen or heard by her servants it would be assumed that after he had interviewed her on her return home the previous night she had let him out herself, re-locking the front door after him.

He had suggested slipping away before daylight in a suit of the Count von Osterberg's clothes, making his way to Berlin and meeting her there again after he had collected those all-important papers, but she would not hear of it. She had pointed out that wherever he went he would be liable to be challenged as a deserter by police, military pickets and railway detectives and, since he had no papers he could produce, promptly arrested. In consequence, she insisted, they must make the journey to Berlin together. She had been granted special permits which allowed her to travel freely everywhere in Germany during wartime, except in the military zones, and she felt confident that they would be able to think up some plausible story by which she could take him with her.

Now that he was on the last stage of his mission he was exceedingly anxious to complete it as soon as possible, so in spite of the personal temptation to linger with Erika he had then suggested that they should both leave the house before the servants were up. She had replied that her sudden disappearance with a Gestapo man—as it was to his visit on the previous night that the servants would attribute her sudden departure—would be certain to arouse their anxiety on her account and they would telephone her friends, who would immediately set an inquiry going. To avoid that she must have her bags packed and leave in a normal manner.

In a last attempt to expose her to as little risk as possible he had put up the idea that he should leave before daylight and conceal himself somewhere in the neighbourhood where she could pick him up later. But this she had also vetoed, on the grounds that once out of the house, either in the S.S. uniform he was wearing or in a suit of civilian clothes, he would be exposed to the gravest risks unless she were with him.

Her reasoning was so sound that he had felt entirely justified in giving way to his own inclinations and agreeing that it was much better to remain there concealed until the following night, which would give them ample time to formulate a really sound plan of campaign, than to rush into unwarranted danger for the sake of trying to save a few hours.

In consequence, when dawn came with Erika still in his arms, despite his grim forebodings he dropped into a blissful doze, and they did not rouse themselves until ten o'clock, when daylight was filtering through the chinks of the heavy curtains.

For a little they talked of themselves and spoke of the wonderful joy of having found each other, their murmurs being interspersed by many kisses and caresses. Then Erika threw back her tumbled golden hair, sat up in bed and fumbled for a cigarette, which he quickly took and lighted for her.

"Breakfast now, *mein Liebling*, I think," she whispered,

smiling at him with heavy-lidded eyes still half-closed from sleep. "It's half-past ten and the war goes on. We must do something about it."

"Damn the war !" he murmured, stretching luxuriously among the tumbled sheets. "Still, you're right, my sweet ; I'd better make myself scarce and leave this Paradise for the outer darkness of the clothes-cupboard, I suppose."

"That's it," she laughed, bending over to kiss him again ; "and if you're very quiet and very good you shall share my breakfast with me."

"Quiet," grinned Gregory, "but not good," and putting his hand round the back of her neck he tilted up her chin and drew her down on top of him.

"Don't !" she gurgled, trying to suppress her laughter. "Stop it, or I'll burn you with my cigarette !"

He promptly stubbed his own out and taking hers from her put that out too. It was eleven o'clock before he had collected his scattered garments to retire into the clothes-closet and she was able to unlock the door and ring for breakfast.

After the maid had brought her tray, turned on a bath and gone again Erika re-locked the door and called him out, upon which they got back into bed to share the hot coffee, home-baked rolls and honey.

"I told Mitzi," she said, "that I twisted my ankle last night, and so that I can keep it up I mean to stay in bed all day."

"Angel !" murmured Gregory. "How clever of you. If you'd said you were ill, that would have meant a light lunch ; whereas people with twisted ankles are entitled to have gargantuan appetites, which means that you can order a highly satisfactory lunch for two !"

"That's just what I thought," she smiled, "and I had the idea, too, that you might prefer to remain in bed all day rather than sit locked in the clothes-closet."

"Bless you !" he laughed, planting a swift kiss on the back of her neck which nearly made her upset the coffee.

When they had finished breakfast they wandered into the bathroom. Fortunately it was well away from the servants' quarters so they were able to fool about in the warm, scented water of the great, sunken bath to their hearts' content providing they kept the sounds of their laughter within reasonable bounds, and Gregory was able to shave himself with the tackle which he had taken such a risk to secure at the same time as he had collected his cap, before leaving the Regina Palast.

Afterwards Erika drew the bolt of a door which was flush with the wall and hardly perceptible among the frescoes of the undersea scene which ran round the whole room. Beyond it was her husband's bedroom, and making Gregory fetch his things she locked him in there while she did her hair and made up her face. Thus she was able to ring again for her maid and let the girl take the breakfast tray, tidy the suite, put away discarded clothes and so on without the least suspicion that her mistress was still entertaining the dark, lean-faced S.S. officer who had been there the night before.

When Erika had finished her toilette she ordered luncheon for one-thirty and as soon as Mitzi had disappeared she let Gregory out of his hiding-place, upon which they curled up in bed again to doze for the next hour. Gregory took refuge in the clothes-closet at twenty-past one and popped out of it again directly Erika's luncheon-tray had been brought up. Having followed the same procedure after the meal, while Mitzi removed the tray, he re-locked the bedroom door and they set about making serious plans for the evening.

He learned that the car in which he had held Erika up outside Coblenz had been temporarily placed at her disposal while she was in that area by her friend General von der Goltz, which accounted for its having a military chauffeur, but that on her return to Munich she had not been able to take the car permanently out of the Rhineland Command. She had three cars of her own but two of them were laid up, and in spite of her influence she had only been able to secure permits for just sufficient petrol to run her in and out of Munich ; so it was impossible for them to go to Berlin by car. On the other hand, Colonel Baron von Buhl, the Chief Railway Transport Officer at Munich, was another old friend of hers, so she thought she would be able to arrange for two sleepers on the night express.

For the purpose of attempting to secure adjacent accommodation on the train a bold step was decided upon. Gregory was to pose as Auguste von Leuterlachen, a cousin of Erika's who had been living in the United States for the past ten years and was there still, as far as she knew. If they said that he had returned to Germany after the outbreak of war, that would account for his not yet being a member of any uniformed service, and even his lack of papers might be got over at a pinch by his long residence in the United States and the disorder into which the permit *bureaux* had been thrown by the outbreak of hostilities. Erika therefore telephoned Colonel Baron von Buhl to ask if he could possibly manage to let her have two sleepers on the night train for Berlin for herself and her cousin.

The gallant old colonel pretended to grumble, chaffed her about her cousin and said he would see what he could do. After keeping her waiting for a few minutes he came on the line again to say that he had fixed the matter up, and demanded that she let him give her lunch on the first day after her return from Berlin as a *quid pro quo* for his good offices.

The conversation was not rendered any easier by the fact that Gregory was tickling her back, but the Colonel put her giggles down to a playful mood and admirable good humour, having little idea that while she was talking to him she was sitting in bed with a British Secret Service agent. She laughingly accepted the invitation and arranged that the sleeper tickets should be left for her at the booking-office. The cousin idea seemed a good one, and it was agreed that Gregory should pose as Auguste von Leuterlachen for the whole of the journey.

The afternoon sped by all too quickly. Erika telephoned down to say that she did not desire *Kaffeetrinken* at four o'clock but would like a bottle of champagne sent up at six. Gregory made himself scarce again when it was brought and then reappeared to drink it with her, remarking how fortunate it was that she liked champagne herself and drank it frequently. They thought it wisest to leave about a third of the wine in the bottle, which they did regretfully, but it was hardly likely that she would have consumed a whole bottle herself at six o'clock in the evening.

After this short interlude she led him through the bathroom to the Count's bedroom, where they selected a grey, London-made lounge-suit, a camel-hair overcoat, tie, shoes, shirt, etc. The Count was a little taller than Gregory and his shoulders were somewhat narrower, so the clothes would have filled with horror the Savile-Row cutter who made them, had he seen them on their borrower ; but the Germans as a whole are a remarkably ill-dressed people so Gregory considered that he would be able to pass in a crowd without undue comment, and very fortunately the shoes were near enough to his own size to be quite comfortable.

While he was dressing in the Count's room Mitzi packed for her mistress and afterwards brought up dinner, so when Erika came along to tell him that the coast was clear again he found her fully dressed and all ready for the journey.

During the meal, from which she fed him with substantial tit-bits on her fork, they discussed the problem of getting him out of the house unseen and Erika said that since darkness had now fallen she thought the best thing for him to do was to go by way of the garden. From the bathroom window he could lower himself on to a flat, out-jutting roof above the billiard-room which was only about fifteen feet above the ground, and from there he could scramble down a drainpipe.

As she had to get him into Munich it was unavoidable that her chauffeur should see him, but that would not matter providing that the man did not actually see him leaving the house, so he was to come round the side of *Das Kleine Schloss* in the darkness, turn left when he reached the road and walk as far as the third corner, where she would pick him up as though by arrangement.

When the time of departure drew near they were tempted to linger, loath to leave the lovely room in which they had both known such brief but glowing happiness for the unknown dangers that might await them outside it. But after a last, long, lingering kiss Gregory threw his leg over the bathroom window-sill and slid down on to the flat roof below.

All worked according to plan and a quarter of an hour later Erika picked him up at the third crossroad half a mile away. After a polite *"guten Abend"* and a few casual remarks about the war, intended to convey that they had not met for some days, they drove into Munich in silence so that the elderly chauffeur should not overhear, through the open section of the glass screen which divided them from him, any remark which might rouse his curiosity.

At the *Hauptbahnhof* Erika collected the tickets, and leaving his with the man on the barrier went straight through to the platform to see that their reservations were all in order. Gregory meanwhile took refuge in the gentlemen's lavatory, as they wished to minimise the risk of his being recognized hanging about on the platform, or in the train before it departed, by anyone who might have seen him in Regina Palast on the previous day.

He had synchronized his watch with the station clock and timed his appearance to a nicety. Running through the crowd as though he feared to miss the train, he gasped out to the man on the barrier : "I am Herr von Leuterlachen. Has the *Frau Gräfin* von Osterberg left a ticket with you for me ?"

The man thrust the ticket into Gregory's hand and he dashed on down the platform until he saw Erika leaning out of the train window and waving to him. Within a minute of his having taken his seat the long train moved out for Berlin.

As soon as it had cleared the station he stretched himself

out on one of the settees and closed his eyes, looking as woe-
begone as possible, while Erika carefully tucked him up in a big
rug she had brought for the purpose. She then rang for the
train-conductor and asked him to make up one of the beds as
soon as possible, telling him that her cousin was travelling to
Berlin to see a famous specialist and was so seriously ill that in
normal times they would never have risked his travelling at all.

The big, portly train-conductor was immediately sympathetic.
The combination of the lovely lady, her unfortunate cousin who
lay at death's door and the generous tip which Erika gave him
before he even set about his business won his heart entirely.
Puffing and panting he made up the bed and offered to help her
get Gregory into it.

"He nearly killed himself running to catch the train," Erika
announced, as between them they divested the groaning Gregory
of his outer garments and got him between the blankets. After
this had been satisfactorily accomplished the conductor asked
Erika for her papers and those of her companion, as in the course
of routine he had to collect them all with the tickets and return
them at the end of the journey.

Erika produced her own and then started to hunt for Gregory's
through all his pockets, but of course, as he had not got any she
naturally failed to find them, at which she simulated acute
dismay.

When they asked Gregory about it he pulled himself together
sufficiently to say that he must have left his wallet at home on
his dressing-table, where he knew he had put it all ready to take
with him, and the explanation was accepted. Had they been
foreigners they would never have got away with it, but as far
as the train-conductor knew they were both perfectly good
German citizens and there was nothing criminal or particularly
extraordinary in a man who was suffering from an acute illness
having forgotten his money and papers at the last moment. As
there were no frontiers to cross passports would not be required
for examination during the journey, so the fat conductor told
Erika she need not worry about it, and the train rumbled on
towards Berlin.

On their arrival the following morning the conductor secured
a porter for Erika, who in turn managed to get one of the few
remaining taxis which had special licences to serve the stations.
The conductor got her baggage out of the train and helped her
to assist Gregory on to the platform. They left him beaming
after them, having thanked her profusely for a second large tip.

Passing the barrier they drove without incident to Erika's apartment in the *Unter den Linden*.

The apartment was a large one on the second floor of a great, modern, luxury block, but as she had arrived unexpectedly she had had no opportunity to transfer any of her permanent staff to it, even had she wished to do so. In consequence, the only servants there were the old caretaker, Franz, who had once been her father's coachman, and his wife, Irmgarde, who had also been for many years in the service of the family. She introduced Gregory to them as her cousin, Auguste—feeling confident that they would not remember Auguste sufficiently well to know the difference—casually stating that he had recently arrived from America and would be staying at the flat for some days.

The old couple were delighted to see her, and having greeted Gregory with deep bows they began to fuss over her as though she were a little girl. All four of them then set to work to pull the covers off the furniture and make the flat habitable.

As she showed Gregory to a comfortable bedroom she remarked laughingly to the old people that, his ship having been torpedoed by the British, the poor fellow had not a rag of clothes except those in which he stood up, and even that suit was badly shrunk, so he would have to use the Count's things until he could get some for himself. Gregory had not yet shaved, as it would not have been in character as an invalid for him to have done so while still on the train, so she left him to his ablutions in the spare bedroom while she went into the kitchen to see about food, though she felt certain that with Franz and Irmgarde there her well-filled store-cupboards would not have been tampered with in her absence.

Once they were alone together again Gregory told her that he intended to go out and try to collect the all-important papers. She knew that it was essential for him to do so but did not at all like the idea of his going out into the street unaccompanied, in case he were challenged by the police or militia, and she begged him to wait while they tried to think of some dodge which might make him immune from such dangers.

For five minutes they sat puzzling their wits, he in an armchair, she on his knee, until she jumped up, exclaiming : "I have it !" And rummaging in a drawer she produced an old black eyeshade such as is sometimes used by tennis players or clerks working on figures by strong electric light.

"This belongs to Kurt," she said. "He wears it when he's working in his laboratory, but it will serve our purpose quite well.

If you fix it so that it comes well down over your eyes and take a stick which I will find for you, you can tap your way along the pavement and pretend that you're a blind man. It's very unlikely that anyone will haul you up and question you then."

"Splendid!" he cried. "Darling, you're a genius. If I manage to pull off this thing it will be entirely owing to you."

A few minutes later, after hugging her to him until she was quite breathless and promising to be back as soon as he possibly could, he left her.

Having adjusted his eyeshade in the corridor he went down in the lift and out of a side-entrance of the block so as to evade the porter. Once in the street he set off, with his head thrown back and tapping with his stick on the pavement, in the direction of the *Tiergarten*. People made way for him as he advanced and he waited on the kerb at each crossing until some kindly pedestrian led him over to the opposite pavement. His progress was slow but he reached the bench in the Berlin Zoo which had been specified as the place of assignation at ten minutes to twelve, so he was in good time and he found it unoccupied.

About five minutes later a woman—as Gregory could see by her feet—strolled up and sat down with the brief greeting of '*Heil Hitler!*'

"*Ein Reich, ein Volk, ein Führer!*" replied Gregory with appropriate patriotism and innuendo, although he had not yet the least idea if the pair of black shoes and dark stockings on the ground near-by could belong to the person he had been instructed to contact.

The rustle of paper immediately afterwards, indicating that the person was about to enjoy a picnic lunch, seemed hopeful, so he proceeded with the conversation.

"I cannot see the time so would you be kind enough to tell me when it is about twenty-five to one, as I should then start to make my way home for *Mittagessen*?"

"Certainly," replied a pleasant treble voice in German with a distinctly foreign accent. "But you have no need to go for a long time yet. It's only just gone one—how stupid of me, twelve I mean."

Good, thought Gregory, this sounds promising; and the voice suddenly came again.

"I'm a hospital nurse and have often had blind people in my care. It's wonderful how cheerful they are, but it's the little things, such as keeping a check on time when they're away from their homes, which are difficult for them. Are you totally blind, or is only *one* eye affected ?"

"Only *one*, fortunately," replied Gregory. "But, as you will appreciate, I have to husband the sight of the other very carefully. That's why I wear a shade over both whenever I am in strong daylight."

"Would you care for *one* of my biscuits ?" the girl asked for a moment.

"How kind !" Gregory stretched out his hand. "I should like *one* very much if you have *one* to spare."

He took the biscuit and munched it slowly while they talked on about a number of things, but into practically every sentence that either of them spoke they managed to introduce the word "one", until both of them were assured byond any doubt that they were speaking to the person with whom they had been instructed to get in touch. It was the girl who gave the first indication that she was satisfied upon this by saying :

"Is your sight very bad or can you see a little ; sufficient, for example, to watch the feet of a person walking in front of you ?"

"There are times," Gregory admitted, "when my sight is perfectly good, and you have such charming feet that I should be delighted to follow them anywhere if you cared to test me out."

"One might almost imagine that you'd come here for that special purpose," she said with a low laugh, "and although your German is excellent I have a feeling, somehow, that you may be a foreigner."

"I am *one*," Gregory replied, mutilating the German language most horribly, as instructed, finally to clinch the point that he was, in fact, British Secret Service agent No. 1.

"We've been expecting you for a long time," she remarked quietly, "and several of us have had to take turns of three or four days apiece in coming here, in case one of the Park police became suspicious at seeing the same person eat lunch on the same bench for so many weeks at a stretch. Thank goodness you've turned up at last and can relieve us of our frightful responsibility !"

"It hasn't been an easy matter to get here," Gregory told her, "but now I am in Berlin I want to get through with the business as quickly as possible."

"We'll go, then." She stood up. "But as you're pretending to be a blind man, I think it would be better if we went off together than if you followed me. After all, a blind man and a hospital nurse happen to go very well together, don't they?"

"Yes. If we'd had the chance, we couldn't have planned it better," Gregory agreed with a smile. "But what sort of a nurse are you? I'm sure you're not a German, from your voice."

"Oh, no. I'm an American and I'm working for the American Red Cross. Of course, they don't know that I'm helping with this sort of thing, as it would be a contravention not only of neutrality but of Red Cross ethics, and there would be a most appalling rumpus if I were found out."

"There'd be worse than a rumpus, I'm afraid!"

"Yes. The Germans shot Nurse Cavell for the same sort of thing, didn't they? And I suppose they'd shoot me. Still, I'm game to take a chance on that. After all, since I happened to be in the Mission here before the outbreak of War I'm giving ninety per cent. of my time to the German wounded; so I reckon I'm entitled to take the other ten per cent. being my own leisure, to do something for the British. Although we're stuck here in Berlin there's not one of us who isn't heart and soul with the Democracies all along the line, though we can't say that except among ourselves."

While they had been talking the American girl had led him out of the park. They traversed several streets, then entered a block of old-fashioned office buildings. Although it was Sunday many of them were open as in Germany a considerable proportion of the professional and business classes work on Sunday mornings. On the first floor they passed through the door of one that had the brass plate of a solicitor on it.

A bespectacled clerk came forward from behind a barrier and greeted the girl, with a strong American accent, as Miss Vanderhoorst, upon which she asked if her brother was in.

"Why yes, Miss Vanderhoorst, I'll let him know right away," said the clerk, and disappeared into an inner office from which he returned a moment later to say that they were to go right in.

A tall, pleasant-faced man of about thirty came forward to meet them. With a cheerful "Hallo, Lorna!" he kissed his sister who, when the door was closed, said simply:

"He's turned up at last, Cornelius; this is No. 1."

"Well, now, I'm delighted to see you." Vanderhoorst shook Gregory warmly by the hand. "I'd sooner have sat with a load of dynamite in my office all these weeks than these two scraps of paper which may mean so much to the Allied cause. But Johnnie Beardmore, of your Embassy, begged me to take charge of them before he had to clear out and I just couldn't say no, because we're all hoping that you're going to wipe these skunks of Nazis right off the face of the earth."

"You and your sister have done us an immense service," said Gregory, as he took off his eyeshade. "The difficulty was we couldn't discover the right man to deliver them to ; that's why I couldn't relieve you of them before. But I'm hoping to be able to hand them over to-night."

"Well, here's the guardian of the treasure !" Vanderhoorst laughed as he waved a hand to an autographed portrait of *Herr Doktor* Joseph Goebbels. "I got landed with that at a charity auction best part of two years ago, but the ugly little blighter's been mighty useful to me since. Any officials who happen along think I'm just one whale of a pro-Nazi from having his dial right on my desk. Wouldn't he throw a fit if he knew what he'd been hiding for us all this time !"

As he spoke Vanderhoorst took the photograph out of its frame, and producing a penknife prepared to remove the actual photographic print from its cardboard mounting.

"One moment," said Gregory. "Are the letter and the list underneath the photo ?"

"Sure ; I took it off, put them under it and carefully stuck the print back in its place again."

"Then may I rob you of the whole thing ?" Gregory asked. "If I could carry it back with me just wrapped in a sheet of paper I'd look a patriotic Nazi directly I produced it to anyone who chanced to stop me, whereas the whole scheme would be blown sky-high, and me with it, if I were searched and they found those two papers loose in my pocket."

"Take it, and welcome !" Vanderhoorst grinned. "You've no idea what a nasty turn the little swine's face gives me when I come along to the office mornings after I've had a bit of a jag. Here, Lorna, there's some paper and string over there, just wrap it up for our friend, will you, there's a dear."

It was the first chance Gregory had had to get a proper look at Lorna Vanderhoorst, and he saw that she was a dark, attractive girl of about twenty-five, with a firm chin and fine, laughing eyes.

While she was doing up the photograph her brother said to Gregory: "Now, about your getaway. Bar accidents, the next underground leaves this city of sin this very night."

"D'you mean that you can get me out of Germany ?" Gregory asked in surprise.

"That's the idea."

Gregory smiled. "I thought you implied just now that the assistance you were rendering us was confined to having taken charge of these papers?"

"Sure thing! It was, originally, but I tumbled to it by pure chance that a friend of mine—another American—who's been living for a long time in Berlin is up to his neck in it with the British. If he'd made that one slip with the Nazis instead of with me it would have cost him his neck, but as it was there was no harm done. He's been acting for your people ever since the war began, as Underground Transport Officer. I don't know the details. It was much better that I shouldn't, because if I'd become mixed up in his show I might have got hauled in myself, then I wouldn't have been here to hand you these papers when you came along, and that was vastly more important. For that reason we've kept clear of each other for some time now, but he's still around so I don't doubt his service is still running.

"I'll let him know you've turned up and'll be wanting a free ride home. To night there will be a taxi waiting with its flag down on the corner of the Ederstrasse and the Wilhelmstrasse, between 10.30 and 10.45. Just ask the driver if he's waiting for me. If he says yes, give him your number, jump in, and leave the rest to him."

"Thanks," said Gregory. "As a matter of fact, though, I should like to stay over and see this thing through now."

"Well, I gather the service is pretty regular. It's run specially to get British agents in and out of Germany and leaves Berlin twice weekly. The car's at the same place every Sunday and Wednesday night. I'll let my friend know you'll be along some time, but if you delay your departure you'll have to take a chance on the Gestapo's not having got wise to the outfit and smashed it up. But, of course, that might happen any time."

"I'll have to risk that," Gregory nodded. "Anyhow, it's a comfort to know that help may be available when I'm ready to beat it for home."

Lorna had tied up the photograph, and turning to a cupboard Cornelius produced a bottle of Scotch whisky and some glasses.

"We have to keep this for state occasions these days," he remarked, "as the old blockade is giving them the works already and you can't get it now outside the Nazis' private palaces. Still, if ever there was a time to have one, it certainly is on this little do."

The three of them drank damnation to Hitler and all his crew ; then, having asked his way back to the *Unter den Linden*, Gregory thanked the two charming Americans for their invaluable help to the Allied cause, and adjusting his eyeshade he left the office.

When he got back to Erika's apartment he found her waiting for him, pale-faced and anxious, but her cry of joy as he entered the hall showed him at once that it was only his absence which had caused her to lose her splendid nerve for a little. Directly he told her that he had got the goods she flung her arms about him deliriously, then, sending him off to his bedroom, she got on the telephone.

Five minutes later she let him out again, and clutching his hand exclaimed : "Everything's all right. He can see me at half-past two, and when I've explained the situation to him I feel sure that he'll manage somehow to arrange to give you an interview this evening."

After they had eaten the luncheon which she had helped to prepare she left him for an hour, getting back at about half-past three to say that her friend was so eager to see the things that Gregory had for him and so anxious that no additional risk should be taken by Gregory's carrying them through the streets, that he had suggested coming in person to her apartment at ten o'clock that night.

The long afternoon seemed interminable, but slowly the grey November day outside the windows began to be lost in the falling shadows. They played the gramophone for a little, and clearing the rugs in the sitting-room danced to it on the parquet floor. At eight o'clock they fed again and at a quarter to ten Erika sent Gregory to his bedroom and locked him in.

Twenty-five minutes later she came to let him out. With him he brought the photograph of Goebbels, still in its paper wrapping, and his automatic. In the sitting-room he found a tall figure in the field-grey uniform of a German General seated in an armchair, but it was quite impossible to identify him because he was wearing his gas-mask.

The General got up and bowed stiffly to Gregory's "Good evening, sir," and Erika said : "This is the English Secret Service agent whom I have told you about."

Without making any reply the General nodded and just held out his hand for the thin packet Gregory was carrying ; but Gregory shook his head and producing his gun laid it on the table near his hand as he said :

"I'm sorry, sir, but I can't part with these papers until I'm satisfied of your identity. I might be handing them to a Gestapo man or a Russian agent dressed in a German General's uniform."

The General coughed, then spoke in a deep, obviously disguised, voice : "I appreciate your reasons for extreme caution. As against that, it may be that these papers are forgeries and just a trick by which you seek to ascertain who I am. Will you allow me, therefore, to look at the papers before I remove my mask ?"

"Yes ; I'm agreeable to that. But I warn you that if you attempt to destroy them or to take them away without my permission I shall shoot you through the heart, if it's the last thing I ever do."

As Gregory undid the packet he had a sudden, appalling thought. It was getting on for nine weeks since Cornelius Vanderhoorst had pasted the photograph over those incredibly valuable papers. All that time it had been left unguarded in his office and at night, or in his absence, anyone might have tampered with it. Supposing someone had stolen the precious list and letter, and they were no longer there !

His fingers trembled so that he could hardly open his pen-knife, but he forced himself to steady them, and sliding the blade under the edges of the print he ripped it off. To his unutterable relief the things were still in place ; a sheet of tissue paper with a long list of names typed on it, and a single page of notepaper bearing the British Arms in a lozenge. Without even a glance at their contents he handed them to the silent, gargoyle-like figure in the hideous mask, and picked up his gun.

The General read them through carefully, then he stood up, laid them on the table, removed his cap and gas-mask, and said :

"I'm quite satisfied that these are not forgeries, because I know the signature to the letter. Also, this list of names conveys exactly what I wished to know about the Inner Gestapo. You will understand how essential it was for me to take every precaution against my being recognized, but I'm happy now to introduce myself to you. I am General Count von Pleisen, Military Governor of Berlin, and on behalf of Germany and the world I thank you, sir, for the great risks you have taken to convey these papers to me."

Gregory laid down his pistol, and picking up the papers handed them back to the General, as he replied : "I, too, am satisfied, Your Excellency, because the second you removed your mask I knew who you were from your photographs in the Press. My name is Gregory Sallust, and I am deeply conscious of the honour done me by the British and French Governments when I was entrusted with this mission. But I must tell you that I should never have succeeded in fulfilling it if it had not been for the magnificent help given to me by the Countess von Osterberg."

"*Ach die Kleine Erika!*" The tall, hawk-faced, grey-haired General laid his hand affectionately on Erika's shoulder. "She is a woman in a thousand and it's a privilege to know her."

Erika smiled. "Dear Uncle Jocheim! You always did believe in me, even when I was the bad girl of the family and disgracing you all. But in this affair co-operation has been easy, because, you see, Gregory and I have fallen desperately in love. I suppose it's quite terrible that two people should fall so shamelessly for each other when their countries are at war. Yet two nights ago we were swept right off our feet. He was crazy enough this afternoon to tell me that he wants me to divorce Kurt and marry him, and I've become so like a silly schoolgirl that I even let myself dream for a little that I might agree."

"So you've regained your lost illusions." Von Pleisen's smile was tinged with gentle cynicism, but very kind, as he went on : "Well, love takes no account of nationalities, and in any case I don't think we can consider Mr. Sallust as an enemy."

Erika slid her hand into Gregory's. "But what are we going to do with him, now he knows that it is you who are to lead the Army against Hitler ? Naturally, I trust him, but then I've been a little mad these last two days, and that's no reason why you should. If you wish to put him behind bars until we've struck our blow for freedom, he's quite willing to go."

"That will not be necessary," replied von Pleisen with a twinkle. "Some of my officers are waiting outside for me. If those papers had been forgeries I should have called them in to arrest Mr. Sallust, and I fear you might never have seen him again. As the letter is genuine that is quite sufficient guarantee of his integrity, and from the look of the two of you I think your eyes will prove better jailers than any prison bars. I'm quite prepared to leave him in your keeping."

"I thank Your Excellency," Gregory smiled. "I should like to remain in Berlin, at least till the *Putsch* is over ; and I don't mind how long my sentence is as long as my presence here isn't likely to bring danger to Erika."

"I can give you your sentence now. It will be three nights and days from this evening."

"You've already made up your mind when to act, then?" Erika exclaimed, in a whisper quick with excitement.

"Yes, my dear." Count von Pleisen lifted the thin sheet of tissue paper. "These are the names of the traitor officers who are in the pay of the Nazis. One thing struck me immediately on looking through the list. At least half of them, to my knowledge—and probably all—belong to a society called the Sons of Siegfried. It's supposed to be an ordinary, military dining-club and they hold their dinners on the eighth of each month at the Hotel Adlon. One of the rules of the Club is that only one officer per Division may be a member, but one officer of each Army Corps and Army Garrison Staff is eligible, as are also a certain number of officers attached to the War Office and General Headquarters. The ostensible reason given for that is to limit the membership yet enable Staff Officers of every Unit in the Army to meet and exchange views.

"Now we know the real reason. Some of these officers are captains, some majors and some colonels, but each is in a situation where he can spy upon a General of importance, and between them this network of espionage covers the whole German Army.

"Many of them will, of course, be with their Units at the front, but it is certain that most of them will manage to obtain leave somehow to attend this monthly dinner in Berlin. Therefore, the majority of them will be gathered together at the Adlon on the night of November the 8th; and what more perfect opportunity could we ask to bag so many of them in one swoop? Three days is ample time, too, for me to issue secret instructions for our friends to arrest those members of the Sons of Siegfried who do not get leave to attend the meeting on the night it takes place. Once they are out of the way we should not have any serious difficulty in dealing with the rank and file of the Nazi party on the following morning."

Erika nodded. "Then the 8th is to be the decisive night and the 9th the glorious morning when we shall raise the flag of Freedom."

"Fateful days for Germany," smiled von Pleisen. "As you will remember, it was on the night of November the 8th, 1923, that Hitler made his first bid for power, in Munich, which ended so ingloriously on the following morning, and it was on November the 9th, 1918, that the first German Revolution was proclaimed by the mutinous sailors at Kiel. That was a sad business for us, but it proved successful, so I take the date as a good omen that our revolution—which will save Germany and make her again a respected nation—will be successful too."

"Are there any means of ascertaining absolutely definitely where Hitler will be on the night of the 8th?" asked Gregory.

"His intended movements are always kept highly secret, and although I always know them, he very often changes his plans at the last moment. But in this case we're exceptionally fortunate—another good omen, I think. Every year on November the 8th the abortive *Putsch* of 1923 is celebrated in the *Buergerbrau Keller* at Munich. All the Old Guard Nazis gather there for a great reunion and so far Hitler has never failed to spend the evening with them. Arrangements are already being made for him to do so this year as usual. It would cause the greatest resentment among many of his staunchest supporters if he failed to put in an appearance, so I feel confident that he won't change his plans on this occasion, unless he has exceptionally grave reasons for doing so."

Erika poured glasses of wine for them and they all drank solemnly to November the 8th, the night that was to free Germany from the chains of the Nazis. Afterwards von Pleisen said that first thing in the morning he would send papers which would cover Gregory from any casual inquiries by showing him to be an American journalist of German origin who had permission to reside temporarily in Berlin, but he requested him not to leave the flat and said that Erika should remain with him to vouch for him in case of a surprise visitation by the police such as were taking place all over Germany. Then, thanking them both most cordially again and wishing them much joy of each other, he took his departure.

The days that followed passed for Gregory and Erika almost as though they were in a dream. They had nothing in the world to do but love each other to their hearts' content. Old Franz and Irmgarde only smiled discreetly, delighted to see their dear mistress so radiantly happy, and Gregory made great friends of the old couple.

The weather was dismal and it rained much of the time, but that did not trouble them as they never went out, and they were glad to see the rain for they knew that it would further delay major operations on the Western Front. Hitler's *Blitzkrieg* was still threatened, but still hung fire. Von Brauchitsch and General Halder, the Chief of the High Command Operations

Council, were both rumoured to have been retired because they had opposed it. Von Keitel, Hitler's yes-man, was prepared to launch the great offensive in the West, but Goering and most of the other high officers counselled prudence and were also against jeopardizing Germany's superiority in planes by launching the Air Force against England. Between them and von Ribbentrop the breach was widening as they differed so violently in their views as to the conduct of the war.

Soon Hitler would be forced to take one side and purge the other, and in a last desperate effort to save himself and his backers von Ribbentrop was now urging an attack on Holland and Belgium. After the bitter disappointment of Molotov's speech in the Kremlin on November the 1st, and Marshal Voroshilov's open hostility to the Germans, there seemed little hope that Russia could be induced to lend her full support against the Allies, or even to provide Germany, without payment, with adequate supplies to defy the Blockade and sit down to sustain a siege of several years' duration.

It had become more urgent than ever, therefore, that Germany should strike while still at the height of her strength and before Britain, with American assistance, could attain complete air superiority. It was argued that with their fast, mechanized columns the German Army could occupy Holland before the water-level of the flooded areas could rise sufficiently to prove a serious barrier. That would give Germany twenty-seven more air bases and bring her bombers within 150 miles of England and thus enable her to strike at the very heart of her principal enemy. Holland and Belgium were both fully mobilised. The King of the Belgians and the Queen of the Netherlands, with their principal advisers, were now in constant consultation, fearing for their countries the fate that had overtaken Poland. Yet certain crack German Divisions were being moved down into Austria, so it might be that the threat to the Low Countries was only a bluff and that the real intention was to defy Russia and strike down at Rumania through Hungary.

In the meantime the world waited, and Erika and Gregory remained on tenterhooks, praying that Goering's counsel of caution might still prevail and that the hundred Divisions which were now in position along Germany's frontiers would not be launched to bring ruin and death to the neutral countries in these last few days which must pass before, all unknown to the soldiers, sailors and airmen in their battle stations, the Jews, Socialists and Bible-Students in the concentration-camps and the millions of anxious families scattered up and down the world, a new hope of unexpected peace and freedom was maturing.

At last the great day arrived, and from the moment they woke in the morning the minutes dragged, each seeming to crawl by so that the hands of the clocks in the flat barely appeared to move. They tried to talk but could not keep on any subject. Neither dance-music, the broadcasts nor the war news could distract them. It all seemed so unimportant now. Their thoughts were riveted upon what would happen that evening somewhere about half-past nine, when the Sons of Siegfried were all assembled and had sat down behind closed doors to their monthly banquet, and von Pleisen's officers were mustering in secret for the *Putsch*. They had drinks in the morning, drinks in the afternoon and smoked endless cigarettes, but they made a pact at tea-time that they would not have another drink until seven o'clock. As the clock chimed seven Gregory got up with a sigh of relief, and leaving the sitting-room went down the passage to the big cupboard round the corner at its far end, near the kitchen, which was used as a cellar.

He had just got out a bottle to make some champagne cocktails when he heard a sharp ring at the bell. Remaining where he was, he waited there, concealed by the angle of the corridor, until Irmgarde went to answer it. Immediately she opened the door he heard a rough voice say:

"Stand aside! We are the Gestapo and we have come to see the Countess von Osterberg."

Irmgarde gave a cry of fright, then there was the sound of trampling feet as the men pushed past her and entered the sitting-room. Gregory stood there very cold and still, his heart hammering in his chest, the bottle of champagne still clutched in his hand.

He had not got his pistol on him and he knew that several men had entered the apartment. All of them were certain to be armed, and his gun was in his bedroom at the other end of the flat. To get it he would have to pass the doors of both the sitting-room and the hall.

Peering round the corner he saw that one S.S. man was still standing by the hall door, clutching Irmgarde by the arm, while the poor old thing wept into her apron. The man's back was to the door, which he had closed behind him, so he was sideways-on to Gregory and there was no possibility of stealing on him from behind and striking him down with the bottle.

As Gregory crouched there, half-crazy with anxiety, a high, effeminate voice came clearly to him from the open sitting-room door.

"So, Countess, we've got you ! What a pretty traitor, to be sure ! I've had my eye on you for a long time, but I never thought I should find that you were mixed up with a British Secret Service man." It was Grauber speaking.

Erika's voice came then. It was perfectly calm and faintly amused. "My dear *Herr Gruppenführer*, I haven't the least idea what you're talking about."

"Oh yes, you have. A man called Sallust impersonated me in Munich. You were seen dancing with him just before I entered the ballroom on that night we supped together at the Regina Palast. Unfortunately I didn't learn that until four days afterwards, but once I did the rest was easy. Your parlourmaid was persuaded to talk. He had been out to see you at *Das Kleine Schloss* that morning and he was waiting to see you when you got home that night. He disappeared after that, but we found his S.S. uniform hidden in your clothes-closet.

"You gave him a change of clothes and helped him to escape, and that is treason in the first degree. I'm afraid you're in for a very unpleasant time, my dear Countess, when we get back to the Gestapo office ; because I mean to have every single thing you know about this man out of you so that we can run him to earth. The new beauty-treatment that I've invented will, I am sure, make you talk. The rapid application of flexible rods to the more tender parts of the body brings a lovely, healthy flush to the skin, and the removal of the eyebrows with a white-hot iron makes it quite unnecessary ever to go to the bother of plucking them again. Then there's an eyelash paste, mainly consisting of red pepper, which gives the eyes a most unusual hue, and a liquid-rouge, made with vitriol, which creates somewhat large but permanent dimples in the cheeks. Even your latest lover would not know you when we've done with you. Come on, now, quick march !"

Erika made no reply, but the sound of footsteps came again and it was clear that she was being led away. Gregory felt a wild urge to dash forward, bottle in hand, but he knew that it was utterly useless. He would be riddled with bullets before he could strike a single one of them down. With the sweat streaming down his face he remained there as they marched her off and the front door was slammed-to with a bang.

Instantly Gregory started forward, but the second his head

was round the corner he halted and drew back. Two of the
S.S. men had remained behind in the hall and one of them was
saying to Irmgarde:

"Old woman, we're now going to search this flat. You'd
better come with us and produce any keys you've got."

With a horrible sense of finality Gregory knew that he was
trapped there. Unarmed, he stood no possible chance of overcoming the two S.S. men. Within a few moments he would be
discovered and arrested or shot, and even as he stood there his
divine Erika was being carried off to the torture-chambers of
the Gestapo.

Chapter XXXI

IN THE HANDS OF THE GESTAPO

FOR once in his life all Gregory's coolness and resource had fallen from him. Wachmuller, Archer, Rosenbaum and Lieutenant Gautier rose before him in a series of horrible pictures. The Pastor with the back of his head blown out, his blood and brains spattering the floor; Archer's tortured face as Karl's torch had flashed upon it, scarred, burned and bleeding; little Rosenbaum hanging crucified from the minstrels' gallery, still dripping blood from the wounds that twelve knives had made in his body; Gautier lying on his back in the shell-hole with the blood streaming from his mouth. And now the awful scarlet trail, which seemed to follow him wherever he went in his impostures, had reached to his beloved Erika.

To his horror and disgust he found that he was trembling from head to foot; his free hand shook as though he had the palsy and the bottle of champagne wobbled in the other. He knew that every moment was precious. Evidently Grauber had as yet no idea that Erika had brought the man she had hidden to Berlin, but he would waste not a moment in putting the question to her directly they reached the underground torture-chambers of the Gestapo.

That high-voiced, sadistic pervert Grauber would spare Erika nothing in an effort to squeeze from her every tiny detail that she could give about the man who had tricked him and posed as the chief of Gestapo Department U.A.-1, in his place. With cold efficiency the Nazis would perform all the fiendish acts that Grauber had threatened just as ruthlessly upon that supremely beautiful body as they would have done on a hunch-backed Jew, until they had dragged out every item of information from their screaming victim.

Gregory made a supreme effort to control himself and to think—to think clearly. There were still two of the S.S. men in the flat. They had gone into the sitting-room with Irmgarde but the door was standing wide open. To get his gun he would have to pass it, and it would be sheer lunacy to launch himself upon them unarmed. What could he do that would not lead to his throwing away his own life quite uselessly?

Any attempt to escape from the flat unseen was equally hopeless, as he would have to pass the open door of the sitting-room to reach the door of the hall. If they did not see him they would hear him as he pulled back the latch, and before he could get out on to the main landing of the block they would shoot him in the back. The only fire-escape was at the other end of the flat so he could not reach that either. He was trapped like a rat. What could he do? What could he do?

Putting the bottle down he turned and tiptoed into the kitchen. Old Franz had been out when the dread visitation had descended upon them, so the kitchen quarters were empty. The whole block having been designed on the most modern, labour-saving principles, there were two service-hatches in the kitchen, one into the dining-room and another into the sitting-room for passing in drinks. The lights were full on just as Irmgarde had left them.

Creeping across to the sitting-room hatch Gregory bent his head a little and listened. The two Black Guards were muttering in there and prising the hatch open a fraction with his finger-nail he was able to see a section of the room. They were busy near-by at Erika's desk, running through her papers. He could just glimpse the top of old Irmgarde's white head as she sat with it bowed, weeping, at the far end of the big room.

The two Nazis were within two feet of Gregory. Had he had a gun he could have thrown open the hatch and had them both at his mercy. As it was, with the hatch open he could have leaned through and touched them, but it was hopeless to try to attack them through the hatch with his bare hands.

At his elbow there was a sizzling and a bubbling as dinner cooked upon the large gas-stove. Very cautiously he closed the hatch again and gingerly lowered the steel shutter, about which Irmgarde was always forgetting but which was there to prevent the smell of the cooking getting into the sitting-room.

Turning to the gas-stove he lowered the flames of each ring until they were no more than glimmers, blew them out, then turned the whole lot full on again. Casting a swift eye round the kitchen he assured himself that there were no naked lights there, tiptoed to the only window and shut it, then retreated to the passage, closing the door gently behind him.

Frantic with impatience he waited there while awful mental pictures of Erika in the hands of the Gestapo seethed through

his brain. He saw her hustled out of the car on her arrival at
Headquarters, just a little dishevelled. He saw one of her high
heels twisting and coming off as she was hurried downstairs to the
basement. He saw her wide-eyed and staring, the touch of rouge
on her cheeks standing out like patches of blood on a dead-white
face as her captors produced the whips with which they meant to
to flay her. He saw her stripped to the skin, naked, gibbering,
her body streaked with red weals, the blood running down her
skin while those blond swine laughed and threw filthy gibes at
her. He knew that no one, neither Statesman, Archbishop,
King nor Saint could keep his dignity in such circumstances.
Nude, defenceless, tortured and screaming, they would lose all
semblance to intelligent humans, and he *knew* that to be the
treatment the Nazis meted out to their victims. Yet he knew
too that he must not act prematurely. For what seemed an
eternity he stood there. Gradually the kitchen became filled
with gas. At last it percolated under the door and he could smell
it strongly where he stood in the passage.

Exercising an iron control he remained still for a further two
minutes, then he tied his handkerchief over his mouth and nose,
opened the kitchen door quietly but quickly and shut it behind
him. He reached the steel shutter in four swift strides on tiptoe,
spent an agonizing thirty seconds easing it up on its well-greased
guides and beat a hasty retreat.

Out in the corridor, with the kitchen door closed again
behind him, he withdrew as far as he could and took up a position
half-way round the corner of the main passage. Producing his
match-box he struck a match and, flinging it towards the kitchen
door, dodged swiftly back.

Holding his breath he waited ; but nothing happened.
Peering round the corner he saw that the match had gone out.
He tried a second, a third and a fourth, dodging back each time.
Suddenly there was a terrific roar which seemed to shake the whole
building.

He was flung sideways against the wall and fell half-stunned
to the floor. Huge flames reached out at him from the angle of
the passage. There was a sound of falling masonry, a high-
pitched scream, then the crackle of swiftly-burning wood.

Staggering to his feet he grabbed up the champagne bottle
and dashed down the passage towards the sitting-room. It was
now or never ! If the Nazis were still conscious they would shoot
him as he came at them. There was no time to get his gun, as
they might have recovered from the shock before he could collect

it and get back to the sitting-room. But as he came hurtling round the corner of the door he saw that he had no need for any weapon.

The desk the Gestapo men had been examining was just under the hatch to the kitchen. The whole of its top was now a mass of splinters and flaming papers. The hatch had disappeared and there was a great hole in the wall through which he could see most of the kitchen. Tables, chairs and curtains were all on fire and billows of smoke were already beginning to blot out the scene of devastation. One Nazi lay groaning on the floor, his face burnt and blackened by the explosion. The other had been stunned and lay still beside the desk, his face bleeding from the place where a great splinter of the hatch had torn it open. Old Irmgarde, still in her chair at the far end of the room, seemed to have escaped injury but had evidently fainted.

There was nothing to show that the explosion had not been an accident and in any case when the Nazis recovered sufficiently to get help they could not blame the old woman, as she had been sitting there with them when it had occurred. There was nowhere Gregory could take her, nothing he could do, and every second was of vital importance.

He knew that the explosion must have alarmed the other tenants of the flats and that already people would be hurrying from upstairs and down to find out what had caused it. After one swift glance round he ran to his bedroom, grabbed his gun, slipped some spare clips of ammunition into his pocket and dashed back into the main hallway.

As he flung open the hall door he saw that a man and a woman were running along the corridor towards him from the left. A porter was hastening up the stairs with a page-boy following close behind. Striding out on to the landing Gregory pushed past the man, and thrusting the boy from his path leaped down the stairs four at a time.

In the main hall below a crowd had gathered. Some people were heading from the staircase, others were running in from the street ; all were calling excitedly to each other, seeking to learn the cause of the loud report they had heard.

He saw instantly that if he attempted to force his way through them they would connect his flight with the explosion and try to stop him. Even if he drew his gun and by threatening them with it succeeded in reaching the street, the crowd would give chase. Armed policemen would join the hue and cry. He would be tripped or cornered and lugged off to jail. That would put a swift end to his last hope of securing help for Erika. Yet if he turned and bolted now that he was in full sight of the crowd, that would equally arouse their suspicions and cause them to chase him upstairs through the block.

There was only one thing for it. Pulling himself up short at the angle of the stairs he yelled : "Help ! Help ! There's been a terrible accident !" And turning, he dashed back the way he had come, waving to the crowd to follow.

The mob came after him at the double and when he had regained the second landing they were hard on his heels, but they had no suspicion that he had had any hand in the explosion. Up there about twenty people from the other flats had now arrived and some of them were forcing their way into Erika's apartment. Thrusting his way forward he mingled with the crush about the door, cursing each second of delay but knowing that he dared not yet attempt to leave the block. The crowd on the stairs joined the crowd on the landing, and with the new additions to it that constantly arrived, a mass of excited people soon choked the whole of the upper hall.

Smoke was now pouring from the doorway of the flat. Everyone was asking questions of his immediate neighbours and wild rumours were already spreading. "What happened ?" "Who did it ?" "An accident." "No. A bomb." "The Gestapo ; they were arresting one of their own people." "Nonsense ! The Communists were at it again. One of them was actually wearing a red shirt." "It killed six S.S. men." "No, eight ; the porter said so."

Firemen and police came on the scene, driving the crowd back. Hoses were brought into action to quell the flames, and the injured Nazis were carried out while the crowd goggled at them from a distance. That was Gregory's opportunity. Easing his way through the back of the crowd he slipped round a corner of the main corridor, along to a back staircase and down it to a side-entrance. With a gasp of relief he reached the street.

He was hatless, coatless, and even had he had the blind man's paraphernalia of shade and stick with him he could never have brought himself to adopt the slow gait necessary to the part for the sake of securing temporary immunity from questioning.

Fortunately, now that darkness had fallen he was much less likely to be halted. Darkness—blessed darkness—was his friend, and the black-out made inconspicuous the fact that he was a youngish, fit-looking man in civilian clothes, except where the

hooded traffic-lights threw up his figure for a moment as he
passed street corners.

Hurrying along, dodging the passers-by and the high piles of
whitewashed sandbags which guarded the entrances to office
blocks, he strode down the street until at last he found a telephone
kiosk. A small, downward-shining light which had been fixed in
one corner enabled him to turn up General Count von Pleisen's
number. The Count, he saw, lived in the Pleisen Palace out at
Potsdam. He might be there; he might be at the War Office;
he might, by now, be at some secret headquarters giving his last
orders for the *Putsch*. In the latter case it would be impossible
to trace him, while if he were at the War Office Gregory knew
that he dared not jeopardize the fate of Germany and perhaps
of the world by speaking to him openly over the telephone about
Erika's arrest. But there was just a chance that he might be at
his home, so Gregory dialled the number.

"This is the Pleisen Palace," said a voice a moment later.

"I wish to speak to His Excellency," said Gregory.

"I'm sorry," said the voice, "that is impossible."

"It's urgent; a matter of life and death," Gregory pleaded
hoarsely. "I must get hold of His Excellency with the least
possible delay."

"I'm sorry," said the voice again, "His Excellency is in conference and no private calls can be put through, however urgent."

"He *is* there, then? All right, I'll come out to Potsdam."

"His Excellency will not see you until the conference is over."

"I'll come out, anyhow." Gregory slammed down the
receiver, flung open the door of the kiosk, and stepping back
into the street ran full-tilt into the arms of a policeman.

For a second they stared at each other, but before the man
had time to speak, Gregory muttered: "Sorry! Trying to get
a doctor—my wife!" And dodging past him he set off at a run
down the street.

Potsdam was fifteen miles from Berlin. How the devil he
could get out there with the maximum speed was the question
which now agitated his overheated brain. He had no car or any
means of obtaining one. It was illegal to take a taxi except for
definitely specified purposes, and in any case they were so few
and far between that he might have to wait there half an hour
before one came crawling down the street. The electric trams
were still running but they were infrequent, they halted every
half-mile and the black-out added to their slowness. To go by
train meant a long walk to the station and then perhaps having

to kick his heels in impotent fury for twenty minutes or more before one was due out.

It had taken time to think of a way of escaping from the two S.S. men, time to get the kitchen filled with gas, time to hang about in the crowd before he had dared leave the block, time to find a telephone kiosk and time to get through to Potsdam. Every second counted now that Erika was in Grauber's hands. Nearly half an hour must have elapsed since her arrest, so she would be at Gestapo Headquarters by now and they would be beginning to question her. The thought was agony to him.

A car pulled up at the kerb about ten yards ahead. As Gregory came level with it a Brown-Shirt officer got out and strutted across the pavement. Gregory waited until he had entered the hall of a big building. It seemed positively suicidal to attempt holding up a Nazi chauffeur right in the middle of the *Unter den Linden*, but there was no time to make elaborate plans —no time even to think coherently, strive as he might to do so. If he could not get help for Erika quickly, those black-clad beasts were quite capable of depriving her of her beauty for life in their determination to wring information from her.

Grabbing the near door of the car he pulled it open. One glance into the black shadows was sufficient to show him that its back was empty; only the driver sat silent and immobile at the wheel.

Next second Gregory had drawn his gun and scrambled in. With one hand he slammed-to the door; with the other he thrust his automatic right into the astonished man's face.

"Drive me to Potsdam!" he snapped. "Come on, step on it!"

The man gasped, lowered a hand towards his own gun, then, as he felt the cold steel ring of the pistol-barrel pressing into his cheek, decided that discretion was the better part of valour.

"Who the hell are you?" he exclaimed.

"Never mind that!" Gregory jerked out. "Get her moving else I'll blow your brains out and drive the damned thing myself!"

Gregory's tone rang with such desperate determination that the man knew that he meant exactly what he said. Letting out the clutch the Nazi put his foot on the accelerator of the already purring engine and the car slid away into the darkness.

"Faster!" said Gregory. "Faster! Unless you want to be put to bed in a coffin to-night. Step on it, man! I'm in a hurry!"

From a crawl the car jumped to a moderate speed, but Gregory was still not satisfied.

"Faster!" he growled. "Faster! Or I'll shoot you where you sit, and drive myself."

"*Gott im Himmel!*" muttered the man. "D'you want to break both our necks? I'll crash one of these islands in the black-out if I don't take care."

They were already driving at a reckless speed for night-time in the darkened city, so Gregory pressed him no further but sat there, now holding his gun pressed into the fellow's ribs and counting the seconds, in an agony of impatience, each time the car had to halt at main crossroads where the traffic-lights were against it.

There was little traffic, and leaving the city the car ran smoothly on along the wide *Autobahn*. Five minutes, ten, fifteen, twenty. Every minute sixty seconds, every second a tensing of Gregory's muscles as the thought of the thrashing Erika might be enduring during those moments struck him like a blow from a whip right over the heart.

At last they came to houses again and the Nazi said: "Whereabouts in Potsdam d'you want me to drop you?"

"D'you know the Pleisen Palace?" Gregory asked.

"Who doesn't, seeing it's the house of the Military Governor of Berlin?"

"To hell with him!" growled Gregory, not wishing the Nazi to know that he wanted to go to the Palace itself. "You're to drop me on its nearest corner. From there I can find the place I want."

For a few minutes more the car twisted through some side-streets, then it slowed down and pulled up. Gregory reached forward across the Nazi's lap, jerked his gun from its holster and rammed it in his own pocket as he said:

"You'll sit here quietly for five minutes, then you can get off back to Berlin. But if you let out a shout while I'm still in this street I'll run back and fill you full of lead. By the living God I will, if it's the last thing I ever do!"

"All right—all right," the man mumbled, now clearly completely terrified of his maniac passenger. "I don't want to die yet, so I'm not starting anything."

"You'd better not!" muttered Gregory. "Because if you do, you'll never live to start anything else."

With this last threat he scrambled from the car and set off down the street towards a just-discernible gateway which appeared to be the main entrance to the Palace. A sentry was on guard there, standing in front of a sentry-box. He halted Gregory and called his Sergeant.

Gregory explained that he had an urgent message for the Military Governor, upon which the Sergeant led him through the gateway into a big courtyard which was surrounded on all four sides by tall buildings.

The yard was chock-full of cars and their military chauffeurs could be dimly seen in the faint light standing about chatting in groups. From the number of cars and people mustered there it was clear to Gregory that von Pleisen had decided to rally the officers who were to take part in the *Putsch* at his own house and that the conference of which the telephonist had spoken concerned their final arrangements. Winding their way through the cars they crossed to the far side of the court and the Sergeant led Gregory up a broad flight of steps to the main entrance of the ancestral home of the Counts von Pleisen, which Gregory saw consisted of this great, four-sided building.

"Civilian with message for His Excellency," said the Sergeant huskily.

"This way," said a voice, as he hurried up the steps, and an overcoated porter on duty there threw open a door, the handle of which it would have been difficult to find in the almost total darkness caused by the overhanging portico, repeating as he did so to somebody inside.

"Civilian with message for His Excellency."

Going in, Gregory passed an A.R.P. light-lock formed by some heavy, hanging tapestries a few feet beyond the door and found himself in a well-lighted vestibule. An elderly manservant in dark clothes stood there, also a Colonel and three Majors, in great-coats and caps, who were talking together in low voices. They had evidently been posted there as a special guard and Gregory realized that although it might be a comparatively easy matter to get into the Pleisen Palace it would be a very difficult business to get out again if its master desired to detain one.

"I want to see His Excellency," said Gregory sharply to the servant.

The man shook his head. "His Excellency is in conference ; he can see no-one."

"If you'll take my name in he will see me," said Gregory with quiet assurance. "My business is of the utmost urgency."

The Colonel suddenly stepped forward. "His Excellency cannot be disturbed. But if you will tell me what your business is, and it really is of an urgent nature, I will give him a message from you directly the conference breaks up."

"*Danke Schön, Herr Oberst*," replied Gregory. "But my business is personal and it is to do with the conference which His Excellency is holding at this moment."

Two of the Majors moved slightly, cutting off Gregory's retreat from the door, while the Colonel said : "I think you'd better tell me."

Gregory took Erika von Epp's little golden swastika from his pocket and held it out. "We're wasting time that may be absolutely vital to the plans that His Excellency is making now. Please take this to him immediately and tell him that Gregory Sallust is here with news of the utmost importance."

The Colonel's face changed instantly, and taking the swastika he handed it to one of the Majors with an abrupt order to carry it with Gregory's message to His Excellency. Two minutes later the Major returned, beckoned to Gregory, and leading him down a broad passage, flung open a door.

It led into the lofty banqueting-hall of the Palace, and between two and three hundred officers were assembled there talking in animated groups. Nearly all of them were either Generals, Colonels or Staff Officers, as Gregory saw at once from the glittering array of gilt foliage and stars which decorated the collars and shoulders of their tunics. Many of them wore distinguished orders hanging from their necks and nearly all had a row or more of medal-ribbons on their breasts. At the far end of the great room Gregory could just see the grey, distinguished head of the tall General Count von Pleisen as the Major who was acting as his guide led him through the crush in that direction.

Gregory caught sight of a big clock at one end of the hall. Its hands pointed to 8.14. Erika had been in the clutches of the Gestapo for just about an hour and a quarter. Grauber was a sadist, so he would derive a personal joy from torturing a beautiful woman. It was probable that he would take his time about the business, and rack her mentally before proceeding to extremities. Gregory could only pray that things were happening so, and now that he had succeeded in getting to von Pleisen he was inclined to take a more optimistic view of Erika's chances. There was no time to lose, not a moment, as during the second hour she was under examination Grauber would certainly begin to apply physical torture. But it would be slow, subtle and ingeniously planned, and if von Pleisen exercised his authority to have Erika transferred under guard to a military prison, an order, telephoned at once, might yet be in time to haul Grauber up short and prevent his satiating his sadistic lust by applying that ghastly "beauty treatment" with which he had threatened Erika.

The Count was engaged in a sharp argument with several other senior officers, but catching sight of Gregory out of the corner of his eye he broke it off and turned swiftly towards him.

"Well? What brings you here? Not bad news, I hope?"

In a few quick sentences Gregory told him of Erika's arrest.

"That's bad," said von Pleisen. "But in an hour or two we'll have her out of it."

"An hour or two!" Gregory repeated, aghast. "But don't you realize, Excellency, what she may be going through as we stand here? Surely you can use your authority as Military Governor. Have one of your people telephone an order that she's to be handed over at once to the Military Police."

Von Pleisen sadly shook his head. "Impossible. An order of that kind is so irregular that it would be challenged and arouse immediate suspicion. I know what you must be suffering, since you love her, and I'm as fond of her myself as if she were my own daughter, but our success to-night must not be jeopardised by the fate of a single woman, however precious she may be to us personally."

"But they may be torturing her! We must stop that some-how—we *must*! And she's your niece. Telephone them your-self and say it's your personal wish that her examination should be held over till the morning."

"Not even I can stay the hand of the Gestapo, and to remind them of the fact that she's my niece would only serve further to jeopardise the success of the *Putsch*. They might send some of their people out here to question me about her recent movements and find out how I'd learned of her arrest. If one of them got to know of this assembly, and succeeded in reaching a telephone, our whole plan of campaign would be ruined."

"Oh God!" Gregory groaned. "Is there nothing we can do?"

"Nothing for the moment. Immediately the *Putsch* is over we will get her out, but until then she must take her chance."

"But don't you see," cried Gregory, swiftly resorting to an impersonal argument, "she's only human and she knows all about your plans. It's not only me they're after. Grauber knows that I was trying to gather together the threads of the anti-Nazi conspiracy, and if he tortures her to tell what she knows about that she may be compelled to give them information which will ruin the whole *Putsch* at the eleventh hour."

Von Pleisen spoke with an effort and his face was grey as he said : "We march at nine o'clock. To advance the hour even by five minutes would throw out our whole schedule, so I am determined not to leave this hall one second before the clock strikes. My niece is a von Epp and she will not betray us."

Gregory looked at the clock again. Its hands now stood at 8.16. Forty-four minutes to go till the hour, at least another twenty to drive back to Berlin, a further half-hour or more before the *Putsch* could become effective. There was now no hope of his reaching Erika until after ten, and by that time she would have been at Grauber's mercy for over three hours.

He knew that von Pleisen was right and that the beauty, sanity or life of one woman, however dearly loved, could not be allowed to weigh against the happiness of millions. Yet he was filled with bitter fury against the General and could have screamed aloud at his own impotence. As he thought of the agony of suspense he had yet to endure, and of the broken, crippled, bleeding state in which he was now certain that he would find his adored Erika, he very nearly fainted.

Chapter XXXII

THE NIGHT OF BLOOD

THERE was nothing further that Gregory could do. Even if the General had been willing to let him, it would have been utterly useless for him to return to Berlin at once in an attempt to save Erika single-handed. It was as hopeless to think of forcing his way into the cells at Gestapo Headquarters as it would have been to contemplate breaking into the vaults of the Bank of England. Agony as it would be, he must wait there until von Pleisen led out his officers. He had done everything in his power to save Erika, and these endless minutes during which he was compelled to remain inactive might mean for her the difference between being rescued while still unharmed or after being disfigured for life. Yet now he could only recommend her to the keeping of the deathless gods who had given her her beauty and her courage.

Almost in a daze he found that von Pleisen was presenting him to the other high officers in his immediate neighbourhood as the brave Englishman who had risked death to bring them the list of the Inner Gestapo and the letter of the Allied Statesmen. To Gregory's amazement, as they stood round bowing and smiling their congratulations von Pleisen took off his own Iron Cross of the First Class and decorated him with it in the name of the future German Government.

As he stuttered his thanks for the honour done him, and clasped hands with the many officers who eagerly offered him their congratulations, von Pleisen turned back to the Generals with whom he had been talking when Gregory had entered the room.

While Gregory shook hand after hand and, forcing a smile, tried to make light of his exploits his eye was constantly switching to the clock, yet the long hand seemed to hardly move at all. At any other time he would have been intensely proud and delighted at receiving the decoration, but what was the Iron Cross of the First Class—the highest award for bravery that Germany could bestow—compared with Erika's safety? It was a worthless piece of tin beside one tendril of her golden hair.

436

In his imagination, while the minute-hand of the clock crept round its dial with maddening slowness, as he saw fat, bespectacled, kindly Rheinhardt being flogged into writing the letter that had duped Madame Dubois, and the horror upon her face as she had opened her parcel of flowers to see it dissolve in the blinding flash of the explosion that had killed her.

In a vague way he knew that Orderly Officers were now constantly arriving through another entrance to report upon completed preparations. Some General or other had everything ready to seize the Central Telephone Exchange ; So-and-So's troops were awaiting the signal to swoop on the Berlin Broadcasting Station ; somebody else was preparing to establish a cordon round the Chancellory ; another General's command was standing to arms in barracks ready to march on the S.S. Headquarters. Soon the darkened streets of the German capital would be alive with marching troops on their way to the railway stations, the great lighting plants, the Templehof aerodrome and the private residences of the leading members of the Nazi Government.

Tanks were to take up positions in the squares, armoured cars were to patrol the streets and corner buildings were to be seized so that machine-gun nests which would command the main thoroughfares could be established in their upper storeys. Artillery was being trained on the Nazi strong points, the barracks of the Brown-Shirts and of the Black Guards and on Gestapo Headquarters.

When it penetrated to Gregory's tortured mind that they were prepared to use guns if they encountered resistance, his face went as white as chalk. Erika was a prisoner in Gestapo Headquarters. If the Army shelled it the searing flame of high explosive or a jagged splinter of steel might complete the mutilation of her dear person on which Grauber would by now have started. Shutting his eyes for a moment Gregory prayed fiercely "Oh God, don't let her die. Oh God, don't let her die. Spare her for me even if she's scarred and crippled."

The argument between the senior Generals was still in progress. One tall, gaunt man, who wore a rimless monocle in a hatchet face and was addressed as *Prinz*, was saying to von Pleisen : "I protest, Excellency ; it would be madness to give these dogs a chance. Everyone of them deserves death, and this is no time to parley."

"*Ja, ja !*" A broad-shouldered, grey-haired man backed him up. "They are certain to be armed. The second we enter the banqueting-room of the Adlon our machine-guns must open and mow them down before they can offer any resistance."

But von Pleisen shook his fine, aristocratic head. "*Nein meine Herrschaften*, I will not have it. You insisted that if Hitler were not killed or arrested within a few minutes of our assault on the Adlon someone would be certain to warn him of our *Putsch* by telephone, and that since we could not be in two places at once in sufficient force to subdue gatherings of several hundred armed Nazis, special measures should be taken in Munich. All against my principles, I consented that a bomb, with sufficient explosive in it to wreck the *Buergerbrau Keller* and kill Hitler and his principal supporters, should be placed in the roof there and timed to go off at the same moment as we open our attack on the Sons of Siegfried. That can only be justified by the fact that we cannot be in Munich ourselves and that the seizing of Berlin, whether Hitler escapes of whether he does not, is the most vital factor in the whole movement. But the brutal massacre of several hundred Nazis, where massacre is not essential, is quite another matter. What you propose is just the sort of thing that Hitler would do, and the German Army must not dishonour itself in its very first move by such brigand methods. The Sons of Siegfried must be given a chance to surrender peacefully before we open fire upon them."

"Hear, hear!" said several others; and von Pleisen went on :

"You have chosen me as your leader for this momentous undertaking and I must ask you to take my decision on this point as an order."

That quelled the protests of the monocled Prince and his supporters, but there were unconvinced shakings of many heads at von Pleisen's humane ruling.

At last the minute-hand of the clock pointed to five to nine. Von Pleisen's adjutant called for silence and the babel of voices was instantly hushed. The Count then spoke briefly but from the heart, of the iniquities of the Nazi régime and of the disgrace and misery that Hitler had brought upon Germany. He ended with a rousing appeal to every man present that night to do his duty, even if he were called on to lay down his life for the salvation of the Fatherland.

Raising his hand he cried : "Follow me! Between us we will see to it that every swastika flag is hauled down and that to-morrow the Imperial Eagles shall float again in the free breeze over Germany's cities. By virtue of your own free will and patriotism I command you to march, in order that Germans may once more lift their faces to the world as an honourable and free people."

As he ceased, the strokes of nine began to chime from the clock and were drowned in a great burst of cheering. The doors of the great room were flung open, and through a lane of wildly enthusiastic officers General Count von Pleisen marched with solemn dignity from the room, followed by the senior Generals and his personal *entourage*.

Gregory found himself next to von Pleisen's Adjutant, von Hohenlaub, a dark, keen-faced man, who took charge of him as the officers streamed out into the courtyard and found him a place beside him in a car.

One by one the cars rolled from the courtyard and took the road to Berlin. Every thing was now very quiet. The big cars sped on smoothly until they reached the centre of the city. Out of the blackness on either side there loomed up patrols of troops. They were the advance guard of the *Putsch* and were taking up their positions to form a cordon round the Adlon. The car in which Gregory had a seat slowed down then drew up before the main entrance of the hotel. On the pavement there were more troops and crowds of officers who were alighting from the other cars. Gregory passed among them into the building. No-one spoke, and the hall of the great luxury hotel was strangely silent.

"The place was taken over five minutes ago," von Hohenlaub informed Gregory. "Since then no one has been allowed into the banqueting-room or out of it, except a certain number of waiters who were on our lists as trusted men but didn't know themselves what was going to happen until the hotel was raided just now and they were given their orders."

At one end of the great lounge the hotel guests were congregated, sitting and standing about covered by officers with sub-machine-guns. Von Pleisen paused for a minute in the hall to speak to the General who had just taken over the hotel, and in the crush Gregory was brought quite near to him again. He glanced for a second at Gregory, then at his adjutant and said:

"Von Hohenlaub, look after Mr. Sallust for me, please. If there's trouble it would be hard luck for him to be killed after having risked his life so often in getting here."

With a pale smile Gregory produced his own automatic and the one he had taken off the Nazi chauffeur whom he had forced to drive him out to Potsdam. "Thank you, Excellency ; but

I can look after myself and, by God, I mean to be in at the finish !"

Von Pleisen nodded and turned away towards the stairs. Officers carrying light machine-guns and automatics followed him, Gregory and von Hohenlaub among them.

On each landing there were squads of officers, and more machine-guns placed in position to command the corridors. Every room had now been searched and its occupant temporarily arrested. Only the Sons of Siegfried, enjoying their monthly dinner, still had no idea that anything unusual was happening.

Von Pleisen advanced down a long corridor. At the end of it was a pair of big double doors. More officers with machine-guns were on guard outside them. At his signal two officers suddenly stepped forward and flung the doors open.

Without any weapon in his hand von Pleisen entered the great banqueting-room, his officers crowding in behind him. Between two heads Gregory was able to catch a glimpse of the long tables, groaning with food while Berlin was already half-starving. There were champagne and hock in the ice-buckets. In the chairman's place of honour, right in the centre of the top table, sat Heinrich Himmler himself, the big-headed but pasty-faced, chinless chief of all the police of the Third Reich, the man who had ordered the torture, mutilation and death of thousands. On his right sat Heyderich and on his left Deutsch, the respective chiefs of the State Police and the Gestapo. The rest of the diners were nearly all officers ; Colonels, Majors or Captains. Most of them wore the tabs of the German General Staff, but here and there there was a black-uniformed S.S. man.

Gregory could not see the whole room, but as far as he could judge three or four hundred of the Sons of Siegfried were present. Their laughter and conversation suddenly ceased as von Pleisen strode straight into the room. Knives and forks clattered to the plates ; some of the diners half-rose in their places.

The momentary hush was broken by von Pleisen as he cried in a ringing voice : "The day of those who have disgraced Germany is done ! In the name of the German Army and the German People I place every man here under arrest. Any show of resistance will be met by . . ."

A solitary pistol shot rang out from somewhere on the left side of the room. General Count von Pleisen's words were cut short. He clutched at his chest, swayed and fell, shot through the heart.

The monocled Prince who was beside him pressed the trigger

of the sub-machine-gun he was holding. Its burst of fire was almost instantly drowned in the crash of shots that followed. The Sons of Siegfried had drawn their guns and were firing straight into the mass of officers jammed in the doorway.

For a second they seemed to waver. Many of them fell, but the mass behind forced the others forward with irresistible pressure and with cries of " Down with Hitler !" they streamed into the room.

Gregory had known battle on the Somme and in the Ypres salient, he had also been in many a gun-fight, but never in his life had he witnessed anything to compare with the incredible carnage that followed. It took place under the thousand-watt lights of the great crystal electroliers, so every detail of the scene was plain and vivid. Six hundred men were fighting there in one hideous mass ; leaping upon tables, hurling chairs, crawling on hands and knees to try and escape the withering fire of the automatics and machine-guns.

Plates, glasses, food and flowers were trampled underfoot. Silver epergnes and wine-coolers crashed over. Bullets hummed, thudded and whined in every direction, and the noise of six hundred weapons all being used at once was utterly deafening.

He saw one man's head severed from his shoulders by a spray of machine-gun bullets. A Nazi shot a General who was within a foot of him, but next instant had his face smashed in with the end of a broken bottle. The banqueting-hall was a hell of curses, shouting, shots and blood—blood everywhere as it streamed and gushed from the wounded and dying men on to the carpets and the white table-cloths.

With both his guns blazing he hurled himself into the fray. He felt certain that he had accounted for two of the Nazis at the top table but could not be dead sure, because such a spate of lead was flying that many of the dying had been absolutely riddled with bullets before toppling over and crashing to the floor.

Within two minutes he found himself practically debarred from taking further part in the slaughter, as von Pleisen's officers had mingled with the Sons of Siegfried who were also nearly all in officers' uniforms. They knew each other, but he did not know which was which and so dared not fire at any of them for fear of killing a friend. He could only look swiftly round him in a wild endeavour to seek out any S.S. men upon whom he could help to execute justice.

Suddenly his eye lit upon a big, paunchy, black-uniformed

figure, with fair hair cut *en brosse*. It was Grauber. With all a maniac's lust to kill Gregory dashed towards him.

The Gestapo chief was in one of the less crowded corners of the room. He shot one of von Pleisen's officers between the eyes as Gregory leaped on to a table. The officer's knees sagged and he fell with blood spurting from his head. Having secured a second's breathing-space Grauber looked swiftly round, his still-smoking automatic clutched in his hand. Suddenly he saw Gregory spring from the table. Recognition and hate dawned in his eyes. Raising his pistol he took calm aim and fired.

Gregory felt the bullet sear through his left shoulder like a white-hot iron. Its impact brought him up short and half-twisted him round. One of his guns dropped from the now nerve-less fingers of his left hand. He staggered, lost his balance and fell.

As he struggled to his knees he felt a hand grab him by his sound arm and pull him to his feet. It was von Hohenlaub carrying out his dead chief's last order, to look after him.

"It's nothing," Gregory gasped. "And I must get Grauber ! He's my pigeon—mine." But as he staggered forward again he saw that Grauber had disappeared.

A moment later he caught sight of his enemy once more. A huge, crop-headed Prussian, who stood six feet four and towered above the others, was rallying the Sons of Siegfried. A hundred or more of them had fought their way to the service-entrance, overwhelmed the officers who had been set to guard it and were now backing out of the banqueting-room, firing as they went. Grauber was among them.

"Quick !" cried Gregory. "I've got to get that devil there !"

The monocled Prince had taken von Pleisen's place as leader of the officers. With a staccato command that rang out even above the hellish din he ordered them to the attack. Shouting "Down with Hitler ! Death to the Gestapo !" they launched themselves forward. Gregory and von Hohenlaub were carried forward in the rush.

People were screaming, cursing, fighting hand to hand. The struggling mass swayed through the service doors. A batch of the Sons of Siegfried was driven into a pantry and massacred there, but the majority of them escaped down the service staircase.

Gregory tried to keep his eyes fixed on Grauber while almost automatically warding off blows with his sound arm. For nearly three minutes he lost him ; then he saw him again, half-way down the stairs.

On the first-floor landing the fight was raging with unabated ferocity. Many of the Sons of Siegfried had now succeeded in reaching the ground floor and were endeavouring to break out of the hotel. Others had scattered, seeking safety in the corridors and rooms around.

"There he goes!" yelled von Hohenlaub as Grauber dashed down a passage, and they pelted after him. For a second they lost him again as he disappeared round a corner, but on reaching it they were just in time to see him fling himself through an open doorway. The door slammed behind him,

"We've got him now!" panted Gregory, and as they reached the door he turned, drew back, and lifting his foot brought the full weight of his boot crashing against it.

The lock gave with a splintering sound and they plunged into the room. Grauber was there, crouching behind a bed, his pistol levelled. For all his hate, Gregory's sanity had returned and he knew that he must take him alive, so he aimed for Grauber's pistol-arm and pressed the trigger of his gun. It gave only a faint click; he had used up all its bullets and its magazine was empty.

Almost at the same instant Grauber fired, but his eyes were wild and his hand shaking. He had lost his nerve, and the bullet sang past Gregory's head to bury itself with a thud in the plaster of the wall.

Grauber fired again, but Gregory had already sprung aside. Next second his arm flew up and he hurled his empty weapon straight into Grauber's face. The heavy pistol struck him with terrific force, its barrel gouging his left cheek and entering his eye. With a shriek of agony he staggered back, dropped his gun and clasped his hand to his injured face.

Gregory's left arm hung limp by his side but he dashed round the bed and with his right hand seized Grauber by the collar. Von Hohenlaub sprang after him and jabbed his automatic into Grauber's stomach.

"Don't kill me!" he screamed, taking his hands from his face and feebly trying to push von Hohenlaub back. "Don't kill me!"

"Take us to the Countess von Osterberg," yelled Gregory.

Grauber stood there rocking from side to side with pain. His left eye was pulped. Blood was trickling from it and from the great gash in his cheek. He put his hand back over the hideous wound and moaned. "If—if I take you to her—you'll only kill me—when we get there."

"You rat !" snarled Gregory. "I'd love to choke you where you stand. But we'll spare your filthy life—anyhow for the moment—by placing you under preventive arrest. That's the best we can do for you."

"All—all right," Grauber gasped, then he lurched and suddenly slid down on to the floor.

"He's fainted," said von Hohenlaub. Stooping, he hauled Grauber up on to the bed.

"Hell !" exclaimed Gregory. "Every second's precious. At any moment now they may start to shell the Gestapo prison. Get some water from that basin and sling it in the swine's face. I'd do it but he winged me and I've only got one arm left to work with."

While von Hohenlaub ran to the fixed basin Gregory examined his own wound as well as he could. Now that the excitement of the fight was over it had begun to pain him badly. The bullet had gone right through his left shoulder and he had lost a lot of blood ; his left sleeve was saturated with it.

Grabbing up a light towel von Hohenlaub soaked it in water and dabbed with it at the horrible mess that had once been Grauber's eye, then he adjusted the towel over the wound as a rough bandage. Grauber began to groan again.

Von Hohenlaub turned to Gregory "Let me look at your shoulder !"

Gregory shook his head. "Thanks, but don't bother. I'm all right, and it would only waste vital moments. You might help me into this overcoat, though."

With his good hand he had taken an Army officer's greatcoat from a peg behind the door. It was a bitterly cold night and he had had to leave Erika's flat without the civilian overcoat of Count von Osterberg's that he had been using. The Army coat probably belonged to one of the Sons of Siegfried who had been staying the night in the hotel for the banquet. In any case he felt that he had earned it, and it would both keep him warm and serve to hide his blood-soaked garments.

As von Hohenlaub helped him into it Grauber opened his good eye and began to biaspheme between his groans of pain. They seized him by the arm, pulled him off the bed and hustled him out into the corridor.

Hauling him along between them they got him down to the lounge. It was empty now except for a little crowd of terrified civilians cowering in one corner, a number of dead and wounded officers scattered about the floor and a small group standing round the telephone at the hall-porter's desk.

Von Hohenlaub paused for a moment to speak to a Colonel who had just finished taking notes from a General who was holding the telephone receiver.

"How's it going ? he asked.

The Colonel grunted. "Hitler, Goebbels, Hess and Streicher have escaped, damn them. The bomb went off all right and the *Buergerbrau Keller* is reported to be in ruins, but for some unknown reason the Führer and his personal gang left the building twenty-five minutes before the explosion was timed to take place."

"*Teufel nochmal!*" swore von Hohenlaub. "What filthy luck ! But if we can hold Berlin there's a good chance we'll be able to hunt him and the rest of his crew down to-morrow."

At that moment there was a terrific explosion.

"God ! What's that ?" Gregory exclaimed.

"Gestapo Headquarters in the Alexanderplatz," replied the Colonel. "We didn't like to tell poor von Pleisen, because he was so squeamish about these rats. But we feared they might make it a rallying-point, so among some cases of wine which were delivered there this morning we put one which was full of T.N.T. It won't wreck the whole building—the place is far too big, of course—but it may have the effect of panicking them so that we can get our men in before they've had a chance to organise any serious resistance."

Beads of perspiration started out on Gregory's forehead. Erika was there, in the Gestapo Headquarters. The wine would have been taken to the cellars, so the explosion might have occurred quite near the cell in which she was confined. If so she would now be crushed to a mass of scarlet pulp beneath a ton of fallen masonry.

"How're things going here ?" von Hohenlaub asked swiftly.

"It's difficult to say," muttered the Colonel. "About half the Siegfrieders managed to fight their way out and they're fighting in the streets now. We've got the Broadcasting Station and the Telephone Exchange so we've been able to cut off all communication with the outside world, but the swine are reported to be barricading themselves into their barracks and those barracks are going to be a hard nut to crack."

Gregory gritted his teeth. They could hear the sharp reports of rifles and the "rat-tat-tat" of machine-guns coming through the open doorway. The Gestapo Headquarters was one of those barracks which the Colonel had mentioned. It was equipped like a fortress with masses of arms and even with light artillery. In spite of the explosion which must have wrecked a portion of its basement, it might become another Alcazar. Its garrison of hundreds of S.S. men might hold it for days and even if Erika had survived the effects of the bomb, it was certain that before the Gestapo surrendered they would kill all their prisoners so that their victims should not give evidence against them.

Out in the street von Hohenlaub's car was still waiting, its military chauffeur at the wheel. As they pushed Grauber into it there was a dull, distant roar ; the artillery had come into action.

"Gestapo Headquarters, quick as you can !" von Hohenlaub ordered.

As the car started off Gregory closed his eyes and began to pray again. "Save her, dear God—save her from those shells. Oh, I beg Thee to give her Thy mighty protection. Guard her and keep her from all ill till I can get there."

There were many more people in the streets than there had been half an hour before. Black-out orders were being ignored. Half a dozen light tanks came rattling by at forty miles an hour with their lights full on. Civilians were running through the streets flashing torches on one another. The firing had told them what was happening, and they were seeking out the Nazis to wreak a terrible vengeance on them. At one crossroad they saw a Brown-Shirt who had been kicked to death and a woman who was still beating his face to a pulp with a broom-handle. An S.S. man dashed across the street right in front of the car, with a howling mob at his heels.

After a few moments the car was forced to slow down by a crowd that spread right across the roadway. The driver hooted but they would not make way, so he had to bring it to a standstill.

Von Hohenlaub thrust his head out of the window and shouted to a man near by : "What's going on here ?"

"It's the Nazis," replied the man. "They've made a sortie from the Gestapo barracks and formed cordons across every street for half a mile around it. They're using hand-grenades and tear-gas."

Gregory dug the nails of his good hand into its palm. Whoever was directing the defence knew his business. Instead of waiting in their barracks to be shelled to hell, the Black Guards had come out to give battle. If the Gestapo were holding a square mile right in the centre of the city other Nazi units might succeed in defending other big areas. The Nazis were all picked men, well-organized and resolute, and they must know now that if they failed to quell the rebelion they would receive no mercy. In their desperation they might yet succeed in overcoming the comparatively small forces that formed the Berlin garrison.

If it had not been for von Pleisen's chivalry such a situation could not have arisen. Had he allowed the Prince to have his way; had he mown down the Sons of Siegfried directly the banqueting-room doors had been thrown open, they would all have been killed or captured. As it was, that moment's respite had enabled them to draw their weapons and give battle. Many of them had escaped and some of them must have succeeded in reaching the telephones and sending out an alarm before the exchange had been seized or the troops had reached their zero-hour positions.

Gregory could only hope now that his Army friends would triumph, but it was anybody's battle. In the meantime the guns continued to thunder, sending shell after shell into the Gestapo barracks. Erika was a prisoner there, and there was no possible way in which he could reach her.

The faces of Rosenbaum, Gautier, Wachmuller and all the others rose again before him. He had done his job but he still dragged that terrible trail of scarlet death behind him. And now it had reached the woman he loved so desperately—the woman he loved as he had never loved anyone in his life before.

Grauber had roused himself and had temporarily ceased his moaning. Suddenly he gave a weak chuckle. "Well, Mr. Sallust, so you're the loser, after all. You'll never get through to Gestapo Headquarters now till the place is a shambles, but you promised me my life if I did my best, and you're the sort of fool who keeps his promises."

"Yes, I keep my promises," said Gregory fiercely, "but you haven't carried out your end of the bargain. You were to take us to the Countess, and you've failed. So I'm going to kill you here and now for the murderous swine you are."

"Stop! Wait!" Grauber exclaimed, shrinking back into his corner as Gregory lifted his gun. "I—I might be able to. But will both of you swear to give me your protection afterwards?"

"You'll have to stand your trial," said von Hohenlaub, "and I expect we'll get enough on you to shoot you a hundred times over. Still, that's better than being torn to pieces by the mob as most of your kind will have been by this time to-morrow, and you'll be safe as long as you're in my custody."

"Ah, to-morrow—" said Grauber quickly. "The tables may have been turned by then. You can see for yourself that the Army's very far from having got the best of us yet, and even if you do win I may be able to wangle things before my trial. 'While there's life there's hope,' you know, as they say in England. It's to-night that worries me. I know Sallust's type, so I can trust him. But he might go off and leave me in your hands. If I take you to the Countess will you swear not to shoot me?"

"Yes, on the word of an officer," said von Hohenlaub.

"Yes, yes," echoed Gregory. "But for God's sake speak, man. Where is Erika?"

"She's not in the prison. I took her to my house—41, Rupprecht Strasse. She's in a private cell there."

As the driver backed and turned the car, Gregory leaned forward. Relief was mingled with fear in his voice as he cried : "Is she all right ? Is she all right, or have you been playing your devil's tricks on her ?"

But the effort to talk coherently while enduring such pain had proved too much for Grauber. He had fallen back in his corner and was again moaning pitifully, and even when Gregory shook him violently he could get no reply to his anxious questioning. Two minutes later Grauber's groaning ceased. He had fainted again.

They had to make several détours to avoid the fighting and twice they were halted by military patrols, but a quarter of an hour later the car pulled up outside 41, Rupprecht Strasse.

Between them they managed to rouse Grauber, and pulling him from the car they supported him across the pavement.

"Is she all right ?" Gregory asked again urgently, as they staggered with the half-conscious man up a short flight of steps to his front door. "And why did you bring her here instead of taking her to Gestapo Headquarters ?"

Grauber was fumbling for his keys. "Had an idea the Army Chiefs were up to something," he mumbled. "Thought I might be able to do a private deal with her, but she wouldn't talk."

"Then you *did* put her through it ?"

As the door swung open Grauber stumbled and nearly fell. Von Hohenlaub caught him and supported him to a chair while Gregory snatched the bunch of keys.

"Which one ?" he cried. "And where's the cell ?"

"It's the longest," Grauber moaned, "and the cell's the first door on the right in the basement." Then he slumped forward.

While von Hohenlaub stood over Grauber, Gregory dashed downstairs. His hand was shaking so that he could hardly get the key in the lock of the cell door. At last he managed it. The cell was in pitch-darkness.

For an agonizing moment he fumbled for the light switch. As it clicked on he saw Erika. She was sitting there on a wooden bench. As she turned her face up to him he almost fainted with relief. From dead white it flushed to sudden radiance, and it was unscarred.

Springing up, she flung her arms about his neck, and pressed her cold cheek to his as she murmured : "Gregory, my darling— my darling."

With a supreme effort he suppressed a cry of pain as her full weight came upon his wounded shoulder. Tears sprang to his eyes, but he buried his face in her neck, and stammered : "You're safe—thank God you're safe ! I—I thought that devil had tortured you."

She shook her head. "He would have done so, but he had no time. He spent twenty minutes trying to get things out of me, then he had to go off to his banquet. Before he went he swore that if I wouldn't talk when he got back he'd make me. But was the *Putsch* successful ? Have we won ?"

"They're still fighting. God alone knows how it will end. But quick, dearest, we must get out of this !"

He hurried her upstairs to the hall, and said to von Hohenlaub : "Can you run us round to the Wilhelmstrasse ?"

Von Hohenlaub smiled his congratulations to Erika on her escape, then turned to Gregory. "I think I'd best remain here with our prisoner. I promised him my protection, and if we take him out into the street again a mob may notice his uniform. If that happens they'll take him off us and hang him to the nearest lamp-post. You can take my car if you like, though."

"Thanks ; and thanks a thousand times for all you've done." Gregory took von Hohenlaub's hand and wrung it. "Best of luck with the *Putsch*, and long life to a new and better Germany !"

He gave one glance at Grauber, who was sitting whimpering on the hall floor with his back against the wall, and pushed Erika out of the front door. In passing the hall he had caught sight of the clock, and it was twenty-five minutes to eleven.

It was Wednesday, November the 8th, a date that would

for ever be fixed in his memory, but all the week he had had it in mind as one of the nights when the gallant, unknown American operated his secret transport system and ran British agents out of Germany.

The taxi was supposed to wait on its corner between half-past ten and a quarter to eleven. They would just have time to catch it *if*, in this night of riot and bloodshed, it were there.

With von Hohenlaub's cheerful cry of "Good luck to you! Come and see us again when it's all settled!" ringing in his ears, Gregory ran Erika down the steps and out to the waiting car. The chauffeur took Gregory's directions, and with Erika beside him in the back the car slid away from the kerb.

Fighting was still in progress. It would last all night, and probably continue for several days, Gregory reckoned. The staccato clatter of the machine-guns and the spasmodic bursts of rifle-fire were punctuated by the dull thud of shells.

At last the car pulled up. Gregory pressed a note into the chauffeur's hand and helped Erika out. With a sigh of thankfulness he saw a stationary taxi just ahead of them. Going up to it he asked the driver:

"Are you waiting for Herr Cornelius Vanderhoorst?"

"*Ja. Sind sie ein Freund des Herren?*" replied the man.

"I'm Number One," said Gregory, "and this lady's with me."

"That's swell." The driver's voice changed at once to rich, homely American. "I've been expecting you, else I wouldn't have come out to-night, with all these palookas banging off their guns. Hop in, friend. The seats are free, and the sooner we're outa this the better my old mother back home would be pleased if she knew what her sonny-boy was up to!"

Gregory was careful to get into the taxi so that his sound arm should be next to Erika. She snuggled down at once with her head on his shoulder, and said dreamily:

"I don't mind where you're taking me, beloved, but—just as a matter of curiosity—where are we going?"

"Listen, my sweet," he said, pressing her to him. He did not wish to tell her of her uncle's death yet, if he could avoid doing so, but he wanted to make the general situation clear to her. "Things didn't go quite as they were planned. Hitler and Goebbels and several other leaders escaped a bomb that it was hoped would kill them to-night in Munich, and by now they're probably hard at it organizing a counter-*Putsch* down there in the south. A lot of the Sons of Siegfried got away from the Adlon, and some of them 'phoned their barracks. There are at least 30,000 of these blasted Nazis in Berlin, and owing to so many regiments being at the Front the garrison here is a long way below peace-time numbers. The Army have got tanks and guns, but the Nazis are better equipped for street-fighting, and have had more practice at it. We've done our bit, and it's their show now. We can only pray that our friends come out on top."

"I see," she murmured doubtfully. "But you still haven't told me where you are taking me."

"Out of it all, beloved. This is the first stage on the under-ground route to England. We may go through Denmark, Holland, Belgium—I don't know. But it's this way. If the Generals win, an Armistice will be declared within twenty-four hours, then you'll be able to return to Germany in safety when-ever you want to. But if they don't, a reign of terror will set in such as even the Nazis have never before instituted. All the officers who have been in this thing to-night and their friends and relatives will be hunted down and shot by the score. It's a thousand to one that you'd be among the victims, and nothing in the world would induce me to risk that."

As the taxi twisted through the streets the sound of the shooting died in the distance ; then only the dull thudding of the guns came faintly through the humming of the engine. When they were clear of the city the cab increased its pace slightly, and about twenty minutes later it pulled up at the side of the road some fifteen miles from the centre of Berlin.

"We're a bare kilo short of Seefeld, and you folks get out here," said the American. Then he pointed to his right. "Walk up that lane. It's no more'n four hundred metres, but I don't want this 'bus seen out there, so I always drop friends on the main road. You'll find a farmhouse on the left ; it's the only building hereabouts. Knock on the door and tell the old palooka who opens it that your car's broken down. He'll offer to put you up for the night, but you'll reply that you've got to cover another 220 kilometres before the morning. Two-twenty, remember ; the rest'll be all right. So long, folks—best of luck !"

Having thanked him warmly for his help Gregory and Erika left him and set off slowly, arm-in-arm, up the lane. They were now both very tired from the appalling strain they had been through, and although he tried not to show it Gregory was feeling very groggy. The blood he had lost had weakened him so much that he found it difficult even to put one foot in front of the other, but he set his teeth and struggled on because he did not want Erika to know that he had been wounded until they reached some place on the way to the frontier where they would be instructed to lie-up for a sleep.

At the farmhouse they followed the directions they had been given, and a grey-haired farmer led them through into a kitchen sitting-room where a bright fire was burning. Before it stood a man who was dressed in airman's kit. The room was lit only by a single oil lamp, and it was not until the second glance that Gregory recognized Flight-Lieutenant Charlton.

"By all that's wonderful!" he muttered. "Fancy finding you here! I thought we should have to spend days of anxiety being smuggled into Denmark or somewhere, but I suppose this means you're going to fly us home?"

Charlton laughed. "I'm one of three pilots on this secret landing game, but I've made eleven successful trips since I set you down outside Cologne two months ago, so if the luck holds I'll have you safely back in London before morning. As you say 'we' I take it the lady's coming with us?"

"No," said Erika suddenly, "I'm not."

"What!" exclaimed Gregory, his pain and tiredness instantly forgotten. "But you must! You said you would back there in Berlin just after we set off in the taxi."

"No," she repeated, "I never said I would. I never meant to come. I'm a German, and I must stick by my people. I can't run away now the thing we've worked for has happened, and the whole future of my country is in the melting-pot. If the Generals win I'll be perfectly all right, and as soon as an Armistice is declared I'll fly over to London. But if things go wrong I've many friends, and I must stand by them as they will stand by me. I'll go to ground and hide from the Nazis somehow. No matter how long the war lasts I'll never think of anyone but you until we meet again, and we will meet somehow, somewhere, in the future."

"Darling, you *must* come, you *must*!" he pleaded wildly. "I *can't* leave you here. If you won't, there's only one thing for it; I shall stay here with you."

"You will not!" With unexpected strength she suddenly seized and gripped his shoulders, staring straight into his face. "You've done your job magnificently, and now you're going home. If I let you stay you might have to remain in hiding for months or years. It's much easier for a woman to conceal

herself in a country that's at war than it is for an able-bodied
man, and for my sake you mustn't risk being caught and shot.
I love you, Gregory. I love you more, even, than I loved Hugo—
much more. I know that now I've got to lose you. I'm still
young in body, but oh, so terribly old in experience, and that's
how I know I'll never love anyone again but you. I'll follow
you anywhere in the wide world you like to ask me, but not
till the war is over."

As she spoke a great pain was stabbing violently down
into his chest from where her right hand gripped his shoulder.
The dimly-lit room went dark, her lovely face blurred and
faded. His knees suddenly gave under him. Charlton jumped
from his place by the fire and just managed to catch him.

Erika glimpsed the palm of her hand in the lamplight. Her
grip had caused the blood to seep through Gregory's greatcoat
on to it.

"*Lieber Gott!*" she cried. "He's wounded!"

"I'll get some warm water," said the grey-haired farmer,
"while you take his coat off. Then we'll bathe and dress his
wound before he starts on his journey."

"That's it," added Charlton. "He'll soon come round.
He's only fainted."

Erika held up her hand quickly. "No," she said. "No.
It's only a flesh-wound in his shoulder. Quick! Take him out
to the plane while he's still unconscious! I've been puzzling
my wits for the past half-hour how to get him out of the country
without me. This is a heaven-sent chance, as I'll never be able
to persuade him to go once he comes round again."

Charlton nodded and, stooping, lifted Gregory in his arms.
With the help of the farmer he carried the limp body out to the
waiting plane and placed it in one of the passenger
seats.

As the engine started up Erika was crying softly. Another
moment and the plane was racing across an open field. It lifted
into the darkness, and she was alone with the farmer.

When Gregory came to he was thousands of feet above
Northern Germany. At first he did not realize what had happened, but his greatcoat had fallen open, and on raising his
hand it came in contact with the Iron Cross that General Count
von Pleisen had pinned upon his breast. Full consciousness
then came back to him.

He knew that he had won and lost and won again. He had
won through with his mission, which might yet bring a speedier

peace to the tortured world through the slaughter of so many heads of the Gestapo. He had lost a place in heaven formed by the arms of that strange, courageous, beautiful woman, Erika von Epp, who had had many lovers. But he had won her heart and would carry it with him like a glorious beacon, through the darkness to the brighter day on which Peace would reunite them.

THE END